ONLY IN YOUR ARMS

"I gather you feel my marriage proposal is not worthy of consideration," Max remarked.

"Get out of my room!"

"It's not your room. This house—and everything in it—is mine."

"Everything but *me*." Nimbly Lysette tried to slip past him, but Max caught her around the waist and closed the door with his foot.

At the touch of his hands she shrieked and tried to kick him. "Stop it," he said, and shook her once, lifting her until her soft-slippered feet were barely touching the floor. "Just what do you think you're going to do if you *don't* marry me? You are ruined, my innocent, for any man but me. You face only two alternatives—to be my wife . . . or my mistress."

Lysette stared at him in shock. "I won't marry you, and I certainly won't be your . . ." she stopped, unable to say the hateful word.

His finger drifted along her jawline. "Say you'll be my wife."

Lysette was stubbornly silent.

"Then I'll make you my mistress. Tonight," he said, and lowered his mouth to hers . . .

ONLY IN YOUR ARMS

LISA KLEYPAS

An Avon Romantic Treasure

AVON BOOKS ◆ NEW YORK

**This book is dedicated to Mother,
who knows that everything I write is really for her.**

ONLY IN YOUR ARMS is an original publication of Avon Books. This work has never before appeared in book form. This work is a novel. Any similarity to actual persons or events is purely coincidental.

AVON BOOKS
A division of
The Hearst Corporation
1350 Avenue of the Americas
New York, New York 10019

Copyright © 1992 by Lisa Kleypas
Lady Legend excerpt copyright © 1992 by Deborah Camp
Published by arrangement with the author
Library of Congress Catalog Card Number: 91-93040
ISBN: 0-380-76150-5

First Avon Books Printing: April 1992

AVON TRADEMARK REG. U.S. PAT. OFF. AND IN OTHER COUNTRIES, MARCA REGISTRADA, HECHO EN U.S.A.

Printed in the U.S.A.

RA 10 9 8 7 6 5 4 3 2 1

Prologue

Natchez, 1805

"We leave for New Orleans *tomorrow*, you little fool!" Gaspard's cold black eyes swept over the trunks pushed back against the bedroom wall. "Why have your belongings not been packed?"

Lysette turned swiftly at the sound of his voice, her long red hair flying around her shoulders. "How *dare* you enter my bedroom!" she cried. It was unthinkable for a man to intrude in an unmarried girl's room, even if he was her stepfather. "Get out! Get out at once!"

Instead of leaving, Gaspard rushed toward her in a burst of fury, seizing her upper arms in a grip that hurt. He was a small man, but he possessed wiry strength as well as an uncontrollable temper. "Stupid, stubborn girl," he said, his face reddening. "Empty trunks are not going to delay our journey. If necessary, we'll leave without your trousseau. You are going to New Orleans with me, and you will marry Etienne Sagesse with every appearance of willingness and gratitude. There is nothing you can do to prevent it."

"I'm not some bit of goods to be sold to the highest bidder," Lysette said in a low voice. She was afraid of Gaspard's temper, and with good reason, but this was one

1

time she could not back down before him. "You profited
from marrying my sister to a man she didn't love—and
now you intend to same for me!"

Her older sister, Jacqueline, had not wanted to marry
the suitor Gaspard had chosen for her, a wealthy old wid-
ower more than three times her age. Now Jacqueline was
resigned to her situation, but she was far from happy. Gaspard was the one who had benefited from the arrangement,
having been paid well for his beautiful stepdaughter's hand.

"There can be no reasonable objection to a match with
Etienne Sagesse," Gaspard said in a self-righteous tone.
"He is a well-bred man, handsome, wealthy . . ."

"You know perfectly well he is a beast!" Lysette retorted, trying to free herself from his painful grasp. "A
complete drunkard, not to mention a braggart. You heard
how he boasted about the young men he has killed in duels. You heard the insolent way he addressed me, and even
Maman. And you know how he behaved toward me in the
garden! He is the most ill-mannered, coarse—"

"You *will* marry Sagesse," Gaspard said through his
teeth. "You will do it for the sake of your family. You
have no right to refuse."

"My feelings—"

"Your feelings matter to no one!"

"Please," Lysette whispered, finally reduced to begging, "there are others who would offer for me if only you
would allow it. Many honorable, kind men here in
Natchez—"

"None of them have Sagesse's wealth, or his influence.
It is my place to decide what is best for you, and I—"

"It is *not* your place," Lysette choked. "You're not my
father. You're nothing but a leech, and you've bled this
family until there's nothing left!"

Gaspard stared at her incredulously as she continued her
reckless outburst.

"I'll never understand how you gulled Maman into
marrying you! I suppose she was too griefstricken by my

father's death to see what kind of man you really are. We could have lived comfortably on the money Papa left us, but you gambled it all away. And now Jacqueline and I have to pay with the rest of our lives because of—"

Gaspard let go of her abruptly, sending her hurtling backward against the wall. Lysette stared at him with wide hazel eyes. She had never seen Gaspard in such a state. He appeared ready to kill her.

"Gaspard?" came the timorous voice of Lysette's plump, prudish aunt. Delphine was referred to as *tante,* one of that category of luckless women who had not caught a husband in her earlier years, and therefore was relegated to chaperoning her niece. "Gaspard," Delphine repeated, creeping into the room, her round face gleaming with perspiration. "If Lysette will allow me to assist her, I will see that her trousseau is packed."

"No, you will not," Lysette said, her knees shaking as Gaspard's features contorted with anger. "I'm not leaving. I'm not marrying anyone. I'm not—"

She broke off with a gasp as Gaspard delivered a numbing blow across her face. Stunned, she raised an unsteady hand to her cheek. Her stepfather's eyes were filled with pure hatred. Quietly Delphine left the room, wanting no part of what was sure to follow.

"I won't do it," Lysette said. "I won't—" Gaspard's fist rose again. In a reflex action, she turned to the side. He struck her ear, and she staggered under the force of the blow. Disoriented, she covered her face with her arms and cried for him to stop, but nothing would stay the punishing fists. Gaspard followed her as she scrambled to a corner of the room. The hard blows to her shoulders and back continued until she collapsed to her knees. Her screams were loud and shrill but no one dared to interfere—not the servants, not Delphine, and not her own mother Jeanne, who was only a few rooms away.

It took a full minute for Lysette to realize Gaspard's assault had ended. Cautiously she unwrapped her arms from around her head and turned her face to the side. He was standing above her, his hands still clenched. She swallowed, tasting blood, and pushed herself up to a sitting position, her muscles twitching in agony. Without thinking, she tried to stand, only to collapse in a heap.

"Now you have learned the price of challenging me," Gaspard muttered. "And from now on, each time you give me so much as an impertinent glance, I'll repay it with *this.*" He held his clenched fist in front of her face. "Do you understand?"

"Yes." Lysette's eyes closed. Let it be over, she thought feverishly. Let it be over . . . She would say or do anything not to have to go through this again.

She was vaguely aware of Gaspard's snort of contempt as he stormed away, then Tante Delphine's hesitant return to the room. Lysette was certain that although Delphine did not like Gaspard, she considered it unnatural for Lysette to oppose his wishes.

"You think I deserved to be punished," Lysette said hoarsely. "I know you do. After all, Gaspard is the head of the house . . . the only man. His decisions are to be accepted without question. Isn't that right?"

"It is fortunate that he did not do worse," Delphine said, managing to sound both pitying and self-righteous. "I did not believe you would take it so far, Lysette." She bent her stout frame with difficulty and took hold of her niece's arm. "Let me help you—"

"Get away from me," Lysette whispered, shaking herself free. At that moment her resentment and humiliation were too great to endure.

"You must accept your fate and not be so spiteful," Delphine said. "Perhaps it will not be as terrible as you anticipate, being married to Etienne Sagesse."

"You don't believe that!"

"Le Bon Dieu has decided for you, and if it is His will that you be the wife of such a man . . ." Delphine shrugged.

"But it wasn't God who decided." Lysette stared at the empty doorway. "It was Gaspard."

Refusing her aunt's help, she made her way to the bed, step by painful step. Her breath hissed between her teeth as she crawled onto the mattress.

"Lysette?" Delphine hovered over her anxiously. "Perhaps some cool water to bathe your—"

"Don't touch me. I . . . I want Jacqueline. Send for her. Please."

"But her husband may not give her permission—"

"Tell her," Lysette insisted, lowering her head to the brocaded counterpane. "Tell her I need her."

There was an unnatural silence after Delphine left the room, the calm following a storm. Lysette fell into a deep sleep that lasted for hours, until the afternoon sun had faded away and the room was dark with evening shadows. She awoke to find her sister sitting beside her.

Once, Jacqueline might have wept over Lysette's pain and held her close to comfort her. But the Jacqueline of the past was gone, and in her place was a restrained, self-contained woman with a brittle expression. Her red hair, the same cinnamon shade as Lysette's, was fashionably arranged, and her face carefully powdered. But no artifice would hide the fact that she had aged twenty years in the past two.

"Jacqueline . . ." Lysette's voice cracked, and she reached out for the slim hand resting on the counterpane.

Her sister's perfume-scented hand did not move. "Oh, Lysette," she said wearily. "Has it finally come to this?"

"He . . . he wants me to marry a planter from New Orleans . . . a man I despise . . ."

"Yes, Etienne Sagesse," came the flat reply. "I knew about it even before Sagesse arrived in Natchez."

"You knew?" Lysette looked at her in bewilderment. "Why didn't you warn me about what Gaspard was planning?"

"From what I've heard, it's not a bad match. If that is what Gaspard wants, then do it. At least you'll be free of him."

"I can't . . . you don't understand what this man is like, you don't—"

"I'm certain Sagesse is no different from any other man," Jacqueline said matter-of-factly. "Marriage is not so very difficult, Lysette—not compared to this. You'll have your own house to manage, and you won't have to wait on Maman hand and foot. After you bear a child or two, your husband won't visit your bed as often. And he will not be unkind to you as long as he has his way."

"But I want more than that," Lysette said in a weak voice. A tear slid down to the tip of her nose.

"There is no more," Jacqueline sighed. "Those ideas we entertained as children were foolish . . . they were just games. I'm sorry if you find me poor comfort. I thought you needed the truth more than platitudes." She leaned over to touch Lysette's shoulder. Lysette couldn't hold back a gasp of pain, and Jacqueline's lips thinned.

"From now on I hope you'll be wise enough to hold your tongue around him. Can you try to give at least a pretense of obedience?"

"Yes," Lysette said, gingerly touching her own swollen lip.

"I'm going to see Maman now. How has she been this week?"

"Worse than usual. The doctor said . . ." Lysette hesitated, and pressed her cheek to the mattress, her eyes fixed on the swath of patterned damask hanging over the headboard. Like the other furnishings in the house, it was shabby and frayed at the edges. "By now Maman couldn't get out of bed if she wanted to," she said. "The past years of playing invalid and never leaving her room have weakened her." She scowled and added, "If it weren't for Gaspard, she would be perfectly healthy. But every time he begins to shout, she takes another dose of tonic, orders the drapes closed, and sleeps for two days. Why did she decide to marry him?''

Jacqueline shook her head thoughtfully. ''Perhaps she was afraid of being alone.''

''But why *him?*''

A hard smile curved her older sister's lips. ''It's possible she thought Gaspard would be more reliable than Papa.''

''More reliable? What do you mean?''

''Papa was too handsome and hot-tempered. Can you imagine how Maman must have felt, having her husband die in a duel in a riverside brothel over some other woman?''

''What?'' Lysette sat up slowly, wincing. She had been very young at the time of their father Lucien's death. Although she had asked many times, no one had ever revealed the cause of his last duel.

''That is the kind of man Papa was,'' Jacqueline said.

''By contrast, Gaspard is not what anyone would call handsome. He is too cowardly to cross swords with anyone and has far more interest in gaming than women. Unfortunately, Maman never anticipated how quickly he would go through her money.'' She stood and straightened her skirts. ''I'll go see her now. Is she aware of what happened between you and Gaspard?''

Lysette smiled bitterly, thinking of the commotion they had raised. ''I don't see how she could have avoided knowing about it.''

''Then she's upset, I'm certain. Well, perhaps with both of us gone, there will be more peace around here. I hope so, for Maman's sake.''

As Jacqueline left, Lysette stared after her older sister and began to ease herself off the bed. Every muscle ached. It even hurt to breathe. ''Somehow,'' she muttered, ''I expected more sympathy.'' She wondered if all Jacqueline had said was true. Would she be better off accepting her lot as Sagesse's wife rather than remaining here? The only thing to do now was hope . . . hope that Etienne Sagesse would not be as repulsive as she'd originally thought.

Chapter 1

New Orleans

Perhaps it was Maximilien Vallerand's deliberateness that most frightened people. He moved as silently as a panther, was self-contained, and utterly intimidating. Although it was not his habit to seek a quarrel with anyone, his lethal sword-arm—and his gift for biting sarcasm—were well-known. A tall, big-boned man, he walked down the street as if it were empty and he was unaware of the stir he caused. He was as handsome as the devil, with black hair and heavy black brows, and riveting eyes a shade of brown so oddly bright that they looked like gold. His features were hard and perfect, his mouth cruel and sensual.

Street peddlers, usually aggressive in proclaiming their wares of coal, palmetto leaves, broom straw, and fruit, fell silent and scuttled out of his way. Superstition ran rampant in New Orleans, and it was rumored that if you actually looked into Vallerand's eyes, you could be struck with an evil curse.

Two Creole women gathered in the window of one of the many shops lining the gridiron streets to peer outside. "Look, look, it is him," one of them murmured, while the other shivered in delicious horror.

A group of small boys ceased their gamboling on the wooden *banquette* where pedestrians walked, and ran to the other side of the unpaved street. The children challenged each other to throw rocks at the tall, distant figure, but none dared, certain he would catch them and maybe even chop off their heads.

Older youths, on the verge of manhood, watched Vallerand with hooded eyes, much in the manner of wolf cubs envying the leader of the pack. "Someday," one of the boys muttered, "I'll be the one to finally best Vallerand in a duel."

The others scoffed at this, but secretly they all cherished the same dream. Over the past ten years Vallerand had engaged in almost thirty duels, and although the number of men he had actually killed was exaggerated, it was true that he had never been defeated. Perhaps in five or ten more years his sword arm would begin to weaken and his reflexes would dull, but for now he was a man in his prime, and to challenge him meant certain death.

"Vallerand. Vallerand, wait."

At the sound of the voice, Maximilien glanced toward the door of a shop and stopped. It was Jacques Clement, a man who had served as his second in many duels. Maximilien raised a black eyebrow inquiringly, not bothering to extend a greeting.

Clement smiled slightly, knowing that was merely Vallerand's way. Max, as his family and closest acquaintances called him, did not like the small talk and social rituals so prized by other Creoles. His lack of affability was a serious character flaw—but truthfully, that was the least of his defects.

"I am waiting for my sister, Henriette," Clement remarked, leaning against the front of the milliner's shop, under the shade provided by an overhanging gallery. "Where have you been? The waterfront?"

Max nodded shortly. "A new shipment arrived this morning." Never content to leave matters in the hands of his managers, he had personally supervised the transfer of fabrics, spices, and luxury goods from his largest frigate to one of his warehouses on the *quai*.

Jacques regarded him quizzically. "With all the Americans pouring into New Orleans now, your business must be thriving."

Max shrugged.

"I have wondered," Jacques murmured, "why you choose to occupy your time in such a manner, when your family's resources are already so . . . extensive."

Max glanced around impatiently. "Because it interests me," he said, in a tone that indicated the conversation was over. "Excuse me, Jacques, I must—"

But just then Henriette Clement emerged from the shop, and Max paused with an inward sigh. It would be ungentlemanly of him to walk away without acknowledging her.

"Jacques," Henriette said with a pleased smile, "I'm having the most exquisite little bonnet designed, brown and green with feathers of—" She stopped with a gasp when she recognized her older brother's companion.

"Mademoiselle Clement," Max said wryly, touching the brim of his planter's hat. Like all the other young women of New Orleans, she seemed to fear he might throw her down on the *banquette* and ravish her in public.

Henriette turned ruddy with embarrassment and unease, drawing closer to her older brother. Max did not attempt to soothe her by offering pleasantries or innocuous smiles. Instead, he merely turned his attention back to Jacques, as if the girl did not exist.

"Henriette," Jacques said, drawing her protectively aside, "why don't you go back into the shop and select some little trifle that pleases you—a new fan, or some gloves—and I'll be inside shortly."

She obeyed immediately, relieved to escape Maximilien Vallerand's brooding presence.

Jacques turned back to Max. "Have you heard the most recent news regarding Etienne Sagesse?"

Max, who had been about to leave, stopped short. "No."

Jacques' delight in being the one to impart the latest gossip faded quickly, and he felt a chill in his blood. Whenever Sagesse's name was mentioned, Max's eyes narrowed in the manner of a predator waiting all too patiently for the chance to attack.

"His fiancée has arrived from Natchez," Jacques said. "They'll be married within the fortnight. I have heard the girl is exquisite, like no one else in New Orleans. But I suppose that is to be expected, considering the number of years it has taken Sagesse to choose a bride." His voice lowered. "*Bon Dieu*, I hope the young women of New Orleans will be safe now. Sagesse's penchant for despoiling innocents is remarkable. It is not girls like Henriette who are in danger from him, but rather those poor merchants' and seamen's daughters, who are overwhelmed by a show of gold and silk and fine airs."

"A wife won't change Sagesse, or his habits," Max said flatly. A cold, introspective smile touched his lips. "My thanks for the information, Jacques. It may be useful."

Clement nearly shivered. It was rare that Max smiled— and when he did, it usually boded ill.

"Delphine, you may leave us," Etienne Sagesse said, motioning to the door, his eyes on Lysette. "Mademoiselle Kersaint and I wish to be alone."

It was no less than Lysette had expected. Since she, Gaspard, and Delphine had arrived in New Orleans yesterday, Etienne had clearly been eager for a moment of privacy with her. Although he had said little to her, he had watched her closely. She was being subjected to the same silent, relentless inspection she remembered from his visit to Natchez, and it sent a cold sensation crawling down her spine.

The parlor was small, but as beautifully appointed as

the other rooms in the Sagesse mansion. Gaspard had prowled through the house with barely concealed delight, running his hands over the fine, carved furniture, silver and brass ornaments, marble-topped tables, and painted linen tapestries. Lysette thought her surroundings were beautiful, but she knew that living in a fine home would hardly compensate for being married to a man she disliked.

Delphine attempted to oppose Etienne in her own flustered way. "But I cannot leave . . . you see, as Lysette's chaperon, it would not be proper if I—"

"She is to be my bride in less than a fortnight," Etienne interrupted. "I believe I have the right to speak with her alone."

Cowed, Delphine sidestepped to the door. "Lysette, I've remembered there are some things I have yet to unpack. I will return soon." She left hurriedly, taking care to leave the door an inch or two ajar.

Lysette returned Etienne's gaze, while inside she felt a profound revulsion. Perhaps some women would consider him handsome. He was a large man, with blue-green eyes, a high forehead, and thick eyebrows that matched his ash-brown hair. But his features were too fleshy, and his eyes were half-hidden by bloated skin underneath the lower lids. His skin was ruddy and spider-veined from an excess of strong drink.

Troubled, Lysette spoke without thinking, "Monsieur, you dislike Tante Delphine, *n'est-ce pas?*"

Etienne continued to watch her in that avid way, and although his tone was indifferent, his expression made her feel violated. "I have no great liking for her. She is more or less typical of your kind."

"My . . . kind? I do not understand."

"Women are generally superficial creatures, and this aunt of yours is no exception."

Lysette frowned slightly. "Superficial in our interests, monsieur? Or intelligence?"

"Oh, women possess intelligence, of a sort. They are clever and manipulative, in the way that children are."

She wondered if he was teasing her, or attempting to anger her for some unfathomable reason. He seemed to be serious. He dislikes women, she thought, just as Gaspard does. Quickly she lowered her eyes, before Etienne could see her expression.

"You are annoyed," he remarked.

Lysette knew she should hold her tongue, but the words slipped out. "I suppose you think women are overly emotional as well."

Etienne laughed. "There is a great deal of spirit behind that demure face of yours. I realized that the first time I saw you." He gestured to her with a flick of his fingers. "Come sit next to me." Her heart quickened unpleasantly. When she did not move, he slid his body closer, neatly pinning her in the corner of the settee. "Do you remember when we were alone in Natchez?" he murmured, his arms creeping around her.

Lysette said nothing, her body rigid with the effort to stay still, when all she wanted to do was shove him away. Remember? How could she forget the sensation of his wet, insulting mouth pressing over her lips and throat, and the greedy urgency of his hands on her body? He had actually torn the sleeve of her gown in his roughness, and worst of all, he had seemed to relish her humiliation. That was what she hated about him, his enjoyment of her helplessness.

"I have desired a wife for many years," he said, "but in every girl I considered, I found a flaw. Not in you." His parted lips touched her neck, and the tip of his tongue slid over her skin. The smell of his breath, like wine gone sour, wafted over her face. "You'll be a pretty ornament indeed," he commented smugly. "After I break your spirit—and believe me, I know how—I'll have you begging to please me."

She turned away and closed her eyes. "Don't," she said thickly, feeling sick.

"You're mine now. I'll do what I like." He passed his hand over the front of her dress in a fumbling swipe.

Gasping in surprise and disgust, Lysette tried to throw him off, but he used his weight to hold her down. His mouth covered hers, and he felt for her breasts again. In the midst of her struggles, she realized he knew exactly how repelled she was by his advances, and was enjoying it all the more because of her unwillingness. Curving her fingers into claws, she dug her nails into his hands and wrists, and suddenly she was released. With a small cry, she sprang to her feet and headed for the door. She was stopped by a tug on the back of her skirts.

Clutching a handful of her gown in his hand, Etienne looked from the red crescents on his wrists to her flushed face. His lips curved with a slow, cruel smile that frightened her far more than anger could have.

"Let go of my gown," she quavered, her chin trembling as she tried to hold back her tears. Oh, she had to get away from him! How had she ever thought she might be able to tolerate him? She felt soiled by his touch. To be his wife and bear his children . . . it was unthinkable.

"We'll settle this later tonight, you and I," Etienne said, with a playful tug or two at her skirt.

Instinctively Lysette knew he meant to come to her bedroom that evening. "D–Delphine will be with me—"

"D–Delphine," he repeated, mimicking her stutter, "will be no hindrance to my plans for you. No one will."

Wildly Lysette tried to think of someone who might intervene should he try to force himself on her. But Gaspard would probably encourage him to do his worst. Etienne's elderly father was too feeble in body and mind to be of any help to anyone. His sister Renée and her husband, Severin Dubois, lived in the huge house with the rest of the clannish Sagesses, but from what Lysette had observed, the family seemed to take Etienne's part no matter what.

"You're very easy to read, my dear." Etienne said. "You're thinking of leaving, aren't you? But there is no place to run, and no one to help you."

Grasping her skirt in both hands, Lysette pulled it away from him and left as quickly as possible, while he snickered behind her. I cannot do it, she thought in panic. I cannot stay. Maybe Etienne is right—it would be foolish to run. But I cannot accept this fate without a struggle.

Max reined in his horse as he neared the large two-story house with its distinctive double stairway in front. He regarded the property with a familiar sense of pride. His father, Victor, had built the mansion over forty years ago. The plantation was the achievement of a man who had begun with nothing in his pockets, but with shrewdness and hard labor had amassed a considerable fortune.

Like other homes in the exclusive bayou district, the Vallerand estate faced the Bayou St. John, a small finger of water that extended from Lake Pontchartrain to the Mississippi River. Victor had chosen the location for a good reason. It was easier for seamen to reach the city along the lake route and Bayou St. John rather than to navigate the tricky currents of the Mississippi river. Pirogues, small flat-bottomed boats, enabled smugglers and pirates to gain surreptitious access to the markets of New Orleans. Although Max currently had no dealings with smugglers, in the past the Vallerands had financed many illegal ventures and profited well by them.

Max's rueful smile faded as he gently spurred his horse into motion. Lately coming home had felt hollow, and though he pondered the reason for it, he could find no answer. All he knew was that his sense of dissatisfaction with life was growing stronger each day.

Frowning, he swung himself off his horse, handed his reins to the slim dark-skinned boy who had bounded off the front steps of the house, and brushed past the butler on the way to the library. But no sooner had he sat down at his desk and flipped open an account book than he was interrupted.

"Max," Irénée said from the doorway, her usually gentle voice filled with exasperation. After the death of her husband twelve years ago, Irénée Vallerand had discarded much of her pretense of proper fragility. In fact, at the age of sixty she displayed more vigor than any of her contemporaries could recall her possessing as a girl. "Max, I wish to speak with you," she said. "I insist you close that book and give me your attention."

Unwillingly he looked up from the desk. "What is it, Maman?"

"I want to discuss the twins."

He sighed tautly. "Have they been causing trouble again?"

"Of *course* they are causing trouble! I sent them outside because they were brawling in the house." She grimaced. "Philippe would not naturally be inclined to such behavior, I think, but Justin encourages him."

Max shrugged carelessly. "What would you have me do? It is the way of fifteen-year-old boys to quarrel. Was I any different? Or Alex and Bernard?"

"*Oui*, you and your brothers were different, without a doubt. You were not half so wild as Justin and Philippe. And when I attempt to upbraid them they pay me no heed, and show not one sign of remorse."

Max's face hardened. "I will discipline them immediately."

"*Non, non,*" Irénée said hurriedly. "There has been enough of that. They fear you enough, my son."

"There is a difference between fear and respect. I have yet to see either of my sons tremble at my censure, or meekly accept chastisement. As you've just pointed out, they are perfect hellions. I will not break their spirits,

Maman, but neither will I spoil them with too light a hand.''

"But they have known so little gentleness. They have come to consider it an unmanly quality, and you know that is because they pattern themselves after their father.''

Max's long fingers began an impatient tapping on the desk. "I cannot change what I am.''

Irénée gazed for a long moment at her handsome, hard-featured son, so different from the warm, compassionate boy he had once been. She had often cursed the circumstances that had changed him so completely. If he were not her son, she would have avoided him as assiduously as everyone else in New Orleans did. Max was intensely private, ruthless, *sans coeur,* almost devilish at times. His sons were learning from the example he set—especially Justin, the most wayward child Irénée had ever encountered.

"Max, it happened ten years ago,'' Irénée murmured, her manner softening. "When are you going to let go of the bitterness? How are you going to learn to trust again, when you close yourself away from everyone, even your own family?''

"Trust again?'' He smiled sardonically. "What purpose would that serve?''

"It would rid your life of its terrible loneliness,'' she said wistfully.

Max laughed. "I am not lonely, truly.'' His needs were more than adequately satisfied. He had work to keep his mind and body active, and a *placée*—a beautiful quadroon mistress who satisfied his physical desires. He had two strapping sons to carry on the family lineage, and more property and money than almost anyone in New Orleans.

Since Victor's death, he had added to the Vallerand fortune by purchasing more land on either side of the city, including a large tract of forest just beyond Lake Pontchartrain. Recently he had invested in a sawmill and a small shipping business to export the cedar, maple, and cypress boards currently in high demand in the West Indies.

And lately Max had taken steps to make his political influence as extensive as his financial means. He had secured appointments for two friends on the legislative council, which the new governor of the Orleans Territory, William Claiborne, had established. Owed favors by numerous members of the city's Creole population and by many of the newly arriving Americans, as well, Max knew he was in a position to have anything he desired. There was nothing wanting in his life.

"Spend your time worrying about your other sons," he advised Irénée. "They need your advice far more than I do."

"Max, you do not know how you have changed."

"If I have, it's for the better."

"Better?" Irénée repeated anxiously. "Is it better to mock and scorn all those who care for you, and treat everyone with contempt? Are you proud of believing only the worst about people?"

"They believe the worst about me," he said with a cynical smile. "And do not try to deny it, Maman. Even you won't allow yourself to be seen with me in town—unless it is unavoidable. And God knows I do not blame you. I'm well aware of the way people scuttle out of my path. I'm also damn tired of the impudent young cockswains who try to bolster their self-esteem by challenging me. No matter how I try to avoid it, I'm forced to duel in sheer self-defense. And each time I kill or wound a man, another seeks to take his place."

His tone was quiet and cool. Long ago Max had seen the way people feared him, and it had made him bury his ability to feel anything deep within himself.

"Why must you be so bitter?" Irénée cried.

Max gazed his mother's worried face, then gave a short laugh. "You can't presume to tell me I don't have the right

to be bitter, Maman. Now, what do you want me to do
about the boys?''

''Nothing,'' Irénée said frostily. ''I see now it was really
you I wished to discuss. And it is no use trying to reach
your heart. Perhaps it is because you have no heart left . . .''
She walked away with a pained expression.

Max stared after her, his lips parting as if to call her
back. But there was something cold and hard lodged inside
his chest that prevented him from entreating her to return.

Philippe and Justin wandered through the woods and
down to the bayou, finding their way around mud holes,
pines, and sycamore trees. The boys were tall for their
age, lanky and thin, having not yet attained their father's
heavily muscled build.

Their features were stamped with the inborn arrogance
of the Vallerands. Heavy black hair fell over their fore-
heads in similar untidy waves, and their blue eyes were
framed with long dark lashes. Strangers were never able
to tell them apart, but inwardly they were as different as
it was possible for two boys to be. Philippe possessed a
sense of honor that led him to be kind to those who were
weak or vulnerable. Justin, on the other hand, was ruthless
and self-serving, resentful of authority.

''What are we going to do?'' Philippe asked. ''Should
we take the pirogue and look for pirates downriver?''

Justin gave a scornful laugh. ''Go find something else
to do. I plan to visit Madeleine today.''

Madeleine Scipion was the pretty black-haired daughter
of a town merchant. A sly, dark-haired minx, she had
lately displayed more than a casual interest in Justin, although she was aware that Philippe was smitten with her.
The girl seemed to delight in pitting one brother against
the other.

Philippe's sensitive face revealed his envy and curiosity.
''Are you in love with her?'' he asked.

Justin grinned and spat. ''Love? Who cares about that?

Did I tell you what Madeleine let me do to her the last time I saw her?''

''What?'' Philippe demanded with rising jealousy.

Their eyes locked. Suddenly Justin cuffed him on the side of the head and laughed, then fled through the trees as Philippe gave chase. ''I'll make you tell me!'' Philippe scooped up a glob of mud and threw it at Justin's back. ''I'll make you . . .''

They both stopped short as they saw a movement near the pirogue. A small boy dressed in ragged clothes and a floppy hat was fumbling with the craft. The tethering rope dropped from his hands as he realized he had been found out. Quickly he picked up a knotted bundle of cloth and fled.

''He's trying to steal it!'' Justin said, and with warlike whoops the twins ran after the vanishing thief, their quarrel with each other discarded.

''Head him off!'' Justin ordered. Philippe swerved to the left, disappearing behind a cluster of cypress trees that trailed their moss down to the soft, muddy brown water. Within minutes he succeeded in cutting the boy off, coming face to face with him just beyond the cypress grove.

Seeing the boy's violent trembling, Philippe grinned triumphantly, drawing a forearm across his sweaty brow. ''You'll be sorry you ever thought of touching our pirogue,'' he panted, advancing on his prey.

With a cry of fright, the thief turned to go in the opposite direction, and ran into Justin, who caught him with one arm and held him dangling sideways. The boy dropped his bundle and gave a high-pitched scream, which caused the twins to laugh.

''Philippe!'' Justin cried, fending off the feeble blows of the youngster. ''Look what I've caught! A little *lutin* with no respect for others' property! What should we do with him?''

Philippe regarded the hapless thief with the censuring

stare of a judge. "You," he barked, swaggering before the wriggling imp, "what's your name?"

"Let go of me! I've done nothing!"

"Only because we interrupted you," Justin drawled.

Philippe whistled as he saw the red welts and bleeding scratches that covered the boy's thin arms and neck. "You've provided a feast for the mosquitos, haven't you? How long have you been in the swamp?"

The child managed to kick Justin in the knee.

"Ah, that hurt!" Justin shook the black hair out of his eyes and glared at the boy. "Now I've lost my patience!"

"Let me go, you mongrel!"

Annoyed, Justin raised his hand to box his captive's ears. "I'll teach you manners, boy."

"Justin, wait," Philippe interrupted. It was impossible not to feel sympathy for the child caught so helplessly in his brother's grasp. "He's too small. Don't be a bully."

"How soft you are," Justin mocked, but his arm lowered. "How do you suggest we make him talk? Dunk him in the bayou?"

"Maybe we shouldn't . . ." Phillip began, but his brother was already heading to the edge of the water, dragging the screaming child behind him.

"Are you aware there are snakes in here?" Justin said, swinging the boy up, preparing to throw him in. "Poisonous ones."

"No! Please!"

"And alligators too, all waiting to snap up a little bite like . . ." His voice trailed off into silence as the boy's floppy hat dropped into the bayou and drifted gently away. Long curls of fiery red hair fell to the ground in a silky cascade.

Their thief was a girl, a girl their age or perhaps even older. She threw her slim arms around Justin's neck, clinging as if he held her over a pit of fire."

"Don't throw me in," she begged. *"Je vous en prie.* Please. I can't swim."

Justin shifted her in his arms, staring down at the small, dirty face so close to his. Her cheekbones were high and delicate, and her trembling lips were exquisitely curved. "Well," Justin said slowly, his voice changing. "It seems we were mistaken, Philippe." He shook the protesting girl to quiet her. "Hush. I'm not going to throw you in. I think I can find a better use for you."

"Justin, give her to me," Philippe said.

Justin smiled darkly and turned away from his brother. "Go amuse yourself somewhere else. She's mine."

"She is just as much mine as yours!"

"I'm the one who caught her," Justin said matter-of-factly.

"With my help!" Philippe cried in outrage. "Besides, you have Madeleine!"

"You take Madeleine. I want this one."

Philippe scowled. "I will fight you for her," he said.

Justin shook his head. "Then she'll run away and neither of us will have her, stupid."

"Then let *her* choose!"

They stared at each other in challenge, and suddenly Justin chuckled. "So be it," he said, his fierceness mellowing to lazy good humor. He jostled the girl in his arms. "Well, imp, which one of us do you choose?"

"Ch–choose?" she whispered, too bewildered and exhausted to understand what was happening. "For what?"

"To go off with," Justin said impatiently. "Which one of us do you prefer?" She began to struggle, and he tightened his grip on her until she subsided with a gasp of pain.

"Mon Dieu, it's not necessary to hurt her," Philippe said.

"I didn't hurt her," Justin replied indignantly. "I just squeezed her a little." He gave the girl a piercing stare. "And I will do it again if she doesn't make up her mind now."

Her lashes lifted, and she looked from the imperious dark face of the boy who held her, to the lighter one of the boy nearby. They were brothers, she thought, identical in appearance. But the one called Philippe seemed a little gentler, and there was a trace of compassion in his blue eyes that she sensed was absent in the other. It was just possible that she could convince him to release her.

"You," she said desperately, looking at Philippe.

"*Him?*" Justin scoffed, letting her feet drop to the ground. "Over *me?* He has no experience at all! He probably has no idea what to do with you."

I can only hope so, she thought, as she was passed from one pair of arms to the other.

"There, do what you want with her," Justin said sullenly. He scooped up the bundle on the ground and searched through it, discovering a handful of coins tied in a handkerchief, a rolled-up dress, and an amber comb.

Philippe put his hands on the girl's narrow shoulders, steadying her. "What is your name?" he asked.

His voice was unexpectedly kind. She bit her lip, feeling the sting of tears. "Lysette," she whispered, her head bent down.

"Why were you taking the pirogue?"

"I cannot tell you."

Philippe's blue eyes took a detailed tour from her glistening red hair down to the shabby, overlarge shoes on her feet. In spite of her outlandish attire, she didn't seem like a common wench, or the kind of girl who might normally be inclined to wildness. She looked innocent and afraid.

"Come with me," Philippe said, sliding his hands down to her wrists. "If you're in trouble, we may be able to help you."

"No, please," she begged, pulling at her imprisoned arms.

"You have no choice."

The words set off an explosion of movement as Lysette tried to twist away from him and began to scream again.

"I'm not going to hurt you," Philippe said, swinging

her over his shoulder and locking his arm behind her knees. She flailed helplessly against his back.

Justin watched his brother's actions closely. "Where are you taking her?" he asked jeeringly.

"To Father."

"*Father?* What are you doing that for? He'll only make you let her go."

"There's something strange about this girl. I have a feeling he will be interested."

"Idiot," Justin muttered underneath his breath, but he followed reluctantly as his brother carried their new acquisition away from the bank of the sluggish stream.

Lysette went limp halfway up the incline, deciding it would be wiser to save what strength she had left to face whatever fate was in store for her. There was no way she was going to escape the clutches of these two arrogant boys. She closed her eyes, feeling sick. If what Philippe had said was true and he was taking her to his father, she would be returned to the Sagesse mansion, and this time there would be no opportunity to escape.

"Please," she managed to wheeze. "Don't carry me upside-down. I . . . I will be ill if you do."

Justin spoke up from behind them. "She does look rather green, Philippe."

"Really?" Philippe stopped and let Lysette's feet slide to the ground. "Would you like to walk?"

"Yes," she said, swaying uncertainly, and the brothers each took an arm, guiding her forward. Dazed, she looked from right to left, realizing the boys must belong to a family of great wealth. The land and buildings were even more impeccably tended than the Sagesse plantation. The intense afternoon sun glared on the main house's white and pale grey exterior. Wide galleries framed by white columns overlooked gardens bordered with luxuriant groves of magnolia, oak, and crêpe myrtle.

The chapel, smokehouse and various storehouses were set a short distance away. Beyond a thick planting of cypress trees was the bell tower, and adjacent to that were the slave quarters, a row of one- and two-room cabins forming a small village.

Lysette's feeling of nausea abated somewhat, and she was clear-headed as they ascended the steps leading to the main house. They passed through the largest front door she had ever seen and reached the great hallway, dark and cool, lined with narrow mahogany benches.

"Father?" Philippe called, and a startled servant gestured to a room just beyond one of the twin parlors bordering the hallway. Smugly the boys paraded their charge into the library, where their father sat at a massive mahogany desk. The room was splendidly furnished, the cushions of the chairs and window seat covered with rich yellow silk that matched the yellow and lapis blue print on the walls. Heavy swags of scarlet wool moreen framed the windows.

Lysette's attention moved from the room to the figure at the desk. His head was bent, so all she could see of him was his lustrous black hair and large, powerful upper body.

"What is it?" came a deep, husky voice that sent a thrill of alarm down her spine. She would not have been surprised if he looked up to reveal the face of the devil.

"Father," Philippe said, "we caught someone by the water trying to steal our pirogue."

The man at the desk shuffled a few papers into a neat pile. "Oh? I hope you made him understand the consequences of tampering with Vallerand property."

"Actually . . ." Philippe began, and coughed nervously. "Actually, Father . . ."

"It's a girl," Justin burst out.

Evidently that was enough to attract Vallerand's attention. He raised his head and looked at Lysette.

He had lean, chiseled features, and eyes that appeared oddly pale against the deep bronze of his face. They were golden eyes, framed with needle-sharp black lashes. Cruelty edged his mocking, beautifully shaped mouth. The same callousness Lysette had glimpsed in Justin was fully developed in this man.

Her heart pounded, and she stared at him in fascinated horror as he stood up. He was a giant, with a long, lean body, and shoulders as wide as church doors. His clothes were simple and perfectly cut, the epitome of elegance. Lysette cowered back against Philippe as the man approached her. She flinched when his warm hand slid under her chin, tipping it upward. She could feel the velvety-rough pads of his fingers as he turned her face from right to left. What kind of gentleman would have calloused hands?

"Who are you?" he asked.

Justin replied eagerly. "She won't tell us, Father!"

Lysette was unable to bear that penetrating golden gaze, but she could not close her eyes. "Why steal the pirogue?" came the next question.

"I–I had to."

"What is your name?" When she didn't reply, his fingers urged her chin up a fraction of an inch higher. "Who is your family?"

"Please . . . I cannot say."

"Are you lost?"

"N–no, not exactly," Lysette replied, feeling the answer dragged out of her against her will.

"Then you're running from someone."

"Yes," she whispered.

"From whom?"

"S–someone like you, monsieur." From her perspective, there were many similarities between him and Etienne Sagesse.

Max smiled slightly. "I doubt that. Do you know who I am?"

"No," she whispered.

"I am Maximilien Vallerand. Have you heard of me?"

"No."

"Then you are not from New Orleans."

Lysette moistened her dry lips with her tongue, and murmured an inaudible *no*. Max was momentarily diverted by the movement, his gaze lowering to her mouth. Lysette fought the overwhelming urge to scream and flee, knowing that an escape attempt would be a useless gesture.

"How old are you?" Max asked tersely.

"I am eighteen, monsieur."

He glanced down at her flat chest with insulting boldness. "You're lying."

Lysette shook her head. She knew she looked younger than eighteen. However, she could not, would not explain that the reason for the childish flatness of her chest was a tightly wound binding cloth.

"How old?" he repeated.

"Eighteen. It is the truth," she managed to say, and his mouth twisted skeptically.

"Where were you planning to go in the pirogue?"

"I have a cousin who lives in Beauvallet, and—"

"Beauvallet?" Justin repeated, staring at her with contempt. The small parish was nearly fifteen miles away. "You were trying to travel there on your own? Haven't you heard of Choctaws? And river pirates? Don't you know what can happen to you in the swamp? What do you think you are? You're just a girl, a silly—"

"Justin," Max interrupted. "Enough."

His son quieted instantly.

"Traveling such a distance by yourself . . . indeed, an ambitious undertaking," Max commented to Lysette. "But perhaps you were not planning to go alone. Could we possibly have interrupted a rendezvous between you and some male admirer?"

Her face went white and her eyes flashed with loathing. He couldn't actually think she would go through this all for the sake of a clandestine meeting with a lover. To be held against her will, questioned, and then insulted—it was beyond indurance. Before she realized what she was doing, her hand shot out in a short arc toward his face. He caught her wrist easily, as if he had anticipated her reaction. Lysette cried with fury and fought against him blindly, striking out with her other hand.

He spun her around and twisted her arm behind her back. Pain knifed through her, and she drew in a sobbing breath. Instantly Max let go of her wrist and slid his arm around her front, imprisoning her arms. The expression on his face became icy as a dark suspicion entered his mind. "Easy," he murmured. "Be still. I won't hurt you again."

He glanced at the twins, who were watching the pair of them with fascination. "Leave, both of you," he said.

"But why?" Justin protested hotly. "We were the ones who found her, and besides—"

"Now," Max said flatly. "And tell your *grand-mère* I wish her to join us in the library."

No! Lysette wanted to cry in panic as she saw the boys leave, dragging their feet and glancing over their shoulders at her. *Don't leave me here alone with him!*

"He has my belongings!" she burst out with an accusing stare at Justin.

"Justin," Max said in a low voice of warning.

The boy grinned, pulling the knotted handkerchief of coins out of his pocket and tossing it to a nearby chair. Then he slipped out the door before his father could reprimand him.

Left alone with Vallerand, Lysette found herself babbling frantically. "Monsieur Vallerand, I am so very terribly sorry I trespassed on your property but since there was no harm done I will disappear and never trouble you again, because surely you must have more important things to bother about than such a little incident as this, and—" She broke off with a squeal of surprise as she felt him raise the back of her shirt. She felt the touch of the humid air on her skin. "No!" she cried in horror, and struggled against his restraining arm. "You mustn't . . . you can't—"

"Of course I can," Max said dryly, stuffing the hem of the shirt into the top of her collar. "You have no reason to fear, mademoiselle, I have no interest in your . . . ," he paused and added sardonically, "feminine charms. Your display of maidenly modesty is quite unnecessary."

Had Lysette not been so shocked, she would have argued the point, but she was learning that her captor would let nothing prevent him from doing what he wanted. "I despise you," she said weakly, and gave a little jump as he located the tail end of the cloth tucked underneath her right arm. For a moment his hand was agonizingly close to her breast. "You are not a gentleman," she muttered, arching away from him as he loosened the binding. "You are heartless and interfering . . . and rude, and insolent . . . cruel, unfeeling, brutal . . ."

While she stated her opinion of him, Max unwound the coarse binding. Frantically she covered her breasts with her hands, beginning with shake with distress.

"Just as I thought," she heard him murmur, and she sensed his eyes on the naked length of her back. The tender skin felt as if it were being burned. A tide of crimson humiliation flooded her. No man had ever seen so much of her body before. Tentatively she tried to step away from him, and his arm tightened around her waist. "Stop wiggling," he said. "I hardly intend to molest you when my mother will be arriving at any moment."

Rigid with humiliation, Lysette endured his inspection. She knew there were many welts where mosquitos had bitten through her clothes. The places she had managed to scratch were smarting. The week-old bruises from Gaspard's beating were now multi-colored splotches that covered her almost everywhere. What was Vallerand thinking? Why didn't he say anything?

As the silence lengthened, Lysette swayed against the steely prison of his arm, almost grateful for its support.

Suddenly she was too exhausted to stand on her own, and it took all her strength just to keep her eyes open. Her chin lowered, and she closed her eyes as she waited for whatever would happen next. She felt peculiarly helpless. Everything was beyond her control. Strangely, it was not unpleasant to lean against that hard, strong arm. Perhaps it was a dream . . . yes, it must be a dream, the featherlight touch of his fingertips on her back, moving from bruise to bruise in a trail that seemed to singe her nerve endings. The tips of her breasts tightened into sensitive, almost painful nubs. She wanted to lean back against that impersonal but soothing hand.

Slowly Max pulled down the back of the shirt and covered her slight body. He turned her to face him, leaving his hands on her shoulders. His expression was impassive, almost inhuman in its granite-like stillness. "Who did it?"

She knew he was asking about the bruises. As before, a irresistible force compelled her to speak. *"Mon beau-père."*

"Who is he?"

"Gaspard . . . Gaspard Médart."

"Ah. And does Monsieur Médart make a habit of this practice?"

Although his tone was casual, nearly indifferent, Lysette sensed a terrible importance connected with her answer. "We have come from Natchez . . . for my wedding. I have refused to marry the man my stepfather has chosen for me. He is very angry with me."

Max's brows raised slightly. Until a Creole girl was married, her father—or stepfather—was considered to be her master, every bit as much as her husband would be. To defy a parent's wishes, especially in the area of marriage, was unthinkable. "Most people would not censure a man for disciplining a rebellious daughter in such circumstances," he said.

"A–and you?"

"I have no respect for a man who would strike a woman. No matter what the provocation."

"That . . . ," Her voice seemed to stick in her throat. "That is fortunate for your wife, monsieur."

Was it her imagination, or was there suddenly a gleam of amusement in his eyes? "I do not have a wife, *petite.*"

"Oh." Lysette looked away from him, the color remaining high in her cheeks. She had sounded coy, something she had not intended.

"Where is your stepfather now? Not too far from here, I would guess."

"Please, monsieur, I *entreat* you—"

"You may as well stop asking me to let you go." Max gave her a mocking smile. "As you may have already suspected, I have no intention of doing so. Where is Médart staying?"

"He is at the home of Monsieur Sagesse." She lowered her head, missing the glint of malice that suddenly appeared in her captor's golden gaze.

"Your betrothed is Etienne Sagesse?"

"*Oui.*"

"And your name," he prompted swiftly.

"Lysette Kersaint," she whispered, and then was too tired to speak anymore.

The situation had taken an unexpected turn. Max studied her with savage satisfaction.

The fiancée of Etienne Sagesse, here at his mercy. Finally the instrument of revenge had been delivered to his hands—by his own sons—and there was little that needed to be done except let things take their natural course.

The voice of his mother interrupted his thoughts. "Max? *Qu'est ce qu' il y a?*" Irénée stopped short at the sight of the miserable little figure held in her son's grasp, like a lamb caught in the jaws of a wolf.

"Mademoiselle Lysette Kersaint, Maman," Max said smoothly. "A visitor from Natchez. Apparently she has become separated from her relatives. The boys encountered her outside and brought her to me. I'm afraid she has experienced an unfortunate mishap and requires our assistance. Perhaps you would be able to see to her welfare and find her something more suitable to wear."

Irénée's curiosity was aroused quickly, but she contented herself with the thought that Max would give her a full explanation at a more suitable time. She regarded the girl, who looked ready to faint, with genuine pity. *"Pauvre petite,"* she said, and clucked her tongue. "I can see how weary you are."

"Madame," Lysette began in a wavering voice. "I must—"

"We will talk later," Irénée said, and moved forward to take her hand. "Come with me, child."

"D'accord, madame,*"* Lysette murmured in agreement, and went willingly, more than eager to escape the presence of Maximilien Vallerand. She could feel his devouring gaze on her as she left. She was inexperienced, ignorant of men and their ways, but she was astute enough to know he had taken an unorthodox interest in her—and that she would not feel safe until she was miles away from him.

Several hours later Irénée approached Max with trepidation. He was standing at the window of the library with a drink in his hand.

"How is she?" he asked without turning.

"She has bathed, eaten a little, and now is resting. Noeline put a paste on the scrapes and insect bites." Irénée joined him at the window and contemplated the sleepy bayou. "I remember making the acquaintance of her mother, Jeanne, many years ago. Jeanne is of the Magniers, a fine family that once lived in New Orleans but regrettably produced no sons to carry on the name. An attractive woman, Jeanne, but certainly she has been eclipsed by her daughter." Irénée's fine brows drew together. "Lysette tried to hide the bruises from me, Max. Are you aware of—"

"Yes," he interrupted. "No matter. They are not serious."

"They appear to be quite painful."

He shrugged impatiently. "The young heal quickly."

Irénée stared at him in wonder. "Max, you are not that callous, are you? Set my heart at ease, because I am beginning to fear . . ." Her voice trailed off into silence as Max turned around. In the gathering shadows of evening his face had taken on a devilish darkness.

"Do you know who she is?" he asked quietly.

"*Oui,* she has told me. She is promised to Etienne Sagesse."

"Yes—Sagesse. The man who brought dishonor on my wife, and on my name."

"It wasn't only his fault!" Irénée cried, eager to talk about the subject he allowed no one to bring up. "Corinne was the one who brought dishonor on herself."

"Nevertheless, it is fitting that I repay Sagesse by dishonoring his fiancée."

"*What?*"

"And then," he mused, "a duel will be inevitable. Etienne's pride is quite sensitive."

"No!" Irénée breathed in horror. "I will not allow it!"

"You cannot prevent it."

"You would ruin an innocent merely to strike at Etienne Sagesse?"

A mocking light glittered in his eyes. "Of course."

"This girl is blameless, Max, more child than woman. She has done nothing to harm you. Would you have her on your conscience for the rest of your life?"

"I have no conscience."

Irénée took a sharp breath. "My son, you must not do this."

"You would rather see her married to a man like Sagesse?"

"Yes, if the only alternative is to see her ruined by you and cast into the streets!"

"She will not be cast into the streets. I can well afford to provide for her. A small price, considering the opportunity she has supplied me."

"Her father will certainly challenge you."

"If he is fool enough, so be it. It would not be the first duel I have fought."

"*Alors,* you intend to violate her innocence, establish her in a residence where she will be scorned by all decent society, and duel with an aging father trying to avenge the honor of his daughter—"

"Stepfather. Who beats her, I might add."

"And so you will undoubtedly expect her to be grateful to you for slaying him! How can I have raised such a wicked man as you? I will not associate with such a man. I will have nothing to do with someone capable of such viciousness!"

Max looked at her coldly. "I warn you, Maman, do not interfere. I have waited years for a chance to gain revenge, and I won't relinquish it, not for anyone's sake. Don't waste your sympathy on the girl. She'll be well-compensated when it's over."

Chapter 2

T he gown Lysette had carried with her was irreparably
stained by her journey through the swamp. Irénée
provided a pale blue gown that fit well, except for a bodice
that strained indecently over her breasts. A high collar and
elbow-length sleeves with lace inserts covered the worst
of the damage done to her arms, chest and neck.

As Irénée stood back to view the results, she realized
with pleasure and dismay that Lysette was beautiful beyond all expectations. Her hair was an impossibly brilliant
red that looked crimson against the porcelain whiteness of
her skin. On any other woman that hair might have seemed
garish, but on this girl it was appropriate, and strangely
elegant. Delicate brows a few shades darker arched over
hazel eyes as clear and round as a child's. Her lips were
shaped in a voluptuous bow that would try the self-restraint
of any man who saw her.

"Your appearance is charming, my dear," Irénée said,
and Lysette murmured her thanks without smiling, crushed
by the fact that her escape attempt had been thwarted. She
was helpless in the hands of the Vallerands.

According to Irénée, a message had been sent to her
stepfather Gaspard. There was little doubt he would be
arriving soon to take her back in disgrace. It would be a
humiliating scene. Lysette ground her teeth together as she

thought of that arrogant monster downstairs observing it all and jeering at her silently. She glanced at Irénée and wondered how such a gentle-spirited woman could have produced such a son.

"Madame Vallerand," she asked, "do you have other children?"

"Oui, I have two younger sons, Alexandre and Bernard, who will be returning soon from a trip to France." Irénée leaned nearer and added conspiratorially, "I have a cousin there with five pretty daughters, all unmarried. I encouraged them to go for an extended visit, hoping that Alexandre or Bernard would take an interest in one of the girls and return with a wife." She frowned. "But either the girls are not as attractive as their mother claimed, or my sons are determined never to marry. They should arrive home in a matter of three weeks."

Privately Lysette thought that if Irénée's two younger sons were as disagreeable as Maximilien, it was likely the girls would not have them!

Seeming to read her mind, Irénée said, "I can assure you, they are very different than their brother. But Maximilien was not always this way, *ma petite.* It is only in the last few years that he has become so embittered. He has suffered much tragedy in the past, and I am afraid it has affected him terribly."

Lysette repressed a disbelieving snort. Suffered? That splendidly healthy, self-assured animal she had met this afternoon had never suffered a day in his life. She promised herself that she would not buckle before him again as she had earlier.

As for facing her father and returning to his guardianship, to be handed over to Etienne Sagesse . . . she would find the resolve to bear that as well. Hadn't her mother told her it was a woman's lot to suffer patiently? Tante Delphine had said that even the worst of husbands was better than no husband at all. In her heart Lysette would never accept Etienne as her husband, but outwardly she would have to endure him.

Lysette accompanied Irénée downstairs, feeling martyred as she consigned the remaining years of her life to be withstood in silent misery. Her husband would never know anything but loyalty from her. Her children would grow to adulthood never realizing how deprived of joy their mother's life had been. And through the years she would always remember that if it had not been for Maximilien Vallerand's interference, she might have made it to her cousin Marie's home in Beauvallet.

Her heart thumped faster as they entered the parlor, a small but airy room decorated in pink, brown and cream-flowered brocade. A rich flemish finish covered the woodwork of white oak. Spotless floor-to-ceiling windows let in the hazy Louisiana sunlight. The moss-green chairs and small baroque sofas were grouped together to invite intimate conversation. Was Maximilien in here? No, thank God, it was empty. Lysette began to relax.

Just then she heard his voice from the doorway behind her.

"Mademoiselle, we have some things to discuss before your stepfather—" Max broke off abruptly as Lysette whirled to face him.

A strained expression crossed his features, then disappeared. Other than that, he showed no reaction to the sight of her. But his insides had twisted themselves into a gordian knot. Valiantly he tried to drag his eyes away from her, but nothing would stop them from traveling over her small body. She was an alluring creature, as trim and dainty as a cat.

"I was not aware, monsieur, that there was anything for us to discuss," Lysette said, lifting her chin. He looked angry. Let him be! she thought defiantly. She would do all she could to vex him. He could not despise her any more than she despised him. "You are sending me back to the

Sagesse plantation with my *beau-père*. Then the matter will be finished.''

"Is that what you want?" Max asked.

She stared directly at him, braving his chilling gaze. "Obviously not, or I would not have left there in the first place." Her voice was soft but undeniably sarcastic.

Irénée watched Lysette in astonishment. It had been years since she had heard anyone speak to Max that way. She prayed silently that Lysette would have the sense to hold her tongue. The poor girl had no conception of how cruel he could be.

"Sit down," Max said.

Although Irénée did so immediately, Lysette remained standing. "I do not wish to."

The golden eyes narrowed, and for a moment Lysette feared she had been dangerously foolhardy. "Have a seat, *s'il vous plaît,*" he said in a nasty mockery of a gentlemanly request. It would do, Lysette thought, and sank into a chair. He sat opposite her and leaned back, casually resting his ankle on the opposite knee.

"I would like to know, mademoiselle, the reason for your dislike of Etienne Sagesse."

Startled by the question, Lysette looked down at her hands. Why would he ask such a thing? It was no concern of his. Perhaps he hoped to make her say something he could hold over her head at some point in the future. "You are taunting me," she said in a low voice.

"It is possible I am trying to help you. If you tell me what I wish to know, we may be able to arrive at some solution to your dilemma other than sending you back with Monsieur Médart."

"Maximilien," Irénée broke in, "The child is not foolish enough to believe she can be kept here against the wishes of her stepfather!"

Max looked at Lysette with a hard smile. "What do you believe, *doucette?*"

The careless endearment had a unnerving effect on her.

She felt his voice deep in the marrow of her bones. The back of her neck felt strangely hot as she returned his gaze. "The reason I do not wish to marry Monsieur Sagesse," she said slowly, "is because I know him to be a dishonorable man."

The image of Etienne's florid, ruddily handsome face, with its full sensuous lips and slumbrous blue eyes, appeared before her. "He does not respect women," she continued. "I know he would not show any degree of fidelity, deference, or consideration toward his wife. And he . . . he frightens me." She felt ashamed to admit such a thing to a man who was undoubtedly incapable of fear.

"An astute young woman," Max commented. "He *should* frighten you."

"My family thinks it most fortunate that Monsieur Sagesse has chosen to wed me."

"As the wife of a Sagesse you will be well provided for," Irénée pointed out, earning a warning glance from Max.

"Then you are acquainted with the Sagesses?" Lysette asked.

Max answered before Irénée had the opportunity to speak. "Not closely," he lied.

"Monsieur Sagesse is difficult to understand," Lysette said, her sensitive features touched with appealing hesitancy. "I cannot understand his determination to make me his wife. He knows I have no tender feelings for him. I do not come from a family of means, and my dowry is not . . ." She shrugged helplessly. "There are hundreds of other women who would serve his purpose equally well, women who would marry him gladly and gratefully . . . and yet for some reason he is intent on me. It makes no sense!"

Neither of the Vallerands replied, but their thoughts were in accord. Yes, there were many other women available to Sagesse, but none with the combination of Lysette's beauty and impeccable lineage. Moreover, her reluctance had un-doubtedly sharpened Sagesse's interest in her.

"What of this cousin in Beauvallet?" Max asked. "What did you hope to accomplish by reaching him?"

"Her," Lysette corrected. "Marie Dufour, and her husband Claude." The Dufours were a prosperous farm-ing family. She remembered Marie as a kind and compas-sionate woman who had eloped with Claude for the sake of love. "Marie and I were very fond of each other as children," she said. "I had hoped that the Dufours would support me in my refusal of my stepfather's wishes, and perhaps allow me to live with them."

"What if we were to delay the wedding long enough for you to send a letter to her and receive her reply?"

The suggestion startled Lysette. "But how?" she asked in confusion.

"We can claim you have been taken ill suddenly. The family doctor will affirm that it is dangerous for you to be moved until your convalescence is complete."

"But the doctor will know I am not ill."

"The doctor will say what I desire him to say."

Perplexed, Lysette considered the proposal. "And I would stay here while we wait for Marie's answer?"

Max nodded briefly. "It will only be a few days. My mother's presence will insure that no harm will come to your reputation. If your cousin agrees to help you, I will have you transported safely to Beauvallet."

Lysette was overwhelmed with a flood of hope. All her mind grasped was the idea of escape. The plan might work! Marie would surely take her side and offer her a place to stay, and then she would not have to marry Etienne. She nearly trembled with excitement.

"The plan is to your liking?" Max asked brusquely.

"*Oui,* monsieur!" she exclaimed. "But . . . why are you willing to help me?"

"Perhaps I do not wish to see you married to a man like Sagesse."

"But—"

"You had better go upstairs now," he interrupted, "before your father arrives."

"*Step*father," Lysette mumbled.

Max acknowledged the correction with a short nod, and turned to Irénée. "Maman, wait here, *s'il vous plaît*, and we will receive Monsieur Médart together." Cupping his hand underneath Lysette's elbow, he guided her out of the parlor to the curving staircase that led to the second floor.

His change of behavior was too sudden, Lysette thought. What was the purpose behind his amiable facade? She glanced up at him as they stopped and pulled her elbow from his grasp. "Monsieur Vallerand, I am sorry to sound ungrateful," she said, "but whether I stay with you or return to Monsieur Sagesse, I am in the predicament of having to place my welfare in the hands of a man I do not trust. It may as well be you. I only hope . . . I pray you will not betray me."

Max looked at her without speaking. Lysette had the sensation of being devoured. The fear that had taken hold of her the first moment she had seen him was beginning to establish tenacious roots. She could not fathom what his motive for helping her might be.

Taking in an agitated breath, Lysette began to question him, when she noticed his gaze slide down to her bodice. The thin cambric was strained to the limit. Blushing and fumbling with the small, high collar of the dress, she looked up at Max uneasily.

"Mademoiselle, there is something that should be made clear if we are to reside in the same house for the next few weeks," he said tersely. "I am not in the least tempted by unseasoned girls with no knowledge of the world, and no art for pleasing a man of my years. Therefore you have no reason to fear any improper advances, and you need not simper and shy away every time I draw breath. Is that clear?"

Her cheeks pinkened, and she gave him a single indignant nod before going up the stairs. The instant she turned her back to him, Max gripped the balustrade until his fingers turned white, and he endeavored to quell the violent pounding of his heart. He watched the nearly indiscernible movement of her hips. Arousal surged through his body and centered in his loins, causing him to wince in discomfort. He decided it would be an excellent idea to visit Mariame, his *placée*, tonight.

When Max returned to the salon, Irénée greeted him with a smile of approval. "I knew you would not go through with it. Not after seeing her and realizing what a sweet, gentle girl she—"

"What are you talking about?" Max interrupted.

"You have changed your mind, *oui?* You are going to help her."

"I haven't changed my mind about anything."

Irénée's face fell as her relief dissolved. "But the letter you are allowing her to write to her cousin—"

"The letter will never be sent."

She stared at him in surprise. "How could you—" she began to berate him, but she was interrupted by the appearance of a servant announcing the arrival of Monsieur Médart. Reluctantly she bid him to show the visitor in.

Gaspard Médart was a short, heavy-set man, graceless in his manner and movements. He was perspiring profusely, clearly upset and eager to see his stepdaughter. Beside him was a woman far taller and wider than he, a matronly woman whose hair had been inexpertly darkened with coffee. She looked frantic. The *tante,* Max surmised, and sent her as pleasant a smile as he could manage.

"Where is she?" Médart demanded before introductions could be made, his keen blue eyes darting around the room. "Where is Lysette?"

Max felt immediate dislike for the man. "Monsieur Médart," he said quietly, "I am Maximilien Vallerand. This is *ma mère,* Madame Irénée Vallerand. I believe she and your wife had the occasion to meet a number of years ago.''

Médart gestured brusquely to his companion. "Delphine, my sister-in-law. Why is Lysette not here?''

Irénée graciously invited both of them to be seated. "We are aware of how worried you must be about Lysette,'' she said. "She is quite a lovely and charming girl.''

"Also willful and spoiled,'' Médart muttered. "Where is she? My intent is to collect her as soon as possible. Let us be done with it!''

Irénée was silent, unable to voice the lie her son had concocted. Max stepped in smoothly. "Unfortunately, monsieur, I must impart some distressing news.''

"She has run away again!'' Médart exploded, turning purple with wrath. "I knew it!''

"No, nothing like that. Do not be alarmed. She has come down with a touch of fever.''

"Fever!'' Delphine exclaimed, her mouth and her eyes round with dismay as she thought of the occasional outbreaks of deadly yellow fever that swept the town.

"It seems to be a mild case,'' Max said reassuringly, "but of course I have summoned the family doctor to examine her. Until he arrives, it would be dangerous to disturb her. She is resting in a guest room upstairs.''

Médart stared at him suspiciously. "I insist on seeing her now.''

"Certainly.'' Max began to rise, then questioned, "I assume you have had the fever before?''

"*Non,* never.''

"If it is a more serious case than we have anticipated, you should be warned it could be life-threatening to a man of your age.''

"Perhaps,'' Delphine interceded hastily, "we should return tomorrow after the doctor has seen her, Gaspard.''

Irénée lent her persuasive voice. "I assure you, we will attend to her every need.''

"But the imposition . . .'' Delphine said.

"It is not an imposition," Irénée replied. "Not in the least. Her company is welcome here."

Médart gave Max his most intimidating glare. "How may I be assured of her well-being? I have no proof that she is even here!"

"She is here, and she is quite comfortable." Max said. "I stake my reputation on it."

Médart scowled. "I am aware of your reputation, monsieur. And I know that you are the enemy of Lysette's betrothed. If you are hatching some kind of plot . . . I . . . I will make you pay!"

Irénée leaned forward and said with conviction, "I promise you, Monsieur Médart, that your daughter is safe with us. No harm will come to her." There was an edge to her voice that only Max could recognize as she added, "I, *personally,* will make certain of that."

After many more minutes of similar persuasion, Gaspard and Delphine left. They had no other choice. Max let out a hearty sigh of relief at the sound of their carriage wheels on the drive outside. "Obnoxious people," he muttered.

Irénée pursed her lips. "They are aware we were lying, Max."

"Of course they are."

"I would have given her over to them gladly if it weren't for the bruises on her back. I am of the opinion she would not long withstand Monsieur Médart's discipline."

"In a week the rumors will begin," Max remarked absently, and grinned. "I'd give a fortune to see Etienne's face then!"

"She might be safer with Etienne. At least he has marriage in mind for her!"

Max's careless smile remained. "She'll find a liaison with me far more agreeable than marriage to him."

"What a man you have become," Irénée said, and continued with venomous softness. "I would never have expected it. Before Corinne came into our lives I saw a certain strength to you, the same strength your father possessed.''

Suddenly Max's face was grim. "I am not my father," he said shortly.

"No, you are not," Irénée said. "Victor was the most resilient man I have ever known. He endured tribulations you can only imagine, and yet he always retained his courage and compassion for others. But you are not strong, and most definitely not resilient. You let a shallow woman destroy all that was good in you, and you have succumbed to the basest human desires. Now you would rather make the weak suffer than admit your own mistakes. It is unmanly of you. Your father would be ashamed, as I am.''

Shock crossed Max's features. Irénée had never criticized him so harshly. To his surprise, her reprimand stung. He stared at her in cold fury. "What is it about this girl that makes you so eager to take her part over mine?''

Irénée realized with despair that he had not listened at all. "I hope," she said, "that one day someone will be able to break through the wall of ice around your heart. But I can't imagine who or what would be able to batter it down. All I am certain of is that you need to be humbled very badly. I pray for it to happen soon, before you ruin someone else's life as well as your own.'' She turned on her heel and left him with her head held at a haughty angle.

Max's foul temper subsided after a night spent in Mariame's welcoming arms. Greatly refreshed, he returned to the Vallerand house in the morning and breakfasted alone, pondering. Why should people marry at all, when there was so much more pleasure to be had without bonding themselves to each other in wedlock?

With Mariame there were no pretenses. She accepted him for what he was and expected nothing, except that he continue to provide for her until it suited him to end the arrangement. In bed she was one of the most accommodating women he had ever encountered. He enjoyed her companionship while knowing that she had no emotional claim on him, or he on her.

Corinne had submitted to him because it was her wifely duty, but always with a proper air of reluctance. Her attitude—commonplace for a well-bred Creole woman—had made the revelation of her infidelity doubly painful. Max smiled bitterly, thinking how much better life was when a man was unencumbered by a wife. Never again would he be jealous, vulnerable, or possessive of a woman.

"Monsieur Vallerand?" a soft voice interrupted his thoughts.

He set down his coffee and stood up as Lysette ventured into the breakfast room. *"Bon matin,"* she said. "Please, do be seated. I do not intend to join you."

Max's good mood began to fade rapidly as he sat down and looked at her. Lysette was wearing a delicate peach muslin frock that fit her as it had never fit his mother. A scowl crept over his face. It was discomfiting to see her in Irénée's clothing.

"Is it possible you might be able to find something more appropriate to wear?" he demanded.

Lysette stopped in front of him, nearly eye to eye with him, though he was seated. "Madame Vallerand and I are in the process of altering some of her gowns," she said.

"I have two impressionable boys to consider," he growled.

Suddenly Lysette smiled. "Monsieur, is that why my presence here annoys you? Or are you always so cross?"

"You do not annoy me. I am indifferent to you. And I am not cross."

"I think you are."

Max's dark brows raised several degrees. "Can this be the same trembling mouse of yesterday?" he said. "From whence comes this excess of bravery?"

"I was not afraid of you yesterday," she said, bristling. "I was merely tired."

He did not reply, but his thoughts were evident from the sarcastic expression on his face.

"I suppose," Lysette said, fishing carefully, "my *beau-père* was very angry last night?"

"Very."

"However he believed what you told him, that I was ill?"

"No, he didn't."

"Oh," Lysette said, taken aback. "But I would have expected him to challenge you, or force his way upstairs to find me, or—"

"Mademoiselle Kersaint, your stepfather is trying to avoid a scandal. Furthermore, no matter what he believes, he is not about to challenge me. It is well-known that I have never been defeated in a duel. And as long as you are in my house, no one can forcibly remove you."

Very few of his remarks, Lysette thought, were conducive to further conversation. It was clear he disliked her company. But before she left, she had to give him her note to Marie. "Monsieur," she said, holding up the carefully creased and sealed letter in her hand, "I have composed the letter to my cousin. May we have it sent today?"

Max grunted noncommittally and took the letter, setting it beside his breakfast plate.

"Er . . . you will not misplace it?" Lysette murmured. "It is important that the letter be delivered as soon as p—"

"I'll see to it."

"Thank you, monsieur." She looked at him curiously, having thought that perhaps her impression of him this morning would be different than yesterday's. After all, she had been exhausted and frightened then. Her imagination may have attributed sinister qualities to him that did not exist.

Unfortunately her first opinion of him continued to hold true. Maximillien Vallerand was every bit as steely and bad-tempered as she had remembered. His manner was self-contained but alert, and every detail of him, from the dark princely head to the tips of his polished boots, bespoke aristocratic blood and breeding.

But if his short speech to her on the steps the night before was to be believed—and she did believe it—there was no reason to feel threatened by him. He would not try to take advantage of a woman he did not find appealing.

Lysette wondered what his wife had been like. Pretty, of course, and most assuredly from a good family. Since the idea of divorce was nonexistent in Creole society, she could only assume the unfortunate woman had died. Later, perhaps, she would find some way to question Irénée about it. Did Max feel sorry he had no wife? Was his rudeness merely a guise to hide his grief? Loneliness? She discarded the idea immediately. No, he did not seem like a man concealing secret grief.

Irritated by her stare, Max frowned. "Mademoiselle, either be seated or leave, but kindly do not hover!"

Lysette started guiltily and left with an inarticulate murmur.

Although Irénée was disgusted with her eldest son, she had not yet given up on the possibility of his redemption. While she had breakfast in her room, she discussed the situation frankly with Noeline. A slim, attractive negress with innate practicality and a penchant for speaking her mind, Noeline had been the housekeeper at the Vallerand plantation for the past fifteen years. As Irénée had expected, no detail of their houseguest, or Max's intentions toward her, had escaped Noeline's observant eyes.

"Ain' never gonna change his mind bout 'dis one," Noeline said in her softly accented voice, shaking her head emphatically. 'Dat woman"—she never referred to Corinne in any other way—"kilt his heart."

"Then you believe he'll follow through with his threats?"

"Madame, *he* believe it," Noeline replied, moving to the dressing table and straightening the tiny flasks and brushes into neat rows.

"Then Lysette is not safe with Max in the house," Irénée said reflectively.

"Might as well tie up a hound wid' a string of sausages." Noeline paused and smiled slightly. "When he look at her, he got more on his mind 'dan revenge. He just don' want to admit it."

"I suspected as much . . . ," Irénée began, then hesitated as an idea occurred to her. "I intended to send her back to the Sagesses right away, in spite of Max's wishes. But perhaps I should delay my plans, to wait and see. The child is coming to no actual harm."

"Non, not yet," Noeline said.

"Oh, Noeline, I hope . . . I wish . . . do you think my son is capable of caring for anyone? After all these years, you know him as well as anyone. Does he seem completely heartless to you?"

As Noeline remained silent, considering the question thoughtfully, Irénée motioned her to sit in a nearby chair. *"Non,* madame," Noeline said, looking uncomfortable, "Ah don'—"

"It's all right, Noeline," Irénée insisted. Gingerly the woman perched on the edge of the chair. "Now, give me your opinion," Irénée continued, "I have lost almost all hope for Max. But this girl is unusual. And I have sensed the attraction between them. Do you think it's possible . . ."

For once Noeline did not give a straightforward answer. "Madame, what 'dat chile gonna give him he ain' already got?"

The point was indisputable. "You're right," Irénée said gloomily.

Now that her initial shock had worn off and Lysette had time to ponder her circumstances, it was difficult to paint a brave face on things. She felt exhausted from the inside out. During her escape from the Sagesse plantation she had been consumed with desperation and wild hope, and at the time of her capture by the Vallerand twins she had been terrified. Now, even after Max had insisted that she stay and Irénée had been so kind to her, she was still uneasy.

It would take some time for word to reach her mother, who remained bedridden in Natchez. What would Jeanne say when she learned of what her daughter had done? Jeanne would most certainly work herself into a state, as she did whenever Gaspard's plans were foiled, and then she would be fretful and distressed for weeks. Jeanne had desired the match between Lysette and Etienne Sagesse, for it would have been a financial boon to the family. Gaspard would have had the Sagesses to prevail upon, just as he did with Jacqueline's family. And what would her sister, Jacqueline, say about all this? Lysette cringed at the thought.

It did not seem so very long ago that she and Jacqueline had been girls sharing childish secrets, dreaming foolishly of dashing cavaliers and true love. Now Jacqueline was too disillusioned to consider anything but practical matters.

Feeling depression sweep over her, Lysette went out into the garden, clutching a balled-up handkerchief in her hand. The garden was fragrant with jasmine, magnolias, and sweet olive. Cautiously Lysette sat on a small stone bench, looking from right to left as if fearing someone might take offense at her intrusion. Not even the barest rustle of a breeze disturbed the stillness. She stared at the luxuriant flower beds and sighed, raising the handkerchief to her face to blot an escaping tear.

Gaspard might find some way to force the wedding to take place, in spite of the Vallerands' protection. And Monsieur Vallerand's attitude toward her was hardly reassuring. He seemed to hate her—well, actually, he seemed to hate everyone.

Max, just returning from the stables after a punishing ride, caught his breath at the sight of the girl sitting alone. The tension he had sought to work off with hard exercise reappeared as he stared at her. For a moment he brooded over the question of why she affected him so greatly, in spite of his will to remain indifferent.

He had known many attractive women, but he had never seen anyone quite like her, with beauty so radiant. The delicate line of her profile was brought into sharp relief by the lush greenery of the garden. She had a softly blunted chin, an impudent nose, a high forehead. Her hair, braided and confined with a narrow ribbon, was a blaze of red in the sunlight.

Max felt a stab of keen hunger to sink his hands into that wealth of hair and bury his lips in the fragile whiteness of her throat. He wanted to pull off the dress that clung so tightly to her breasts, and fill his hands and mouth with her warm female flesh. He wanted to crush and consume her. The desire propelled him a few steps forward before he could stop himself.

Lysette heard the muffled sound of footsteps. Halfblinded by the sun, she nevertheless recognized Maximilien Vallerand's tall, lean-hipped form dressed in riding clothes. She blinked in apprehension as he approached her. There was a finely-toned grace in his stride that made her think of a prowling animal.

His eyes locked with hers, and Max forced back the fierce need that had so inexplicably overwhelmed him. After last night with Mariame, he should not be contemplating a woman, especially not an innocent. "Good afternoon," he said coolly.

She nodded, and tried to tuck the handkerchief behind her where he couldn't see it.

He sat beside her without asking for permission, his muscled thigh close to hers, one large, booted foot settling near her small slippered one. His masculine scent, of horses and sweat-dampened skin, a trace of starch and salt, drifted subtly to her nostrils. Confused, she started to turn away from him, and felt him take her wrist.

He held her hand and regarded the wadded handkerchief. "You are unhappy," he murmured.

"No . . . I . . ." Lysette was having difficulty breathing. The heat of his touch seemed to flow into her bloodstream. "Isn't that to be expected?"

"Is it that you're displeased with our hospitality?" he asked. "Is there anything you require?"

"Oh, no . . . it's not that at all . . . your hospitality has been above . . ." Lysette broke off with a slight sound of distress, and tugged at her wrist. Immediately the gentle clasp was broken.

"I was thinking of my family," she said, gathering her wits. "My mother and sister will not take my part against my stepfather. I should marry Monsieur Sagesse without complaint. I was taught that my parents know what is best for me, but this time I cannot allow myself to believe that." Lysette lowered her head in shame. "What I am doing is wrong, a sin, but I can't help myself. I am not a good daughter. I am not obedient. I—"

"Stop," Max interrupted, his eyes glinting with sudden amusement. "There is no crime, little one, in not wanting to marry a man you suspect will not treat you well."

"Of course there is." She looked up at him in surprise. "You know how wrong it is to do what I have done."

He shrugged. "It is true that most females would not have dared to resist the match. However, were I in your position, I might have chosen the same course of action."

Lysette regarded him doubtfully. It was impossible to imagine him in the position of having to accept something he did not want to accept. "I . . . I am not usually as willful as I may seem to you, monsieur."

Max smiled, remembering the sight of her in boys' clothes. "Now why don't I believe that?"

"Because your impression of me is wrong, monsieur!"

Max slid his fingers under her chin and lifted her face upward, the smile still lingering on his lips. "It would take something drastic to change it, *doucette.*" He looked much younger than before, the ever-present shadow leaving his expression.

"You have been so kind to me," Lysette murmured, her throat feeling thick. "I hope your efforts will not have been in vain. You seem to understand my feelings about Monsieur Sagesse, and if my father were alive, I know he would thank you—"

Max's hand fell away from her, and he stood up from the bench, the customary scowl back on his face. Lysette wondered what she had said to make him angry. She had been trying to thank him!

"Your gratitude is useless to me," Max muttered.

"Nevertheless, I felt I should tell you."

"What happened to your father?"

"He died from a dueling wound when I was a child." Her father, Lucien, had been dark and formidable, his moods as changeable as Max's. When he had been gentle, he could charm and cajole anyone into doing whatever he wanted, but when his temper was stormy, everyone had scurried out of his path. He had often been cruel to those he loved, but he had been undeniably protective of his children. Lysette was certain her father would not have forced her to marry Etienne Sagesse.

"In some ways you remind me of him," she said.

Max glared at her. "I am not your father," he snapped, "nor do I have any desire to be cast in such a role."

"I was not—"

"Spare me your infantile fantasies. I have no desire to serve as the object of some girl's immature attraction!"

Lysette shot up from her seat. "I was merely remarking on a *slight resemblance!* And as for *fantasies* . . . it is your own conceit, monsieur, to assume that I think about you at all! You are not the kind of man I admire or find even remotely attractive! You are the most arrogant, swaggering bully I have ever met!''

They were both distracted from the argument by the sound of a muffled snicker nearby. Startled, Lysette glanced over her shoulder to see the twins watching them, Philippe with a baffled expression, Justin doing his best to look worldly. A sneer curled Max's lips, and he left with a curse while the boys scooted out of his way. Mortified, Lysette sank back down on the bench and flapped her hand to stir the air against her hot face.

Philippe was the first to speak. "Mademoiselle?"

"*Oui?*" she responded grimly as he walked closer. She wondered if the boys intended to be insolent. A tinge of healthy pink crept across Philippe's tanned cheeks and the bridge of his nose. In his perfectly honed features there was a disturbing trace of Max, but when she glanced at Justin the resemblance was overpowering.

"Mademoiselle," Philippe said abashedly, "about yesterday . . . we must apologize for the way we treated—"

"Don't apologize for me," Justin interrupted, growling in a creditable imitation of his father. "I'm not sorry for anything. If mademoiselle had not pretended to be something she wasn't, we would have treated her appropriately."

"Of course," Lysette said matter-of-factly, sensing that the way to deal with him was not to let him provoke her. "There is nothing to apologize for. Since I will be staying here for a few days, I hope we may regard each other as friends. Considering what has already transpired between the three of us, an attempt at formality would be rather ridiculous."

"Is your offer of friendship extended only to Philippe?" Justin demanded.

Lysette's eyes moved to his sullen face. "I was speaking to both of you."

Justin grinned suddenly. "Fearless little girl, aren't you?"

"Older than you," Lysette pointed out. Patronizing boy!

"Standing up to Father that way . . ." he continued. "Courageous, but not very wise."

"I'm certainly not afraid of him."

Justin's smile turned sly. "No? Then why were you shaking in your shoes yesterday when father—"

Philippe exploded before his brother could finish the sentence. "Justin, shut up!"

"Or what?" Justin taunted.

"Or I'll make you!"

"You wish you could!"

As they began to bicker, Lysette left unnoticed, shaking her head and smiling to herself. Having been brought up with no brothers and only limited exposure to her male relatives, she had had little opportunity until now to form an opinion on those of the opposite sex. They seemed excessively quarrelsome.

"Back again this evening?" Mariame purred, opening the door wider and welcoming Max into her white one-story house, located in the quadroon quarter of the Vieux Carré, near Rampart Street.

Mariame's thick lashes lowered as she concentrated on loosening Max's starched necktie. "I thought I had satisfied all your desires last night." She gave him a good-natured smile and wrapped her strong, slender arms around his shoulders. Lean-bodied and tall, she found it an easy task to rise on her toes and brush her lips against his. But tonight Max did not respond as usual. He was preoccupied, troubled about something.

"I didn't come here for that," Max said, disentangling himself from her grasp and frowning as if a new burden had been added to those he already carried.

Obligingly Mariame let go and went to pour him a drink. "Oh?" she said over her shoulder. Her wavy black hair fell down her back. "Then what are you here for, Max?"

"Just . . . a little companionship." He paced around the room restlessly.

"That is something you've never asked of me before," Mariame remarked. "Sit down, please, *mon ami*. It makes me nervous to see you pace like a hungry tiger. Companionship . . . are you referring to a simple conversation, perhaps?"

Max gave a short nod.

"Well," she said, "we've never done that before. It might be interesting."

She settled comfortably on the sofa beside him, her long, sleek legs dangling carelessly over one of his thighs. She handed him the glass of bourbon. "What are we to talk about, Max?"

"Damned if I know," he said, taking a deep swallow of liquor.

Mariame's fingers walked up his thigh on a path they had often frequented before. "Are you sure you do not want to—"

"No," he snapped, brushing her hand away.

Mariame shrugged. *"D'accord."* A sly, interested smile touched her lips. *"Alors,* you might tell me more about this woman staying at the house."

"Her? There's nothing to tell. And she's not a woman. She's just a girl. A child."

"Child," Mariame repeated. "How old did you say she was? Seventeen?"

"Eighteen."

"At that age I was a full-grown woman. My maman made an arrangement for a young man to become my protector, and he established me in my own home. Eighteen? . . . I would not call her a child, Max."

"Impudent wench," Max said gruffly. "Why has everyone begun to contradict me of late?"

"Your little houseguest—does *she* find you fearsome?"

"Yes." Max smiled darkly. "Although she doesn't know why. And she does her utmost to hide it."

Mariame looked at him curiously. "What are your plans for her? No, no, do not tell me. I do not wish to know. I already pity her."

Max traced the elegant curve of her jaw with a sensitive fingertip. "Mariame," he said, abruptly changing the subject, "you know that I would never abandon you without providing for you."

Mariame nodded, remembering the day she had met Max. Eight years ago her first lover had broken off their arrangement callously, leaving her and the child she had had by him with no money or home. In despair, she had been packing her belongings to move back in with her mother. Maximilien, who had long admired her, heard of her lover's desertion. He rode up to the house on his gleaming black thoroughbred and boldly invited himself inside.

Back then Mariame had been as afraid of Max as everyone else. She had been astonished by his offer to become her protector. He had his pick of younger and more beautiful women, untouched women. Most men wanted virgins. Apparently Max did not. Throughout the years his casual generosity had overwhelmed her. Although he had never sired any children by her, he had paid for her son to be educated in Paris. The jewels and clothes he had given her through the years would be enough to keep her in luxury for the rest of her life. She knew Max was closer to her than anyone else, but he still remained an enigma.

Once Mariame had tried to express her feelings to Max, her appreciation of his kindness, only to have him mock her for thinking his motives were anything but self-interest. His gifts to her, as he said, were incentive for her to continue pleasing him in bed. She had not argued with him, although they both knew she had no need for that kind of incentive.

As a lover, Max was experienced and wildly exciting, understanding women and how to satisfy them to a degree that no gentleman really should. He had given her extraordinary pleasure, something she would miss when he eventually ended their relationship. Oh, he claimed that he would never marry again, but Mariame suspected that would change.

Mariame was a perceptive woman, and she had seen signs that Max was not as ruthless as he and others thought. It was possible there was a vein of compassion in the granite-like region of his heart. Because Max had been kind to her, she had resolved long ago never to stand in the way of what he wanted. When he decided to end their relationship, she would let him go without protest. She had no wish to chain him to her, and she was glad there was no spark of love between them. He would be cruel to someone who loved him, and that would be impossible to bear.

"I never fear that you will leave me destitute," Mariame said, her eyes unblinking as she looked at him. Was this, perhaps, the first sign that his interest in her was waning? "You are not that kind of man."

He smiled wryly, making no reply.

"Someday," Mariame said idly, unfolding her legs from his, "I would like to run my own boardinghouse. I would be quite successful at it."

"Yes, you would."

"Should I begin to make plans?"

"Someday. If that's what you want." He caressed her cheek dispassionately. "But not yet."

Mariame smiled, content in the knowledge that for now he still wanted her.

Thursday was the Vallerands' usual at home day, when Irénée's friends and acquaintances came to visit and chat over a cup of strong chicory-laced coffee. Lysette regretted that Irénée had been forced to turn away visitors because of her.

"My stay with you is disrupting your usual habits," Lysette said.

Irénée shushed her cheerfully. *"Non, non,* we will have

coffee together, just the two of us. Presently I find your company much more diverting than that of my friends, who bring the same gossip to chew over week after week. You must tell me all about your mother, and your friends in Natchez, and about your beaux. Such a pretty girl—you must have had many handsome admirers!''

Lysette blushed slightly. ''Actually, madame, I have led a very secluded life. My sister and I were not allowed to have beaux. In fact, we seldom associated with even our male cousins or relatives.''

Irénée nodded in understanding. ''By standards nowadays, that is an old-fashioned upbringing. It was that way with me. I never read a newspaper until after I was married. I was well-educated in manners, art, and languages, but knew nothing of the outside world. It was frightening when the time came to leave the cocoon of my family and assume my place as Victor Vallerand's wife.'' Irénée smiled, her dark eyes soft with amusement as she remembered the girl she had once been. ''My Tante Marie and my mother accompanied me to my marriage bed, and left me there alone to wait for my husband. Oh, how I begged them to take me back home! I did not want to be a wife at all, much less the wife of a Vallerand. Victor was a big bear of a man, and very intimidating. I was terrified of what he would require of me.''

The color in Lysette's cheeks deepened, but she listened intently to the older woman, hoping Irénée might reveal something about the mysterious marital relationship everyone took such pains to keep her ignorant of. There were many questions she wanted to ask, but it would be improper. Irénée noticed Lysette's obvious interest and smiled in pity. It was not her place to tell an innocent girl the things she would discover on her wedding night.

It was a man's right to instruct and educate his young wife as he wished. Some men liked their wives to take pleasure in their union, while others had been known to abandon their brides on their wedding night because they displayed unseemly desire. More often than not a man wanted his wife to remain docile, submitting only reluctantly to his animal passions.

"Lysette," Irénée said, abruptly changing the subject, "do you think we might enlist your Tante Delphine's help in this little fiction of ours about your supposed illness? Your stepfather will be coming back soon—more upset than before, and with just cause—and perhaps it will set his mind at ease if we invite her to stay with us. Could we depend on Delphine to keep our secret?"

"No, we could not," Lysette said sadly. "Tante Delphine would not take my part in something she disapproves of. She chastised me for expressing my dislike of Etienne Sagesse, and she repeated everything I had told her to my stepfather. That was when he became angry and . . . ," she broke off and winced. Irénée knew what she was thinking.

"Then we will not speak of it again," Irénée said. Picking up her cup, she tasted the strong brew and decided to stir more sugar into it. Like other Creoles, she preferred her coffee "black as the devil and sweet as sin."

"In the past," Irénée said, concentrating on swirling her tiny silver spoon in the cup, "some young women have found Monsieur Sagesse . . . er . . . not without appeal."

Lysette could not prevent her strong reaction to the gently inquisitive comment, and her voice trembled with heedless temper. "I find him *entirely* without appeal. I hated him the first time I saw him. He came to Natchez at my stepfather's invitation, and inspected me as if . . . I were a horse to be purchased. And the second day of his visit . . ." She stopped, turning crimson.

Irénée leaned forward. "Yes?"

"I-I should not say."

Immediately Irénée was as intent as a bloodhound with a fresh scent to investigate. A new bit of gossip about Etienne Sagesse could not fall on more appreciative ears.

"I am certain there is nothing you could say that would surprise me," she said in an encouraging tone.

Lysette sighed morosely. "The second day of his visit, Monsieur Sagesse accompanied me on a walk in the garden. It was the first time I had ever been alone with a man. I was trying very hard to like him, madame, since I knew my stepfather had given him leave to court me. But the moment we reached a secluded spot far enough from the house, he—" she faltered. "He took liberties . . ."

"I see," Irénée said after a moment, when it was clear Lysette would not describe the scene.

"After I managed to elude him, I told my *tante* what had happened, and then my mother. But no one seemed willing to censure Etienne Sagesse. Maman explained that sometimes men simply cannot control themselves."

"True," Irénée replied, nodding wisely.

"Later," Lysette continued, "when my stepfather and Delphine brought me to New Orleans, Monsieur Sagesse came to my bedroom door the first night and tried to come in, but I had locked it. Had I not, I'm certain that no one in the house would have lifted a finger to prevent him from doing whatever he wished. The next evening I found the lock on my door was broken, and I was afraid. I did not stop to think. I went to the stables, gave the stableboy a coin for his clothes, and left immediately. I traveled the night along the edge of the bayou." She paused and smiled ruefully, remembering the darkness, the slithering reptiles, and worst of all, the plaguing insects that had stung and tormented her mercilessly. "I hope never to have such a night again. The next morning I encountered the twins, and subsequently Monsieur Vallerand. And how grateful I am that I did!"

"As am I," Irénée said. "I fear there have been others, Lysette, who were not as successful at evading Etienne's advances as you. In the past years he has seduced several girls in New Orleans and threatened to shame their families and ruin their hopes for marriage by revealing what he had done. Some poor innocents have been forced to enter the convent because of him.''

''Yes,'' Lysette said earnestly, ''I am not surprised. But what frightened me about Monsieur Sagesse was not merely his displays of passion. I believe he *enjoys* to humiliate . . . that he despises women, and it satisfies him to hurt them. I could feel it whenever he looked at me.'' She glanced at Irénée, who looked vaguely puzzled.

''Despises women, you say? I do not think so. There is no reason for it.''

Lysette shrugged. Reason or not, she was certain Sagesse felt that way. ''Has no one ever called him out?'' Lysette asked.

''It has occurred a few times. Etienne has killed some of the fathers and brothers of his victims in duels. He has never been bested.''

''Monsieur Vallerand made a similar claim to me,'' Lysette said absently.

''But there is a difference,'' Irénée said emphatically. ''Maximilien only duels when there is no other alternative, and his honor is at stake. Etienne, on the other hand, has instigated nearly all the duels he has fought.''

''I do not see the difference,'' Lysette said. ''Killing is killing, no matter who provokes the duel.''

Irénée looked offended. ''Not in New Orleans, *petite*. Here it is justifiable and at times quite necessary.''

''Of course,'' Lysette said quickly. ''Forgive me. I did not mean to sound judgmental. And in any case, it does not matter what I think.'' She smiled slightly. ''Certainly no one will ever duel over *me*, and the members of my family are not the kind to become involved in such matters.''

Irénée stirred a lump of sugar into her coffee, making no reply.

The Vallerand household was frequently disrupted by Justin's antics. Sometimes the hapless Philippe would be drawn into his brother's devilry, but most often Justin mis-behaved on his own. The only one capable of dealing with the boy was Max. When they argued, the house seemed to shake down to its foundations. Max would become dangerously quiet and sarcastic, while Justin would shout at the top of his lungs. Everyone else would retreat to their rooms, far removed from the line of fire.

The most recent battle had occurred when Justin tried to sneak in the house well past midnight, bloodied and battered from one of his frequent brawls. Max cornered him immediately, dragging him into the kitchen and giving him a scalding lecture. Lysette could hear the clash from her room on the second floor.

"You cannot treat me as if I were a child!" Justin bellowed, and grunted as Max applied a cold rag none too gently to his blood-smeared face. "I'm a man!"

"So you claim," Max sneered. "But a man does not bully others into fighting him merely for his own entertainment."

"It's not for entertainment," Justin said hotly.

"Then why do you fight?"

"To prove something!"

"To prove you're not as agile and sharp-witted as you seem to fancy yourself. Perhaps you are quick with your fists. That won't take you far. Soon, my boy, you will reach the age when your heavy-handed tactics will earn you the challenge to a duel, and then you'll have a man's lifeblood on your hands. Either that, or you'll end in an early grave."

"You cannot attack me for being like you," Justin said, ripping himself away from his father's grasp, glaring at him through a shock of black hair.

"I'm not attacking you," Max said, unimpressed by the boy's dramatics.

"I'm doing nothing worse than you! I know what you are!" Justin sneered as he added, "And I know about your plans for Sagesse."

Max went still. After a long, nerve-wracking pause, he finally growled, "I have reasons you know nothing of."

"Don't I?" Justin taunted.

Max's breath hissed between his teeth as he sought to control his temper. "If you were not my son, I—"

"I hate being your son," Justin said in a near-whisper. "I *hate* it. Because I know all about you."

For a moment they were both shocked into silence by what Justin had said. Max studied him with hard eyes, his mouth set grimly, his hand tightening around the bloodied rag. "So you've heard the rumors," he said.

"I have heard the truth!"

"Rumors," Max said flatly, "until they are confirmed by me."

Justin's blue eyes glittered, and a grimace of misery twisted his face. "I *know* it is true," he said gruffly, and fled from the room as if the devil were at his heels.

Chapter 3

$\sim\!\!\!\mathcal{GC}\!\!\!\sim$

Max was gone all the next day, attending to business in town. In response to Lysette's questions, Irénée replied rather indifferently that he was meeting with Governor Claiborne.

"But why?" Lysette asked, fascinated. "What could the governor want from Monsieur Vallerand?"

Irénée shrugged. "I suppose it is because Max is owed many favors and has a good sense of politics. I have heard there is much unrest in the city, especially among the Americans—but then, they are such a troublesome people."

Like most Creoles, Irénée considered Americans to be barbarians, with few exceptions. Rough and unrefined, Americans were preoccupied with money, fond of drinking to excess, and impatient with the Creoles' leisurely way of doing things. Only Americans would be tasteless enough to replace the Creoles' waltz and cotillion with the reel and jig. Only the hypocritical Americans would criticize the Creole habit of relaxing on Sunday instead of sitting in stiff-backed pews from morning till night.

"Why is there unrest in the city?" Lysette asked.

"Who knows? It is for men to occupy themselves with these things. They will resolve the situation one way or another."

Lysette knew the older woman was right, but she could not help being curious. Fretfully she turned her attention to the light needlework Irénée had provided, until the nagging in her temples became a full-fledged headache. The morning stretched into early afternoon, and the blazing heat seemed to invade even the most shadowy parts of the house. Perspiration glued her garments to her skin, and Lysette pulled at her clothes irritably.

When Irénée retired to take a midday nap, declaring herself fatigued from the heat, Lysette did the same. She trudged into her own room, stripped down to her undergarments and stretched out on the cool white sheets. A housemaid unrolled the *baire,* a gossamer net that kept mosquitos away from the bed. Staring up at the fourteen-foot-high chintz canopy of the bed, Lysette waited for sleep to overtake her. Although it had been three days since her journey along the bayou, she had still not fully recovered from it. She was exhausted, and she ached down to her very bones. Strange, that she should be so weary when she had done nothing but rest ever since she had arrived here.''

Quietly Justin slipped into the library, his gaze darting from one end of the room to the other. The library was stuffy in the afternoon heat. Books lined up in endless rows seemed to look down from their shelves like sentinels.

The bulk of Max's staunch mahogany desk, with all its mysterious drawers and cubbyholes, stood between the draped windows. The sight of it sent a shiver down Justin's spine. How often he had seen his father sitting at that desk, his black head bent over documents and books. The drawers were filed with keys, receipts, papers and strongboxes—and hopefully the object Justin was looking for. Swiftly he moved to the desk and rifled through it, his fingers peeling through the contents of each drawer.

Justin used the hairpin purloined from Irénée's room to

unlock a small gray document box. It opened with a protesting click, and he threw a wary glance over his shoulder before looking inside. More receipts, and a letter. An unopened letter. Justin's eyes glittered with triumph. Carefully he tucked it inside his shirt, closed the box and put it back where he found it. A vengeful glow of warmth rose up his neck to his face. "This," he muttered to himself, "will go far toward squaring my account with you, *mon père.*"

Lysette slept heavily, well past the supper hour, but Irénée saw to it that she was not interrupted. When she awoke, the room was dark and the coolness of evening had settled into it. She felt better, but still sluggish, and her eyelids were swollen. Disgruntled, Lysette dressed in a light yellow gown and left her bedchamber. As she stepped out into the hall, she thought she heard some light footsteps behind her. Turning swiftly, she looked but could not detect any presence in the shadows. Lysette frowned and made her way downstairs.

"Ah, you have finally awakened," came Irénée's buoyant voice. "I thought it better to let you sleep as long as you wished. You must be hungry now, hmm?" The older woman took Lysette's arm and squeezed it affectionately. "The twins and I have already eaten. Max arrived just a moment ago and is having supper. You can join him in the *salle à manger.*"

The thought of food made Lysette nauseous. *"Non, merci,"* she managed to say. "I find I am not very hungry tonight."

"But you must have something," Irénée argued, propelling her towards the dining room. "We have delicious gumbo, and pompano stuffed with crab, and hot rice cakes—"

"Oh, I can't," Lysette said weakly.

"You must try. You are too thin, my dear."

As they went into the dining room, Lysette could see

Max's reflection in the gold-framed mirror over the marble fireplace. He was seated at the table, the lamplight gleaming on his raven hair.

"Good evening, mademoiselle," he said. With a perfunctory show of courtesy, he stood up and assisted her into a chair. "Irénée tells me you have slept a long time." He gave her an assessing glance. "Are you feeling well?"

"Yes, quite well. Just not hungry." Lysette looked at the plate of food in front of him, which ordinarily would have been quite appetizing.

Irénée clucked her tongue. "See that she eats something, Maximilien. I will be in the next room with my embroidery."

Lysette smiled after the older woman as she left. "Your mother is very strong-willed, monsieur."

"There is no disputing that," Max agreed, and tore a chunk of bread in two. There was a mocking gleam in his eyes. "Irénée will not rest until she's added more substance to your frame."

"I like the way I am," Lysette replied, lifting the glass of water to her lips and taking a sip. She nearly choked on it as his gaze traveled audaciously from her face down to her throat and bosom. He gave no sign as to whether he approved of what he saw or not. She stared at his bronzed face defiantly until the heavy-lashed eyes met hers. One corner of his mouth tilted in a sardonic half-smile. "Madame Vallerand told me you met with Governor Claiborne today," she said, trying to sound casual.

The expression on his face did not change. "Yes," he said, his white teeth biting into the golden-crusted bread.

"Why did he desire such a meeting?" she asked.

"His administration is under siege. He is trying to gather all the information he can before his enemies destroy him."

"Who are his enemies? The Creoles?"

Max shook his head. "No, not Creoles. Refugees from France and Santo Domingo, and a small but noisy handful of Americans.'' Including, he might have added, the former vice-president of the United States, Aaron Burr, who was at this moment in Natchez. It was rumored Burr was on a reconnaisance mission to enlist men in a plot to take possession of the Orleans territory. Claiborne was justifiably agitated.

"Why are they his enemies?'' Lysette asked. "What do they want?''

"They would like to discredit Claiborne and separate the territory from the Union. Unfortunately, the governor seems too young and inexperienced to prevent it from happening.''

"Are you one of those, monsieur, who wish Louisiana to attain statehood?''

Max's brow arched at her untoward interest. "I'm counting on it,'' he replied. "When the Americans took over the territory two years ago, I placed my loyalties with Claiborne. Unfortunately the Americans have not kept their promise to admit Louisiana into the Union.''

"But why?''

"They claim that our population is not ready for citizenship.''

"I don't see why . . . ,'' Lysette began, and fell silent as dizziness swept over her. She closed her eyes, and when she opened them, Max was staring at her closely, like a cat stalking a small, flighty bird. "I . . . I'm rather tired, monsieur,'' she murmured, pushing back from the table. "I cannot stay any longer. If you will excuse me . . .''

"Of course.'' He helped her up, and grinned as she jerked away from his touch. "I'm beginning to wonder, *doucette,* why my proximity seems to distress you so.''

Annoyance at his gibe burned in her chest. "I don't understand what you mean,'' she said. "And I do not find you amusing.''

"But I find *you* amusing,'' he replied. "Endlessly.''

He was the most insufferable man she had ever met. He had such contempt for her, and for everyone else as well.

If only she knew how to put him in his place! Filled with loathing, Lysette glared at him and turned her back, leaving as quickly as possible, while the sound of his laughter carried to her ears. She felt more relieved with each step she put between them.

It took almost all her energy to climb the stairs. As she neared her room, Lysette put her hand to her face, knowing something was not right. Her skin felt clammy. Perhaps she should tell Irénée—but it might turn out to be nothing, and Lysette did not want to cause the older woman further inconvenience. Not only that, she was determined not to earn Maximilien's censure by proving to be in need of constant attention. He would probably say she was feigning illness in order to gain sympathy! She decided to go back to bed, certain she would feel better in the morning.

There was a white square of paper in the doorway. Curiously Lysette bent and picked it up, holding onto the doorframe to keep her balance. A tingle crept down the back of her neck, a feeling that someone was watching her. She turned and glanced up and down the hallway, but no one was there. Moistening her dry lips, she looked down at the object in her hand. Her heart stopped beating as she saw what it was.

"The letter," she whispered, suddenly finding it painful to breathe. The envelope trembled in her hands. It was her letter to Marie, unopened, undelivered! What did it mean? Max had not sent it. But why? What was his purpose in keeping it? Oh, God . . . she had known she couldn't trust him, but she'd had no other choice!

Lysette's bewilderment changed to anger and a hard knot in her stomach prompted her to move. Step by step she made her way to the stairs. The ache in her back and head intensified. She would face Vallerand this moment and make him explain! She would know his purpose before another minute passed! Shaking with rage, she gripped the balustrade in her slippery hand and began the long descent. Halfway down she saw Max walking out of the dining room.

"Monsieur Vallerand!" she cried, stopping abruptly. "You will explain this to me now!"

Nonchalantly he glanced at her. "Explain what, mademoiselle?"

She held up the letter. "Why was *this* not sent? What are you trying to accomplish?"

Max's eyes narrowed on her. "What is that?"

Lysette felt herself turn white with fury. "My letter to Marie! You kept it! You never intended to send it!" Her concentration was disrupted by a sharp ringing in her ears. "I do not understand," she said, clumsily trying to back away as he walked up the stairs to her. "There is no reason . . . why did you do it? Why?" It was difficult to move her feet, and she nearly tripped. "St–stay away from me!"

Max's face was inhumanly calm, but there was something in his eyes that frightened her. "How did you get it?"

"It doesn't matter. Tell me . . . *why* . . . ," Lysette gasped, lifting her arm weakly and throwing the letter at him for emphasis. It missed him completely, fluttering to the steps. "I am going back to my father . . . I would rather be with Sagesse th–than stay here another minute. I am leaving!"

"No, you're not," he said coolly. "I have plans for you. You're staying here."

"I hate you," she whispered, her eyes stinging. "I *hate* you . . . what do you want from me?" She raised her hands to her head in an effort to stop the pounding inside. If only it would stop. If only she could calm herself enough to think clearly.

Suddenly Max's face changed. "Lysette," he murmured. He reached out to steady her swaying form, his hands closing around her waist. Those unbearably keen eyes raked over her.

Wildly she pushed at his arms. "No . . . don't touch me . . ."

His arm slid around her back. "Let me help you upstairs."

"No—"

But even as Lysette fought to be free of him, she felt herself stumble and slump against him. Her head fell against his shoulder while her arms hung uselessly at her sides.

"Max?" Irénée questioned, having come out of the salon when she heard the commotion. At the same time Noeline appeared close behind. "Is something wrong? *Mon Dieu*, what has happened?"

He didn't spare her a glance. "Send for the doctor," he said tersely, and picked Lysette up, hooking his arms underneath her knees and back. Her body was unexpectedly light and fragile.

Lysette whimpered in pain and protest as Max carried her up the rest of the stairs. Hot tears seeped from the corners of her eyes. Being held by him was intolerable. Using the last of her strength, she tried to make him let her go. "I can walk," she sobbed, prying at his hands. "I can . . . let me down—"

"Hush," he said quietly. "Don't struggle."

The trip to her room took only a few seconds, but to Lysette it seemed to last forever. Her cheek rested on his shoulder, while her tears dampened the crisp linen of his shirt. She was hot and nauseous, and wretchedly dizzy. The only solid thing in the world was the broad chest she was clasped against. Somehow, in her misery, she forgot how much she hated him, and was grateful for the vital beat of his heart, the iron-thewed arms supporting her aching back.

For a moment she was certain she was beginning to feel better, but then he set her on the bed, and the room whirled around her. She was falling into suffocating darkness, and there was nothing, no one, to hold onto. Blindly she reached out in an effort to save herself. The tear tracks on her face were dried away, and the soothing voice of a stranger drifted to her ears. She could not understand what he said. A gentle hand smoothed back the hair from her burning forehead. "Help me," she whispered, thinking he might protect her from the Vallerands, unaware that it was Max she was holding onto so desperately.

Fitfully Lysette turned to escape the scorching cloud that had descended on her. The stranger was still above her, blurred in a fiery white blaze. She tried to explain something to him, and he seemed to understand her frantic babble. "It's all right," he murmured. "It's all right."

Noeline, who had followed them into the room, looked over Max's shoulder and folded her arms, shaking her head. "Yellow fever," she said. "Don' need no doctor to tell you. It's bad when it comes on 'dis quick. Ah seen some walk around healthy one day an' drap dead 'de next." She sent a pitying glance at the suffering figure on the bed, as if a quick demise were a certainty.

Max threw the housekeeper a thunderous scowl, but he was careful to keep his voice even. "Bring a pitcher of cold water, and some of that powder—what was it we gave the twins when they had it?"

"Calomel and jalap, monsieur."

"Be quick about it," he growled, and Noeline left immediately.

Max looked down at Lysette, who was muttering incoherently. Gently he disentangled her hands from his shirt, and while his touch was tender, his face was set in grim lines. He wished he could give vent to the curses hovering on his lips.

Irénée came up behind him, saw the rigid set of his shoulders, and knew he was angry. But why? she puzzled. Was it because he had some compassion for the girl? Or was it because Lysette's illness was an inconvenience to him? She could not resist probing to find out. "Her death would certainly foil your plans, *mon fils*," she said.

"She's not going to die."

Irénée regarded Lysette gravely. The illness had come on too quickly, and with too much force. The girl was already out of her head with fever. "There are things we cannot control—"

"No," Max interrupted. "I won't hear it. And don't speak of it around her again."

"But Max, she cannot understand—"

"She can hear what's being said. I don't want any morbid speculation distressing her." He stood up from the bed and added, "I'll leave her in your care. When the doctor arrives, tell him he's not to do anything without my permission. I don't want her bled."

Irénée nodded, remembering how they had nearly lost Justin during his bout with the fever, when he had been bled too copiously. Like Max, she had long entertained doubts about the effects of the procedure. Her own mother had died after being weakened by excessive bleeding.

Max left the room without another glance at Lysette. Irénée looked after him, at a loss to know what he was thinking. It made her feel inadequate as a mother, to be so unaware of what was in her own son's heart. Her other children were so easy to understand. Bernard, her second oldest, sometimes showed a touch of moodiness, but never Max's complexity or callousness. Alexandre was more like her than the others, good-humored and even-tempered. But Max, so pitiless and solitary, seemed at times to be what others had called him, the spawn of the devil.

Irénée and Noeline took turns sitting with Lysette the first forty-eight hours. Irénée had forgotten the work and patience it required to nurse a yellow fever patient. Her back ached from bending over the bed and sponging Lysette with cold water. The violent bouts of vomiting, delirious raving and nightmares, the pungent smell of the vinegar baths they gave her—all of it was repellent and exhausting.

Max frequently asked about the girl's condition, but

propriety barred him from entering the room and seeing
for himself. Surprisingly, he stayed on the plantation within
close reach, curtailing his usual roaming and occupying
himself with record books and business matters he could
attend to at his desk.

To Justin he said not a word, leaving the boy to worry
in silence over whether a reprisal would take place. Although nothing was discussed or admitted, Max suspected
Justin's involvement with the letter, knowing his son's
penchant for stirring up trouble. The boy slunk around the
house, avoiding his father and brother, while Irénée was
too concerned about Lysette to bother with him.

At such times, when all the adults were otherwise occupied, the twins usually took the opportunity to run wild,
dodge their lessons with the tutor, and sneak off to see
friends or cause mischief in the city. Now, however, they
were unusually docile. Justin suffered pangs of guilt for
what he had done, while Philippe was burdened with sympathy for the bedridden girl. A fog of gloom seemed to
have descended on the house, the silence interrupted only
by the Lysette's incoherent cries during the worst periods
of delirium.

This time, when the Kersaints returned to the Vallerand
house, they departed with no doubt that Lysette was indeed extremely ill. Delphine was allowed to visit the sickroom, but the girl did not recognize her. They left greatly
subdued, Gaspard swallowing the threats and suspicions
he had intended to voice.

"How terribly ironic," Irénée had commented to Max
later, "that the lie you told has now become the truth."

Max had shrugged. "I have her, and Etienne Sagesse
does not. That is all that matters."

"Do you mean to say it is of no import if she is ill or
not? You don't care that she is suffering? That she'll probably die?"

"She's not going to die," he replied in a chilling voice.

Irénée left him in disgust, knowing it would be a waste of breath to upbraid him for his heartlessness.

Being unused to sickness, Justin grumbled about the nuisance it was to have an ailing houseguest. "I wish it would end one way or the other," he said dully. "I can't stand everyone having to walk on tiptoe, and the noises she makes, and the whole house stinking of vinegar."

"It won't last much longer," Philippe commented. "I heard *Grand-mère* say she will not last another day."

They froze as they heard a weak cry from upstairs. Suddenly Max emerged from the library, brushing by them without a word. He went up the stairs two at a time. The twins glanced at each other in surprise.

"Do you think he is worried?" Philippe asked.

Justin's young face hardened in contempt. "Only that she'll die before she is of any use to him."

"What? What do you mean?"

"Idiot, you don't think he cares for her, do you? He doesn't care for anyone."

Alerted to the fact that his brother was hiding something from him, Philippe caught him by the sleeve. "Justin, what do you know that I don't?"

Justin took his arm free impatiently. "I won't tell you. You'd only try to defend him."

Irénée tried in vain to quiet the girl who twisted in the clutches of a nightmare. *"Pauvre petite,"* Irénée exclaimed under her breath, aware of how weakened Lysette was. But nothing would bring tranquility. There was nothing that could be done for her. She slumped back in the chair by the bed, watching Lysette's restless twitching.

"Don't . . . don't let him . . . oh, please . . . someone stop him . . ." The thin voice rose and fell monotonously.

Wearily Irénée began to reach for the sponge and basin, hoping to cool the fever with more water. She fell back in surprise as Max appeared in the darkened room.

"Max?" she exclaimed. "What are you doing? What do you want?"

He ignored her questions, swatting aside the filmy folds of the *baire* and sitting on the edge of the bed. His dark head bent over the girl's writhing form. "M–Max," Irénée stuttered, "you should not be in here. It is indecent. You must leave!"

Max pulled away the knotted mass of sheets from Lysette's scantily clad body, stroked the tangled hair off her face, and pulled her into his arms.

"Max," Irénée gasped in astonishment.

He did not reply, the force of his will concentrated on the small, shivering figure folded against his chest. "Shhh," he whispered against Lysette's temple, cupping her head in his hand, rocking her gently. "Don't be afraid. You're safe now. Shhh. Nothing will harm you."

The girl clung to him convulsively. ". . . he's there . . . I see . . . don't let him near . . . don't . . ."

Max shifted her higher against him and reached for the wet sponge. He drew it over her face and chest, squeezing until the cool water ran in rivulets over her skin. "No, I won't let him near," he murmured. "I'm right here. You're safe."

After a while the stroking and the quiet words soothed Lysette, and she went limp against him.

The nightmare had been banished. Irénée exhaled slowly, discovering she had been holding her breath. Was she dreaming? She could not recognize the man before her as her cold-hearted son. Max's face was not visible to her, but she heard his voice, and it was filled with a tenderness she had not believed him capable of.

Max picked up the cup from the bedside and pressed it to Lysette's lips. Helplessly the girl choked and tried to resist, but he forced her to swallow. When she had drained the medicine from the cup, he eased her back down on the bed, straightened her gown and covered her with the sheet.

Irénée finally found her voice. "Noeline and I were not able to make her drink any of it."

Max's lips were touched by the shadow of a derisive smile. "Obviously she heeds a man's voice better than a woman's." His attention shifted back to the sleeping girl, and he toyed with a lock of her hair. "Don't you, my sweet?"

Irénée was unsettled by the way he looked at Lysette. "Thank you for your help, Max," she said. "That is enough. I will see to her now."

Max didn't move. "You are exhausted, Maman. Why don't you get some rest? I'll take care of her."

Irénée did not know how to reply to such an outrageous statement. *"What?* What a ridiculous suggestion! Completely out of the bounds of propriety. Her reputation would be destroyed!"

"It already is." His lips curved cynically. "Or will be soon. My presence in her room makes no difference."

"Max, be sensible," Irénée begged. "You don't know about nursing. It is a woman's concern. There are duties required—"

"A woman's body is hardly a mystery to me. As for nursing the fever, I tended the twins when they had it." He paused deliberately. "Remember?"

That silenced Irénée for a few seconds. Indeed, she had forgotten. Max had been very good with the twins when they were ill. "But . . . ," she faltered, "they were boys, your sons, and this is . . . an unprotected girl . . ."

"Do you think I'll attempt to ravish her?" Max asked with a twisted smile. "Even I am not that degenerate, Maman."

Irénée was not reassured. The darkest suspicions filled her mind. *"Mon fils,"* she asked apprehensively, "why do you wish to take this upon yourself?"

"Why shouldn't I? I have a vested interest in her welfare. Now go and rest. I'm capable of looking after her for a few hours."

She stood up reluctantly. "I–I am sending Noeline to take your place."

But Max did not allow Noeline or anyone else to replace him. From that moment on he spent every minute by Lysette's bed, his shirtsleeves rolled above his elbows as he labored to break the girl's raging fever. He was inexhaustible and astonishingly patient.

Irénée had never heard of even a husband doing as much for a wife. It was all too shocking. She was dismayed, but unable to think of a way to intercede. She had no control over Max, and precious little influence. Perhaps if his brothers had been home they would have volunteered to coerce him out of the sickroom, but day after day went by without bringing their arrival—and Max remained in the girl's bedchamber as if it were his right.

A black wolf with yellow eyes prowled through Lysette's dreams, stalking until she ran and stumbled to the ground. He loomed closer, his teeth gleaming as he crouched over her prone body, and suddenly he was ripping her to pieces. She screamed as she felt herself being savaged, torn apart by sharp white teeth. Then suddenly the wolf was gone, disappearing at the sound of a low voice. "I'm here . . . it's all right. Shhh . . . I have you now . . ." She reached out to the source of the voice and clung until darkness swept her away from the comforting arms.

She was surrounded by sweltering heat that scorched her skin and blistered her lungs. Crying out in agony, she fought to escape it. She felt a cool hand stroke her forehead. Restlessly she sought more "Please," she gasped, aching upward. "Please . . ." She groaned with relief as the life-giving caress returned, coolness moving over her body, easing the unbearable fire.

The wolf-eyes were watching her again, glowing devilishly in the darkness. She whirled away in panic and came up against a man's hard chest and taut arms. "Please help me—"

"You've been promised to me," she heard the voice of Etienne Sagesse, and she looked up at his face in horror. "I want a taste of what is mine." Desire flickered bright in his heavy-lidded eyes, and his lips shone with moisture. He made her feel unclean. She choked on a denial and fought him desperately, twisted away, and came face to face with her stepfather.

Gaspard's face was blotched with rage. "You will marry him!" He struck her, and raised his hand again.

"Maman," she cried, seeing her mother nearby, but Jeanne backed away, shaking her head.

"Do what your *beau-père* says. You must obey him."

"I can't . . ."

The hard rim of a cup pressed against her lips, and she recoiled from a bitter taste. A steely band around her shoulders would not let her retreat.

"No . . . no," she choked, her head falling back against an unyielding shoulder.

"Don't fight me, little one. Drink it all." She opened her mouth with a gasp, obeying the gentle prompting.

She saw the dark, slim shape of her father, half-obscured in a thick mist. He would help her . . . he must. "Papa," she pleaded, and tears sprang to her eyes as she saw him begin to disappear. Frantically she chased after him, ran and ran until her way was blocked by a tall iron gate. She grasped the bars and shook them violently. "Wait! Let me in! Wait . . ."

The wolf was behind her. She could feel him drawing near. His low snarl pierced the misty night. Terrified, she tugged at the gate, but it would not open. Powerful jaws closed around her neck, and she screamed.

"Don't. Don't be afraid." Suddenly Maximilien Vallerand's face was above her.

"Don't let him hurt me," she whispered.

"No, never, my sweet."

She was falling, falling into a pit a fire, caught in a current of flames that closed over her head. Writhing in torment, she begged for respite. A wet cloth stroked over her back, legs, neck, arms. Again the cup was raised to her mouth. "I c–can't," she moaned, turning to press her face against a hard shoulder. "Please . . . oh, please . . ."

"Once more," came a quiet command. "Once more."

She submitted while the wolf watched and waited, his yellow eyes gleaming. Lysette whimpered in fear as she felt the protective arms begin to withdraw from around her. If she were left alone, she would be at the wolf's mercy. "It's all right," she heard someone murmur. "I won't let go."

But the the wolf approached stealthily. Just before he reached her, his form changed into that of a man, and she looked in horror at the dark, mocking face of Maximilien Vallerand. He snatched her up greedily in bruising arms, carrying her away deep into the shadows while she cried in terror for him to stop . . . but he would not let her go . . . he would never let her go . . .

"You look so much better today," Irénée exclaimed.

Lysette nodded feebly. For the past few days she had been too listless to move at all, but finally she could feel some of her strength returning. From the moment she had awakened to see Irénée sitting by the bed, she had been aware of how much the older woman had done for her, and how carefully she had been nursed back to health. "Madame," she whispered, "I can never repay you . . . what you have done for me . . ."

Irénée reached out and grasping her slender hand. "It will be repayment enough to see you recover completely, Lysette. We were terribly distraught over your illness."

"We?" Lysette repeated.

"Why, all of us! The twins, and Noeline, and Maximilien."

The mention of Max stirred Lysette's interest. She had

not seen nor heard from him since the night she had been taken ill. But her dreams had been riddled with such strange images. Her memory played tricks, recalling moments when a stranger had held her in his arms. She reassured herself that it had not happened. It was her imagination—that, and the fever.

"Madame," she said, her fingers plucking at the hem of the delicate white sheet that covered her, "Monsieur Vallerand was not . . . in here . . . during my illness, was he?"

Irénée appeared flabbergasted by the question. "Max? *Mais non!* He asked after you frequently, but that is all."

"Of course," Lysette murmured, mortified that she had asked such a foolish question. It was just that the images were impossible to dispel.

Irénée looked at her closely, her expression so intent that for the first time she reminded Lysette of Max. "Why would you think such a thing?"

"I just . . . had a strange dream . . . it made no sense . . ."

"You were delirious," Irénée said serenely, settling back.

"Yes . . ." Lysette let her eyes close as she felt a tide of exhaustion wash over her. "Madame, I am so tired—"

"Go to sleep," Irénée said, patting her arm gently. "That is the best thing for you."

When Lysette had recovered enough to desire a change of scene, Irénée let her sit for a while in the parlor downstairs. Lysette experienced an agony of embarrassment worse than anything she had ever known when Irénée summoned Max to carry her.

"I can do it on my own," Lysette insisted, keeping her eyes from the dark figure in the doorway and clutching the ruffled white pelisse more closely her body. The pelisse and bedgown she wore were as concealing as regular clothes, but under Max's scrutiny she felt completely undressed. "I am much stronger now, I don't need help, especially not . . ." She stopped, realizing the rude comment she had been about to make.

"Especially not mine?" Max inquired softly.

Lysette flushed and looked up at him. It was the first time she had seen him since the night the fever had struck, and she had forgotten how overpowering he was. He was even taller than she remembered, and his presence in the room was almost oppressive. She remembered the humiliation of collapsing in his arms and having him carry her upstairs. Not for any price would she ever allow him that close to her again.

Carefully Lysette stood up by the bed, holding onto the bedpost. A rush of dizziness overtook her, and then the room was clear. The sensation of being on her feet was invigorating. "I'm definitely strong enough to walk by myself," she said.

"Lysette, we do not want a relapse," Irénée fretted, moving to stand beside her and grasp her arm. "It is too soon for you to be exerting yourself. Isn't that right, Max?"

"That's right," he agreed smoothly. "However, I will not restrain Mademoiselle Kersaint from taking a few steps to find out for herself."

Annoyed by his arrogance, Lysette decided she would walk the entire way if it killed her. Unfortunately even with Irénée's help, her legs were too weak to carry her to the hallway. At the exact moment that her knees began to tremble in warning, Max was at her side, sliding his arms around her and lifting her up.

"No," Lysette said through her teeth, wedging her arms against his chest. "I would rather stay in bed than have you carry me anywhere."

A biting rejoinder sprang to Max's lips, but he managed to quell it. It was far too easy to embarrass Lysette. There was little sport in it. And her youthful awkwardness touched him as nothing had in a long time. How long had it been since he had known a woman capable of genuine shyness? "Come now," he said, "you won't let my bad manners deprive you of a trip downstairs. You've been confined to this one room for days."

Although his voice was mocking, there was a caressing note in it that spoke to some deep-lodged impulse within her. Lysette capitulated sullenly, pulling her arms from between them. "Well . . . don't take your time about it." She was sorry for her incivility, but there was something about him that made it impossible to be gracious.

Max chuckled softly and carried her to the salon, where Noeline was waiting with a large embroidered shawl for covering her knees. Lysette settled back against the pillows on the brocaded sofa, disturbed by the feelings that had awakened during the short journey downstairs.

It was an ordeal to be held by him, even impersonally. Although he was being gentle with her, the hard muscles underneath his clothes reminded her of his capacity for cruelty. So far Lysette hadn't had the strength to mention the letter to Marie. Until she recovered enough to defy him, she was a pawn in whatever game he had chosen to play. She detested the situation. Still, it was preferable to being in the clutches of Etienne Sagesse.

"Oh," Lysette gasped in surprise as she felt a painful tug on her scalp. A few strands of her hair had caught in one of the buttons on Max's shirt. Realizing what had happened, he leaned over her to undo the tangle. Lysette reached for the button at the same time. Their fingers caught together, and she recoiled in confusion. "Monsieur," she protested, but he interrupted brusquely.

"Let me."

The warm puff of his breath against her cheek unloosed a blaze of sensations that stunned her. With a dreamlike slowness Lysette let her hands fall, while her heart thundered in her breast. Deftly Max freed the tiny snarl of hair, dismantling the silken bond that had held them together. The scent of his skin floated to her nostrils. She was close enough to see the shadow of bristle on his smooth-shaven jaw, and the spikiness of his eyelashes. Then his amber eyes were staring into hers.

"Thank you," she said, shrinking away from him. But he remained bent over her, one arm braced on the back of the rosewood sofa, the other hand resting close to her hip. He was staring at her so strangely. With a pang of fear Lysette realized this was exactly how the wolf in her dreams had looked.

Her mind raced. Something about this was horribly familiar. It wasn't her imagination. Something had happened while she was ill—he had been there with her. Oh God, the arms that had held her couldn't have been his. She tried to look away from him, to hide her burgeoning suspicions, but she couldn't tear her eyes from his. Yes, Irénée had lied to her. Max *had* been there in her room. Oh, it can't be the truth, Lysette thought dazedly, please don't let it be!

When Max spoke, Lysette could hardly hear him over the wild beating of her heart. "Don't be afraid of me," he said. There was a huskiness in his voice she had not heard before.

Her eyes widened. She was cornered. There was nothing to do but snap back at him. "I'm not," she managed to say. "Not in the least. I–I hate you."

Irénée's voice broke the spellbinding silence. "Max? Is she all right?"

Max's peculiar expression vanished and he stood up. "She's fine," he said curtly, striding to the door. "I'll be in the library."

As he left, Irénée looked after him and shook her head. "I do not understand. He is behaving so oddly. What did he say to you?"

Hastily Lysette lowered her eyes. "Oh, nothing, nothing." Perhaps she was wrong. Surely Irénée would not have allowed Max in her room when she was ill. The idea was so improper it was not worth considering. Moreover,

Maximilien Vallerand would have no interest in caring for her. He despised those weaker than himself. He had shown no compunction in manipulating her for his own purposes.

Lost in her truths, Lysette stared out the window, stirring occasionally to respond to Irénée's chatter. The scene outside was lovely. On the other side of a small clearing was a fruit orchard and shadowed pathways among rose and camellia bushes. The Vallerand house was more secluded than others she had seen, close-guarded and private. It had become her sanctuary, but it was obvious she would not be safe here much longer. Her illness had been only a temporary reprieve from whatever plans Maximilien had concocted.

"Madame," she said slowly. "Monsieur Vallerand has not sent the letter to my cousin Marie."

Irénée frowned. "Lysette, we should wait until you are stronger to discuss—"

"He wishes to keep me here. Why? Is it because of Etienne Sagesse? He and Monsieur are enemies, *non?*"

Irénée nodded reluctantly. "They are enemies."

"Then he is using me to provoke Etienne Sagesse?" Lysette asked, already knowing the answer.

"I wish I could tell you *non* . . . but I fear that is Maximilien's intention."

Lysette closed her eyes, leaning her head back against the pillow. "He is trying to dishonor me," she murmured, wrapping her arms protectively around her middle. "That will indeed make Monsieur Sagesse angry enough to demand a duel."

Irénée was silent for a long moment. "Lysette," she finally said, "it is still not too late for you to be returned to Sagesse. If that is what you wish, I will see that it is done."

Lysette shook her head. "I don't know. I have no idea what to do. I . . . I am caught between two men who are equally selfish and dangerous. I cannot trust either of them. But I cannot return home because of my *beau-père*. Tante

Delphine would say it is the will of God that I am in such a predicament. What have I done to deserve it?''

Irénée was spared from replying by the appearance of Noeline in the doorway. ''Madame,'' the housekeeper said, rolling her eyes heavenward, ''it is Monsieur Médart, come to take Mademoiselle Lysette back wid' him.''

Chapter 4

"**S**he appears to be in perfect health," Gaspard said, his black eyes surveying Lysette's face.

Max shrugged, remaining at the back of the room as if he had little interest in the proceedings. "Our family doctor is of a different opinion."

"But she is certainly well enough to travel!" Gaspard exclaimed, and Tante Delphine hurried forward to allay his frustration. She positioned herself beside Lysette, straightening the shawl over her lap.

"There, there, *enfant*," she cooed, pushing a lock of red hair behind Lysette's ear. "Can it be that you fear we will not take good care of you? Our sweet, beloved little Lysette?"

Lysette turned away irritably from the encroaching hands. "Please don't," she said through her teeth.

"Do not be difficult," Delphine whispered too softly for the others to hear. "You don't know what you have done. You have nearly ruined yourself through your own willfulness. We must remove you from here at once. Trust Gaspard and me, your family, to know what is best for you."

Lysette looked away only to meet Irénée's sympathetic eyes. "Lysette," Irénée said, astonishing them all, "I do not think it would be harmful for you to leave with them. It might be the wisest course of action.''

"Yes, it would," Gaspard added, his swarthy face losing its thunderous cast. "I am happy to see that you have such a sensible attitude, Madame Vallerand."

"We must consider Lysette's welfare above all else," Irénée replied, glancing cautiously at Max.

"I am not welcome here?" Lysette asked, unable to understand why Irénée had withdrawn her hospitality. Hurt struggled with surprise. Had Irénée wearied of her company? Small wonder in that, considering she had been nothing but trouble to the Vallerands. Or was Irénée trying to protect her from Max's plans?

"Of course you are welcome to stay," Irénée said quickly. "It is just that—"

"It is just that Madame Vallerand recognizes the impropriety of your presence under this roof," Gaspard interrupted, moving toward Lysette. "Enough of this foolish chatter. *Allons,* Lysette. There is a carriage waiting outside, the finest carriage you have ever seen. The Sagesses have anticipated everything you might require." He reached out for her, intending to lift her in his arms and carry her outside.

Lysette stared at his outstretched hands, and rebellion knotted in her throat. She did not want to go anywhere with him, no matter what the consequences of staying here would be. Shrinking back, she shook vehemently, but she was too weak to fight him. "I'll run away again," she said.

"You will not have the opportunity," Gaspard assured her testily, pulling off the shawl and curving his arm behind her back.

Max had been so quiet no one had noticed his approach. Suddenly Lysette found herself snatched out of Gaspard's grasp. Startled, Delphine scuttled out of the way, her movements nimble for one of her girth. Lysette curved her arms around Max's neck, and held on until he deposited her in the other corner of the sofa. Then he looked at her, and the possessiveness in his eyes made her nervous and strangely giddy. As far as he was concerned, she was not going anywhere.

Casually Max interposed himself between Lysette and the other occupants of the room. "It appears further discussion is called for," he said.

Gaspard made the mistake of trying to move past Max to reach Lysette. He was stopped by Max's soft snarl.

"Don't." The golden eyes were brilliant with vengeful promise. "I'll warn you only once. Don't so much as disarrange a hair on her head."

"But she . . ." Gaspard blustered, staring in shock at the grim-visaged giant in front of him. "She is my daughter—"

*"Step*daughter," Lysette muttered.

Max turned to look down at her, the corner of his mouth twitching in amusement. Although he said not a word, Lysette understood his intent. He was going to to take her part in the dispute, because it served his purpose to keep her here. The thought struck Lysette that she had little to lose by allowing Max to handle the others as he would.

Given the choice, she would rather stay here than cast herself at the mercy of her stepfather and Etienne Sagesse. Perhaps there was still a chance she could persuade Maximilien to send her letter to Marie, or failing all else, she would flee to the sanctuary of the Ursuline Convent—anything, rather than marry Sagesse.

"What right have you to interefere?" Gaspard demanded, glaring as Max seated himself beside Lysette. Furiously he turned to Irénée, who was speechless. "What has gone on between the two of them that she allows him such privileges? What illicit liason, what scandalous goings-on—"

"Mademoiselle Kersaint afforded me that right when she took refuge in my home," Max said. "And nothing improper has taken place."

"The rest of New Orleans is not inclined to believe that!" Gaspard cried, turning an apoplectic red. He glared at Lysette. "Sagesse has said that if you are not returned by this afternoon, he will *not have you!* He will consider you tainted, defiled, corrupted! Do you understand, you little fool? *No one* will want you. You'll be useless to me, because no decent man will ever offer for you! You will not only have blemished your own name, but also Sagesse's honor, and this is *exactly* what Monsieur Vallerand intends. You are nothing but an excuse for him to finish a feud that began years ago. Once it is done, you will have no recourse, no hope of anything close to the life you might have led as the wife of a Sagesse. Save yourself, Lysette. Come with me now and end this madness! Don't let your feelings toward me lead you to do such harm to yourself."

Lysette was pale with fatigue. She met Max's eyes. As always, it was impossible to see any clue to his thoughts. But she understood everything, perhaps far more than even he suspected. She voiced the question that needed no asking. "Monsieur Vallerand, everything he says is true, *n'est-ce pas?*"

Max began to utter some glib reply, but something in her gaze stopped him. She was so young, incapable of hurting anyone, in need of protection. Something stirred inside him, some far-away emotion he shied from immediately. Elusive as the feeling had been, Max was troubled enough to consider giving her back to Sagesse. He didn't want her near him . . . he didn't want to feel anything for her.

Lysette still waited for the answer to her question. Max saw no reason to lie to her.

"It is all true," he said bluntly.

"And what had you planned to do with me when your game is over?" she asked.

"Repay you for the opportunity you afforded me," he replied, with no visible trace of shame. "Provide for you in whatever manner you wish. I am not an ungenerous man, Mademoiselle Kersaint, and my gratitude for the chance to duel with Sagesse will prove boundless.''

''Why? What has he done to earn your enmity?''

Max did not reply. In his eyes a small, cold flame burned, and he looked so pitiless and determined that it was all Lysette could do not to cower away from him. There were depths of darkness within him she could only imagine. He was using her as a weapon of revenge for a wrong that had occurred years ago. Certainly there was no spark of forgiveness or any other Christian sentiment lurking inside that broad chest. Lysette's hand crept to the hollow of her throat to conceal her pulse's throbbing.

Suddenly a vivid image rose up before her, and she heard the dream-echo of a low voice, remembered gentle hands, strong, unyielding arms, and a tenderness that had driven away the most fearsome nightmares. Bewildered, she stared at the man at her side. *Could* it have been him? Oh, it didn't seem possible! Her head ached fiercely as she wondered what to do.

Seeing her pain, Max scowled at the room in general. ''She should be resting. This is too much for her.''

''Then let us have her!'' Gaspard spat.

''No.'' Lysette faced her stepfather, knowing he would take great pleasure in throttling her. ''I told you I would not marry Monsieur Sagesse, no matter how you attempted to coerce me,'' she said, ignoring Delphine's horrified gasp. ''I will not return with you. Although Monsieur Vallerand has turned the circumstances to his own benefit, I will continue to accept his hospitality. I will gladly face the consequences of remaining here, rather than become the wife of Monsieur Sagesse.''

''It is decided,'' Max said, and stood up to indicate the dispute was over.

Gaspard's eyes bulged as he looked at Lysette. ''You foolish, simple-minded girl! What do you think is going to happen to you?''

Irénée crossed the room swiftly, placing her hand on Max's steely arm. "My son," she said urgently, "it is not your place to come between them. Think of someone besides yourself—you will ruin her! I cannot bear it on my conscience, even if you can!"

Max looked from Lysette to his mother. A careless smile touched his lips. "Don't look so disillusioned, Maman," he murmured. "I could hardly allow your conscience to remain troubled for long." He bent his dark head to whisper in her ear.

Whatever Max told Irénée astonished her. She turned to stare at Lysette, her jaw slack, and then again focused her attention on her son's impassive countenance. "Oh, Maximilien," she whispered, and her chin trembled with some cryptic emotion.

"Madame?" Lysette questioned, wondering what Max has said to her.

Max approached Gaspard and Delphine, who were both frozen. "I must ask you to leave," he said.

"I will not! I will not accept this!" Gaspard stormed. "Not when there is a chance Sagesse will still have her!"

"Why don't you take a message to Sagesse?" Max invited softly. "Tell him to come here and retrieve her himself, if he so desires."

Trembling, Delphine held her hands out to Lysette in a beseeching gesture. "Lysette, how has this all happened?"

Lysette smiled humorlessly. "I don't know."

"Your maman will never forgive me. Please. You must listen. You are cutting yourself off from your family forever. There will be no second chance."

"I don't want one."

Gaspard pointed a finger at Maximilien. "I assure you, this matter is not concluded, Vallerand!"

Max's brows arched sardonically. "I'm glad to hear it."

As Gaspard and Delphine left, Lysette slumped back against the sofa, exhausted. Later she would try to make sense of her whirling thoughts, but for the moment she had to rest. "Madame," she said, "I must know what Monsieur Vallerand told you."

"He merely set my mind at ease about something," Irénée replied evasively.

"But what did he—"

"Enough," Max interrupted. "I will take you upstairs."

Lysette closed her eyes, loath to feel his arms around her but eager to be returned to her bedchamber. She desperately wanted to be alone. She sensed the power of his well-muscled body as he picked her up, and her ears tingled at the sound of his voice. "How submissive you suddenly are, mademoiselle. I find it rather appealing."

"You know I find it very *un*appealing, monsieur, to be touched by you at all."

The smile still lingered on his lips. "Do you know, for every step you've taken in this house I've carried you twice as far?"

They concentrated on each other, unaware of Noeline trailing behind them. "Monsieur," Lysette asked, "what did you tell your mother back in the salon?"

Max ignored her question. "Explain something to me," he said abruptly. "What did Sagesse do to make you dislike him so? Did he try to force himself on you?"

Lysette blushed. Not for the world would she tell him something so private. "Perhaps you should ask your mother. She is aware of what happened."

"I have asked her," he said dryly. "Repeatedly. She won't divulge a thing."

Lysette smiled at the thought of Max badgering Irénée for information she would not give him. "I like your mother quite well, monsieur."

Max glanced at her mouth, intrigued by the soft curve of her lips. "She feels the same about you," he said, sounding displeased. "Now tell me what Sagesse did."

"I cannot see why it would matter to you."

"No, I'm certain you can't. Tell me nonetheless."

Lysette was too tired to think before she spoke. "First I would like to know what transpired between Sagesse and *you,* all those years ago." She thought her impudent request would have stirred Max's temper, but instead he smiled.

"My mother hasn't told you?" he inquired.

"Madame Vallerand will not say anything about it."

"Evidently she is a more trustworthy confidante than I had supposed," he mused. "I must remember to compliment her. Most women are unable to hold their tongues when they come across a tidy bit of gossip."

"Now that I have chosen to stay, Monsieur Sagesse will challenge you soon, *oui?*"

"Most assuredly."

"And after . . . What about me?"

"What fate do you envision for yourself?"

"I–I have been educated. I could find a position as a teacher somewhere."

Max seemed to find her remark amusing. "In what subjects are you educated?"

"English, geography, history, floral arrangement, latin—"

"Arranging flowers, hmm? I was not aware there was a need for teachers of that art."

"You mock me," Lysette said. "Evidently you think me a fool."

"I think of you in many ways, my sweet, but that is not one of them."

"D-don't call me that," she stuttered.

"Sweet? But you are," Max said with sarcastic softness. "A sweet, gentle creature who would never have been stirred from her quiet ways were it not for the caprice of fate. Winsome, kind, selfless . . . you possess all the qualities a man desires in a wife. And yet you wonder why Etienne Sagesse wants you. Such modesty is overwhelming."

Max was not certain what impulse had caused him to deride her, except that the very sweetness he had spoken of affected him far too powerfully. She was, after all, a woman, and would someday be prey to all the vanities and treacheries a woman was capable of. Allowing himself to forget that would be a mistake indeed, the same mistake he had once made with Corinne.

"You don't know me at all," Lysette said, words tumbling from her lips in childish haste. "You imagine you do, but you don't!"

Suddenly his bitterness faded into amusement. "Is it possible you have taken offense at my description of you?" he asked. "I meant to be complimentary."

"No, you didn't!"

His grin was wicked and vibrantly warm. "I meant every word. Now calm yourself, or I'll be accused of spurring you into a relapse."

Lysette's mouth tightened, and she turned her face away from him, glancing over his shoulder. She encountered Noeline's thoughtful gaze. Quietly the housekeeper followed them into the bedroom, turning down the sheets and drawing the curtains together. Odd, the long, speculative glance Noeline sent toward Max. Lysette wondered what she was thinking.

Lysette's hair was still damp after a thorough washing that had left it gleaming like fire. Carefully Noeline separated the tangles and began to comb the silken locks, while Irénée sat nearby and looked out the window. The morning sunlight shone bright on the oak trees lining the drive, filtering down to the wet ground beneath. Irénée watched as Max rode away from the house on his black stallion. When she was assured her son was well away from the house and there was no chance of a precipitous return, Irénée turned to Lysette and spoke softly.

"You have a right to know, Lysette, what happened between Max and Etienne Sagesse." Irénée had pondered over the wisdom of revealing the secrets of the past to the girl, but Noeline had assured her that it would be better to hear of it from Maximilien's mother than another source. "Max will never speak of it," she continued, "and so it falls to me to tell you. You may learn to understand my son better, and perhaps out of that some gentler feeling for him might come."

Lysette was bewildered. "Madame," she said, "if you're hoping that I might grow fond of him . . . well, I cannot lie and say it is even remotely possible. And why would you want—"

"First hear what I have to say."

"Very well." Lysette watched her in the mirror as Noeline continued to work on her hair.

"I should begin," Irénée said, "by telling you Max has always been a man of unbridled emotions."

Lysette could not help interrupting. "I've formed quite the opposite impression. He is the most emotionless person I've ever encountered."

Noeline paused in her brushing. "Just because you ain' seen it, chile, don' mean it ain' dere. Down deep is all de stronges' kind of feelin's."

"Exactly," Irénée said. "If you had seen him many years ago, Lysette, you would not doubt what I say. Max had a hunger for life, an abandon, unmatched by anyone else. His brothers possessed nothing like it." Her face became soft with wistfulness. "Do not discount any part of what I tell you, although I am certain you will think it is just a mother's boasting. Max exceeded all the hopes his father and I had for him. He was a wild boy, to be sure, given to mischief, utterly fearless, but tender and kind to the helpless, and full of laughter and charm. At that time Max had many friends. He would risk his life to defend the honor of anyone he cared for. Nearly every woman in New Orleans, young or old, matron or maiden, was in love with him. In those days he was dashing, and very handsome."

''But he still is,'' Lysette said without thinking, and then went crimson at her slip of the tongue.

Irénée smiled wryly. ''His attraction is of a different sort now.''

Lysette knew exactly what Irénée meant. Only women with no heed for their reputations would want to consort with a man like Max. She tried to envision him as a young man, without the cynicism in his eyes or the mocking smile on his lips, but it was impossible.

''His downfall, *naturellement*,'' Irénée continued, ''was a woman. Corinne Quérand, the daughter of a respectable family in New Orleans. Max was not much older than you are now. He was completely blind to her true character. Corinne was very beautiful and alluring, but her charm concealed a selfishness that knew no bounds. The first year of their marriage she gave Max the twins, and he was overcome with joy. He would have done anything to keep her happy, but . . .'' Irénée paused and shook her head.

''What happened?'' Lysette demanded, unable to curb the impatience in her voice.

''Corinne changed.''

''Changed? How?''

''The beautiful mask simply dropped away, and the woman underneath proved to be as cold as ice. She claimed to be bored . . . she began to discard her morals and self-respect as garments she was simply tired of wearing. Corinne had no interest in her children. She did not wish to belong to just one man, *alors* she took a lover. I think, Lysette, you can guess who that was.''

Lysette swallowed hard. ''Etienne Sagesse,'' she whispered.

''*Oui, c'etait lui*. Corinne flaunted her indiscretion with Etienne in Maximilien's face. She knew Max still loved her, and that drove her to such cruelty . . . *Mon Dieu*, my son suffered as no mother would ever want to see her child suffer. He desired to call Etienne out, but his pride would not let him admit before the world that his wife had been unfaithful to him. Finally Max was driven to challenge Etienne, but before the appointment could be kept, he . . . he . . .''

Noeline secured Lysette's hair at the nape of her neck and moved to hand Irénée a handkerchief.

"Merci, Noeline,'' Irénée said, swabbing at her tearful eyes. "It is not for Corinne I grieve, you understand.'' Lysette waited in anxious silence until Irénée spoke again. "Anyone could understand why it would happen. Corinne was a cruel woman, and she had tortured Max with his own feelings for her, until he couldn't stop himself from . . . it was justified, wasn't it, Noeline?''

"Oui, madame.''

"What happened?'' Lysette burst out, her hands clenched.

Noeline was the one who answered. "Dey found Madame Corinne in de empty overseer's house, set back in de woods. Strangle' dead.''

"Max claimed he found her that way,'' Irénée whispered. "He said he didn't kill her, but he had no alibi. The authorities considered the circumstances and chose to be lenient. They can on occasion be persuaded to look the other way, especially in the matter of an unfaithful wife. The duel with Etienne never took place. Max continued to insist he was innocent of the crime, but no one had faith in his claim. His friends proved to be unsteadfast. His family wished to believe him but could not, and Max was left alone with his grief. I was certain that after time had passed he would recover and become something like his former self. But the bitterness consumed him. He became incapable of expressing affection, of trusting anyone, of allowing himself to care for anyone.''

"Madame, do you believe in his innocence?'' Lysette asked shakily.

Irénée paused an unbearably long time. "I am his mother,'' she finally answered.

Did that mean yes or no? "What if he didn't do it?''

Lysette asked. "Perhaps there was someone else who had reason to kill her?"

"No one else," Irénée said with terrible certainty.

Lysette shivered, crossing her arms over her midriff. So Monsieur Vallerand was a murderer. Those lean, powerful hands had wrapped around a woman's neck and strangled the life out of her.

"Max must be pitied," Irénée said. "He was victim of his own emotions."

Lysette's eyes were round with horror as she stared at the older woman. "How could I pity a man capable of murdering his own wife?"

"You must understand. It was the circumstances . . ."

"Oh, madame," Lysette said fervently, "I wish you had not told me."

"Now you know why he could not stop himself from taking advantage of your sudden appearance here. He saw you as the means to force Etienne into a duel which he regards as his opportunity to avenge the past. I have little doubt he will kill Etienne. Perhaps then Maximilien will find himself able to stop looking back, and put the entire tragedy to rest."

"Yes," Lysette whispered, "after having executed his wife and then her lover. How evil."

"You must not think of him that way," Irénée said. "He is not evil. Somewhere within him remains the essence of the gentle, loving boy he once was. I did not believe that until you came to us, Lysette, and I saw how he is with you."

"With *me?*" Lysette exclaimed. "He has never been anything but mocking and insulting! He has made his contempt for me clear!"

Irénée and Noeline exchanged a look over her head that perplexed her greatly. What did everyone know that she did not? "Madame," she asked, "you would not let any harm come to me, would you?"

"Oh, I do not believe that *you* have anything to fear from Max."

Lysette stared at her incredulously. "But another woman might? Why in heaven's name would *I* be safe from him if others are not?"

Irénée considered the question, looking sheepish, then resolutely optimistic. "Maximilien seems to feel rather protective of you, dear. I think you bring out very good qualities in him."

"I don't know why you think that!" Lysette exclaimed. "And even if it were true, that doesn't mean that if I annoy him he won't lose his temper and . . . oh, *how* could you have let me decide to stay here without first telling me about his past?"

Irénée looked surprised. "Not a moment ago you said you wished I had *not* told you."

"I know . . . but I . . . well, this changes everything. I must leave!"

"It is too late for that now," Irénée said serenely. "And I did not tell you about Maximilien to frighten you, Lysette, but to help you to understand the trials he has been through."

"Madame, surely you do not intend to leave my fate in Monsieur Vallerand's hands!"

"I must remind you, *ma petite,* that is where you yourself placed it."

Irénée could not help but be gratified by the number of visitors she received on Thursday. All her female friends and relatives came from far and wide, eagerly seeking information on the most thrilling gossip to be passed around in years. The controversy had spread to every corner of New Orleans. It was obvious a duel was forthcoming. Everyone knew Maximilien Vallerand had virtually stolen Etienne Sagesse's fiancée from under his nose and ruined her.

"The rumors are absolutely untrue," Irénée said placidly, reigning over the crowd in the parlor like a queen, handing around plates of cakes and *langues de chat,* tiny pastries that dissolved on the tongue. "How can anyone believe my son could assault the virtue of a girl living under my roof? Not only was I there to chaperon her, but she was ill with fever! I myself nursed her through it!"

Four gray, lace-capped heads nodded together. Claire and Nicole Laloux, Marie-Therese Robert, and Fleurette Grenet were Irénée's staunchest friends, supporting her through the direst circumstances. Even in the dark days of Corinne Quérand's murder, they had not stopped paying calls and had never thought to withdraw their friendship. Irénée was a gentle and generous woman, and everyone knew her to be a lady of the highest refinement. Her son, on the other hand . . .

Still, most Creoles tolerated Maximilien. The Vallerands had been a significant New Orleans family for decades. Regardless of his shameful past, he was invited to the important social events of the year . . . but not to the small, intimate family gatherings, where real attachments were formed and deepened.

"We all know you would *never* have condoned anything improper, Irénée," spoke up Catherine Gauthier, a young matron who was friends with some of the younger Vallerand cousins. "But the poor girl has been ruined just the same. The fact is, she has spent two weeks under the same roof with Maximilien, who is undeniably the city's most notorious . . . gentleman. No one blames Etienne Sagesse for not wanting her now."

Everyone murmured agreement, held out their cups to be filled with more coffee, finished the last crumbs of pastry and began on a new plate.

"Has a duel been arranged yet?" Marie-Therese asked.

"Duel?" Irénée repeated. "No one has mentioned anything about a duel until this moment! There is no need for it."

"Irénée," Claire scolded gently, "Of course there will

be a duel. It is the only recourse left to Sagesse. Otherwise his honor would be forever besmirched.''

"Yes, everyone knows that," Fleurette said, daintily dabbing at the corners of her mouth with a napkin. She assumed an expression of objective interest. "Irénée, what did Maximilien *do* to make this girl decide to stay here rather than return to Sagesse?"

"He did nothing at all," Irénée said primly.

Claire and Fleurette looked at each other knowingly. It was obvious the girl had been seduced. Either that or threatened with violence. Maximilen—handsome devil— was such a wicked man!

A native of Virginia, William Charles Cole Claiborne was only eight-and-twenty when President Jefferson appointed him the first American governor of the Orleans Territory. Although Creoles had been opposed to him, it was a coalition of money-hungry Americans and refugees from France who constituted the greatest threat to Claiborne's administration now.

Among those whom Claiborne wisely considered a danger were Edward Livingston, a New Yorker who had come to New Orleans to make his fortune, and General Wilkinson, the ranking officer of the army and newly-appointed governor of the Upper Louisiana Territory. Both men had more or less allied themselves with Aaron Burr, who was encouraging them to stir up strife among the most powerful residents of the territory.

Max had many doubts about Claiborne's ability to withstand the events that were taking shape. Although clever and determined, he was still grieving over the loss of his wife and only daughter to yellow fever the year before. The press attacked him ruthlessly, alleging he was a gambler, a reprobate, and had treated his wife cruelly before her death. Worse still, Claiborne's attention was frequently distracted from the Burr problem by the increasing number of pirates infesting Barataria Bay and the bayous to the south of New Orleans.

"The problem," Claiborne said ruefully to Max as they sat in heavy mahogany chairs and discussed the latest events in the city, "is that the bandits know the swamps better than my own police force, and they are far better supplied and organized. President Jefferson has promised a number of gunboats with which we may combat the pirates, but I fear they will not all be in suitable condition. Nor will there be a great number of enlisted men to choose from."

Max smiled wryly. "I should point out that most Creoles will not be in favor of strong measures to oppose privateering. The local merchants will cause quite an uproar if you remove their access to duty-free merchandise. The fortunes of many respectable families have been founded on smuggling. Here it is not always considered a dishonorable vocation."

"Oh! And which respectable families are you referring to?"

The question, asked in a tone of suspicion, might have caused many to recoil in unease. Max only laughed. "I would be surprised if my own father had not contributed to the pirates' cause," he replied.

Claiborne looked at him sharply, startled by the bold revelation. "And with whom do your sympathies rest in this matter, Vallerand?"

"If you're asking whether or not I have a hand in smuggling, the answer is . . ." Max paused, drew on his thin black cigar, and blew out an even stream of smoke. "Not at the moment."

Claiborne was torn between annoyance and amusement at the man's insolence. The latter won out, and he chuckled. "Sometimes I wonder, Vallerand, if I should count you as friend or foe."

"Were I your enemy, sir, you would have no cause to wonder."

"Let us talk of *your* enemies for a moment. What is this my aides tell me of the rivalry between you and Etienne Sagesse over some woman? And some ridiculous talk of a duel? Merely a rumor, I hope?"

"All true."

An expression of surprise appeared on the governor's face. "You would not be so impetuous as to duel over a woman. A man of your maturity?"

Max's brow arched. "I am five-and-thirty, monsieur—hardly in the doddering years of infirmity."

"Not by any means, but . . . ," Claiborne shook his head in dismay. "Although I haven't known you long, Vallerand, I consider you to be a sensible man, not a wild-blooded youth who would sacrifice all in the heat of a jealous rage. Dueling over a woman? I would have thought you above such behavior."

Max's lips twitched in amusement. "I am Creole. God willing, I will never be above such behavior."

"I have no hopes of understanding the Creoles," Claiborne said with a slight scowl, thinking of his brother-in-law, who had recently been killed in a duel while defending the memory of his sister. "With your women, and dueling, and hot tempers . . ."

"You will discover, Governor, that dueling is an inevitable aspect of life in New Orleans. You might someday find it necessary to defend your own honor in such a way."

"Never!"

Like all Americans in New Orleans, Claiborne did not understand the Creoles' penchant for dueling over what seemed to be trifling matters. Rapiers were the preferred weapon, and the art of fencing was taught by a flourishing group of academies. The garden behind the cathedral had absorbed the lifeblood of many gallants who had sacrificed their lives merely to avenge an imagined slight. Sometimes a single misspoken word or the tiniest breach of etiquette was enough to result in a challenge.

"My God, man," Claiborne continued, "how can you

involve yourself in something like this when you may still be of use to me? You know it is imperative that I avoid antagonizing the population of this city, and if the Creoles' dislike of me worsens—''

"The Creoles do not dislike you," Max interrupted matter-of-factly.

"They don't?" Claiborne began to look mollified.

"They are largely indifferent to you. It is your own countrymen who dislike you."

"Dammit, I know that." The Governor gave him a dark look. "Much help you'll be to me if Sagesse wins the duel."

Max half-smiled. "That is unlikely. However, if I prove unsuccessful against Sagesse, my absence will not make as much of a difference as you seem to believe."

"The hell it won't! Colonel Burr is in Natchez at this moment, plotting to stir Louisiana to revolt and wreak havoc on God knows what other portions of the continent. He'll be here in a matter of weeks looking for supporters. By that time you'll most likely be buried at the foot of a tree instead of doing what you can to verify the reports I'm receiving. And if Burr succeeds, your property will be confiscated, your family's wealth plundered, and your desire to see Louisiana attain statehood will never be realized."

A gleam of malice appeared in Max's golden eyes. "Yes, they'll alight over the territory like a flock of buzzards. No one can scavenge and pillage quite like the Americans."

Claiborne ignored the observation. "Vallerand, the duel can't really be necessary."

"It has been necessary for ten years."

"Ten years? Why?"

"I must go. I'm certain you can find someone willing to help you," Max said, standing up and proferring his hand on the short businesslike shake the Americans seemed to prefer to the Creole custom of kissing both cheeks. A strange lot, the Anglo-Saxons—so squeamish, solitary and hypocritical.

"Why must you go?" Claiborne demanded. "I have more to discuss with you."

"The news of my presence here will have circulated by now. I'm expecting to receive a challenge on your very doorstep." Max gave him a slight, mocking bow. "At your service, as always, Governor."

"And what if you are dead by the morrow?"

Max gave him a saturnine grin. "If you require advice from the netherworld, I'll be pleased to oblige."

Claiborne laughed. "Are you saying you'll haunt me?"

"You wouldn't be the first to encounter a Vallerand ghost," Max assured him, replacing the wide-brimmed planter's hat on his dark head and striding nonchalantly away.

As Max reached the outer door of the run-down Governor's Palace, he was approached by a small crowd of men. The air snapped with excitement, for the Creoles had been roused from their leisurely routine by the prospect of a duel involving Vallerand.

"Gentlemen?" Max prompted lazily. "May I be of assistance?"

One of them stepped forward, breathing fast, his gaze riveted on Max's dark face. In a sudden jerking movement, he whipped a glove against Max's cheek. "I challenge you on behalf of Etienne Gerard Sagesse," he said.

Max smiled in a way that sent chills down the spine of every man present. "I accept."

"You will appoint a second to arrange the details of the meeting?'

"Jacques Clement will serve in that capacity. Make the arrangements with him."

Clement was an agile negotiator who had twice been able to reconcile a dispute before swords were crossed. This time, however, Max had made it clear to him that negotiations would not be required. The duel would be fought to the death, with rapiers, on the shores of Lake Pontchartrain. More privacy would be afforded there, as well as fewer distractions.

"And the doctor?" the second asked. "Who will choose—"

"You appoint him," Max replied indifferently, knowing that at the outcome of this particular duel, a doctor would be of no use.

Excited by the rumors flying through the city, Justin and Philippe tore through the house barefooted, staging mock duels with walking sticks and brooms and upsetting small knick-knacks from their perches as they bumped into tables, bureaus, and shelves. Neither of them entertained any doubt that their renowned and fearsome father would best Etienne Sagesse. As they had boasted to their friends, Maximilien had proved himself without peer, whether the weapon was pistols or swords.

Irénée had taken to her room, praying feverishly for the safety of her son on the morrow, and asking forgiveness for his ruthlessness and unholy desire for vengeance. Lysette sat in the salon, bewildered and tense, trying to convince herself she did not care what happened to Maximilien Vallerand. She stared out the window at the hazy sky which gleamed with an opalescent shimmer. In New Orleans, the moisture in the air was never completely burned off by the sun, making the twilights lovelier than any she had ever seen.

Where was Maximilien now? He had appeared earlier in the day, then left without partaking of supper. Noeline had hinted archly that he was visiting his mistress. The idea had caused a perplexing emotion to spill inside Lysette's chest. "I don't care if he has a hundred women," she said to herself, but the words sounded false to her ears.

She could not stop her imagination from alighting on thoughts of Max with his mistress at this very moment.

What would a man say to a woman when he knew he might die the next day? Lysette's eyes half-closed as she pictured a woman with an unseen face leading Max to her bed, her slender hips swaying in invitation, her hand caught in his. And Max looking down with a sardonic smile, his head lowering as he stole a kiss, his hands moving to unfasten her clothes. *I had to spend my last night with you,* he might be whispering. *Put your arms around me . . .* And as the woman arched up to him, her head falling back willingly, Lysette saw her own face tilted upwards, her own arms stealing around his broad back . . .

With a gasp, she shook her head and blinked in confusion. "Ah, *Mon Dieu*, what am I doing?" she whispered, pressing her hands to the sides of her head as if to force out the wicked images. "How could I, how *could* I be thinking . . ."

"Mademoiselle!" Philippe's voice interrupted her, and Lysette looked up as he approached. Justin followed at a slower pace, sauntering in a way that reminded her of his father. "Why so downcast?" Philippe inquired, his blue eyes dancing with exhilaration. "Are you not pleased that *mon père* will be dueling for the sake of your honor tomorrow?"

"Pleased?" she repeated. "How could I be pleased? It is dreadful!"

"But it is the highest compliment that can be paid a woman. Just imagine what it will be like, the clashing swords, the blood, all for your sake!"

"The duel is not being fought for her sake," Justin said flatly, his blue eyes locked on her pale face. "Isn't that true, Lysette?"

"Yes," she said dully. "That is true."

"What?" Philippe looked puzzled. "But of course the duel is over you. That is what everyone says."

"Idiot," Justin muttered, and sat on the sofa beside Lysette, staring at her curiously, seeming to understand her fear. "He won't lose, you know. He never does."

She lifted her chin, forcing herself to return Justin's stare. "What happens to your father is not my concern."

"Isn't it? Then why are you waiting and watching for his return?"

"I am not!"

"Yes, you are. And you might wait all night. Sometimes he doesn't come back until dawn. You do know who he is with, *oui?*"

"No, and I don't . . ." Lysette's voice trailed off, and she flushed. "Who?"

Philippe broke in angrily. "Justin, do not tell her such things!"

"He is with Mariame," Justin said, giving Lysette a knowing smile. "She's been his *placée* for years. But he doesn't love her."

Lysette swallowed back more questions with extreme difficulty. It was undignified to be listening to a boy's ill-intentioned gossip. "I don't care to hear any more," she said, and Justin gave a jeering laugh.

"You would love to hear more," he said, "but I won't tell you."

Suddenly there was a feminine cry of outrage from upstairs. "Justin! Philippe! Ah, the mischief you have done! Come here *immédiatement!*"

When Justin made no move to rise from the sofa, Philippe tugged impatiently at his sleeve. "Justin, come now! *Grand-mère* is calling us!"

"Go see what she wants," Justin said lazily.

Philippe's blue eyes narrowed with annoyance. "Not without you!" He waited while Irénée called, but Justin continued to sit calmly without stirring. Making an exasperated noise, Philippe left the room.

Lysette folded her arms and regarded the boy in front of her with all the cynicism she could dredge up. "Is there some other bit of gossip you wished to impart?" she asked.

"I wondered if you knew the story of what Maximilien

did to my mother,'' Justin said idly, a thin smile on his lips.

He was a malicious boy, Lysette thought, and yet somehow she felt sorry for him. It must be terrible to live with such a suspicion of his own father, terrible to know that his mother had been an adulteress.

"It's not necessary to speak of it," she said. "It has nothing to do with me."

"Oh, but it does," Justin countered, his voice lowering. "You see, my father is going to marry you."

Her breath was driven out of her lungs in a whoosh. She looked at him as if he'd gone mad. "No, he isn't!"

"Don't be a fool. Why else would *Grand-mère* allow him to compromise you, if she wasn't assured he will make the proper amends?"

She began to tremble. "I will not allow him to make amends. I am not going to marry anyone."

Justin laughed. "We'll see. My father always gets what he wants."

"He doesn't want me," Lysette persisted. "All he wants is revenge. The duel with Monsieur Sagesse."

Standing up and bowing, Justin smiled in satisfaction at her distress. "You'll be a Vallerand before the week is out. Unless, of course, he is defeated—and he won't be."

The scratch of a quill on thin parchment was the only sound in the room as Etienne Sagesse bent over the small desk. Word after scrawling word filled the ivory sheet, while the face above it turned ruddy with effort.

Carefully he blotted the letter, folded and sealed it, then held it in his hands with exceeding lightness, as if it were a delicate weapon. For just an instant a long-forgotten softness appeared in his turquoise eyes, while old memories danced before him.

"Etienne?" His older sister Renée entered the room. She was a striking woman of unusual height, admired for her self-contained ways, respected for being a dutiful wife and the mother of three healthy children. For years she had worried over Etienne every bit as earnestly as their own mother had, and although she turned a blind eye to some of his misdeeds, she could not help be aware of his true character. "What are you doing?" she inquired.

He gestured with the letter in response. "In case events do not turn out as I wish tomorrow," he said, "I want this to be given to Maximilien Vallerand."

"But why?" Renée asked with a frown. "What does it say?"

"That is only for Max to know."

Renée came to stand by his chair, resting her long hand on the back of it. "Why must you duel over that creature?" she asked, her voice for once impassioned.

"Many reasons. Not the least of which is the fact that Lysette Kersaint is the only woman I ever desired to marry."

"But *why?* She is not remarkable in any way! Pretty, yes, and of good blood . . . but there are so many like her!"

"Another woman would see her that way, perhaps."

"Why could you not have chosen to marry one of the girls you—" Renée stopped abruptly, but Etienne knew exactly what she had been about to say.

"So you know about them, eh?" he asked unconcernedly.

"Oh, yes, I know," Renée muttered. "I and the rest of New Orleans. Why must you seduce these naive girls instead of frequenting . . . others more suitable for such attentions?"

"Such questions from my decorous sister," Etienne sneered softly, and smiled. "If you really care to know, I have never been particularly excited by whores."

"Etienne," she protested in embarrassment.

"It is the hunt and conquest I enjoy," he continued. "After that is accomplished, my interest wanes quickly. Innocence is such a transient quality, and most pretty young women are surprisingly corruptible, no matter what station they are born to."

"Then what is it about this Kersaint girl—"

"She is beautiful without conceit. Intelligent, but so very unworldly. Any man would be glad to have a wife so fundamentally gentle in disposition . . . but there is a touch of fire in her, and *that, ma soeur,* is what makes her remarkable."

"And therefore you consider her worth a duel? Worth your life?"

"The duel would have taken place in any event," Etienne replied. "As you know already, it has little to do with Lysette."

"Will you be able to live with yourself if you kill Maximilien?" Renee murmured.

An odd smile shaped Etienne's lips. "Perhaps. That remains to be seen. I can be certain, however, that Max will not be able to live with himself if he emerges the victor." He set the letter down on the desk. "If that happens, do not forget this note. I will be watching from the grave while he reads it."

Renée's blue eyes crackled with anger. "I have never understood your attitude toward that cruel, embittered man. Maximilien Vallerand is not worthy of a single moment of your time, and yet you insist on risking your life to indulge his need for vengeance!"

Etienne appeared to have only half-heard her. "Remember how he was?" he said absently. "Remember how everyone loved him. Even you."

A blush edged up to the tips of her ears, but Renée was too straightforward to deny it. Like so many other women, she had been in love with Maximilien back in the days when his tawny eyes had glowed with warmth and innocence, and he had possessed a boyish gallantry that had set her heart beating all too fast.

"Yes, of course I remember," she answered. "But that

was *not* the same man, Etienne. The Maximilien Valler-
and whom you go to duel with is the devil himself."

Lake Pontchartrain was a shallow body of water, perhaps
sixteen feet at its deepest. Nonetheless, the seemingly tame
lake could turn dangerous. Sometimes a strong wind would
flail the surface until the waves grew violent enough to over-
turn vessels and take the lives of many men.

This morning, however, the water was serene, a glassy
gray mirror poised against the pale dawn sky. Only the
hint of a breeze skimmed the lake and touched the shore.
The duel between Max and Etienne would take place away
from the beach, on the edge of a pine forest where the
ground was firm and even and the air was filled with a
crisp verdant scent.

While the seconds and the small group of onlookers
stood by, Max and Etienne drew aside for a private meeting.

The men were similar in height and reach, both experienced and well-trained in the art of swordsmanship. None
of the witnesses present would dare to choose which opponent they would rather face, though several had noted
that an excess of fine living would soon begin to take a
toll on Sagesse's agility, if it had not already. He indulged
too often in the rich wines and cuisines the Creoles loved,
and led a dissipated life that would not long allow him his
current preeminence as a duelist. Max, by contrast, was
in superb physical condition, moving lightly for a man of
his size, his limbs developed to their full power and flex-
ibility.

Etienne Sagesse confronted Max with a faint smile on
his coarsely handsome face. "Vallerand," he murmured.
"It need not have waited this long. You could have found
some other excuse years ago. Why did you use my little
fiancée to provoke the duel? There was no need to deprive
me of such a sweet tidbit."

A sneer pulled at Max's lips. "It seemed appropriate."

"I suppose it might have seemed appropriate to you, but it was hardly an equal exchange. Lysette was chaste and modest, of far greater value than your harlot of a wife."

Max drew in his breath. "I'm going to kill you."

"As you did Corinne?" Etienne smiled casually. "I never had the opportunity to tell you what a relief that was. She was so tiresome. You must admit, my taste in women far surpasses yours. Tell me, was Lysette as delectable as I anticipated? I had only a taste of her charms before she slipped from my grasp."

Strangely, the thought of Sagesse holding Lysette in his arms was more enraging than the knowledge of his affair with Corinne. Max struggled to contain his fury.

"Careful," Sagesse murmured. "You'll give me the advantage by letting your emotions get the better of you."

"My emotions have already won out where you're concerned," Max sneered. "That's why we're here."

Sagesse's smile dimmed. "So it is. Let us be about it, then."

They exchanged one last look before turning to take up their weapons. Max pushed away an unwanted memory that hovered entreatingly on the edge of his awareness, a memory of childhood. He wondered if Etienne had given a thought to a fact few people in New Orleans remembered—that once they had been inseparable friends.

Chapter 5

In the privacy of his own thoughts Max had pondered the question of why Sagesse would have stooped to adultery with his wife, and decided it had been inevitable. Although he and Etienne had not spoken in years, the competition between them had not waned. Even at the height of their boyhood friendship, when they had sworn to be blood brothers, Etienne had also been Max's most jealous rival.

It had never failed to gall him that Max lived in a charmed circle, favored by all who knew him. Handsome, willful, intelligent, subtle but determined in his ambitions, Max had been the boy all parents wanted for their daughters, the kind that older women watched with secret, speculative expressions and men measured their own sons against.

Because they were friends, Etienne struggled to subdue his jealousy. But eventually their friendship was overshadowed by too many arguments and an increasing sense of competition, and for several years they kept a careful distance.

When Max fell in love and married Corinne Quérand, a sultry, dark beauty, it had not taken long for the idea of seducing her to take root in Etienne's mind. Like his other conquests, it had been born of an inner compulsion that would not be stayed.

His very first woman had been older, almost two decades older than he, and she had controlled, manipulated and expertly wielded her power over him. Maddened by love, Etienne had begged her to run away with him, and she had merely laughed at his ardor. Their affair had ended when her husband, a Spanish diplomat, had taken her back to his native country. Since then, Etienne had only wanted young women, artless and vulnerable, who would never be able to put him through such misery.

With Corinne, the chase and the victory had been sweet, but once Etienne had succeeded in possessing her, her charm had worn off quickly. Now that Max had repaid the debt by ruining his betrothed, Etienne was determined to settle the score between them. He could not shrug off the loss of Lysette, not merely for the sake of his pride, but because she had been a prize of great value to him, tender and unspoiled, shy and graceful. He had fancied himself half in love with her, and Max would pay for taking that away from him.

After making the customary salute, they crossed swords, the blades whipping through the air and clashing with surprising force. Etienne lunged swiftly, was blocked by a deft parry, then lunged again, advancing several steps. Max responded with a rapid series of feints and lunges that drove Etienne back again.

"Mon Dieu," Jacques Clement said under his breath, his eyes wide.

Another man nearby agreed softly. "Just wait . . . it will be more vicious yet."

It was one of the most singular beginnings to a duel any of the spectators had ever seen. Usually a number of simple exchanges first started things off to warm up the combatants and ease them into the more vigorous fighting. But

Vallerand and Sagesse opened the match with explosive force, neither man seeming to require any kind of prelude.

Calling forth all his skill, Etienne wielded his rapier in a search for an opening in Max's guard, but he could find none. He risked a quick glance at Max's set face, and sneered, "I suppose you think . . . if I died by your hand . . . it would set the past to rest."

"I won't know until I've tried it," Max muttered, parrying a forceful thrust and countering with one of his own. He was filled with a peculiar exhilaration, as if some inner demon had been unleashed and was guiding his every movement.

"Damn you . . . ," Etienne breathed. "This should have taken place years ago!"

Max did not answer. For once, they were in agreement.

Lysette walked down the stairs dispiritedly after a sleepless night. The house was still, the hour too early for the twins to have awakened. There was a heavy feeling in her heart, and she could not pretend it was anything other than concern for Maximilien. Just why she should care what happened to him was impossible to understand, but she was very definitely afraid that word would come that he had been killed.

Going to the morning room, she peered through the window and saw that dawn had arrived. Perhaps at this moment Sagesse and Max were dueling, rapiers scissoring and flashing in the pale light, feet stepping lightly in the singular grace of a swordfight.

"By now it is over," she heard Irénée say behind her, and she turned to see the older woman sitting at the empty breakfast table.

"Are you certain?" Lysette asked, frowning as she saw how haggard Irénée looked.

"It seems I have been through a hundred mornings such as this," Irénée said. "This is hardly the first duel Maximilien has fought, nor is he the only son of mine to have taken up swords. No one understands what grief a woman bears when the life of her son is threatened.''

Lysette drew closer, her green-brown eyes touched with pity. ''I think I understand,'' she said, and rested her hands on the woman's slight shoulders.

Irénée gave a tremulous sigh. ''My poor Max.''

''I do not think he will fail, madame.''

''And if he doesn't? How much more will his heart be blackened when he tries to live with Etienne's death on his conscience? Perhaps it would be better for him to . . . to lose this duel than to become so embittered.''

''Don't,'' Lysette murmured, unwilling to hear Irénée's fear voiced. It was frightening to imagine. Oh, if only Irénée's other son's were here to comfort their mother! She was wholly inadequate to the task, especially in light of her own feelings about Max. ''It will be as you said,'' she continued lamely. ''He . . . he will be able to put the past to rest after today.''

Irénée seized on Lysette's consoling words eagerly. ''Ah, it *must* be so! Yes, you are right. He will, he will!''

The minutes seemed to drag by at a fraction of their usual pace. Lysette's throat became tight as still no message came. Surely if Max were all right he would have returned by now. But no . . . Sagesse could not have bested him in a duel! From what little she knew about the two men, she was certain Max would emerge as the victor. Where was he? Why had there been no word?

''Madame!'' she heard Noeline's voice exclaim. Irénée and Lysette both turned with a start. The housekeeper stood in the doorway, her wiry arms bracketing either side of the door frame. ''Retta's boy just run up to say Monsieur comin' up de road!''

''He's all right?'' Irénée asked in a quavering voice.

''Jus' fine!''

Irénée jumped to her feet with surprising alacrity and hurried to the entrance hall. Lysette followed, her heart pounding with some inexplicable emotion. She clasped her hands together, her eyes trained on the front door. The tension was severed as Max burst through the house, his expression dark with frustration, his brows drawn nearly together. He slammed the massive door, scowled at the two women in front of him and strode to the library. Irénée was immediately at his heels, while Lysette stood frozen in the hall.

"Max?" she heard Irénée's muffled plea. "Maximilien? What has transpired?"

There was no reply.

"You won the duel?" Irénée pressed. "Etienne Sagesse is dead?"

"No. Sagesse isn't dead."

"Mais . . . Je ne comprends pas. What happened?"

"I wish I knew," he said savagely. "I planned it all to the last detail—and it was going to be even easier than I had expected."

"I do not understand."

Max strode to the mahogany desk and braced his arm on the bookcase above it, staring at the colored spines of the leather-bound volumes. "For all his vaunted expertise, I had Sagesse at my mercy. Less than a minute after it began, he knew it, too. His reflexes have gone soft. He couldn't best anyone but the rankest novice."

Max looked down at his right hand as if he still held the rapier. "Child's play," he continued with a curl of his lip. "I gave him a scratch, barely enough to draw blood. Then the seconds conferred and inquired if honor had been satisfied. Sagesse's arm was being wrapped by the doctor. I was about to say no—honor required that I fight to the death. And then he stared at me with this peculiar expression, because he *knew* I was going to kill him—" Max groaned and swiveled around, clutching his black head in his hands. "My God, I don't know what made me do it. I wanted to kill him so badly. It would have been so easy, so *damned* easy."

"You let it end there," Irénée said, her eyes disbelieving. "You did not kill him."

Max nodded, his face twisting in baffled self-hatred. "Much to the disappointment of all concerned, excepting Sagesse."

Irénée did not bother to hold back her tears of happiness. "Not to my disappointment," she managed to say. "Unlike your other duels, it would have been . . ."

"Murder?" he suggested with a snarl.

"Yes. And instead you let him go free."

"And now I still haven't succeeded in claiming my revenge."

"*Non.* Your actions this morning have redeemed you!"

Max made a sound of disgust. "I need a drink," he said, looking around for the silver tray of decanters, his emotions threatening to rage out of control unless they were soon dulled by alcohol.

"It is too early," Irénée said.

Max was about to bite out a scathing reply when he noticed Lysette's slender figure in the doorway. She was wearing a soft pink morning dress of thin jaconet muslin, trimmed with ribbon-threaded lace. Her flaming red hair was pulled back haphazardly, untidy curls escaping around her face. Even in the weak morning light, her beauty was incandescent. His eyes narrowed, and he stared at her consideringly.

Lysette felt warning chills chase over her body. "Monsieur . . . you are angry at yourself because you did not kill Etienne Sagesse?"

"How perceptive you are," he said nastily.

Her cheeks colored, and she backed away, knowing better than to ask another question. Unfortunately, now that she had attracted Max's attention, she would not escape unscathed. "It seems," he continued, "that you have been delivered from the fate of lifelong solitude you had envisioned for yourself, mademoiselle."

"H–how?" she stammered. The answer was immediately forthcoming.

"You'd better make plans for an immediate marriage." Max seemed to enjoy her dawning horror.

"To Monsieur Sagesse?" she whispered.

"No. To me."

"To . . . to . . ." The idea was so ludicrous that Lysette felt a hysterical smile threatening to creep across her lips. "Oh, no," she said, shaking her head. "No, I will not be marrying *you*. It would be no different from having Monsieur Sagesse as a husband!"

"But Sagesse doesn't want you anymore," came the soft parry. "I, on the other hand, find that the idea of marrying you holds some merit. It would be a convenient arrangement."

"It wouldn't!" she said wildly.

"I have need of a wife," Max said.

"Because of what you did to the first one!" Lysette cried.

Max glanced at his mother with a sardonic smile. Irénée shrugged apologetically, looking guilty. "I see Maman is not quite as close-mouthed as I thought," he said. "So she warned you about me, hmm?" He took a step toward Lysette, who whirled and fled into the hall. She propelled herself up the shallow steps to her room, her legs tangling in the rush of scalloped skirts.

"I do not think she is receptive to the idea," Irénée said worriedly.

Max laughed at the understatement, some of his fury seeming to abate. He walked over to her and dropped a light kiss on her furrowed forehead. "Maman," he murmured, "you must not go around telling my prospective brides I murdered my first wife. It casts a definite shadow on my appeal."

"But, *mon fils,* I had to tell her. She does not understand you. Better to hear the truth from me than someone else."

His faint smile remained. "I understand."

The worry did not disappear from Irénée's face. "Do you think you will be able to persuade her to marry you, Max?"

"Begin making plans for a wedding one week from yesterday."

"Less than a week? But how could I possible prepare . . . no, no, it cannot be done."

"A *small* wedding. I know you, Maman. You could arrange it in a quarter-hour if you wished."

"But this haste—"

"Is entirely necessary. I'm afraid my beloved fiancée's reputation could not withstand a lengthier engagement."

"If we could wait two weeks, Alexandre and Bernard will have arrived. Your brothers would want to be here, Max!"

"I assure you," he said with a wry grin, "my wedding will lose none of its poignancy for their absence. Now if you will excuse me, I'll go upstairs to have a private talk with Lysette." He paused meaningfully. "Make certain we are not disturbed, hmm?"

The impropriety of his intent was not lost on Irénée. She frowned, aware that her son was capable of bullying the poor child in unscrupulous ways. "Max," she said, trying to express her concern tactfully, "you will not spend too long with her alone, will you? And you must not frighten her."

Max paused and turned to look at her over his shoulder. Irénée remembered that same expression on his father's face. It heralded trouble for anyone or anything that dared to stand in the way of what he wanted. Of all the Vallerand sons, Maximilien relished a challenge the most.

"I might have to," Max said. "After the confidences you shared with Lysette, it will take strong measures to convince her to marry me, *n'est-ce pas?*"

"What kind of measures?"

Now her son truly looked devilish. "Don't ask questions, Maman, when you know you would not like the answers.''

Lysette hunted through the chest of drawers in her room, snatching up the ragged clothes and the knotted kerchief of coins she had carried with her during her escape from the Sagesses. The same panic that had enveloped her then had returned tenfold now. The prospect of marrying Etienne Sagesse had been horrifying, but at least *he* had not been a murderer! Now her circumstances were more dire than she had ever dreamed possible.

She could not possibly marry Maximilien Vallerand, with his wolflike presence and past dark deeds, a man whose cruelty she imagined could be far more subtle than Etienne Sagesse's. A wife was at the mercy of her husband, her happiness dependent on his kindness and goodwill. No one faulted a man for meting out the treatment he felt his wife deserved—and here in New Orleans it seemed that even murder was overlooked, especially when it involved someone as powerful as a Vallerand.

There was a noise behind her. She spun around, bumping her hip on the corner of the chest of drawers, but she didn't feel the pain. Max had entered the room and was watching her.

''I gather you feel my proposal is not worthy of consideration,'' he remarked.

''Get out of my room!''

''It's not your room. This house—and everything in it—is mine.''

''Everything but *me.* '' Nimbly she tried to slip past him. ''Madame Vallerand,'' she called, aiming her voice at the half-open door, ''he is in my bedchamber! Please, tell him to leave me—''

''She is not coming,'' Max drawled, catching her around the waist and closing the door with his foot. At the touch of his hands, she shrieked and tried to kick him. Her toes glanced off his booted shin. ''Stop it,'' he said, and shook her once, lifting her until her soft-slippered feet were barely touching the floor. "We are going to discuss your rather short-sighted approach to the future."

"Let go of me!"

The corner of his mouth tilted mockingly. "My sweet, just what do you think you're going to do if you *don't* marry me?"

"I–I have alternatives."

"Such as?"

"I could teach—"

"With your reputation? No one would have you."

"Then the convent—"

"They won't take you in. I have more influence than you realize."

"My cousin—"

"You'd never get that far. There is no place you can go where I won't be able to ferret you out and bring you back here. And you can discard any hope of returning to the bosom of your family. My guess is they've renounced all responsibility for their disobedient daughter."

"No," Lysette said, although she knew his assessment was accurate. Gaspard had most definitely washed his hands of her.

"And even if they did take you back, they would make your life a living hell," Max continued heartlessly. "In the estimation of any decent family, placing yourself in my custody was choosing a fate worse than death. You are ruined, my innocent, for any man but me. You face only two alternatives—to be my wife . . . or my mistress."

Lysette stared at him in shock. "I can't," she finally said. "I won't marry you, and I certainly won't be your . . ." She stopped, unable to say the hateful word.

"In actuality, there would be little difference between the two. Wife or paramour, you're going to be mine." His hand lifted to her face, and the backs of his fingers drifted along the curve of her jawline. Idly he rubbed her earlobe between his thumb and forefinger. Lysette's entire body tensed. "There's no need to cringe so fearfully, sweet. The arrangement might turn out to be pleasant for you."

"Pleasant?" How, Lysette wondered wildly, could he dare make such a claim?

"You'll be the wife of a wealthy man. I'll dress you in clothes and jewelry that will properly display your beauty. I'll give you whatever you desire."

"I don't care about money."

"I'll be a considerate husband in all ways." Max paused, and let the silence draw out. "You'll be well satisfied, Lysette."

What? Just what did *that* mean? "It does not matter how considerate you would try to be," she said through dry lips. "I don't want . . . I–I don't like you at all—"

"You won't have to like me." He drew her closer, his arm taut around her waist.

Lysette was paralyzed as his hand moved down the side of her throat and smoothed over her breast. Her nipple ached at the light touch and contracted into a hard peak. Shocked by the intimate gesture, she stared up at him, while a surge of tingling warmth seemed to collect underneath his hand.

"Don't," she breathed, red with shame. "Oh, stop it!"

Ignoring the feeble protest, Max cupped his hand over her breast, then brushed his thumb against the sensitive bud. "You enjoy my touch, don't you?"

"No!" Trembling, Lysette tried to push his hand away, but he resisted her effort easily, sliding his palm over her breast.

His lips moved against her temple as he spoke, causing the delicate hairs to rise on the back of her neck. "Tell me the truth, *doucette.*"

Somewhere in the back of her mind Lysette prayed she would faint, that something would happen to release her from this nightmare.

"I . . . I don't . . ." She faltered, and her voice caught in the back of her throat.

His warm, teasing mouth moved over her face, traveling to the corners of her lips, the curve of her cheek, the tiny space between her eyebrows. Lysette tried to turn away, but his arm tightened around her back, and his hand slipped inside her bodice. At the touch of his hand on her naked flesh, she gasped weakly and felt her knees wobble. If not for his supporting arm, she would have collapsed.

Max smiled against her forehead, while his fingers continued their gentle play. "You're not indifferent to me," he said. "The truth is, Lysette, you have no reason *not* to marry me."

"No!" She writhed helplessly, but he caught her even tighter against his body.

"Yes," he said softly. "Would you like further proof of our compatibility?"

"You could have another woman for *that!* And as for marriage, there is no reason for you to marry again!"

Max's eyebrow quirked at her presumption. "Since we first met I've come to fancy the prospect of starting afresh. You possess all the necessary qualities to be an adequate wife—"

"Adequate!" Lysette repeated in outrage, straining away from him.

"—and I have no doubt of my capability to make you content in that position."

"Make someone else content! I don't want you!"

"You have need of my protection."

"I don't want the protection of a man I'm afraid of!"

"What reason have I given you to fear me?"

"You killed your first . . . you k–killed Corinne."

"So it is said." Max's face was emotionless. "Do you believe that?"

"Why should I not?"

"What if I told you I had nothing to do with her death?"

Lysette glared at him. "You've lied to me before."

"Then perhaps I did kill her." Max gave her a chilling

smile. "You, however, will not provoke me as she did. So you have nothing to fear."

"What could you possibly stand to gain from this?"

"I should think that would be quite obvious. One, it would amuse me to flaunt you before Sagesse."

"Oh, how I despise you!" Lysette was shaken by a new awareness as she felt the heat of his body through her clothes. She bit her lip as she saw that the pupils of his eyes had contracted to startling points of black in the cool golden irises. Max had never looked more predatory.

"It would also please me," he said, "to have you in my bed."

She shivered. "You told me once I don't know how to satisfy a man of your experience."

"I didn't mean," he countered in a quiet, deliberate manner, "that I would be unwilling to tutor you."

"Let me go!" Lysette heard her own voice as if it came from far away. Suddenly his eyes were closer, boring into hers, mesmerizing in their intensity. She tried to turn her head, only to discover it was cradled in his hand, positioned exactly as he wanted. "Let me go," she said again, flinching as she felt his warm breath touch her lips. "Monsieur . . ."

Max's expression changed as he experienced a surge of potent desire. The feel of her in his arms caused his blood to stir hotly in his veins. Her lips, so close to his, were sweetly vulnerable, while her thick lashes were lowering over her eyes in an unconscious submissiveness his male instincts responded to instantly. "Max," he prompted, wanting to hear her say his name.

Unable to make a sound, Lysette pushed against him. There was a full, tickling sensation in her breasts, relieved only slightly by the pressure of his chest against hers. His thighs were taut and unyielding as iron, and high against her abdomen there was an alarming ridge of heat and throbbing pressure. She twisted to escape from him, succeeding only in arousing his further.

"Say my name," he urged. "Say you'll be my wife."
Lysette was stubbornly silent.

"Then I'll make you my mistress. Tonight." His head
bent closer, his features half-concealed in shadow. "No,
now," he said gruffly, and lowered his mouth to hers.

Her gasp of protest was smothered as his mouth crushed
hers relentlessly. His arms confined her against his hard,
insistent body. She couldn't move . . . couldn't breathe.
Pressing her lips together, she made an imploring sound
. . . and then his hand came to the side of her face, and
his fingers stroked her cheek with startling gentleness.
Dazed, she relaxed against him, unable to help herself.

Slowly Max broke the kiss and stared down at her.
Opening her heavy-lidded eyes, Lysette felt herself swallowed in the depths of amber fire.

"Open your mouth," Max said huskily, his lips brushing against hers.

"W–what?"

"Open your mouth when I kiss you."

"No—"

Max bent over her again, assaulting her senses with a
slow, sultry kiss, his tongue thrusting gently between her
lips. Lysette gave a small cry and tried to retreat, but she
was anchored firmly against him. There was no use in
fighting him—he would not let her go until he was finished. Her head fell back against his arm, and her hands
flattened on his shoulders. The world shook and crumbled
away until nothing was left but darkness and the powerful
body that enveloped her in its driving possessiveness.

And then all too soon, shamefully, there was no need
for coercion. Her own senses betrayed her, responding to
the touch and taste of the man above her. The pressure of
his lips eased, and her mouth clung frantically lest the kiss
be broken. She reached out for him, her slender arms
curving around his back, her spine arching until her breast
was urged deeper into the confinement of his hand.

When she had surrendered completely, Max lifted her

in his arms and carried her to the bed. His lips began a devastating foray down the side of her neck. Impatiently he nuzzled past the perfumed cluster of ribbons that concealed her cleavage, and buried his mouth in the valley between her breasts.

Suddenly Lysette realized what was happening. She tried to push him away. "Please . . . don't—"

"I won't hurt you," Max said thickly, catching her wrists in his hands and pinning her arms over her head. Her nearness had driven him nearly mad—he, who had always controlled his passions with ease. Suddenly he was too hungry to care whether Lysette yielded freely to him or not. Her protests were trapped in his mouth as he kissed her again. Lysette quivered as she felt the hard pressure of his loins through her gown. Even in her inexperience, she recognized how close he was to forcing her maidenhead. If she did not stop him this moment, it would be too late.

"P-please, Max," she stammered. "I . . . I am afraid."

To her surprise, he lifted his head, his breath pelting unsteadily against her skin. She shrank back into the snowy pillows.

Max turned his face away, his hands clenching in her disheveled hair. After a long time he looked back at her, and she was reassured to see that the frightening hunger had gone from his gaze.

"I need to rest," she said timidly, longing for him to go away. It had not been all that long since her illness, and she'd slept little the previous night. "I . . . need to be alone."

"Of course." Max did not move. "As soon as you consent to my proposal."

"I cannot think—"

"What is there to think about? You know it's pointless to deny me."

"You are cruel!"

"Only when I don't get my way." Max shifted his position, making certain his elbows bore the brunt of his weight. "Tell me you'll marry me."

"I can't—"

His fingers clamped on her jaw, forcing her mouth upward. The tip of his tongue tested the even edge of her teeth, traced the silkiness of her inner cheeks. Her hands fluttered beseechingly to his head . . . and her fingers slid into his thick hair, clasping him closer.

The weight of his body pressed hers deep into the mattress, and his breath scalded her ear as he took her earlobe between his teeth. Lightly he bit the soft flesh and touched the tiny spot with his tongue. *"Maintenant, petite,"* he whispered, "are we going to do this with or without the benediction of marriage? Tell me before the answer becomes immaterial. In case you do not understand, Lysette, I wouldn't be averse to taking you right now."

As he waited for her reply, his body covering hers, his arm solid beneath her neck, Lysette stared at his handsome, intent face. Every instinct told her he would not hurt her. His taste was on her lips, his touch imprinted on her skin. Her cheeks tingled from the scrape of his bristled jaw. She already felt as if she belonged to him.

"I would consent to your proposal," she said haltingly, "if . . ."

"If what?" Max asked swiftly.

"If you would allow me some time before . . ." She stopped, trying to find the right words.

"Before we consummate the marriage," Max finished for her, seeming unsurprised by the request.

"Yes."

Max was quiet for a moment. When he spoke, his voice was oddly gentle. "Had you married Sagesse, would you have requested such a reprieve from him?"

Lysette shook her head abashedly, wondering if he found her utterly contemptible.

"Then why ask it of me? Do you think I am any less a

man than he? That I would look forward to our marital
relations with less anticipation than he might have? I
thought I had demonstrated my desire for you quite effec-
tively, but if not—''

"Oh, no, no, it's not that, not at all," Lysette said with
such haste that she missed the flash of amusement in his
eyes. "It's . . . I would like to be more accustomed to you
before we . . .'' She tried to recall the unfamiliar word he
had used before, ''. . . consummate.''

Max smiled at that, and wound a lock of her hair around
his finger. Lazily he traced a path from her collarbone to
the center of her chest. Following his gaze, Lysette saw
that her bodice had shifted down to the tips of her breasts,
revealing the pink crescent of her nipple. Automatically
she made a move to cover herself.

"No, don't," he said, pressing her wrist down against
the mattress. "I want to look at you." Lysette went crimson as she was forced to lay exposed to his gaze.

"I won't be generous with your reprieve," Max remarked. His loins throbbed, his body urging him to pull
up the twisted hem of her gown and continue what they
had begun. "It all depends," he continued, "on how
sorely you test me. I advise you to accustom yourself to
me rather quickly.''

"Yes, Max," she whispered.

"And as long as we are being honest with each other,
enfant, tell me . . . are you harboring any suspicions that
I will attempt to dispose of you as I did my first wife?''

Lysette gave him a startled look. "You said you didn't
kill her!''

"And you intimated that you didn't believe me.''

"But I do believe you," she said. It was the truth, she
suddenly realized. If he were a murderer, he would not
have spared Etienne Sagesse's life that morning. His actions had betrayed a sense of honor too intrinsic to ignore.

Max was silent with surprise. Granted, her words hardly
rang with confidence, but she was the first woman in years

to voice any kind of faith in him. The strength of his own reaction surprised him.

"What a trusting creature you are," he finally said.

"Sh—should I be suspicious of you?" she dared to ask.

Suddenly Max grinned. "Yes, my sweet. Just a little." He bent his head to press his mouth to the small, delicate point of her breast. Although he knew the gesture would shock her, he was too tempted to resist.

Lysette shuddered at the gentle lash of his tongue, the sensation stealing her breath away. The heat of his mouth seemed to touch every nerve in her body. When he ended the shattering caress and stared at her with a trace of smugness, she could hardly speak. "You promised," she said raggedly. "You said you . . . would allow me time!"

"I said I wouldn't do any . . . ," Max paused and added with a lazy smile, "consummating. I did not say I wouldn't kiss you."

After Lysette's trousseau was transferred from the Sagesse mansion to the Vallerand's, Irénée inspected each garment with distress. The styles were fashionable enough, and the fabrics were acceptable, but the gowns were not of the quality she herself was accustomed to. The dressmaker had obviously been second-rate. Gathers were not sewn correctly, colors had been chosen poorly, the hems were not all even, and in many cases the styles did not flatter Lysette's petite form. Fortunately the wedding gown was tolerable, but only just.

Anxiously Lysette questioned her, wondering why Irénée should seem so displeased. "Madame, my trousseau is suitable, is it not? Maman and I gave it much thought."

"Ah . . ." Irénée exclaimed noncommittally, as she held up a pelisse of zephyrne silk in the most peculiar shade of lavender she had ever seen. Irénée met Noeline's eyes, and they exchanged a look of dismay. The room was filled with heaps of clothes, none of which were appropriate for the wife of a Vallerand.

Lysette picked up a bonnet of ruby velvet and twilled levantine silk, absently toying with the blond lace lining the brim. "Everything is new," she said, now guessing their thoughts. "It would be wasteful to dispense with any of it."

"My dear, it is not for you to think of expense anymore! We, er . . ." Irénée wondered how to say what must be said and yet avoid hurting the girl's feelings. "We must *add* to your wardrobe, however. You do not seem to have enough."

Lysette lifted her chin proudly, aware that the older woman would contrive to get rid of the clothes as soon as possible. Having been raised in a frugal manner, Lysette could not abide the idea of disposing of perfectly decent gowns. The Vallerands might be a wealthy family, but she could not change who or what she was. "I'm certain I have everything I'll require," she said.

An uncomfortable silence filled the room. Irénée did not know what to say. There were many families such as Lysette's in New Orleans, fine families forced to contend with limited financial means. To many Creoles, frugality was a badge of honor, and having too much money was regarded as vulgar, *comme les Americains*. But for Maximilien's bride to be dressed in clothes so obviously inferior . . . ah, it would not do!

"My dear," she said, "it would please Maximilien to see you in gowns more suited to your position."

Lysette shook her head firmly, holding a dress in front of her and fluffing the sleeves as if that would make the garment more presentable. "I am certain Monsieur Vallerand will not even notice. Men do not pay close attention to such things, do they?"

"Not usually, but Max—"

"Then there is nothing more to be discussed. I am quite satisfied with these gowns. Perhaps some of them can be altered, *si vous voudriez.*"

"No 'mount of cuttin' and sewin' ain' gonna help dem,'' Noeline commented, unable to resist airing her opinion on the matter.

When Max returned from a visit to his warehouse in town two hours later, Lysette discovered that Irénée was more than willing to take any and all grievances to Max, and that he tolerated little opposition to his mother's wishes. What Irénée wanted, Irénée would have.

As soon as Max entered the house, his mother drew him aside for a whispered conference. Lysette saw the pair of them as she ventured downstairs, and she knew immediately what they were discussing. Her steps became slower and slower as Max's gaze traveled from Irénée's upturned face to Lysette.

"Good evening, monsieur," Lysette said with forced lightness, reaching the bottom step and preparing to scuttle past him on her way to the dining room.

"Just a moment," Max said, reaching out to catch her slim upper arm. "I would like to talk with you privately."

"Oh, but I am very hungry—"

"It will not take long," he assured her.

"Well," Irénée said brightly, not meeting Lysette's eyes, "I will have supper delayed for a minute or two."

"Don't on my account," Max advised. "Lysette will join you momentarily. I intend to wash now and eat later."

"Ah, yes, after your ride to town . . . of course." Irénée left them with a nervous laugh.

Lysette stared after Irénée ruefully. Without speaking, Max pulled her into the parlor and closed the door behind him. Even in her apprehension, Lysette could not help noticing the pleasant masculine scent that clung to him, of horses and sweat, and a trace of dry burgundy. His gaze moved over her consideringly as he loosened his cravat.

"She told you about the gowns," Lysette said. "I did

not wish her to. Really, there is no reason for her to interfere in the matter of my trousseau—"

"I'm afraid you'll have to tolerate it," Max interrupted, leaning against the back of a settee and crossing his legs. "My mother takes great pleasure in attending to such matters, as trivial as they may seem. I should have warned you before that Maman would want to examine your trousseau. She does have excellent taste, sweet. For her sake, you will allow her to furnish you with some new gowns." He smiled wryly. "It will give her something to plan and worry over."

"But mine *are* new," Lysette protested. "It would be a terrible waste to replace them. The expense, and the—"

"I can afford the expense."

"Still, what I already have is more than adequate." Lysette did not want to be argumentative, but she would not be bullied—even in a kindly way—by any of the Vallerands, not even Irénée. "I have been coerced into this marriage, monsieur, but that does not mean I must accept every one of your dictates!"

"Now is not the time to make a stand," Max warned. "My patience is wearing thin."

"So is mine! It is my right to wear whatever I wish, and I will not wear anything but the clothes I brought from Natchez."

"Even if I forbid it?"

"If you forbid it," Lysette said triumphantly, "I will wear them until every last one is nothing but rags!"

Readily taking up the challenge, Max reached out and locked his fingers in the top of her gown, pulling her closer. "You won't be wearing them long, then. Because every time I see you in one, *this* will happen!"

Lysette gasped as she felt a quick tug at the front of her dress, and her ears were assailed by a rending sound. The bodice of her gown fell open down the middle. Her modesty was saved only by the chemise covering her breasts.

Fury warred with absolute astonishment. "How *could* you?" she demanded, trying in vain to pull the torn cloth together with one hand and slap him with the other. "You *ruined* my gown!"

"If it had been of better quality, it would not have ripped so easily," Max said, deftly avoiding her flying fist.

"I will never speak to you again!" she cried, her face burning. "You arrogant . . . tormenting . . . bullying . . . you have no consideration . . . no respect—"

"*Au contraire.* My respect for you is the reason I won't allow you to wear such ill-made garments."

"Hah! You *enjoyed* ripping my . . . my—"

"Not at all," Max said. "I was merely making a point."

She sensed the pure masculine satisfaction underlying his words. Suddenly she understood that he was in a playful mood, a wolf unaware of the sharpness of his own teeth.

"You're *impossible,*" she said with frustration, trying in an agony of modesty to hold her bodice together.

Max caught her hips in his hands and pulled her between his thighs. Lysette spun around, intending to leave, but his grasp on her hips tightened, and he pulled her back against him.

"Do not touch me so," she muttered, detesting the way he handled her so casually. Her spine went rigid as it touched the hard surface of his chest.

Max's breath stirred her hair as he spoke. "My promise still holds, *chérie.* The same thing will happen every time I see you in one of those damnable gowns." He paused, and Lysette could picture the sardonic slant of his smile as he added, "How many of them do you have?"

Lysette did not reply, plucking ineffectually at the large hands that imprisoned her.

"You're going to humor my mother, then?" he prompted.

"Oui," Lysette said under her breath. What other answer could she give?

"What?"

"I said *yes!*" She threw a baleful glance over her shoulder. "But it will take a few weeks to have new ones made, *alors,* you will have to tolerate mine until then."

"Certainement." Then Max was quiet. Only *le Bon Dieu* knew what he was thinking. Slowly he turned her to face him, and Lysette saw that his amusement had died away. She bit her lip as she recognized his expression, and what it heralded. "Put your arms down," he said softly.

At first Lysette did not understand. "Wh–why?"

"Because I told you to."

Lysette's fingers tightened on the material, while her heart beat fast enough to cause a visible pulse in her throat. Something between fear and excitement shook her from her head to her toes.

"Don't be afraid," Max said, his gaze roving over her slight body, then returning to her face. "Go on. Let me see you."

Did she have a choice? What would he do if she refused?"

"No," she said weakly.

"Lysette." His eyes narrowed.

Little by little her arms eased down to her sides, and the bodice sagged open. The outlines of her breasts with their small pink aureoles were visible through the thin chemise. Lysette flushed deeply, aware that the tips of her breasts had hardened into distinct points. She kept her eyes on the center of his chest as she tried to quell her trembling.

Grimly Max thought it was fortunate for Lysette that she had no conception of how difficult it was for him to let the episode end there. His hands itched to pull her closer between his thighs, and his mouth went dry with craving. After a long inner struggle, he reined in his desire enough to speak evenly. "You're very beautiful," he murmured, and with extreme care he pulled the torn material back over her bosom. Instantly her hands flew upward to anchor the covering, and she turned away from him.

Max began to say something else, but Lysette interrupted, her voice high-pitched with desperation. *"Please."*

His hands spread wide, setting her free, and she left without looking back.

The Vallerand clan reacted with scandalized delight to the news of Maximilien's wedding. Always absorbed in the subject of courtship and marriage, the Creoles had already begun to make predictions about the fate of the hapless bride. Some said the wedding would never take place, while others claimed to have heard from a reliable source that the girl was already *enceinte.* One thing was certain: If and when a child was born, there would be an assiduous counting of days to determine when it had been conceived.

Lysette's genealogy was analyzed in every Creole parlor. No fault could be found with her bloodlines, but that did little to quell the rumors flying around New Orleans. After all, not one member of the bride's family would attend the wedding. Parents held Lysette's situation up to their daughters as an example of the hazards that would most certainly befall a disobedient girl. It would have been far better for Lysette to have accepted Etienne Sagesse's troth. Granted, Sagesse was not known as a saint, but at least he—unlike Maximilien Vallerand—did not have the blood of a first wife on his hands!

Owing to the events leading up to the proposal, there would not be a large wedding at St. Louis Cathedral, but rather a small at-home affair, not unlike the kind the Protestants held. The ceremony itself would be brief, but afterwards there would be a large banquet at the Vallerand plantation. All sought invitations eagerly—unseemly rumors not withstanding.

It was expected that the music, food and wine at the

wedding banquet would make the occasion one to be remembered for years to come. In the old days Vallerand hospitality had been known as the finest in the territory. At Irénée's petition, an old cakemaker by the name of Pasquet had come out of retirement to bake the many-tiered wedding cake. For anyone who had ever sampled his cakes, the flavor of his genius was a tantalizing and all-too-distant memory. Long ago Monsieur Pasquet, over-worked by the demands for the sumptuous confections, had declared he would no longer make them. However, the personal request of a lady as great as Irénée Vallerand was not something Pasquet could refuse.

The wedding would fall on a Monday, not a bad choice although Tuesday was currently the most fashionable. It was considered vulgar to marry on Saturday, or Friday, usually the day on which public executions were held. As tradition demanded, Lysette was kept in strict seclusion, while everyone debated whether she could really be as beautiful as it was said. Some claimed that a face and form like hers could only have been fashioned by the devil. After all, *le Bon Dieu* gave each of his creations a flaw to ward off sinful pride. Only crafty Lucifer would make someone so exquisite. And *vraiment*, what other kind of girl would Maximilien deign to marry after all these years?

Chapter 6

L ysette sat at the dressing table with her head in her
hands. Noeline would be here soon to arrange
her hair, and in the meanwhile, she had time to collect
her thoughts. It was the morning of the wedding, exactly three weeks since she had first stumbled onto the
Vallerands' property.

Twenty-one days . . . how could the course of her entire
life have changed in so short a time? She had been brought
to New Orleans to marry a man against her will. Now she
would be marrying an entirely different man . . . still
against her will. Was her situation any better than before?

Irénée walked through the double parlors with a satisfied smile, checking to make certain the guests would find
no flaw in her house, no fingerprints on the glass, no wilted
flowers. As Creole tradition dictated, the wedding ceremony would take place in the afternoon.

The morning was warm and clear, and Irénée was
pleased with the results of her hastily made plans. The
house was filled with huge garlands of roses, the silver
had been polished, the servants were busy with last minute
preparations for the reception after the ceremony. The
wedding cake was a splendid creation. Now, with four

hours remaining until the wedding, there was little to worry about.

Her smile faded slightly as she heard a minor commotion out in the hall. Certain the twins were up to some mischief, she rushed to the doorway with scolding words on her lips. "Justin! Philippe! *Pas de ce charabia! Pas de ce—*"

She stopped with a gasp as she saw the two tall figures of her younger sons. Alexandre and Bernard were home.

"My sons," she exclaimed in disbelief, "what are you doing here?"

The two tall, dark-haired brothers glanced at each other, and then back at her. Alexandre replied in a quizzical tone. "I was under the impression we lived here, Maman. Isn't the sight of us welcome?"

"Yes, but . . ."

"We decided we had seen enough of France, and all it had to offer," Bernard said dryly. "Those Fontaine daughters, Maman . . . good Lord, some of our *horses* are more attractive than the choicest of the lot."

"Bernard, how uncharitable! I am certain you exaggerate."

Alexandre was turning slow circles, gazing at the flower-bedecked house. "What is all this?" he asked in bewilderment. "Has someone died?"

Bernard frowned. "Maman . . . has Max been in another duel?"

While Lysette remained safely tucked away upstairs and Noeline arranged her hair, the Vallerands drew together for a family conference in the parlor. Rumpled, dusty and stiff-jointed from the long journey, Alexandre and Bernard stared at their mother and older brother disbelievingly.

"You are going to be *married?*" Alexandre exclaimed, leaning his hip on the back of the settee and folding his lanky arms across his chest. He snickered and looked at Max, who favored him with a cool stare. "Of all things I had expected to find on my arrival . . ." For some reason, the sight of his oldest brother clad in wedding finery tickled Alex's fancy. The most whimsical of Irénée's sons, he had never been above irreverence. *"Bien sûr,* he's finally been caught! I would never have gambled on it!" He choked with laughter, and even Bernard's sober demeanor cracked with a smile.

"I fail to see what is so amusing," Max said with a scowl.

Alexandre had nearly fallen to the floor by now. "I would like to know what kind of woman managed to drag you to the altar! Did she use a very big club?"

"Alex," Irénée murmured, "do not make your brother angry."

"Bah, he is always angry!"

Bernard regarded Max more seriously. "Who is she?" he asked. "Not anyone we know, I would guess. You've never taken a second glance at any of the women around here."

Irénée answered quickly. "She is a young, beautiful girl of excellent family, from Natchez. *Te souviens de* Jeanne Magnier? Max's bride is Jeanne's daughter."

"A Magnier?" Bernard repeated, looking at Max speculatively. "An attractive family, as I recall. I would wager there was little need for her to carry a club."

Max smiled unexpectedly. "You would win your wager, *mon frère.*"

"But she must be remarkable indeed for you to risk marriage again," Bernard remarked.

They were all quiet then, remembering that other wedding so many years ago. Corinne's dark loveliness had been striking against the ivory of her wedding gown and lace veil. And Max . . . good-natured and audacious, dazzling in his charm and youthful handsomeness.

Irénée broke the spell by speaking briskly. "Lysette will make Max very happy, you will see. Finally the past is behind us all."

* * *

Lysette's hand shook so badly that Max could hardly slide the gold band onto her finger. The ceremony was not a joyful occasion for either of them. While Lysette was obviously terrified, Max had been wrestling with a trapped feeling. His first marriage had been the worst mistake of his life. Max knew he had only himself to blame for marrying Lysette, for wanting her even though there was a possibility his second marriage would become a living hell just as the first had.

Like Corinne, Lysette was young, delicately bred, high-spirited, and armed with great beauty. Bitterly Max reflected that what his father had once told him about women had been the truth: A man who trusted them would sooner or later be proven a fool. Max detested the need he felt to take this woman to wife, instead of retaining his precious freedom. Ridiculously, he was angry with Lysette for being so desirable. But as she made a move to pull her hand away, he kept it in his until the iciness was thawed from her fingers.

Lysette's mouth had been dry as she spoke the vows that would chain her forever to the man beside her. In a scant few seconds she would be his possession, chatelaine, wife, and someday she would bear his children. Such a virile man would have no difficulty in fathering many offspring. In the eyes of all, Maximilien would have the power to punish, abuse, cherish, favor, subject her to any whim he desired. Lysette could only pray that he would be merciful. The color faded from her face as she reflected on the twist of fate that had brought her from Etienne Sagesse's household to this man's arms. Perhaps destiny had played a hand more than she realized. She could not dispel the feeling that no matter what she had done, all paths would have led to this point.

Incense lent its sweet, pungent scent to the air as Lysette knelt before the priest and prayed for God's blessing on the marriage. Silently she pleaded that there might be some moments of happiness found in the long years ahead, and that her husband might find it in his heart to be kind to her. Meekly she placed her hands in Max's and allowed him to help her to her feet.

The wedding feast was attended by more guests than Lysette could count. For a while she lost sight of Max, who was monopolized by small crowds of relatives suddenly eager to be in his presence. In their eyes, the marriage served to diminish the aura of danger about him, at least for the present. Lysette stayed close by Irénée's side, trying to ignore the snatches of conversation she heard as the woman gossiped over her.

"Pretty . . . but *vraiment,* so little charm . . ."

"She doesn't *look* ruined, Maman."

"That red hair . . ."

"It will not be long before he strays . . ."

". . . ah, I would not be in her place for any amount of money!"

Irénée drew her to the table where the massive wedding cake towered in icy-white splendor. "It is time to cut the cake, Lysette," she said. At that, all the unmarried maidens gathered around them expectantly. According to tradition, each maiden was to receive a slice, which she would take home and put under her pillow along with the names of three eligible men, one of whom might then be moved to propose to her.

The cake was daunting in its size, a fortress of sugar and roses. Lysette did not relish the task before her, or the multitude of gazes pinned on her so intently. Everyone was watching, listening to every word she spoke, measuring and evaluating her. "Must I?" she asked with a strained smile.

Irénée pushed her more firmly toward the table. "Oh, but of course you must!"

There was a tingling sensation on the back of Lysette's neck. Knowing Max must be near, she turned and nearly bumped into his chest. Her heart jumped into her throat and began a laborious descent. Max's presence would make the ritual even more of an ordeal.

Clad in immaculate black and white, he was breathtakingly handsome, his tawny eyes startling in their brilliance. An excited titter ran through the cluster of girls as he placed his hand on Lysette's back and murmured softly in her ear. "You look fearful, my sweet. Is it possible you're more afraid of them than of me?"

"N-no . . . I . . . yes . . ." Lysette glared at him, her nervousness driven away by a spurt of annoyance. Distractedly she leaned over the table, grasped the knife and began to cut the first slice of cake. The blade plunged unevenly through the smooth white icing. Her hand was not steady at all. Before she made a second incision, Max's large hand closed over hers and he pulled her back lightly but firmly against his chest.

The guests chuckled and offered encouragement as Max helped his bride cut several slices, his hand engulfing hers as he guided the knife. Lysette's face was deeply flushed, her eyes locked on the hateful cake, her body intensely aware of the warmth that was generated wherever Max touched her. There was nothing for her to do but lean back against him and follow his movements.

When all the maidens' slices had been served, Max took the knife, set it on the table and lifted Lysette's hand to his lips. He smiled down at her and kissed the tip of her thumb, where a spot of icing had collected. She suppressed a gasp as she felt his tongue remove the dab of sweetness.

Hastily Lysette tried to pull her hand away, but Max retained it with ease. His smile, sported solely for the benefit of the guests, remained on his lips. "Stay by my side, wife," he said in a low voice. "If you stray even a foot away, I might be tempted to take full advantage of my wedding night."

Her resistance fled, and Lysette stood by him docilely. For the rest of the evening it was as if there was an invis-

ible chain between them. Max would not allow her to leave
him, forcing her to talk and even smile, trapping her in a
charade for which she was ill-equipped. In mute despair
Lysette realized this was what he would always expect of
her when others were present, to pretend wifely devotion
she did not feel.

Max pressed a goblet of wine in her hand, his warm
fingers curving over hers, and she glanced at him with
refusal on her lips. She did not like wine. "Monsieur, I
am not thirs—''

"Have some," he said quietly, meaningfully.

Too cowardly to argue, Lysette took a tiny sip, resolving
to set the goblet down somewhere when he wasn't looking.

Shyly she began to respond to some of the guests'
friendly inquiries, while always aware that her husband
was close by. Eventually the dancing began, signaling the
time when the bride was to be led to the bedchamber to
wait for the ordeal yet to come. Irénée appeared and looked
at Lysette anxiously.

"Ma petite—" Irénée began, but Max interrupted
brusquely.

"There is no need for you to leave the guests, Maman."

Irénée frowned at her son. "But I must take Lysette
upstairs. And Noeline must help her change . . . Max,
you must wait."

"I'll see to my own wife," he said inflexibly.

Lysette and Irénée stared at him in dismay. Irénée protested softly, mindful of the attention their discreet conversation might attract. *"Mon fils,* what will all these
people think if you disappear with Lysette like that?''

"They'll think whatever they wish. They always do."

Irénée took hold of his arm. "Maximilien," she said
through her teeth, "I will put this to you as plainly as
possible. Lysette has not yet been prepared for what is to
happen tonight. I have not explained *one detail* to her. I
had intended to tell her while you were down here—''

"And you think," Max inquired lazily, "that a few

words whispered in her ear before I visit the bedchamber would adequately inform her about tonight?'' The shadow of a smile crossed his lips. ''Let us go, Maman.''

''But for Lysette's sake—''

''Lysette has no need of anyone's ministrations or advice, save mine.''

''Maximilien, this is indecent,'' Irénée said, folding her arms in disapproval.

Max cast a mocking look at Lysette, who had been silent. ''I intend to go upstairs with you now,'' he said. ''Does my little bride have any objections?''

Her hazel eyes lifted to his. It was too late to object to anything he wished to do. Max was her husband. He had given her a promise, and she did not think he would not break his word this evening.

''Whatever you decide, monsieur,'' she murmured.

Max smiled. ''A proper and dutiful response. How gratifying. Come, Lysette.'' He began to lead her out of the room, quietly murmuring goodbye to a few of the guests. A more ostentatious departure would have been in bad taste, since all were aware of where the couple was headed, and what would soon happen between them.

Alexandre stopped them at the door, taking hold of Lysette's shoulders and kissing her heartily on each cheek. His dark eyes twinkled at her. ''You are, little sister, a most welcome addition to the family. Max is fortunate I did not meet you first, or—''

Max pulled his wife away from his brother's grasp. ''I am fortunate, Alex, but not for that reason.''

As they approached the stairs, she picked up the skirts of her wedding gown, and noticed that her feet felt as heavy as lead. She did not want to go the bedroom with him. She had never been so afraid in her life. She stumbled on the first step, and his arm went around her waist.

It was then that Max felt the tremors running through her body. Looking at her sharply, he saw the blind panic on her face. ''Did you drink the wine I gave you earlier?''

"No," she admitted in a small voice.

"I didn't think so," he said with a short sigh. "It would have helped, little one."

Helped? Helped what? Lysette fumbled with her skirts, gathered them again in her fists, and continued up the stairs, feeling more awkward with every movement. Apparently annoyed by her slow progress, Max bent and scooped her up in his arms, carrying her the rest of the way.

Noeline was waiting in the bedroom, an expression of surprise on her face as she saw that it was Max, and not Irénée, who had accompanied Lysette. "Monsieur?" she asked. But he motioned her out with a decisive gesture. Immediately the housekeeper left, closing the door behind her.

Lysette stared fiercely at the floor as Max set her down. Her heart began to thud in her chest. "Monsieur," she said, "your promise to me—"

"From now on use my name."

She swallowed hard and nodded. "Max. Your promise . . ."

His fingertips grazed the side of her face, lingering on the downy curve of her cheek. "I'll keep my promise to you, *cherie*. But I reserve the right to educate you as I wish."

"Educate?"

Max took her face in both hands, cupping her jaw in his palms. Lysette felt a slow warmth course through her body, and her eyelashes lowered in response.

"Look at me," he murmured, and waited until she complied. The pad of his thumbs etched a trail down her throat, sending a shaft of fire to the pit of her belly. "I want you to ignore what Irénée, Noeline, or anyone else may tell you about the marital relationship," he said. "Any questions you have will be answered by me."

"I don't understand—"

"Because I alone will be completely honest with you."

Lysette blinked in confusion. "And they would not?"

"No, they would not," Max said flatly.

"Why?"

"They believe a wife is not meant to take pleasure in the time she spends with her husband in bed." His brows quirked slightly. "And I would rather you did."

A blush climbed high in Lysette's cheeks. Moistening her lips, she tried to object. "But if it is not proper—"

"In this I would rather you be improper, *ma petite femme.*"

Max's frankness embarrassed her, but at the same time it was intriguing. Lysette had always wondered about the differences between wives and mistresses, and why a man's relationship with one should be an obligation and with the other a sinful pleasure. A question occurred to her, but she was hesitant to voice it.

"The morning you proposed . . ." she began, then paused as she remembered how Max had coerced her into accepting his proposal, and the way he had touched her. Each time she thought about it afterward, it aroused both shame and pleasure inside.

"Yes?" Max encouraged, removing his exquisitely tailored black coat and starched cravat. "What about it?"

"Were you displeased when I . . ."

When it was clear Lysette would not finish the question, Max regarded her downbent head thoughtfully and began to loosen the pins and orange blossoms entwined in her hair. "Was I displeased because you responded to me?"

She answered with a half nod.

Max smiled slightly as he freed the mass of red hair and watched it tumble down her back. "No, I was not displeased. It would not have been flattering to discover my desire for you was not returned."

His strong fingers sifted through her hair, his fingertips rubbing her scalp gently. Lysette did not move, unable to suppress the quiver of pure bliss that went down the back of her neck. The tiny aches where the pins had pulled her hair dissolved in a tingle of comfort. "Max," she breathed, while the thought drifted hazily through her mind that he might intend to seduce her even in spite of his promise. And somehow that thought was not as alarming as it should have been. "Max, I . . . have no questions tonight."

"Oh, yes you do. And I intend to answer them—even if you won't bring yourself to ask them."

"No, truly—"

"Sit down." He pushed her into the chair at the tiny walnut Louis XIV dressing table. Lysette confronted the reflection in the mirror, stifling her uneasiness as she watched those large, tanned hands slide over her shoulders to the base of her neck.

His fingers wrapped around the silver handle of a brush. Lysette closed her eyes, unnerved by the strangely intimate sight of her husband attending to her hair. He brushed with long, thorough strokes, over the side of her head, up from the back of her neck, smoothing and untangling snarls without pulling a single strand. Drawing the mass of hair together, he tied it at the nape of her neck with a blue silk ribbon and pulled her up from the chair, his fingers going to the fastenings of her gown. Lysette was unexpectedly compliant, soothed by the gentle assurance of his hands on her body.

The satin folds of her wedding gown rustled as Max released the tiny buttons from their tethers. Lazily the fine cloth fell from her shoulders and bosom, slipping downwards as each fastening was undone. Then the gown was a pristine white heap on the floor, and her slim body was clad only in a chemise and pantaloons. Lysette clasped her arms over her breasts, not daring to look at Max's face.

Lightly his warm hands glided over her ivory shoulders, until his thumbs hooked in the edge of the chemise. Lysette bit her lip in surprise and dismay as she felt her nipples tautening underneath the folds of silk. She knew Max saw, knew he was aware of every breath she took, every beat of her heart. His golden eyes were hot and searching, seeming to strip away the fragile concealment of her garments, while his thumbs stroked the border of the chemise in a restless movement.

The tension spun out until Max let go of her with an indistinguishable curse. He strode to the canopied bed and scooped up the nightgown draped across the foot of it. "Here," he said, thrusting the garment into her hands.

Awkwardly Lysette held the diaphanous material to her bosom and retreated to the Chinese screen in the corner. While she changed into the nightgown in privacy, she listened for the sound of Max's footsteps going to the door. The room was quiet. He was waiting for her, she realized, and found it difficult to push her shaking hands through the puffed sleeves of the gown. She waited as long as possible before peering around the side of the screen. Max was still there, a brooding expression on his face.

Without a word he walked over to her, picked up her still form, and carried her to the bed as if she were a child. She could feel the play of muscles underneath his shirt, their tension betraying some sternly repressed emotion. Lysette stared up at the hard edge of his jawline, wondering if he were angry with her. As soon as he set her down on the mattress, she cowered against the pillows and pulled the sheet protectively up to her neck. He sat on the bed, pinning her in place with an intent stare.

"Do you know," he asked, "anything about what goes on between a man and a woman? Anything at all?"

Lysette sank lower under the sheet. "No, *mons* . . . Max."

"Would you care to have me explain it to you?"

Lysette inhaled sharply. Was Max testing her in some way? Would he scorn her if she gave the wrong response? "I—I . . . don't know," she said, her fingers curling around the edge of the linen sheet.

In the glow of the *veilleuse*, the tiny oil lamp on the

dresser, Lysette seemed too young to be a married woman. Max watched her for a moment, a frown gathering on his face. She did not belong with a man as jaded as he, nor would she fare well if she trod on the wrong side of his abominable temper. She would have been better off had she never encountered him—he was fully aware of that fact, and yet his body was already clamoring to pull her underneath him. He needed release from the desire she had aroused in him from the first moment they had met.

He couldn't hold back the thought that appeared in his mind. Why not take her now? She was his. Force would not be necessary—he could seduce her before she could even think of denying him. He could make her purr with pleasure, have her writhing underneath him in ecstasy . . . it would be so very easy . . . she was so close by . . . and he wanted her so damn badly.

Lysette pulled the sheet a little higher, seeming to read his mind. With an effort Max controlled his mounting lust. His lips twisted with self-mockery. He laced his fingers through hers and surveyed their entwined hands thoughtfully. "Do you trust me, Lysette?"

"I–I am trying to."

He smiled suddenly. "You don't make it easy to be trustworthy, *cherie*. You're far too tempting, and I'm not accustomed to denying myself anything I want."

"But tonight you won't force me to . . ." She floundered for a moment and finished, "You won't force me?"

"No."

She stared down at their joined hands as he had a moment earlier. "You . . . may tell me what you wish, Max."

Lysette would never forget the intimate conversation that followed, or Max's gentle manner as he explained things even mothers did not tell their daughters. As he talked, she listened intently but did not dare make a sound, her blush turning from deep pink to scarlet. Gradually the mystery of all she had only been able to guess at before was removed. Lysette could not bring herself to look at him when he finished, but he forced her to, lifting her chin in his hand and surveying her flushed face.

"Is there anything you wish to ask now, *enfant?*" he drawled.

Lysette resented the touch of sarcasm in his voice, not knowing how hard it had been for Max to keep his frustrated desire reined in during the long explanation. "Yes," she said, stung by the way he was looking at her, as if he were jeering silently. Why did his mood have to change so swiftly, when he had been so nice for the past several minutes? "I would like to know i–if you are going to visit your *placée* tonight."

Good women were never supposed to mention that word. They were required to pretend complete ignorance of the quadroon mistresses almost all Creole men kept. Lysette did not know what had prompted her to ask such a bold question. She held her breath as she waited for his response.

"Yes," Max said flatly, a dangerous glint in his eyes. "Unless, my virgin wife, you would rather I shared your bed."

"No," she said automatically.

Max smiled unpleasantly. *"Bien.* Mariame will be less trouble—and I seem to have exhausted my patience tonight. *Bonne nuit."*

As he left, Lysette glared after him, aware for the first time of the discomforting taste of jealousy.

In her sleep Mariame shifted away from Max, curling her arms around a fluffy pillow and sighing softly. He tucked his hands behind his head and stared at the shadowed wall, a frown riding on his brow. Mariame had been as generously uninhibited as always, and yet he had never been left so unsatisfied after love-making. There was a feeling of incompleteness, an appetite that had not been fulfilled.

He should have seduced Lysette this evening instead of holding to his promise. Damning his lack of control over his feelings about her, he wished his life were as it had been before she had stumbled into it.

On the surface everything was the same, but underneath it was all different. His firmly moored emotions had been set adrift on a swift-moving current. He had thwarted his own plans for revenge, gone against his oath never to take a wife again, and had ended up in his mistress's bed on his wedding night. Max smiled grimly, appreciating the irony of his situation.

Had he wanted Corinne this badly? The recollection of that first night was little more than a blur, but he did remember that Corinne—the first and only virgin he had ever bedded—had regarded him with resentment and reproach forever afterward. In spite of his efforts to be gentle, it had been a painful and mortifying experience for her. Corinne had been raised to dread any kind of intimacy with her husband, just as Max had been brought up to think that love for a wife was entirely different than love for a mistress.

"Max . . ." Mariame's drowsy voice drifted to him through the darkness. "Why did you not make love to your wife tonight?"

Lazily he caressed the curve of her shoulder. "I wanted you."

"Ah . . ." Mariame rolled onto her back until he could see the glint of her eyes. "The familiar is always so much safer than the unknown, n'est-ce pas?"

"It's not that," Max said abruptly, disliking the trace of amusement in her voice.

"It is exactly that, mon ami. I think you are a little bit afraid of her."

"Afraid?" he repeated with stinging lightness.

"Oui, of what she makes you feel."

Annoyed, Max sat up in bed, the sheet falling to his hips. "She is a convenience to me, nothing more."

Casually Mariame traced her fingertips over his lean golden torso, and through the thick hair on his chest. "Max, we have know each other far too long."

"Your point?" he asked curtly.

"How could I not notice the difference in you? I have been thinking—"

"You shouldn't waste your time thinking," Max said coldly. "Not when it leads to such inaccurate conclusions."

"Why can't you allow yourself some happiness?" Mariame continued.

"What gives you the idea she could make me happy?"

"The fact that she is making you so miserable."

"That's enough," he said, irritably brushing her hand away.

Mariame shrugged and dropped her head back to her pillow. "You have always puzzled me, *mon amour.* I have never pretended otherwise."

Max swung his legs over the edge of the bed, scooped up his breeches and pulled them up over his hips. Mariame watched his lean, muscled form admiringly as he strode to the window and braced one hand on the sill.

"Are you going home now?" she asked.

"No, damn you."

He was upset. A feline smile hovered on her mouth. Mariame had never been able to tease Max before—he had never been open to it. It was because of the girl, that was clear. How interesting, she mused, that the most invulnerable of men—even Maximilien Vallerand—were sooner or later prey to their own wayward hearts. They could not escape it, although they insisted on trying.

"Why do men always make things more difficult than they need to be?" Mariame asked. "She is yours. Why not admit you have feelings for her?"

Max glanced at her over his shoulder, the moonlight gilding the side of his face with silver. His lashes lowered, casting spiked shadows over the high plane of his cheek.

"Feelings are, for the most part, inconsequential. Haven't you realized that by now?"

A long time went by before Mariame answered softly. "Oh, Max. In some ways you are as innocent as she is."

Bernard held a glass of rich red wine between his long fingers, drinking slowly and contemplating his older brother. This was their first opportunity in three months to talk privately. Max had been gone all day, superintending the repair of a faulty bridge on the property. He had come into the library without changing, intending to have a drink while his bath was being drawn. The mud-covered condition of Max's clothes attested to his active involvement in the repair of the bridge.

Bernard could not help being amused by his brother's inclination to lend his back to a task when there were more than enough slaves to do the work. "Not the way I would have expected you to spend the day after your wedding," Bernard said.

"Nor I," Max replied wryly as he sat down and crossed his legs, heedless of the crusts of mud that fell from his boots to the fine rug.

"I see you have not changed in one regard: nothing is right unless you do it yourself. There is no call for you to wallow in the mud and sweat like a field hand, is there?"

"I thought we had agreed you would run the plantation, Bernard. Unfortunately, in the light of your frequent absences, I seem to be the only one available to make decisions. I'll gladly stop wallowing and sweating, *mon frère,* the moment you decide you're equal to the task."

Bernard flushed slightly, remembering the number of occasions on which he had neglected his responsibilities, knowing that Max always took care of unfinished business. "Our father decided long ago what roles we would assume," he said with a philosophical shrug. "You were to be the paragon, the choicest of all the aristocratic offspring in New Orleans . . . the head of the family. I was to be the prodigal, the spendthrift, always returning home with a penitent heart and outstretched hand. And Alexandre . . . the baby, the libertine . . . lover of drink and women. How dare we step outside the parts we were cast in?''

Max gave him a skeptical glance. "Victor is gone now. You can discard the role whenever you like.''

"It's too late. I don't wish to. I want neither responsibility nor a family of my own.''

Suddenly there was silence between them, and Bernard studied his boots while Max considered ways of broaching the subject that had to be discussed. "Were the Fontaine daughters truly that unappealing, Bernard?'' he finally asked.

Bernard gave a weary sigh. "No, no . . . but how could I possibly consider marriage, when I know that somewhere out there I have a woman and an illegitimate child who need my protection?''

"It's been ten years,'' Max said flatly. "By now she's probably found a husband.''

"And that is supposed to comfort me? That some other man is raising *my* child? My God, every night for the past ten years I've wondered why she left without telling me or her family where she went!''

"I'm sorry, Bernard,'' Max said quietly. "Back then I might have been able to do something about it, but instead I was concerned with—''

He fell silent. At the time he had been too involved in the turmoil of Corinne's murder to give a damn about his younger brother's unfortunate affair with Ryla Curran, the daughter of an American boatman. Bernard and the girl had known that marriage between a Catholic and a Protestant would have meant disaster for one or both of them. When Ryla discovered she was pregnant, she virtually disappeared. In spite of Bernard's efforts to find her and the baby, ten years had gone by without a sign of them.

"Bernard," Max said slowly, "you have searched long enough for them. Perhaps now you should try to let go of the past."

"Is that what *you've* decided to do?" Bernard asked, changing the subject abruptly. "Is that the reason for this precipitous marriage?"

"There is more than one reason for this marriage."

"Is Lysette as frightened of you as she seems?" Bernard asked.

Max smiled unpleasantly. "I hope not."

"You did not stay the night with her—the entire household knows."

"The household be damned. It's my marriage, and I'll conduct it however I wish."

"I know you will," Bernard said lightly. "But I think you are a fool for discarding the tradition. Remember . . . you should spend at least a week alone with your new bride." He smiled suggestively. *"Vraiment,* it is your duty as her husband to break her in properly."

Max scowled. "Perhaps someday I'll ask for your opinion. In the meanwhile—"

"Yes, yes, I know." Bernard's dark eyes flickered with humor. "By the way, have you decided to give Mariame up?"

"Why do you ask?"

"Well, she is a bewitching creature. How did she react to your marriage? Distraught, I imagine."

"Not at all."

"Poor Maximilien." Bernard laughed quietly. "Has any woman ever loved you, aside from Maman?"

Max stared at him emotionlessly, making no reply.

"Love really is impossible for you to tolerate, isn't it?"

"Is there any particular reason," Max asked mildly, "for this pointless inquiry?"

"Oh, every now and again I try to discover if there's a

heart beating somewhere inside that chest of yours. I always fail to discern one.''

"Then perhaps you should stop trying.''

Bernard smiled. "I like to occupy myself with trivial matters.''

"So I've noticed,'' Max replied.

Lysette stood frozen in the doorway, having overheard the last minute of their conversation, her heart constricting oddly at the question: *Has any woman ever loved you?* She felt moved by something between pity and fear, and suddenly she wished she had the courage to go to Max and kiss him in front of his brother, so that Bernard would think she loved her husband. It was ridiculous, really, to feel there was some need for her to protect Max from his own brother's opinion . . . certainly mere words could not wound him.

Timidly Lysette cleared her throat and advanced a few steps into the room. Both men looked at her, Max half-turning in his chair, his golden eyes finding hers instantly. He was more disheveled than she had ever seen him, his shirt sweat-blotched and open at the throat, his hair clinging damply to his forehead and the nape of his neck. There was a smudge of dirt underneath his right cheekbone, and another on his neck where he must have pulled at the collar of his shirt. In the sudden fluttering of her senses, she wondered how it could be that Max was more handsome now than when dressed in the finest of garments.

"Good evening,'' she said breathlessly.

They had not seen each other since the night before. Max set down his glass of wine, looking at her in the way that never failed to make her uneasy, filling his eyes with her the way a starving man might stare at a bit of pastry. One snap of his jaws, and she would be devoured.

"There are things we need to discuss later, Bernard,''

Max murmured, still focusing on Lysette. "In the meanwhile, I believe my bath is waiting."

Bernard murmured an indistinguishable reply, all the while watching the pair of them with great interest. Max accompanied his wife from the room. Feeling the light but secure grip of his hand on her arm, Lysette realized he intended to pull her upstairs with him. "I merely wished to say hello . . . and then I thought I might take a walk in the garden," she said. Max did not reply, continuing to climb the steps with her in tow. She offered no resistance, although her pulse was becoming uncomfortably fast.

The silence seemed ominous. She had to say something to break it, no matter how inane. "You are very dirty," she said.

Max chose to ignore the observation. "I suppose Irénée made mention of my departure last night?" he asked.

"Yes."

"What did she say to you?"

"That . . . well . . . although you might have . . . neglected me last night, you would be a good husband in time."

"Oh, I intend to be," he assured her. "An excellent husband. Extremely attentive to my wife's needs."

"At present there is nothing I need, monsieur."

"Perhaps you would have less difficulty using my name," he suggested silkily, "if we became more familiar with each other."

"*Max,*" she said quickly, her steps slowing as they approached his bedroom. "Would you like me to call Josiah to come help you with your bath, Max?"

"No. I would like your assistance." He seemed to relish the crimson wave that swept over her face.

"But . . . Max . . ."

"It's not a punishment, my sweet. In fact, there are some women who would even enjoy the prospect."

"I wouldn't," she said weakly.

As he closed the bedroom door behind them, Lysette was transfixed by the sight of the enormous tub in the center of the room. Steam rose from the water in gentle wisps and a cake of hard-milled soap was perched on the edge of a bucket nearby.

Lysette remained with her back plastered to the door while Max casually stripped off his shirt. Horror assailed her. Immediately she closed her eyes, but an overpowering curiosity caused them to open a slit, and widen . . . and widen. He was lean and very tan, his skin gleaming like the bronze of a warrior's shield. Heavy black hair covered his chest and narrowed into a silkier pelt over the muscled tautness of his abdomen. His bare arms were corded and heavily muscled from work on the plantation, supple and finely toned from years of fencing. Lysette stopped breathing as she watched him stride to the bed and sit on the edge of it.

Max stared at her with those warm topaz eyes, and then a smile tipped one corner of his mouth. "Help me off with my boots, wife."

Like a sleepwalker Lysette approached him while he extended one long, muscled leg. She grasped the heel of his boot with both hands, working it off with difficulty. The smell of him—sweat, skin, and horses—wound its way to her nostrils, causing her to quiver in alarm. He seemed so unbearably primitive, as if he might reach out and snatch her at any moment. After she had tugged one boot free, she glanced from her dirt-streaked hands to his broadening smile.

"You're going to need a bath as well," he commented.

Doggedly Lysette took hold of the other boot and labored to remove it. When she'd succeeded in easing it off his foot, she dropped it and tried to brush the dried mud from her hands. Max stood up, and she froze, intensely aware of the huge half-naked body standing so close that her breath stirred the hair on his chest. He made no attempt to touch her, only stood there looking down at the top of her head, his fingers moving slightly as if itching to reach out and slide around her. Lysette began to tremble, but she remained still, sensing that one move on her part would break his self-restraint.

His head bent, and she felt his warm mouth touch her forehead, lingering briefly and then sliding to her temple. "Thank you," he said, and the heat of his breath caused a shiver to start at the back of her neck and work its way down her spine.

Her eyes wandered over his chest and midriff, stopping at a twisted pattern of scars, darker than the surrounding skin. "How did these happen?" she asked tentatively.

His lips lifted from her temple, but remained close as he replied, "Dueling wounds. My honor, insubstantial as it may seem, took many contests of skill to preserve."

Rapiers had made those marks. How many times had he faced the point of a sword? How close to death had he come? With an inarticulate sound, Lysette turned away. "You must be tired after all the work you have done today."

"Not really," he said evenly.

There was a rustling sound. Automatically Lysette glanced over her shoulder, and her face blanched as she saw that her husband had discarded his close-fitting breeches and was sliding into the tub. She looked away quickly again, but not before the sight of his tight-muscled buttocks and hair-dusted legs was emblazoned across her memory. Breathing hard from embarrassment and something she couldn't name, she wrapped her arms around her middle and spoke rapidly.

"Since you no longer need my assistance, I have things to—"

"But I do," came the soft contradiction. *"Viens, petite."*

He had commanded her to come to him. Why? What more did he want from her?

Lysette's feet were leaden as she forced herself to cross the distance to the tub. She stared at his face—there was no other safe place to look—and she was chagrined to see a mocking smile on his lips. Silently he leaned forward, bracing his forearms on his knees, waiting for her to scrub his back.

Slowly Lysette sank beside the tub, fishing a sodden sponge out of the bucket of warm water. Wringing it out, she lathered it with the cake of soap and began to wash the broad expanse of his back. The water ran in rivulets down his coppery skin, droplets collecting in every indentation of muscle and sinew. She became flushed from the steam, and the nearness of his naked body.

It seemed an unspeakably intimate thing, to wash his hair, but she did that as well, her soapy fingers working through the dark wet locks and scrubbing the scalp underneath. Max enjoyed her ministrations unabashedly, closing his eyes and tilting his head like a tomcat starved for attention. She rose on her knees to tip the bucket of fresh water over his head, rinsing the suds away.

Carefully she set the bucket down, watching warily as Max pushed the hair back from his forehead. His water-spiked eyelashes lifted. "It appears you have some uses, wife," he said.

As he had intended, the comment provoked her. "You're far too kind, monsieur."

He took her shoulders in his wet hands, pulling her close to the edge of the tub before she had time to react. "Max," he said, and grinned before crushing her lips underneath his, indulging himself in the kiss he had craved for so long. Lysette squeaked in protest and tried to jerk away, her arms splashing in the water until her dress was soaked. Her nostrils flared as she took a deep breath of the steam-filled air. The water from his hair and skin trickled down her cheeks and the curve of her neck.

Determined to gain her response, Max slanted his head and forced her lips apart, kissing her until every coherent thought hurtled into oblivion and her heart beat sluggishly underneath his fingertips. His tongue ventured deep into her mouth, gently marauding, exploring the sweet warmth and taste of her. A plea caught in her throat, and died in a muted moan. Her hands came to rest on the furry surface of his chest, one palm tingling as it covered a flat male nipple. Max made a soft sound and sank his fingers into her hair, pulling her mouth harder against his.

The edge of the tub cut into her midriff, and she flinched in discomfort. Immediately Max's grip eased, and he let her retreat several inches. Lysette stared at him in disbelief, struggling with the honey-sweet ache of newly kindled passion. Part of her wanted to flee from him, while part of her wanted his mouth on hers again, and his hands on her body, and—

"Why don't you join me in here?" Max said huskily.

Pulling her wrist from his grasp, Lysette wiped ineffectually at the water on her face and neck. She was surprised at the sound of her own voice, so tremulous and high-pitched. "Is that an invitation or a command?"

His smile was dazzling in its wicked sweetness. "A suggestion."

"One which I . . . do not choose to follow." Lysette was overwhelmed by the side of her husband she had not see before—playful, sensual, teasing.

"There's more than enough room for both of us," he said, tracing the curve of her chin with his fingertips. "You would enjoy it." He leaned over and kissed her neck. She quivered but did not move away. "You told me before you're not afraid of me. I'm going to have you sooner or later, my sweet . . . why not let it be now? There's nothing wrong in giving yourself to your husband.''

''I don't want—''

''You want me. Don't you think I know how you felt when I kissed you? How you're feeling right now?'' Max found a particularly sensitive spot on her neck and nibbled lightly. The scrape of his jaw against her skin was not at all unpleasant. ''Give yourself to me,'' he murmured.

''I . . . n–not yet.'' She was shy, and afraid, but at the same time she longed to sink into the warm, soap-scented water with him and relinquish herself to his desire. Something inside would not allow her to consent to Max's urging.

Reluctantly he held her at arms' length, regarding her shivering, water-drenched form with no small degree of interest. ''But soon,'' he said, his eyes traveling slowly down to her breasts and back up to her face.

Lysette's long lashes fell to her cheeks. ''Perhaps,'' she was surprised to hear herself murmur.

Max chuckled at the reply, appreciating her first timid attempt to play the coquette with him. His thumb removed a drop of water from the highest curve of her breast, and he let go of her.

Although Lysette would have liked to leave right then, she stayed, even venturing to dry his back when the bath was finished. She frowned as she noticed the twisted path of another scar extending from his midriff to his side. ''Max?'' she asked, her movements slower as she wiped the cloth over his shoulders.

''Mmm?'' He stepped out of the tub and bent to dry his legs.

''You do not intend to duel anymore, do you?''

He smiled as he reached for a burgundy-hued robe and belted it at his lean waist. ''I've never sought to duel. Except with Etienne Sagesse. Why do you ask?''

She turned to the side, striving to keep her tone careless. "Oh, no reason at all . . . it is just so dangerous . . . and you have tempted fate many times, *oui?*"

Max laughed softly. "No one will make you a widow, Lysette. I plan on being your husband for a long time."

But she could not banish her worry. "Many younger men seek to test the skill of your sword. You would not duel for such frivolous reasons, would you?"

"Never for frivolous reasons," he said, aware that she was angling for some kind of promise not to duel again. A promise he would not give. However, it was rather pleasing, the notion of her wifely concern.

"It would be foolish for a man of your responsibilities—and age—to put his life at risk merely for some empty principle."

"Honor is not what I would call an empty principle," he interrupted. "And my age has little to do with it, although thirty-five must seem far advanced to one of your tender years."

Lysette was annoyed by his patronizing tone. "It's not that. And I'm not *that* young."

He grinned. "I'm not that old, *enfant.*"

"Don't call me that," she said, further irritated. When would he start treating her with the respect husbands were supposed to give to their wives? He always seemed to be amused by her, and superior and smug. "I'm not a child, I'm a woman!"

"Are you?" Max caught the damp sleeves of her gown and pulled her close to him. The corners of his mouth were still tipped in a smile. "Then show me how much of a woman you are. Give me proof of your claim."

"I don't have to prove . . ." she protested as his arms stole around her and urged her slender form against the length of his. His broad shoulders loomed above her, while the warm, hard body underneath his robe was obviously aroused. She started at the intimate clasp of his hand on the curve of her buttock.

"As I mentioned last night," Max said, "it causes a man considerable discomfort to be aroused for long periods of time without gaining relief. I fervently hope you took the point as it was intended."

He smiled as she twisted away with a smothered denial.

Chapter 7

Although Lysette knew the Vallerand family considered it exceedingly odd that the newlyweds spent so little time together, no one ever made mention of it in her presence. Not even Justin dared to comment on the separate sleeping arrangements between his father and stepmother, although there was sometimes an insolent gleam in his eyes when he looked at Lysette that betrayed his thoughts exactly.

It would take time for her to become accustomed to the Vallerands. She had been brought up in an almost exclusively female household. She, Jacqueline, and Jeanne had pandered to all of Gaspard's whims. Now with all three of the Vallerand brothers home, not to mention the twins, Lysette found herself surrounded by men—and they were very different from her stepfather.

The Vallerands were no less volatile than Gaspard, but even in a temper they were soft-spoken. Unlike Gaspard and his ineffectual rantings, they knew how to wound with a few expertly chosen words, and at times the brothers were merciless with each other. When a woman was present, however, all arguments were restrained, and the conversation was steered into gentler channels.

Lysette was beginning to believe the wry statement Noeline made one day, that the Vallerand men were born with the knowledge of how to charm women. Since childhood Lysette had been accustomed to Gaspard's poorly veiled dislike, which was why, at first, she had actually been disconcerted by the Vallerands' compliments and courtly manners.

Alexandre often made a great show of taking her aside to ask her advice on matters of the heart, claiming with a roguish wink that any woman who had managed to catch his brother was certainly a great authority. Bernard regaled her with tales of his travels abroad and sometimes conversed with her in English, complimenting her increasing skill in the language. Philippe shared his favorite books with her, selecting those he thought she would particularly enjoy. Even Justin accompanied her on rides around the plantation, discarding his usual surliness and proving to be quite courteous.

Max, however, was seldom there. For two weeks the family saw almost nothing of him. Irénée's assurances that there were many demands on Max's time did little to console Lysette. Hungry for knowledge of him, she plied Irénée with questions, but even after hours of discussion she still knew far too little about Max. No amount of Irénée's fond reminiscences would make up for the distance between husband and wife. When he was gone at night, Lysette was plagued by thoughts of him with his mistress. She had not dared to mention the subject since their wedding, but her frustration increased until she finally brought herself to confront him.

Max strode in just as the clock struck one, crossing through the entrance hall and heading upstairs. Since he had told his valet Zac that morning not to wait up for him, he didn't expect anyone to be awake. A soft sound alerted him, and he paused with his foot on the first step, glancing over his shoulder. One of the parlor lamps was burning. Shrugging off his coat, he went to the doorway and saw the tiny form of his wife snuggled in the corner of the settee. Lysette rubbed her eyes and spoke his name again, having awakened at the sound of his arrival.

"Lysette?" Max frowned curiously, going to her and dropping to his haunches before her. He brushed a wave of hair off her forehead with a gentle hand. "What are you doing here at this hour?"

"I–I was waiting for you," she said, still disoriented. "I didn't mean to fall asleep . . . I . . ."

"Waiting for me? Why?"

Had Lysette been more awake, she might have been less blunt, but she heard herself blurt out, "You were with Mariame again, weren't you?"

Max regarded her emotionlessly, and then a slow half-smile appeared. "Not tonight, no."

She hadn't expected a denial. Sitting up straighter, she uncurled her legs and tried to gather her scattered wits. "Then what were you doing? And why do you come home late so many nights? Irénée says it isn't like you. Irénée says—"

"I would prefer," Max interrupted, the smile still playing on his lips, "that you refrain from paying quite so much attention to everything Irénée says." Moving to sit beside her, he regarded her averted face and took both her hands in one of his. "So you believe I've been whiling away the nights in Mariame's bed, hmm? Has it bothered you?" He laughed softly when she refused to answer. "Well, she is there to welcome me whenever I have need of her. But most of these past evenings I've been attending to business concerning my shipping operations."

Her brow creased. "Is that true?" she asked doubtfully. "Why can't such work be done during the day?"

"Some business, sweet, is better conducted at night."

She looked at him closely, trying to see beyond his bland expression. "Max, you're not doing anything . . . illegal, are you?"

He paused for a few moments, then held up his thumb and forefinger an inch apart. "Just a little illegal." He grinned suddenly. "But nothing more harmful than a cargo of silk stockings, cinnamon bales . . . and several thousand English pounds."

"English pounds? But why—"

"The supply of hard money from Mexico was cut off when the Americans took possession, and New Orleans has little confidence in the French and Spanish paper money that is available. I fear Governor Claiborne's plan to distribute American paper will have several false starts, and in the meanwhile . . ." He shrugged casually.

"But don't you want to support Governor Claiborne's efforts?"

"Oh, I'm under no obligation to Claiborne. I help him when I'm able. I also help myself, when the opportunity arises."

Lysette didn't like the idea of her husband dealing in contraband goods, no matter how minor, but she was relieved that he had not spent all those missing hours in the arms of his mistress. "Then *that* is the only reason you've been away so much of the time?"

"No. I've also been negotiating to buy another ship. I'm planning to add another route to the West Indies and appoint a manager to open an office there. And I'm having another warehouse built on the riverfront." He raised an eyebrow. "Should I begin describing what I've done around the plantation?"

"That won't be necessary," she said gruffly, and tried to move her hands, but his fingers tightened, keeping them clasped in his.

"Then perhaps you should explain your concern about Mariame. Have you decided you would like me to begin visiting your bed instead of hers?"

Lysette blushed violently. "Max, I . . . it is merely that . . . I find it difficult to become accustomed to you when you are always gone!"

"I see." He slid an arm around her shoulders and gathered her against his side. She heard the smile in his voice as he spoke over her head. "Then, my sweet, we most definitely have a problem. Because I find it difficult to be near you for any length of time and not take you to bed."

Instead of being alarmed by the bold statement, Lysette was aware of a distinctly pleasant sensation. She felt comfortable and oddly safe, crushed against his warm side, her head close to his hard, inviting shoulder. She even tried to think of some way to prolong the moment, but before she could say anything, Max had released her.

"Come, before you fall asleep again." He pulled her up from the settee, extinguished the lamp and walked with her to the stairs. Lysette kept her hand tucked in the crook of his arm. Several times she glanced at his hard-edged profile, wishing she knew him well enough to guess at his mood. "I understand you have been busy these past two weeks," he remarked.

"Yes, that is true," Lysette said cautiously. For her the days had been filled with much activity, familiarizing herself with a new household and all the aspects of managing it.

It was up to the mistress of a plantation to see that it ran efficiently, down to the smallest detail. There were always supplies to be ordered, bookkeeping to be done, cooking and baking, cleaning of furniture, rugs, drapes and linens, clothing to be made and mended, and endless laundering. The mistress was expected to take care of minor medical emergencies, mediate disputes between family members or servants, and she was to preside over all rituals of childbirth and death. Men concerned themselves with matters of the outside world, but they, like all others on the plantation, entrusted their basic well-being to the woman at home.

Lysette had few doubts about her ability to handle such responsibility—after all, she had been the only one to take care of the Kersaint home when Jacqueline had left. But this situation wasn't entirely the same. Irénée and Noeline had been running the Vallerand plantation for years, and they might take great offense were she to alter any of their long-standing practices. And there certainly were some things that needed to be changed.

"Max," she said, unconsciously tightening her hand on his arm, "I would like your opinion about something."

"Yes?"

"Don't you think that some of the ways things are done in this house are rather . . . old-fashioned?"

He stopped in front of her bedchamber, seeming to consider the question with undue interest. "Actually, I hadn't noticed."

"Oh, I suppose it's nothing a man would give much thought to. A hundred little things, really . . ." It would be necessary to train at least two more housemaids to keep the huge mansion as scrupulously clean as she would like. There were sun-faded drapes in several rooms that needed to be replaced. She had discovered treasure troves of silver that hadn't been polished in years. From what she had observed, there was never enough fresh linen on hand. That was only the beginning of the list. At Irénée's age, there were things she simply didn't see. But how to assume her rightful place without upsetting Irénée—that was the problem.

"I think I understand," Max said wryly, taking her narrow shoulders in his hands. "Now listen well, *cherie*. You have the right to turn the entire house upside-down, if you so desire. Noeline will do as you tell her, even if she doesn't happen to agree. As for Irénée, it won't be long before she'll appreciate having the leisure other women her age enjoy. In the meanwhile, I have no doubt about your ability to match her stubbornness. Just agree with what she says, and then do things the way you want. That is the only way to handle her."

"But I do not wish to distress her—"

"Oh, I don't think you'll provide her with more distress than she can bear, sweet. That is something only her grandsons can do."

Lysette nodded. "All right, Max."

His thumbs caressed the edge of her collarbone, and he smiled lazily before brushing a kiss against her forehead. "Good night."

She expected him to let go of her then, but he hesitated, his hands flexing on her shoulders, all traces of his smile vanishing. His golden eyes held hers with an intensity that would not let her look away. Her heart skipped several beats. She kept very still, but she could not stop the sudden trembling of her knees.

Now it would happen, the thought raced through her mind, now he would insist on his husbandly rights—and she no longer had the excuse of unfamiliarity to hold him at bay. To her amazement, she realized she actually wanted to end the waiting. The moment seemed to last for hours, while she wondered frantically what he would do.

His hands fell away, and he turned and left her with rude abruptness. Staring after his departing figure, she battled with relief and a peculiar sense of disappointment, wanting to call him back but discovering she was not quite able.

"Burr will arrive tomorrow, without a doubt," Governor Claiborne said, wiping his perspiring face with a handkerchief. "Damn this heat! And I'm told that the barge he will arrive on was a gift from Wilkinson! *Our* Wilkinson!" He sent a glare out the window as if the governor of the Upper Louisiana Territory were in plain sight.

Max settled more comfortably in his chair. Amusement touched his expression. "Ours?" he repeated. "He might be *your* Wilkinson, sir, but I don't care to claim him."

"Blast it, how can you smile? Are you in the least bit concerned about what might happen? The two of them, Burr and Wilkinson, make a powerful pair!"

"I'm concerned, yes. But if Burr's plans are, as we suspect, to seize the Louisiana Territory and Texas—"

"And Mexico!" Claiborne reminded him testily.

"And Mexico," Max continued, "he'll need considerable funds from many sources. Funds he won't be able to get, with or without Wilkinson's influence. The Creoles have a saying, sir . . . *il va croquer d'une dent.*"

"Which means?"

"He'll munch with only one tooth."

Claiborne refused to smile at the quip. "There's a possibility Burr will procure all the money he needs from Britain. Last August he was cozy with Anthony Merry, the ambassador from Great Britain."

"The British won't finance him."

"They might. At the moment the United States and Britain are hardly on friendly terms."

"However, the British are currently at war with France, which means they can't afford to back a losing cause—and Burr's tongue is too loose for his plans to ultimately prove successful."

"Well." Claiborne was silent for a moment. "That's true enough. His enterprise depends on utter secrecy, and I have been surprised by the rumors of things he has said publicly. It is not like Burr to be quite so overblown in his speechmaking, nor foolhardy with his words. Overconfident rascal!" He frowned. "If the British won't finance Burr, he'll turn to Spain."

"How do you know that?"

"I and many others have suspected for some time that Wilkinson is secretly in the Spanish pay."

"Is there any proof?"

"No, but the suspicion is not unjustified."

"And of course," Max said slowly, "His Catholic Majesty would like to take Louisiana back under Spanish protection. Yes, it would be logical for Spain to become a patron of Burr." Suddenly his brows slanted down as they did when he was occupied with troubling thoughts.

"Wilkinson is close to the Spanish high commissioner in New Orleans, the Marquis de Casa Yrujo," Claiborne remarked. "Burr will probably spend some time with Yrujo during this visit. But none of my people have been able to get any information. At the moment, relations between the Spanish and Americans are too hostile. The quarrel over who is entitled to the Floridas might eventually start a war!"

"I am acquainted with Yrujo," Max replied. "I'll see what I can find out from him."

Claiborne mopped his face yet again. "He'll know something. The Spanish talent for intrigue is unmatched. They're probably aware of every move Burr makes. I hope you can get Yrujo to reveal a little of what he knows, Vallerand—for all our sakes."

"So do I," Max said dryly.

"Good Lord, what a tangle. What kind of man could manipulate people and even countries to such an extent? Where does Burr get the will, the nerve, the ambition?" At Max's silence, Claiborne continued as if to himself. "A close acquaintance of Burr has a theory, that Burr would not be involved in such disreputable schemes had his wife not been taken from him some years ago. She had a cancer of some sort—unfortunately it was a long death."

Max's fingers began an idle tapping on the arm of his chair. "I can hardly believe that would influence his political ambitions, sir."

"Oh, well, Burr doted on her, and when she was gone . . ." The governor's eyes grew distant as he thought of his own wife, who had passed away so recently. "Losing a woman, a wife, can change everything inside a man . . . although you certainly would know—"

Claiborne stopped abruptly as he met Max's emotionless stare.

There was silence until Max spoke. "There are wives," he said flatly, "and wives. My first was no great loss."

Claiborne nearly shivered at the coldness of the man. What boldness, to admit his dislike of the woman he had purportedly murdered. Every now and then Claiborne was forcibly reminded of what his aides had warned him, that Maximilien Vallerand was acutely intelligent and sometimes even charming, but completely ruthless.

"And . . . how do you find your second marriage?" Claiborne could not resist asking.

Max shrugged slightly. "More—and less—than what I had expected."

"I have heard the new Madame Vallerand is a great beauty."

Max's brow arched at the governor's comment. It was rare that their conversation turned to personal matters. Because their goals and political views were similar, they were on friendly terms, but they did not talk of family, children, or personal sentiments, and each was aware that they would not associate with the other were it not for political necessity.

"I expect it will not be long before you have the opportunity to meet my wife," Max replied.

"I look forward to it. I must admit, I find Creole women damnably intriguing. Lovely creatures, and so spirited."

Max frowned impatiently. "You plan to welcome Burr when he arrives?"

Claiborne nodded ruefully. "I have the speech already written."

"Good." Suddenly Max's eyes flickered with amusement. "You may as well maintain the pretense of having nothing to fear from him."

"I thought we had just agreed there was no reason to be afraid of Burr!"

"But then," Max rejoined lightly, "I'm not *always* right."

Lysette combed through the tiny kitchen garden at the back of the house, picking herbs which would be dried and used for seasoning. Discontent creased the smooth plane of her forehead, and she sighed as she regarded the shadow her sunbonnet cast on the ground.

It was the tradition that a bride could not go calling or
be seen in public for five weeks after the marriage. She
was compelled to stay at home while everyone else was
gone. Bernard and Alexandre had been absent last night
and all this morning, in pursuit of amusements that would
keep them occupied until much later in the day. As usual,
Max was not there. The twins were busy inside the house
with their lessons.

Irénée had left early in the morning with the cook to go
to market. It was Irénée's special pleasure to be known as
une plaquemine, a green persimmon, or tight with her
money. All the merchants had considerable respect for her
ability to bargain for the cheapest prices. After talking
with everyone of note in the marketplace, Irénée would
return home with all the latest gossip and repeat several
bits of conversation. In the meantime, there was little for
Lysette to do but wait.

Her ears caught the sound of muffled whispers and
stealthy footsteps approaching from the side of the house.
Setting down her shallow basket, she watched as two dark
heads came into view. It was Justin and Philippe, furtively
carrying some bulky object in a dripping sack. They carried it between them, glancing from right to left as they
rounded the corner and turned toward the grove of cypress
trees near the bell tower. Justin saw Lysette and stopped
abruptly, causing Philippe to bump into him. They nearly
dropped the heavy sack.

Justin threw an annoyed glance at his brother. "I thought
you said no one was out here!"

"I didn't see her!" Philippe retorted.

Lysette stared at them quizzically. "What are you carrying?"

The twins looked at each other. Justin scowled pirati-
cally. "Now she'll go inside and tell," he grumbled.

Philippe sighed. "What'll we do with her?"

"Are you stealing something?" Lysette asked.

Justin took the heavy object in both arms and gestured

to Lysette with a jerk of his head. "Kidnap her," he said brusquely. "If we make her a part of it, she can't tell anyone."

"A part of what?" Lysette asked.

"Shhh . . . do you want us all to get caught?" Cheerfully Philippe grasped her wrists and dragged her along with them.

"You're both supposed to be studying," Lysette admonished in a whisper. "Where are we going? What is in that sack? If you *do* get into trouble, I want it to be clear that I was an unwilling partner . . . a victim . . . why is that dripping?"

"It's from the kitchen," Philippe said in a tantalizing voice.

Lysette knew what it was immediately. "You haven't," she said. "Oh, you couldn't have." A huge watermelon shipped in from across the lake had been soaking for hours in a tub of cold water in the kitchen. It was intended as a special after-dinner treat for the family that night. Stealing it was a serious crime, indeed. Berté the cook would have an apoplectic stroke when she discovered its disappearance. "Can't you wait until tonight?" Lysette suggested. "Stealing it isn't worth the trouble you'll cause—"

"Yes it is," Justin said firmly.

"Hurry, let's take it back before they realize it's gone. Right away. Philippe, how could you let Justin talk you into this?"

"It was my idea," Philippe said mildly.

They took cover in the trees and deposited their booty on a large stump. Lysette sat on a fallen tree trunk watched with a mixture of dismay and amusement as the twins unwrapped the glistening emerald melon. "I'll do the honors," Justin said, and lifted the melon, grunting slightly at its weight.

"I can't look," Lysette said, and Philippe put one of his hands over her eyes as the watermelon was cracked against the tree stump. She heard a juicy splitting sound, and Justin's triumphant chortle.

"We've come too far to turn back now," Philippe commented, sounding enormously pleased. Gingerly Lysette pried his hand away from her face and peered at the splendid sight. Appalled as she was at the crime, she could not stop her mouth from watering at the sight of the cold red fruit.

"You should feel guilty," she said, "depriving the rest of the family."

"They should have known what would happen to an unguarded watermelon," Justin retorted, pulling an ancient but carefully sharpened knife from the kerchief knotted around his thigh, and hacking away at the red and green bounty. "Besides, they've deprived us of lots of things. This little watermelon only *begins* to settle the score."

"It's not a little watermelon," Lysette said. "It's a big one, very big."

Justin thrust a glistening wedge toward her. "Try some."

"Are you attempting to buy my silence?" Lysette asked with a severe expression.

"It's not a bribe," Philippe cajoled. "Just a gift."

"It's a bribe," Justin corrected. "And she'll take it. Won't you, Lysette?"

"I don't think I could enjoy a stolen watermelon."

"It tastes much better when it's stolen," Justin assured her. "Try it."

Lysette arranged her apron over her lap and took the offering. As she bit into it, the sugary juice ran down her chin, and she blotted it with a corner of the apron. The watermelon was sweet and crisp, heavenly on a day as hot as this. She had never tasted anything as satisfying. "You're right," she said with her mouth full. "It *is* better when it's stolen."

For the next few minutes there was no conversation as

they concentrated on the melon. It was only when Lysette was comfortably full, her eyes heavy-lidded and the ground around her feet littered with crescents of rind that she looked up to discover Max's tall form approaching.

"Justin? Philippe?" she said slowly. "Your father is coming this way."

"Run!" Justin said, already on his feet.

"What for?" Philippe countered, watching Maximilien. "He's already seen us." He sighed briefly. "He looks annoyed."

"He always does," Justin said, and Lysette had to suppress a fervent agreement.

Guiltily the three of them sat still and waited until he reached them. Max's gaze traveled over the despoiled melon, the sticky-faced twins, and lastly his red-haired wife. His expression was grave, but there was a twinkle in his eyes.

"It seems we have a conspiracy," he said softly.

Lysette smiled up at him. "It was not my fault. I was kidnapped, *mon mari*," she said, and Max found to his disconcertion that being called *husband* in that engaging way went to his head like too much burgundy.

"Traitor," Justin muttered under his breath, but he could not help grinning.

Philippe turned innocent blue eyes to his father's face. "You won't tell Berté, will you, father?"

Max smiled wryly. "No, but you'll give yourselves away by the amount of food you leave untouched on your plates tonight."

"It's still afternoon," Justin said. "We'll have an appetite by supper."

"I have no doubt my two growing boys will," Max replied, and looked at Lysette speculatively. "I wonder about my small wife, however."

He was so handsome as he stood there in a mixture of sunlight and shadow that Lysette caught her breath. "You will have to help me think of something," she said. "It is your duty to defend me, *n'est-ce pas?*"

"Indeed it is." Max lowered himself to the space beside her, gesturing for Justin to cut him a portion of the melon.

"How did you find us?" Lysette removed her apron and passed it to the boys to wipe their hands and faces with.

"According to Noeline, you were in the herb garden. As soon as I went to look for you, I found your basket and a set of tracks." Max took an appreciative bite of watermelon.

Lysette saw that one of his shirt-sleeves was threatening to fall down his forearm. Cautiously she reached out to roll it more snugly. "Why were you looking for me?" she asked, her eyes on the sleeve she was attending to.

"Because I wanted to see you," he said.

"But why—"

"Isn't that reason enough?" he interrupted gently, and Lysette knew from the closeness of his voice that his head was bent to hers.

Suddenly Lysette wanted another excuse to touch him. She was aware of sensations ready to burst forth at his slightest caress. What had happened to cause this undeniable gladness to be near him? Did he feel it too?

"Of course," she said, and glanced at the twins to see their eyes fixed on her.

"Would you like us to leave?" Justin asked mockingly, and was immediately cowed by a punch in the arm from his brother and a warning glance from Max.

"I assume," Max said meaningfully, "that all lessons have been learned thoroughly, or the two of you would not have time for stealing watermelons."

Neither of the boys met his eyes. "There was only a little left to study," Philippe said.

Max stood up, taking Lysette's elbow and pulling her to her feet. "Then I suggest you finish it before supper,"

he said. "In the meantime, find some way to dispose of
this mess."

"What about Berté?" Justin asked. "Are you going to
talk to her?"

"I'll handle Berté, *mons fils.*"

"Thank you, father," the twins mumbled in unison,
nudging the melon rinds with their bare feet as Max walked
away with Lysette.

Troubled, Lysette eased her elbow from Max's grip as
they headed toward the house. "Max?" she asked, and
cleared her throat. "Don't you ever laugh with them?"

His reply was distant, as if he were thinking of other
matters. "Laugh? About what?"

"Oh, just . . . things."

Max stopped and turned her to face him, his hands coming to her waist. He had suspected that sooner or later
they would come to this turn. No woman could resist attempting to reform the man she married, and God knew
Lysette probably had a long list of grievances. "I know
exactly where this conversation is leading," he said dryly,
"and I've already heard everything you're about to say
from Irénée. I'm a dictatorial father. Strict and unsympa-
thetic, *oui?*"

"Well, I—"

"I've been that way too long to change, Lysette. Besides, the twins are used to it."

"But what if—"

"I will not discuss it again. *D'accord?*"

That should have been the end of it. But Lysette could
not let it go. It was so clear that both the boys, especially
Justin, hungered for their father's approval. Why did Max
seem so indifferent to them when she knew he was not?
She saw the way he glanced at them sometimes, with a
father's love and pride. Much as he would like to, it was
impossible for him to hide. Why was Max so determined
to keep such a distance between himself and everyone else,
including his own children?

"You could be nicer to them," she persisted. "It would not take much effort."

"*Nice?*" Max repeated, taken aback. The corner of his mouth curled in jeering amusement. "Nowhere has it ever been written, my sweet, that a father is under any obligation to be *nice* to his children. I've provided for them—"

"Material things only," Lysette interrupted.

"Educated them—"

"History, fencing, mathematics? Is that all there is to an education? What about kindness and compassion? You give them nothing of yourself. And you want nothing your children have to give in return! They want to love you, Max, but you make it impossible!"

His face went cold. He let go of her instantly and continued to the house without her. Lysette hurried to catch up to him, exerting herself to keep pace with his long-legged stride. Her temper asserted itself, and she decided grimly that she would not stop until she had gotten *some* reaction from him. "Are you trying to punish them?" she demanded, her voice low but perfectly audible. "For being Corinne's children? It's not their fault she was—"

In a lightning-fast movement Max stopped and seized her, holding her by the shoulders until her toes barely touched the ground. A dark flush covered his face, and he was so angry he had to speak through clenched teeth. "Don't ever say her name again." He glared at her up-turned face.

Lysette sensed the steely tension in his limbs and realized it would take little effort for him to break her in half. She should have been afraid, but instead she was filled with a strange elation. Max's heart was definitely not made of stone—and his self-control was not absolute.

A deep-seated instinct prompted her to speak very softly. "Max, I am sorry. I did not mean to make you so angry."

He let go of her roughly. "There's no need for self-congratulation,'' he muttered, striving for a measure of his usual indifference. "I'm not angry. Merely annoyed.''

But it was too late, Lysette thought in triumph. She had seen a glimpse of the inner man, and he was not buried as deep beneath the surface as Max liked to think.

"They are your sons, of course . . ." she began to say, but he ignored her, presenting her with an excellent view of his back as he walked to the house.

Lysette was infuriated. *Don't walk away from me!* she wanted to shout after him, but considering his mood, she decided to hold her tongue.

Max thought he had mastered his emotions by the time he reached the library, but there was a tightness in his chest that refused to go away. He closed the door with unnatural quietness and downed a drink, welcoming its fiery smoothness. The frustration of living with Lysette and not having her was driving him out of his mind.

For years he had been able to keep himself protected, shutting the past behind doors he had thought would never be opened. Feelings, needs, vulnerabilities, all seething behind the barriers he had constructed. And if just one of those doors were unlocked, the rest would follow rapidly. That was something he could not afford. But even now he could feel the splintering within himself, impossible to hold back.

Love had cost him everything before. In a way, it had been as fatal to him as it had to Corinne. His old self had died ten years ago—permanently, he had hoped. But it seemed that after all this time there was still something left of his heart, and it ached every moment Lysette was near.

He left, unable to stand another minute under the same roof with her. Rudely he brushed by Lysette in the hall, averting his eyes. If he looked at her, he was afraid he would carry her upstairs and force himself upon her. *That* was how little self-control he had.

"Max?" she asked. "Where are you going?"

"It shouldn't be difficult to guess," he muttered. "I occasionally enjoy the company of a woman who knows not to pry."

Lysette felt as if he had struck her. He was going to visit his mistress? In the afternoon? Her heart twisted in her chest, and she wanted to slap the taunting expression she knew was on his dark face. "How indiscreet of you," she said acidly. "I hope you'll have the taste not to leave your carriage in front of her home."

He laughed bitterly, continuing to the front door. "Concerned for my reputation? Or yours? Rest assured, neither of us has enough left to damage."

"And whose fault is that?" she demanded, clenching her fists in impotent rage as he left without replying.

Contrary to his promise, Max had done nothing to soothe Berté's indignation about the stolen watermelon, and so the twins had made a shamefaced confession. Lysette had tried to intercede on their behalf and tell of her involvement, but Justin interrupted with loud apologies and shoved her out of the kitchen while Philippe wrung his hands before the cook. Finally, confronted by two pairs of appealing blue eyes and expressions of sincere penitence, Berté relented, and the household was again at peace.

During dinner Lysette was too upset to eat. She pushed her food around her plate while staring at the empty place at the head of the table. Sensing her distress, the family talked with forced animation, exchanging light comments and directing few questions to her. Living in the same house, they could not help but know of the state of affairs between the newlyweds.

It was Lysette's misfortune that she overheard the private conversation between Bernard and Alexandre as they partook of wine and cigars in one of the double parlours after dinner. Heading there to find the needlework she had left earlier, she heard their low voices through the half-closed door, and she hesitated as she caught mention of her name.

"I can't help but pity Lysette," Alexandre was saying a trifle nonchalantly. "The problem is, she's too young, and she can't do a damn thing about that."

Bernard's voice was quieter and more thoughtful. "I would not say that is the problem, Alex. For all her youth, she is more intelligent and educated than most of the women in New Orleans—"

"Since when," Alex asked dryly, "is intelligence something of value in a woman? I know *I* never look for it!"

"Which is why I have never complimented your taste in women."

Alex chuckled. *"Dites-moi, mon frère . . .* what is your learned opinion of our sweet sister-in-law's inability to keep Maximilien home at night?"

"Very simple." There was a deliberate pause. "She is not Corinne."

Alexandre sounded startled. "Forgive me, but I would have thought that speaks quite well of Lysette. Corinne was a harlot, a complete—"

"Yes," Bernard said calmly. "But she was also the most beautiful woman New Orleans has ever known."

"Bah, I'd say Lysette is just as beautiful."

"No, it is not the same. Corinne was . . . hypnotic. No woman could ever equal her. In Max's eyes, that is."

"Apparently not in yours either," Alexandre said slowly. "I never knew she had such an effect on you."

"She did on every man she encountered, little brother. You were just too young to notice."

"Perhaps," came Alexandre's doubt-filled reply. "But as to this one, do you think there's a chance Max will ever come to . . . appreciate her?"

"He'll bed her, most certainly. But love? Someone like Max is capable of love only once. The best we can hope

for our little *belle-soeur* is that Max doesn't crush and
bully her, as so often happens when a stronger nature is
paired with a much weaker one.''

Lysette edged back down the hall, the color running
high in her cheeks. Hurt feelings battled with anger. Unconsciously she reached a hand up to her hair—the unruly
red hair that had caused her such displeasure when she
was younger and made her look so dreadful when she
blushed. Corinne must have had the smooth, dark hair that
Creoles prized so greatly. Corinne must have flirted to
perfection with the men who admired her, and hypnotized
them with her beauty. How could Lysette ever hope to
equal such a predecessor?

''But Max does want me,'' Lysette murmured to herself. ''He does, and I . . .'' Absorbed in her thoughts, she
stopped and leaned against the wall. Her jaw tensed with
determination. She would prove hardier than the Vallerands considered her. She would be a wife to Max in all
ways. The thought of him with Mariame at this moment
was intolerable. Fiercely she promised herself that she
would learn whatever was necessary in order to please him
so that he would get rid of his mistress. It was time to
assume her place as his wife.

She felt a presence behind her. Whirling, she began to
speak a name, but her lips were stayed when she saw nothing but empty space. Although the hall was softly lit, she
felt as if she were standing in darkness. The past that she
knew so little about seemed to form a cavernous gulf behind her. She could almost sense Corinne's dark, superior
smile, as if Corinne had some eternal claim on Max that
Lysette could never hope to break.

Max returned two hours past midnight, ushering in a
sheet of rain and a dull crack of thunder from outside as
he opened and closed the front door. The heavy rain had
started early in the evening, breaking the oppressive heat
and spreading its cooling touch over the hot Louisiana

marsh and swamps. The downpour had turned the streets
and roads into deep mud, almost impossible for horses'
hooves to slog through, more difficult yet for carriage
wheels.

Max narrowed his eyes to peer through the somnolent
atmosphere of the house, and his lip curled as he thought
of his wife sleeping peacefully upstairs. For him the nights
brought no rest, only torment, restless tossing and turning. He made his way to the curving staircase with the
overcautious movements of a man who had raised his cup
too many times that evening.

Water fell from his hair and clothes to the summer mat-
ting on the floor and the carpet on the stairs. It gave him
a petty sense of satisfaction, knowing Noeline would fume
tomorrow when she saw the muddy boot marks, but
wouldn't dare utter a word. No one dared reprove him for
anything he did, except for Irénée—and even she had been
quiet lately. It was always that way during the periods
when his temper was unusually foul. The entire family,
including the servants, stayed well out of his way, knowing from experience it was unwise to cross his path.

"Max," he heard a voice as he reached the top of the
stairs. His face was implacable as he looked at Lysette,
who appeared in the doorway of her room. She was
wrapped in an ivory nightgown and pelisse festooned with
tiny silk ribbons. A loose braid of red hair fell over her
shoulder and down to her waist.

"What do you want?" he asked, taking a step or two
closer to her, then stopping as if encountering an invisible
wall.

"I heard you come in," she said. "It's very late."

The depth of his eyes contained a moody resentment
that startled her. "I've come home later than this before."

Lysette could smell the liquor on him—strong spirits,
not the refined burgundies and ports Creole men usually
restricted themselves to. "Your clothes are wet—you'll

need help,'' she said, beginning to move forward, but he stopped her with a gesture of his hand.

"Go back to bed.''

Lysette regarded Max with a perplexed frown, wondering if he were less intoxicated than she had first thought. He was speaking clearly, and he seemed steady on his feet. Certainly he would be able to understand what she wished to tell him. "There is something I must talk to you about,'' she said.

Max gave a sneering laugh. "Oh, I don't think so. Not now.'' He turned and headed toward his room, throwing over his shoulder the casual words, "—it's been *quite* a tiring evening.''

Lysette followed him without thinking, not bothering to conceal the impetuous demand in her voice. "And that, monsieur, is exactly what I intend to discuss!''

Max felt the hard tug she gave to the back of his coat. He stopped, outrage exploding in his brain. So she had decided to start making demands . . . but by God, he would make it clear that she had done nothing to earn that privilege!

"It wasn't business tonight, was it?'' Lysette asked.

"I'll be damned if I answer to anyone,'' Max said, his tone not quite even, "about where I go or what I choose to do.''

"Not even to your wife?''

Max dragged her in front of him, resting his hands heavily on her shoulders. "Let me point out that your usefulness as a wife has yet to be proven.''

She inhaled sharply. "Let *me* point out that you're hardly an exemplary husband!''

He laughed. "And you wish my philandering ways to end?''

"Yes!''

"But why?'' he asked silkily. "Aren't you satisfied with our arrangement? You wanted me to stay out of your bed. I've done just that. However, I'm a man, not a fledgling boy. I have needs that must be met. If my visits to Mariame must cease, I'll have to turn my attentions to *someone* . . . and *you*, my innocent, are the only other candidate. What do you want?''

Lysette stared up at him helplessly, trembling with the force of her feelings. Seconds passed by . . . and the silence proved eloquent in itself. Max's sarcastic expression faded. The hairs on the back of Lysette's neck prickled as she saw the first flicker of understanding in his eyes. Lightning flashed outside, sending its blue-white glow through the windows on the front of the house. The drops of rain in Max's black hair and on his clothes glittered like diamonds. Then all was dark again, and he had let go of her.

His back was to the windows and his face shrouded in shadows. She squinted but could not see anything save the outline of his head and the wolflike gleam of his eyes. He knew now, she thought, and her heart began to pound.

"Max?" she breathed, backing away until she came up against the wall. Her fingers tightened on the edges of her pelisse and brought it more closely around her body.

"What do you want?" he asked again, his voice husky.

Overcome by emotions frightening in their intensity, she could not speak. The lightning burst forth again, illuminating Max's broad-shouldered form as he stalked her slowly, braced his hands on either side of her head, imprisoning her against the wall. "I know exactly what you want," he said thickly, and bent his head, his mouth possessing hers with a completeness that wiped every thought from her mind. His lips forced hers wide apart, and his tongue roamed eagerly inside her mouth.

Max groaned, his senses feeding on the taste and feel of the woman he wanted so desperately. He reached for the opening of her pelisse, roughly pushed her hands aside when she tried to help, found the warmth of her flesh covered only by the thin white cambric.

His hands slid over her breasts, caressing until he felt

her nipples hardening in his palms. Pressing the soft weight upwards, he tore his mouth from hers and bent his head to her breasts, nipping and biting through the fragile gown. With a shuddering sigh, Lysette raised her arms to his shoulders.

"Lysette . . ." His breath burned through the veil of cambric, scorching the tender skin underneath. "I want you . . . ah, Christ . . . I can't turn back now."

"I–I wouldn't ask you to," she whispered. That was the last sound she made for a long time as he kissed her in a way he never had before, his mouth seducing hers with slow velvet heat. She began to tremble, and clawed helplessly at his cloth-covered back, needing to feel his skin under her hands.

Max interrupted the kiss only long enough to tell her something that suddenly seemed important for her to know. "Lysette, I . . . wasn't with her tonight."

Her eyes were soft and dazed. "N–No?"

He curved his hands over her sleek buttocks, pulled her warm body against his. "I haven't touched her, or any other woman," he said into the curve of her neck. "Not since our wedding night. I only wanted *you.*"

"I'm glad . . . I am so glad," she said brokenly, shivering as his lips found her pulse. "I shouldn't have denied you, but . . . oh, Max—"

His mouth crushed hers, while his hand moved down between her thighs, seeking the feminine warmth of her. Lysette recoiled from the intimate touch, but he would not let her pull way. His mouth was at her ear, whispering indistinguishable words as his fingers gently searched through the veil of her gown, seeming to know exactly where the sweet ache of desire was centered.

She threaded her fingers into his cool, wet hair and pulled his head down to hers, her lips welcoming his eagerly.

Once more he grasped her hips and lifted her, fitting the hard, swollen length of his manhood against her pliant

softness. With a soft growl, he rocked against her insistently, aware of nothing but the need to find release within
her slender body. The fire in his loins raged wildly, and
he obeyed the primitive urging without hesitation.

Scooping Lysette up in his arms, he carried her to his
bedchamber, closing the door with a nudge of his heel.
He set her down by the bed and pulled off the ribbon that
fastened her hair with hands that shook slightly. "Loosen
it," he said, more roughly than he had intended, and
shrugged off his coat.

Lysette unbraided the length of hair, running her fingers
through it until it fell to her waist. Pushing the pelisse
away from her shoulders, she let it drop to the floor.

Max removed his white shirt and sat on the bed to shed
his boots. Wordlessly she went to help him, grimacing as
her hands came away muddied. She looked up at him with
a rueful smile, but there was no answering amusement in
his eyes. His face was taut with fierce hunger.

After tugging the boots off, Lysette cast them aside and
rose to her feet. Max stripped back the covers on the bed
while Lysette went to the nightstand to wash her hands.
The stubby candle of the *veilleuse* made a faltering attempt
to pierce the darkness of the room. She stared at the little
flame, her hands gripping the edge of the nightstand as
she tried to muster the courage to turn and go to her husband.

Chapter 8

~~~OO~~~

S eeing her hesitation, Max strode across the room to her and pulled her back against his body. One arm slid across her chest, while his free hand swept from her breasts to her stomach. Lysette closed her eyes, leaning her head against his hard-muscled chest.

"From the first moment I saw you," he said against her hair, "I knew I would have you. You had no choice."

Lysette waited, trembling, while he pulled the sleeves of her gown down to her elbows. His warm mouth touched her neck and shoulders. A soft gasp escaped her lips as the gown fell in a crumpled circle around her feet.

Max turned her to face him, his eyes filled with a hot, urgent light as they swept over her. His hand sank into her hair, tilting her head upward, and she felt her blood turn to liquid fire at the feel of his gently ravaging kiss. The hair on his chest was thick and springy against her palms, the sleek surface of his shoulders and back unyielding. Her naked body quivered against his tautly aroused one, and suddenly her heartbeat became a roar that swallowed all other sound.

Max carried her to the bed and lowered her to the mattress, and for a moment her pale form was lost in the darkness of his shadow. His black hair fell untidily over his forehead as he looked down at her. Instinctively she slid her arms over her chest and drew up her thighs, trying to cover herself in a spasm of modesty.

Leaning over her, he took one of her hands and kissed the inside of her wrist, his lips searching over the delicate tracery of veins until he found a racing pulse. His tongue touched the throbbing spot lightly, and she felt her toes curl in pleasure. He took her other wrist and administered the same treatment, and then spread her arms wide.

His dark head bent over her breasts, his tongue finding the hardened points of her nipples and swirling over them until her entire body writhed in response. Lazily his fingertips wandered over the vault of her ribs, and his palm coasted over her fine-boned shoulders and spine. Lysette arched closer to him in feverish longing, wanting more kisses, craving more of the gentle torture of his hands and mouth.

Driven by needs she had never been aware of before, she touched his back, sides, stomach, her hands inexperienced and hesitant. She heard his breath catch sharply, and she realized with wonder that she had the power to excite him. She hesitated . . . and Max caught her wrist with hungry impatience, pulling her hand down below his waist.

"Max, I can't—" she whispered in agitation. Her words were jolted back in her throat as he pressed her palm against the hot, engorged surface of his manhood. His fingers folded over hers, and the vital force of his flesh throbbed against her hand. Insistently he guided her in a rhythmic stroke, murmuring passionate encouragements against her lips.

Her eyes half-closed, and she gave in to the wanton desires that flooded her body. Later, perhaps, she would be mortified at the memory of her shamelessness . . . but for now, pleasure had made a willing captive of her.

When he cradled her head in his hands, she parted her lips and returned his deep kisses with languid sensuality. When he touched the tangled silken hair between her thighs, her legs opened to allow whatever intimacy he wished. His fingers, so gentle and sensitive, glided over her flesh until she began to moan softly, and then his touch slipped inside her, warm and deeply probing. She twisted against him with a faint cry, trying to escape the agony of pleasure that had surrounded her, but he would not relent until she had dissolved into shuddering sobs beneath him, her body weak in the aftermath of ecstasy.

Murmuring her name, he kissed her temples, her eyelids, the bridge of her nose. She sighed against his neck and wrapped her arms around his back, cradling his hips between her thighs as he braced himself over her. The muscles in his arms tautened as he began to broach the virginal barrier of her body with a slow thrust. Although he tried to be gentle, he knew he was hurting her. The need to bury himself completely was almost unendurable, but he stopped before he was fully sheathed, letting her adjust to the invasion of his swollen length.

Gasping in sudden pain, Lysette thrashed ineffectually, trying to push him away. A low growl emanated from his throat, and he held her wrists down as he sank inside her. She cried out and went rigid, her arms straining against his grip.

"Easy . . . don't struggle, *ma petite*," he said hoarsely as she twisted beneath him. "Lysette, *je vous en prie*." His hands came up to the sides of her face, while his mouth moved gently over hers. "Put your arms around me," he whispered in the soft indentation beneath her ear. "It will be better, I promise."

She obeyed, her hands slipping on the sheen of sweat that covered his back. His breath rasped close to her ear, his knees nudged her thighs wider still, and he pressed full and heavy within her, thrusting rhythmically. Suddenly he groaned and moved in a deep lunge that made her gasp. His hands tightened in her hair, and he succumbed to an acute explosion of pleasure, the hot burst of his seed released inside her.

Lysette offered no resistance as he gathered her against his chest and reclined back against the pillows, his body still a part of hers. Her hand crept to the center of his chest, and her cheek came to rest on his hard, warm shoulder. Max sighed, weary and utterly fulfilled. His hands drifted over her limbs, apprehending the change from tension to languor.

Lysette had never felt so peaceful as she did in this moment. The storm still raged outside, but in here she was safe, held securely against her husband's side. The smell of rain came in through a crack in the window, mingling headily with the scent of Max's skin.

"*Mon mari,*" she said, her fingertip twirling in the hair on his chest. "I . . . I'm glad I am finally your wife." She closed her eyes at the gentle stroke of his hand over her breast.

"So am I," he murmured.

"Is it true, what you said about Mariame? You have not . . . been with her?"

Max hesitated before replying. "Yes."

"But you are still keeping her, *oui?* She is still living in a house you have paid for, and running up expenses that you assume in return for . . . her company."

"Let's not talk about Mariame," Max said, his voice cooling a degree or two. "She has nothing to do with our marriage, *doucette.*"

Lysette swallowed hard, but the questions and the concern were an indissoluble knot in her throat. "Max, do men usually love their *placées?* Or is it just a matter of physical pleasure?"

"I cannot speak for other men." Max disentangled his body from hers and sat up, the cool white sheet barely covering his loins. The line where sun-darkened skin faded into the paler skin of his hip was clearly visible. Lysette wanted very much to touch that tantalizing strip of dark and light, but she restrained herself, still not entirely at ease with him.

"After Corinne's death I thought I would never want a woman again," Max said, stroking the wisps of red hair away from her face. "Every woman in New Orleans was afraid of me, and I . . ." He stopped, the words catching in his throat. Lysette said nothing, waiting with hard-won patience for him to continue. "In a way I was afraid of myself," he finally said. "Everything was different. I was celibate for at least a year. Then I heard that Mariame had been abandoned by the man who had been keeping her. I had seen her before, and admired her beauty. She needed someone to provide for her and her child . . . and I needed someone like her."

Lysette felt a stab of jealousy. "What is she like?" she asked.

"Comfortable," he said after a moment. "The arrangement has suited both of us for a number of years. She's had no children by me, nor has either of us ever desired a close attachment." Max smiled cynically. "I think Mariame's heart still belongs—will always belong—to the knave who deserted her. The finest hearts are often ruined by a first love."

"Was yours?" Lysette asked in a half-whisper.

The motion of his hand in her hair ceased. "Oh, I was ruined, sweet, but not by love."

Lysette was silent for a moment. "Max . . . what are you going to do about Mariame now?"

He smiled slightly. "I wasn't aware there was a need to do anything about her."

Then he still planned to keep Mariame? Visit her bed

occasionally, even after tonight? Hot, affronted words hovered on her lips, but she managed to bite them back. Everyone knew a man had a right to have a mistress as well as a wife, if he could afford to provide for them both. Everyone knew a wife had no recourse except to ignore the situation gracefully. Lysette turned away from him and lay on her side, worrying her lower lip with her teeth.

"After all," Max continued lazily, "I've already made a handsome settlement on her. I believe she plans to run a boardinghouse."

"You mean you . . ." Lysette rolled over, raising herself on her elbows as she stared at him. "She is not your *placée* any longer? You won't be visiting her?"

"No." Max pulled her up against his body. "As I told you, Madame Vallerand, you're the only woman I want."

"Oh," she said breathlessly, sudden happiness rippling through her.

"Somehow I don't think I'll find fidelity too confining," he said, his voice softening. He slipped his fingers under her chin and urged her close for a kiss. Lysette curved against him with no thought of denial, trusting him now as she had not before. She circled her arms around his neck as he pressed her back to the pillows.

"Don't," she whispered as she felt him pull away. "Stay with me."

Max hushed her with a kiss and unhooked her arms as he stood up. At the nightstand he poured fresh water from the pitcher into a bowl and brought it with a soft cloth to the bed. Abashed, Lysette could not meet his eyes as he washed the blood and residue of his passion from her thighs. Impassively he moved the cloth over the smooth surface of her hips and legs, but she could feel the warm touch of his gaze as it strayed over the slim curve of her waist and the rise of her breasts.

When he was finished and reclining again by her side, Lysette turned to him. Her arm draped around his neck, and she lowered her lips to his shoulder. Immediately she felt his response as his desire was aroused.

"Are you trying to tempt me?" he murmured, the trace of a smile in his voice.

She nodded, rubbing her cheek into the juncture of his neck and shoulder.

"It's too soon after your first time." But even as he spoke, Max could not prevent the yearning caress of his hand down her back. Her body fitted against his so perfectly, and the memory of their lovemaking still hovered around them like exotic perfume. Suddenly passion swept through him with blinding force, and he was powerless to subdue it. He sought her lips, pulled her closer, and found her body curving willingly against his.

His fingers slid between her thighs, delving into the secret warmth, and Lysette shivered, her body opening for him. Gentle, teasing kisses swept over her throat and breasts, and then he drew her leg over his hip, his hand gripping her thigh. Gasping against his shoulder, she did not try to move away, not caring what he did, even if it brought pain again.

His knowing hands moved softly over her body, rearranging her trembling limbs, and then he eased inside her, mindful of her newly broached virginity. This time she found pleasure in his possession, and her low moans held more than a trace of astonishment. Max gathered her in his arms, kissing her face, her hair, the vulnerable hollow behind her ear, moving unhurriedly until she sobbed and clung to him in a burst of exquisite fulfillment. He let himself follow her then, closing his eyes and shuddering against her.

As the slim form of his wife relaxed against him, Max cradled her head on his chest, staring at the rain-spattered window. "Lysette," he whispered, his golden eyes sweeping down to her pale shoulders. Even after she fell asleep, he found no rest, his mind plagued by wonderings he could not dispel.

Chapter 9

Lysette awakened to a ray of sunshine slanting across her eyelids. Stirring with a disgruntled sound, she turned away from the window and encountered the hairy surface of her husband's chest. She blinked in confusion, then remembered what had happened during the night. Were it not for waking up beside him, she might have convinced herself it had all been a dream. For hours she had drifted in and out of sleep, drowsily surprised to find herself snuggled against a hard, warm body, the touch of his breath in her hair, the feel of his arm underneath her neck.

"Bon matin," Max said huskily, smiling as she inched the sheet up to her breasts. He was enchanted by her blush. "I'm afraid it's too late for modesty, *petite.*" His hand moved across the sheet that draped over her hips, and rested at the soft juncture of her thighs. "I've been watching you for some time."

Lysette's color deepened as she realized that by now the household was aware she and Max were in the same room. She was certain the events of the night were written on her face. Irénée would be pleased, as well as Noeline. Suddenly a smile pulled at her lips.

"What is it?" Max asked, his mouth moving against her temple.

"I was just thinking that perhaps now I'll stop finding those scraps of red cloth under my pillow."

"Red cloth?" Max repeated. His hand strayed up and down the naked length of her back.

"Oui. Noeline hides them there to attract *le Miché Agoussou."*

Max laughed softly. "The Creole demon of love. But there was no need for such charms. There hasn't been a moment I haven't wanted you."

"Then why did you wait so long to consummate our marriage?" Lysette asked, turning and burying her face in his chest. She breathed in his scent, thinking how odd it was to feel so safe in his arms, when she had once been so afraid of him.

Max drew his head back and looked at her with a trace of surprise. "You rejected my advances often enough, madame. I was under the impression you would not welcome my presence in your bed."

"That was true at first," she admitted in a muffled voice, "but then . . ."

"Then what?"

Lysette looked up with an innocent smile. "I changed my mind."

One of his eyebrows arched. "I gather my appeal has increased since the wedding ceremony?"

"Oui . . . somewhat."

Max rolled onto his back in a lithe movement and dragged her on top of him. "You're not easy on a man's pride." He cupped her head in his hands. "Count yourself fortunate that I consider you worth the frustration I've suffered."

"Max," she said, her eyes alight with amusement, "you have a right to a measure of pride. I know you well enough to say that with certainty."

"Oh, I disagree." Max pulled her head down until his breath touched her lips. "You don't know me well enough at all, my love."

The careless endearment threw Lysette into silent consternation. She knew after last night that he desired her . . . but there had been no sign of love . . . had there? Her thoughts were interrupted as Max kissed her, his unshaven cheek abrading her skin. Lysette smiled against his lips and leaned down, her hair enshrouding them in a ruby curtain.

Agilely Max nibbled on her chin and throat, while his hands pushed the tangled sheet away. Last night he had not expected her to give of herself with such abandon, but after her initial shyness, she had responded with a warmth that had taken his breath away. After hours of holding her in his arms, he had thought himself fully sated, but he wanted her again.

"The night was far too short," he said gruffly, and Lysette smiled.

"Morning arrived at the usual time, I believe."

"How would you know, madame?" He nuzzled the sweet-scented valley between her breasts. "You were asleep then." The heat of desire collected in his loins, refusing to abate until he took his pleasure within her again. "I want you," he said thickly. "I can't get enough of you. God knows if I ever will."

Her breath quickening, Lysette allowed him to guide her further on top of him, her thighs fitting on either side of his hips. Their naked loins brushed together, and a current of wanton excitement rippled through her.

Wordlessly Max eased her closer, until his mouth captured the budded peak of her breast and his tongue nudged it gently. Lifting a trembling hand to his bristled cheek, Lysette held his face there for a long, explosive moment. Finally she dropped her head to his shoulder and gasped his name. She felt the hard ridge of his manhood just beneath her, and her body clamored with the need for release.

Her hands wandered over his chest, stopped at the flat male nipples, her fingertips circling them curiously. With a ragged groan, Max gently sucked her tongue into his mouth. Until now it hadn't occurred to Lysette to kiss him that way. She explored the inside of his mouth as he had hers, learning the textures of his teeth and tongue.

Dazed by a maelstrom of emotions, she made no sound when Max put his hands to her cheeks and eased their heads apart. They stared at each other, his golden eyes burning into hers. Slowly Max stroked her flat stomach with the backs of his fingers, watching her eyes dilate with pleasure. Her body tensed above his as his fingers wandered down through the silky-rough triangle and beyond. Her breath caught, and then she gasped his name.

"Don't move," he said in a gravelly whisper, still holding her gaze, willing her to be patient. She bit her lip and trembled as she felt his teasing fingers slide inside the moistening inlet of her body. The tip of his thumb found the aching center of desire, and he manipulated it with feather-lightness. Shaken, she tried to pull away.

"*Non, petite . . . laisse-moi entrer,*" he urged. At the command to let him inside her, she relaxed, trusting him, allowing whatever he wished. Slowly Max lowered her onto his swollen shaft, their bodies interlocking with stunning completeness. Lysette moaned as her body widened to engulf his hard, thrusting length.

Max pushed deeper into her welcoming sheath, encompassed by a need more primitive than anything he had ever felt. His hands were tight on her hips as he guided her undulating body in an insistent rhythm. Suddenly he felt her arch above him, every muscle taut, and he muffled her low cry with an openmouthed kiss.

Lysette surrendered helplessly to the ecstasy that seared every nerve with white-hot flames. As the furor abated, she was aware of Max's body tensing underneath hers in fulfillment. A curious emotion filled her, something bittersweet and overpowering. Too replete to move, she kept her arms around his neck as he rolled over, taking her

with him. Her eyes remained closed as she felt him stroking her hair away from her face.

Languorously Max captured her lips with a long kiss.
"It seems," he said huskily, "that moderation is not possible where you're concerned."

Since he seemed to have no intention of moving, Lysette wondered if he planned for them to stay in bed all
day. She dared to ask as much, and he gave her an attractive grin. "Would you like that?" he asked, and disconcerted, she did not know how to answer. Max dropped a
kiss on her forehead. "I'll ring for breakfast and a bath,"
he murmured. "Much as I'd like to spend the day with
you, I have obligations that cannot be ignored."

He stood and hunted through the armoire for a robe.
Tall and sinewy, he moved with unselfconscious ease, as
comfortable in his nakedness as he was in clothes. For the
first time Lysette felt a tingle of pride that Max was her
husband. Distrustful, dangerous, unpredictable, he had so
many faults . . . but so much strength.

When Noeline arrived with a large tray of food and *café
au lait*, Max was at the marble-topped nightstand, where
he sharpened the blade of his razor on a leather strop. Two
housemaids busied themselves emptying kettles of heated
water into the bath. Lysette sat in bed with the covers
pulled high under her arms, pulling her fingers through
her tangled hair and braiding it. She blushed slightly as
she smiled good-morning to the housekeeper.

Evidently the situation met with Noeline's approval. Her
expression was as serene as usual, but there was satisfaction in her dark eyes as she set the tray down on a small
table by the window. *"Bon matin,"* she said placidly.
"Bout time I find you in here, *demoiselle.*"

Max began to shave, and Lysette occupied herself with
a flaky croissant and a cup of hot, milky coffee. Noeline
felt compelled to bestow a benediction on the scene.
"Now," the housekeeper observed, "if it please God,

dey'll be babies in de house again. Been far too long since de twins.''

"I believe it's rather soon to think about babies," Lysette replied, her smile deepening as she saw Max's scowling soap-spattered reflection in the mirror. "May I have more coffee, please?" she asked, hoping Noeline would not aggravate Max with another remark.

Noeline complied, glancing at the readied bath and the clothes laid out on the bed. "You go out today, monsieur?" she asked with displeasure. "An' leave a pretty wife wid' no babies?" As far as Creoles were concerned, it was a man's first responsibility to give his wife children.

Max pinned the housekeeper with an ominous stare. "Air your opinions on my marriage elsewhere, Noeline."

"Oui, monsieur," Noeline replied, unruffled, and muttered to herself as she left, ". . . how she gonna get babies by herself ah don' know."

Closing the door with a distinct slam, Max dropped his robe and stepped into the tub. Sinking into the steaming water, he leaned back with a sigh. Out of the corner of his eye he saw Lysette snatch up the discarded robe. He turned his head to watch her put it on. The corner of his mouth twitched in amusement as he saw how the hem of the garment trailed along the floor.

Lysette rolled up the overlong sleeves industriously and went to the tub, reaching for the soap. Max leaned forward, accepting her attentions as if they were his due.

"Max, you don't really mind what Noeline said, do you?" She lathered the soap over his broad back and shoulders. "She did not mean to annoy you."

"I'll tolerate no one's interference in this marriage—no matter how well-intentioned." Max frowned and added darkly, "I had enough of people prying and poking in my first one."

Lysette regarded him curiously, wondering why his marriage to Corinne had turned so bitter. "Max . . . why did Corinne—'' she began to ask, but stopped as she sensed a wall dropping in place between them.

Max slid a wet hand under her chin, searching her hazel eyes. "Ask what you like," he finally said, "though I won't promise to answer."

She pulled back until his fingers slipped from her chin. "Why did Corinne turn to another man?"

"She was angry with me."

"Why?"

"Because I was not the husband she imagined I would be—nor was marriage what she expected."

Lysette was quiet for a moment. "What *did* she expect?" she finally asked, not certain if she had the right to know. But she was desperately curious.

"Unending excitement and activity. She wanted more attention than any one person could give her. In many ways, she wanted to remain a child. I should have seen that she was the kind of woman who would eventually regard marriage as a prison . . ." He frowned and shrugged.

"Did you . . . know at the time that she had taken a lover?" she asked.

His mouth twisted in a hard smile. "Of course."

"What did you do about it? Did you tell her—"

"I did nothing. By that time we were both disillusioned. I didn't care what she did."

Lysette nodded, although she sensed that wasn't quite true. He had still cared, she thought, if only because Corinne was the mother of his children.

Abruptly Max scowled, noting the whisker burns on her delicate skin, one near the corner of her mouth, one on her throat. His fingers traced the edge of the robe and pulled it to the side far enough to reveal more reddened patches on the inside curve of her breast.

"Qu'est-ce que c'est?" Lysette asked, wondering why he looked so annoyed.

Max did not explain the reason for his displeasure, only

rebuked himself silently for not being more careful with her. Letting go of the robe, he rested his elbows on the edges of the tub, his scowl remaining.

"Max, did Corinne—"

"Enough," he said curtly. The mention of his first wife had been enough to cast a shadow over his mood.

Lysette rinsed the soap off his back contritely , realizing it was too soon to pry into his history with Corinne. It would take time and patience to gain his trust. "Why is it that neither of your brothers has ever married?" she eventually asked.

"No need. They have all they desire—all the benefits of marriage and none of the responsibility."

"No need?" Lysette repeated with a touch of indignation. "What about children?"

Max regarded her sardonically. "It's likely that after watching the twins grow up, my brothers have received a rather negative impression of the joys of fatherhood."

"But not all children are like the twins."

"Thank God for that," Max said under his breath.

"Don't your brothers realize they need wives to take care of them when they're ill, or—"

"Married women, my sweet, all share the same inexplicable need to see to it that everyone else is married as well. But I warn you, don't try to play matchmaker for either of my brothers. Bachelorhood is not a condition some men care to remedy."

"Why did you marry *me,* then?" she asked pertly.

"I thought I made that clear when I proposed." His eyes glinted as he added, "And I *know* I made it clear last night." As Lysette blushed, Max stepped out of the tub, water running in rivulets down his lean body. She handed him a towel. Modesty compelled her to wait until his back was turned before attending to her own bath. Quickly she dropped the robe and slid into the water, flinging her braid back until it draped over the back of the tub.

"When will you return home?" she asked, watching

him dress in tan breeches, a black coat and black cravat. The clothes were simple but elegant and perfectly fitted, their quality betraying the fact that his work today would take him beyond the perimeters of the plantation.

"This afternoon, if possible."

"I think I'll go riding around the plantation today," she said. "There are still parts of it I've never seen."

Max glanced at her speculatively, and she met his eyes with perfect innocence, hoping he would not guess her intentions. "Take someone with you," he finally said.

"Yes, Max," she agreed with a satisfied smile.

Perhaps it was her own self-consciousness, but Lysette felt herself to be the object of unusual scrutiny when she joined the Vallerands in the morning room. Even Alexandre, who was clearly suffering from a bout of heavy drinking and carousing in town the night before, dragged his bloodshot eyes to her face. "Good morning," Lysette said, looking from Bernard to Irénée, while her ears grew warm.

Justin, who lounged in the corner with a sugar-dusted roll, broke the tension with his typical bluntness. "Are we trying to see how she fared the night with father? She looks well enough to me." But it was not said in malice; indeed, there was a twinkle in his blue eyes that was impossible to resist. Lysette found herself smiling at him even as the rest of the family reacted with annoyance, demanding that he leave the room. She touched his shoulder as he sauntered toward the doorway. Justin stopped, arching an eyebrow questioningly in a way that reminded her of his father.

"It's not necessary for you to leave," she said.

"Yes, it is. Philippe and I have a fencing lesson in town."

"I hope it goes well for you."

Justin grinned, raking his fingers through his shaggy black hair. "It always does. I'm an excellent swordsman."

He slid his hands into his pockets and rested his weight on one leg, a carelessly handsome pose that suited him well. Lysette felt a flicker of pity for all the girls whose hearts he would break. "You look very pretty today, *Belle-mère*," he said, his expression angelic.

"Thank you so much," she replied dryly, and Justin grinned once more before going in search of his brother.

"That boy . . ." Irénée did not finish the complaint, but her irritation was clear.

"Max should have taken a switch to him far more often," Alexandre said grimly, taking a tiny sip of coffee and holding his head as if it were about to fall off.

"It's only his way of making himself noticed," Lysette replied, advancing further into the room and seating herself beside Irénée. "Philippe earns attention through his good behavior. Naturally the only course left to Justin is to be bad."

The group stared at her in surprise. It was the first time Lysette had dared to state an opinion in the presence of the family. No one thought to respond to her remark until Bernard cleared his throat.

"Whatever the reason for it, Justin is beyond redemption."

"He is rather young for such a pronouncement," Lysette said. "I think eventually he will change."

Bernard and Alexandre exchanged glances, both of them wondering what had happened to unloosen their sister-in-law's tongue. The fact that she had contradicted one of them was a source of amazement. That, and the air of contentment about her, revealed that Maximilien's treatment of her must have been better than everyone had expected.

"You may be right, Lysette," Irénée said doubtfully. "One can only hope."

"All the hope in the world will not change the way Max raised the boy," Bernard commented.

Lysette turned to Irénée, determined to change the subject. "I thought I might ride around the plantation today."

"Have Elias accompany you," Irénée replied. "He is a good boy, quiet and well-mannered."

Bernard's eyes narrowed as he looked at Lysette. "Where in particular are you going?"

She shrugged. "Perhaps toward the east, beyond the cypress grove."

"There is little there to see," Bernard replied with a frown. "Except . . . ," he paused in discomfort, "the ruins of the old overseer's house."

Everyone was quiet at the mention of the place. Lysette looked at Irénée, who seemed to be devoting all her attention to stirring more sugar into her coffee. "It's still standing, then?" she asked.

"In spite of my wishes, Max has always refused to have the house torn down," Irénée said, her voice empty of emotion. "It is a blemish on the plantation—a useless eyesore standing on a plot of land that should be cultivated. Some have foolishly claimed to have seen ghosts there. Even Justin . . . although I suspect he was merely out to make mischief."

"None of the slaves will go near it," Bernard said. "Their superstitions are too strong." A flicker of satisfaction crossed his face. "You won't get within a hundred feet of it before Elias refuses to go further."

That afternoon Lysette discovered that Bernard was right. Elias, riding a placid mule behind her dappled mare, stopped short when he saw the broken outline of the overseer's house rising before them. The structure was situated well out of sight of the main house. It was set on the edge of fields that had once been productive, but had been left untouched during the last ten years. The land was overgrown and richly green. Given enough time, the tropical climate would accomplish the destruction of the rickety overseer's house, which had already decayed from mold, dampness, and insects.

"Elias?" Lysette questioned, glancing back and seeing the tense set of the boy's thin frame. He was staring, not at her, but at the house, his eyes wide and nostrils flared.

"Dat where you plannin' to go, madame?" he asked softly.

"I am going to take a look at it," she said, urging her horse a few steps. *"Allons."*

Elias did not move. "We cain', madame, dey's hants in dere."

"I will not ask you to go in with me," Lysette said soothingly. "Just wait outside until I return, *d'accord?"*

But as she met his eyes, she saw that he was deeply upset. A suspicious brightness had sprung in his eyes, betraying the fact that he was torn between his fear of going near the house and his reluctance to displease her. He remained silent, looking from her to the ominous structure before them.

"Elias, stay here. I will be back soon."

"But madame—"

"Nothing will happen to me. I'll only be a few minutes."

Terrified, Elias watched her ride toward the house, knowing he would face serious consequences for allowing Monsieur's Vallerand's new wife to go there unaccompanied. But the deepest instinct of self-preservation held him back. There were demons in that place, and one ghost in particular that haunted it in search of revenge for her death. Sometimes mournful groans of the master's first wife could be heard at night. Any token of the house—a stick, a chip of brick or molding plaster—carried with it the essence of evil. Such fragments could be used to make a powerful *gris-gris* that would bring death and everlasting grief to a victim. And Madame Vallerand was going in there alone.

His face ashen, Elias turned the mule around and urged it back to the main house as fast as it would go.

Lysette tethered her horse to the cankered wooden railing of the house's tiny porch. Absently she untied the ribbon streamers of her glazed straw hat and set it on a
sway-backed step. The house was braced a foot or two
from the ground in deference to the nearby bayou's occasional habit of flooding its banks. Gingerly she set her foot
on one of the steps, wondering if it would hold her weight.
It creaked loudly but held fast. Slowly Lysette went to the
door, which hung askew, its edges covered with slime. An
air of gloom and oppression hung around the place. It was
as if the crime that had occurred there had become a part
of each board and beam.

She tried to imagine what the house had been like a
decade earlier, when Corinne Vallerand had slipped inside
for her clandestine meetings with Etienne Sagesse. How
could Corinne have betrayed Maximilien in a place so close
to the home they shared? It was almost as if she had wanted
to be discovered, wanted Max to be aware of her infidelity.

Pushing the door to the side, Lysette crept into the
house, ducking under a mass of cobwebs. The room was
dank and foul-smelling, its walls shaded with moss. Inches
of dust and yellowish matter caked the tiny-paned windows, blocking out most of the sunlight. Spiders scuttled
into the corners and cracks of the walls, fleeing from her
intrusion. It seemed like a tomb, Lysette thought, and
shivered.

Drawn on by curiosity, she advanced to the back rooms,
picking her way around broken furniture and shards of
pottery. She stopped in the northeast corner of the house,
in a room filled with rubble. As she looked from side to
side, the hairs on her arms stood on end. Nothing tangible
set this room apart from the others . . . but she knew
somehow that this was where Corinne had been murdered.
A feeling of devastation gripped her, and she froze where
she stood, unable to move.

The room darkened, the shadows turning scarlet. Her
knees wobbled, and she felt light-headed. She saw Max

bending over the form of a woman, his hands clenched around her neck, his arms trembling with strain. He was killing her. Lysette's heart seemed to explode. Her lips moved in a soundless whisper. *No, it wasn't you, it wasn't—*

"Lysette."

At the sound of her husband's voice, Lysette whirled around, her hand flying to her throat. The blood drained from her face. Max was standing in the doorway, staring at her as if he hated her. His features seemed to be carved in granite. His brows were gathered in a demonic slant. The sound of his voice, so soft and caustic, and strangely detached, made her feel slightly ill.

"Tell me what you're doing here, Lysette."

She was too startled to speak.

"Answer me!"

"Don't look at me like that," she said, swallowing painfully, her hand falling to her side. "I–I was merely curious."

"Curious about the place where your husband murdered his first wife?"

"Y–yes . . . no, I . . ." She stopped and gathered her wits. "I know you didn't do it, Max."

"I might have," he said. "It's only logical that I did." His eyes were cold. "God knows I wanted to often enough."

"This morning you said you didn't care—"

"It was a lie. I hated her. I wanted to kill her."

"But you didn't," she whispered. "Etienne Sagesse—"

"Had many people with him that night. He had no opportunity to kill her, whereas I certainly did." A malicious quirk appeared at the corner of his mouth. "Still have faith in my innocence, my steadfast little wife?"

Lysette had never felt so helpless, so uncertain of what to do or say. Her heart pounded frantically as she wondered how to turn the stranger before her back into her husband. Had she severed the fragile bond between them so soon that it could never be rebuilt? Why was he trying to plant suspicions in her mind? Why did he seem to want her to be frightened of him?

"How did you know I was here?" she managed to ask.

"You're very predictable, Lysette—a quality I appreciate in a wife. When you said you planned to tour the plantation today, you looked damnably guilty, so I decided to follow you. Elias, by the way, is heading back to the main house as fast as that sorry mule can take him."

"I didn't mean to upset him," Lysette murmured.

"You'd do better to worry about upsetting *me,* my sweet." The endearment was spoken in a tone that chilled her. "You knew I didn't want you to come here."

"I didn't think you would be so angry." Miserably Lysette wondered what had possessed her to cross him so soon. "I–I just wanted to see this place."

"Well, you've seen it," Max snarled. "If I ever find you here again, you won't be spared the consequences. Now get out."

Lysette took a hesitant step forward. "You are coming with me?" she asked.

When Max did not answer, she realized he intended to stay, for what reason she couldn't guess. She couldn't bear the thought of him being here alone, steeped in ugly memories and self-hatred . . . it would be the worst mistake for her to allow it. Already she could see the dreadful effect the place had on him. No one who saw him right now would have any doubt he was capable of murder. "Max, take me home," she whispered. "Please."

Max didn't move, didn't seem even to have heard her. Driven to cast aside all caution, Lysette went to him and pressed the length of her body against his, as if to warm the chill from him. Startled, Max began to push her away, but her arms slid around his waist, and she buried her face against his chest. "Please," she repeated desperately.

With aching relief, she felt his hands come to rest on her back. Max was still for a few moments, and then something seemed to snap inside him. He gathered her in his arms, burying his face in her hair, pulling her against him until her toes left the ground. A shudder racked his body, and he dug his fingers into her soft flesh, unconsciously leaving bruises. Lysette was pliant against him, letting him do what he would.

Hungrily Max searched for her lips. She made no protest as her mouth was forced open in a savage kiss. His breath burned like steam against her cheek, his arms crushed her deeper into his embrace. He pulled her head against his shoulder, still ravaging her lips, kissing her as if he would draw the soul from her body. Through their clothes she felt the hot, gouging impression of his manhood, and the thought crossed her mind that he was going to take her right there. Feverishly his hands ran over her back, and he groaned against her mouth. Suddenly wild excitement coursed through her veins, and she didn't care what would happen, as long as he didn't let go of her.

It took inhuman strength for Max to lift his mouth from hers, but he managed it, aware that if he didn't curb his passion, he would pull her down to the rotting floor like an animal. Disgusted with his own lack of control, he rested his chin on top of her head.

For a long time Lysette listened to the sound of his breathing, at first raw and unsteady, then slowing into a gentler rhythm.

"You haven't been back here, have you?" she asked. "Not since you found her that day."

He shook his head in a nearly imperceptible movement.

"Why don't you have it torn down?" she murmured.

"It wouldn't change anything."

"It would. This way it is a constant reminder—"

"I would still remember," he said. There was a note in his voice that warned her not to argue. Lysette relinquished the battle for now, but inwardly she promised herself that the house would be torn down if she had to do it herself, board by board.

"How stubborn you are," she muttered.

"Yes. And let us hope you are not," Max said, finally able to take his arms from around her. "It wouldn't be wise to gainsay my wishes, *doucette*. I'm not a forgiving man."

They rode home side-by-side, but there might as well have been miles between them. Max was more distant than ever before, barely replying to any comment she made, looking at her only when absolutely necessary. There was a cool indifference about the way he helped her down from her horse, and he made no move to touch her as they went into the house.

At dinner Max did not meet her eyes. Unsociable and quiet, he ate methodically while the light chatter of the family filtered around him. The food was as savory as usual—smothered cabbage, peppers, rich yellow corn bread, roast pork and sweet potatoes. Accustomed to Max's spates of moodiness, the Vallerands chose their words carefully, none of them wishing to draw his attention. Irénée and Lysette exchanged a long look, one questioning, the other troubled.

The older woman sighed, wishing she knew how to help her daughter-in-law. At times Maximilien could be such a bully, unwilling to forgive someone who had thwarted him. There was nothing that could be done with him on these occasions except to let him have his way and hope the storm would pass quickly. *Be patient,* she wanted to tell Lysette. *You've already done more for him than you know.*

Annoyed by her husband's deliberate rudeness, Lysette decided that this would be the last time she would bear the brunt of his temper. Perhaps, she thought, he was looking for an argument everyone was too afraid to give him. If that was what he wanted, he would have it. After all, she had not done anything wrong, and it was unjust for him to vent his displeasure on her!

As if he sensed her resolve, Max finally glanced at her.

His mouth curved in a jeering smile. Tossing his napkin on the table, he stood up and left without a word. With relief, the family turned their attention back to the meal. Lysette picked up a glass of wine and twirled it slowly by the stem as she stared into the vintage's pale golden depths.

Bernard looked at her and spoke idly. "You must have gone to the old overseer's house today."

Justin replied before Lysette had the opportunity. "How clever of you, Uncle Bernard. *I* never would have guessed it."

"Impudent whelp," Bernard muttered.

Justin would have retorted, but Philippe elbowed him roughly.

Bernard's attention was directed at Lysette once more. "I could have told you how Max would react."

"I do not require advice about my husband from you," Lysette said, standing up and leaving as abruptly as Max had.

Justin grinned after her, pleased by the display of temper. Philippe turned his serious blue eyes to Irénée. *"Grand-mère,* why is father angry with Lysette?"

Irénée smiled. "It is difficult for the newly-married, Philippe. They must adjust to many changes. And . . . Maximilien does not like the way Lysette makes him feel."

"I'll *never* marry," Justin remarked sourly. "What's the good of it?"

"Every man has need of a helpmate," Irénée replied. "You will understand someday. It is not good for a man's life to be barren of love."

Bernard regarded Irénée with vexation. "Max is certainly not in love with the girl, Mother."

"Then why so much anger?" Irénée pointed out, and was pleased that he was unable to answer her.

Lysette found Max in the library with a drink in his hand. He pretended not to see her, tossing the liquor to the back of his throat and pouring himself another. She stood in the doorway, waiting until he gave her his attention.

"You are trying to punish me for something," Lysette said, her voice controlled. "It's more than what I did today, isn't it? What is wrong?"

"Let me make something clear. I am accountable to no one for the things I do, not for my damnable moods, not for anything I choose to do or say."

"What Corinne did is in the past, and I—"

"Don't," Max interrupted violently. "Don't mention her name once more or I'll . . ." He bit back his next words and swung around, staring out the window.

"I do not understand you," Lysette said. "You are the most unreasonable, perplexing . . . What is the *matter?*" Knowing he would not answer, she left the room.

It was Lysette's misfortune to pass by Bernard near the entrance hall. Having just finished dinner, he was heading out to the small guest house where he was wont to spend most of his nights. Glancing from left to right to make certain they would not be overheard, Bernard spoke to her in a voice that chilled her almost as much as Max's had.

"I'll say this once, Lysette, not only for your sake but for Max's. Rid yourself of this curiosity you have about Corinne. It is dangerous, do you understand? Leave the past alone—or I'll personally put a stop to your meddling."

She was too astonished to reply.

Glancing at her with dark eyes that for the first time held an expression of dislike, Bernard turned on his heel and strode to the front door.

It was long after bedtime when Lysette finally heard Max climbing the stairs. How much had he been drinking? Her heart began to hammer as she wondered if he would come to her room. For the past hour she had been rehearsing apologies. It was impossible to sleep with the heavy feeling in her chest. Sitting up, she smoothed her hair and arranged her nightgown.

Her wide eyes flew to the half-open door, and she waited . . . but the footsteps passed her suite. Evidently Max intended to sleep alone. She had thought that after last night they would be sharing a bed from now on.

What would he do if she confronted him? Deciding she had little to lose, she jumped out of bed and went through the small dressing room to the connecting door beyond. Finding it locked, she tried the key, which was more difficult to move than she had expected. It seemed brittle enough to snap in the lock. Holding her breath, she twisted it until she heard a click. As she pushed against the door, it creaked from years of disuse, but gave way as she lent her weight to it.

Max was staring at her, having paused in the act of disrobing. His shirt was open to his waist, his breeches unfastened and his feet bare.

"I had hoped you would come to my room," she said.

"Not tonight," he said tonelessly.

"Because you're angry?"

"I'm not angry," he said. His face was so devoid of emotion that she had no choice but to believe him.

"Max . . ." Lysette was bewildered. "Help me to understand." She flushed as she heard the note of pleading in her own voice, but she couldn't hold it back. "What do you want me to do? How can I make things right?"

"Go back to your room." He dropped the shirt to the floor. "I'm just tired. No more questions tonight, Lysette."

"Let me stay here," she persisted.

"No."

Her cheeks burned scarlet. "I just want to sleep near you. I know you don't wish to be . . . intimate. I . . ." As she looked at him, she wondered how his face could be so blank, when she stood there with her feelings so recklessly exposed.

"I don't sleep with a woman unless I wish to bed her," he replied indifferently. "We have separate rooms for a reason. I value my privacy. Marriage to you won't change that."

Suddenly Lysette was filled with anger. "How dare you speak to me that way," she said, her eyes flashing. "I merit some kind of place in your life. You have no right to be so callous when I'm trying to be a wife to you! And I won't be confined to my room when you're in a mood!"

"If you don't leave," Max said evenly, "then I will." As she didn't move, his mouth hardened into a cruel line. "You overestimate your charms, my dear. Is it really that difficult to understand I don't want you?"

Her face turned from scarlet to white, and there was a shock of nothingness before she felt pain and embarrassment. She looked away from him. An intolerable ache welled up behind her eyes and in her throat. "No . . . of course not," she heard herself say. "I won't bother you again."

Expecting to feel relieved, Max watched her walk to the connecting door, but with each step she took the cold emptiness inside him expanded. He knew it was better this way, that he would only end up hurting her more if she stayed. A second passed . . . then two . . . three . . . and suddenly it hurt to breathe. He couldn't stand the sight of her walking away, despised himself for having lied, for hurting her.

"Lysette."

She quickened her step, desperate to flee from him. Max tried to let her go, but at the last moment he covered the distance between them in three strides, and slammed the door just as she reached it. His arms formed a cage around her. Blinded by a rush of tears, Lysette grasped the tiny golden doorknob in both hands, pulling at it frantically. She couldn't let him see her cry—she would hate herself forever.

"I am leaving," she said hoarsely. "Just as you wanted. Stop tormenting me!"

With a tortured groan Max turned her around and pulled her against his chest, ignoring her small pummeling fists. "Lysette, I didn't mean it. I do want you. I want you too goddamn much. Don't cry . . . don't."

Her fists stilled against his chest, and she continued to cry, damning him with every sobbing breath. His arms wrapped around her, and he felt his defenses crumble for good. It was precisely what he had been trying so hard to avoid. He clenched his hand in her hair, kissed her wet cheeks, held her shuddering body protectively against his. "Forgive me," he said, desperate to make her stop crying. It was agony to feel her tears against his skin, knowing he was the cause.

"You *enjoy* hurting people," she wept, her arms encircling his neck.

"No," he murmured against her hair. "No."

"Why did you make me your wife if you wanted to be alone?"

"Because . . . I . . ." Max struggled to explain and could not. "Dammit!" All he knew was that some terrible, unfamiliar emotion had taken hold of him, something he had tried to fight ever since he had first met her—and he had just lost the battle. He would do anything rather than hurt her again, no matter what it cost him. "I want you," he said hoarsely. "Always."

Her silence let him know that those few words were not enough. She waited for him to continue. Doggedly Max tried to tell her the reason for his behavior, but for a man not given to self-analysis, the task was grueling. "It is just that," he said, nearly at his wit's end, "I am not accustomed to a woman—or anyone—being . . . close, and I feel . . . it's not easy to discover that I . . ." he stopped with a curse and scooped her up in his arms, carrying her to the bed.

As soon as he eased her down to the mattress, Lysette

tried to roll away, the pain of his cutting words of a few
minutes ago still fresh. She did not want to make love
with him now, not when she felt so vulnerable. Gently he
held her still and lowered his mouth to hers. She tried to
escape, but his head followed hers, and he parted her lips
with devastating skill.

Max lifted his head and Lysette stared up at him, her
lips trembling as she saw the primitive expression in his
eyes. He let go of her wrists, his black lashes lowering as
he glanced down the length of her body. His gaze was
devouring, but he remained motionless, giving her the
chance to refuse him.

Lysette's eyes watered once more, but for a different
reason this time, as she realized how much Max needed
her forgiveness. He was fighting his feelings at every turn,
afraid to admit them even to himself. That had been the
reason for his coldness that afternoon. Holding his gaze,
she slid her hand to the back of his dark head and pulled
him down to her.

"Lysette," he rasped, kissing her hungrily. The blood
smoldered in his veins, and excitement drove through him
with feverish intensity. He pulled the nightclothes from
her body, his lips questing from her shoulders to her
breasts. She moved restlessly underneath him, quivering
as he stroked and fondled her, evoking sensations that
burned through her skin and singed every nerve.

He left her for a moment to remove his breeches, she
felt his absence, the empty space where his body had been,
as intensely as if half of herself had been torn away. Blindly
she reached for him, moaning as his arms slid around her.
She turned her face into the side of his neck, kissed the
smooth, tanned skin, loving the taste of him.

Max covered her nipple with his mouth, awakening the
tender flesh until it tightened into a rosy peak. Reveling
in the sweet cries that escaped her lips, he moved to her
other breast. He had never wanted to possess a woman so
completely, to own her thoughts, every breath and sound

she made. He would make her forget everything but the pleasure he could give her.

Drawing up her knees, Lysette curled around him, clinging like ivy to a strong oak. His kisses trailed from her breasts to her smooth, flat abdomen, and down to her hip, where he softly bit the ridge of her hipbone. She took a sharp breath and half-turned, uneasy with this new familiarity. He stayed her movement, grasping her hips, and his mouth ventured to the edge of the triangle between her thighs.

"No, no . . . please," she gasped, and twisted onto her stomach.

Instantly Max pulled her back against him, his mouth at her ear. "I won't hurt you . . . darling, let me—"

"No," she said shakily.

He kissed the nape of her neck, while his hands wandered over her back and buttocks. "Someday," he whispered, "I'll kiss every inch of you."

Lysette closed her eyes as his teeth scored the sensitive back of her neck. His fingers glided between her thighs, and she groaned, helpless at his touch. Soon she moved to embrace him, but he pressed her on her stomach, his palm curving over her buttock. Feeling a pang of trepidation, she lay prostrate beneath him, aware of his quickening breath. His hands slid over her body, arousing every nerve . . . and then his arm was beneath her hips, lifting the lower half of her body, holding her steady. Lysette's heart jumped as she felt his thighs braced behind hers.

"Max, I–I—"

"It's alright," he said huskily. "I won't hurt you."

She moistened her chafed lips, but she could not form a single word, wondering desperately if they were committing some cardinal sin. Her thoughts went scattering as he pressed inside the welcoming cache of her body. Lysette shivered, yielding to the exciting intrusion, her world careening wildly. Driven by elemental need, Max caught her hips tighter against his, and instinctively Lysette arched

her back to fit closer to him. She was floating higher and
higher, approaching a peak of aching pleasure . . . but just
as she tensed in anticipation, she felt him withdraw from
her.

"Max," she gasped, "don't s–stop, don't—"

He turned her onto her back, spreading her thighs. His
features were concealed in shadow as he loomed over her,
but she sensed the triumph and possessiveness that gov-
erned him. Eyes half-closed, she looked up at the dark
shape of his head and shoulders, edged in gold from the
sparse lamplight. Slowly he eased inside her, and her body
jolted with pleasure as she received him once again. The
rhythm he set was steady and deliberate, causing her to
twist wildly beneath him.

Their open mouths meshed in a deep-reaching kiss, and
her nails clawed down his tense back as she wavered on
the brink of ecstasy. Astonished, she felt him pull away,
once more holding fulfillment out of reach. Her eyes widened, and she clutched at him frantically, but he would
not move until she subsided beneath him.

The torment continued for what seemed to be hours,
Max bringing her to a near-climax and then withholding
it, over and over, knowing exactly how to stretch her
nerves to a point of excruciating tension. She begged incoherently, aware of nothing but the hard, bronzed body
over hers, the rigid length inside her, the sensations that
had reached an intolerable pitch, until the blistering ecstasy overcame her. Pressing her face against his shoulder,
she shuddered convulsively, feeling the world fall away
until there was nothing left but the two of them. Max
allowed himself to follow her, his fingers tunneling into
the pillow beneath her head as he gasped from the force
of his own release.

When at last Lysette was able to move, she put her arms
around his neck, tangling her fingers in his sweat-
dampened hair. She felt his lips wander across her cheek
and down to her chin, and she turned her mouth to his

languidly. Max seemed to relax then, stretching out beside her, draping a heavy arm over her waist.

Sometime after midnight, Lysette's eyes opened in the semi-darkness. Wistfully she looked at the velvet-draped window, thinking of the world beyond these walls, the home she had left in Natchez, and all the familiar things that were gone. It was impossible to believe that a few months ago she had never even heard of Maximilien Vallerand. Now she was his wife, and he had changed her life completely.

Her gaze wandered over his profile, the sharp-edged cheekbones and long black lashes, the bold nose and chin, the surprisingly sensual lips that were capable of casual cruelty and disarming smiles. In sleep, Max's face was touched with a softness that was missing in his waking hours. He looked almost innocent, all frowns and arrogance and narrow-eyed glances smoothed away.

Chapter 10

"**A**nother letter to Jeanne?" Max inquired, coming to the tiny satinwood table where Lysette sat.

"It is more difficult than I expected," she grumbled, indicating several crumpled sheets of fine parchment.

Max smiled as he contemplated the scene. Days ago the writing table and matching clawfoot chair had been mysteriously moved from her bedchamber to his. It was yet another sign of the feminine invasion that seemed to be taking place.

Wryly he supposed he should be grateful for the considerable size of his room. At this rate it would not be long before Lysette's possessions occupied every inch of available space. He had always liked his surroundings to be uncluttered and spare, but each day he discovered new articles strewn over his bureau, dresser, and bedtables. There were bottles of scent and boxes of powder, fans and gloves and flowered hair ornaments, pins and combs, stockings, garters and laces.

It was the custom for husbands and wives to maintain separate rooms—a custom Lysette seemed to be unaware of. When Max retired each evening, he found her in his bed waiting for him. Evidently no one had informed her that a wife should remain in her own bed and allow the husband the choice of visiting her. It wasn't that Max found the situation *unpleasant,* it was just . . . different.

He could have offered some objection to the lack of privacy, but for some reason it did not annoy him. Perhaps, he reflected, he'd had too much privacy over the last ten years. And there were distinct benefits to having Lysette so close at hand. He had an unlimited view of her bathing, tending her hair, dressing . . . and undressing. Rarely was a man privileged to see so much of a woman's toilette—wives and mistresses alike were seldom inclined to allow such intimacy.

Turning his attention to the matter at hand, he braced his arms on either side of her and leaned over the table, reading the unfinished letter.

"Neither Maman nor Jacqueline answered the first letters I wrote," Lysette said glumly. "Perhaps Gaspard won't let Maman write to me. Perhaps he won't even allow her to *receive* anything from me . . . but I expected some sort of a reply from Jacqueline!"

Max brushed his lips against the top of her head. "Give them time," he murmured. "It's been less than a month since the wedding. And you did marry one of the more notable scoundrels of New Orleans."

"You're too modest, *mon mari,*" she said with a small smile. "As a scoundrel, you're without peer."

He grinned and tilted her chair back, causing her to gasp with surprised laughter. She clutched at his arms. "Max!"

"Relax, sweet . . . I wouldn't let you fall."

"Max, let me up!"

Slowly the chair was raised to its original position, and she jumped to her feet, warily backing away, not trusting his casual smile.

Holding her gaze, he advanced forward, reached down to the desk, and crumpled her letter in one hand.

Lysette's mouth fell open. "Why did you do that?" she demanded indignantly.

"Because I didn't like it," he said without remorse. "I won't have you begging and pleading for their favor."

Her small jaw firmed, and she glared at him. "I'll write whatever I wish to my mother!"

"And have that toad of a stepfather gloating over every tearful entreaty?" He shook his head decisively. "You're a Vallerand now, and I won't allow—" As he saw her outrage, he stopped and looked away. When his gaze returned to hers, his face was expressionless. "Lysette," he said in a quieter tone, "right now a mountain of penitent letters wouldn't do any good. From what little I know of them, your family will take the opportunity to use any sign of weakness against you. As I said before, give them time."

"Are you forbidding me to write to them?" she asked unsteadily.

There was a long silence. When he answered, he sounded indifferent. *"Petite,* I'm not forbidding you to do a goddamn thing."

She cleared her throat and walked to the desk, taking the ball of paper he had crushed, holding it in both her hands. "I–I want to try to make them understand." She was afraid he would be angry then, or give her one of those glances that chilled the blood. But Max only shrugged casually.

"It's on your head, then." He watched the quick succession of emotions cross her features: stubbornness, curiosity, contrition. "Do you plan to begin another letter this very moment?" he asked.

"I . . . no, I think I'll do it later," she said uncertainly.

"Good. I'd hoped you would accompany me to town. An important visitor arrived this morning, and I have an interest in some of the speechmaking that will be done."

"A visitor? Who? Oh, I would enjoy leaving the plantation. I haven't set foot off it since I first came here."

"I know that."

"But it will be another week before I can properly be seen in public, and I know Irénée would not like—"

"We'll stay in the carriage," Max interrupted, amused by her excitement. "There will be too much of an uproar to move about in the crowd—cannon fire, parades, music. All to celebrate the arrival of one Aaron Burr."

"When are we leaving? Now? Oh, I hope we won't be late!"

Max shook his head, watching as Lysette flew to the bureau and rummaged through his top drawer for her gloves.

The Place D'Armes, the town square built to face the river, was filled with a noisy crowd that had gathered from miles around to see and hear Aaron Burr. This morning, the twenty-fifth of June, he had arrived in New Orleans after a long western tour through Ohio, Kentucky, Tennessee, and Natchez, paying visits to powerful allies and making speeches to approving crowds. Burr had been received everywhere with hospitality and acclaim, for he stated that he had the interests of the West at heart, and that he only wanted to help the territory grow and flourish.

It was remarkable that in all the upheaval of the welcome festivities, the distinctive black and gold Vallerand carriage drew almost as much attention as the sight of Aaron Burr himself. The rumor that Maximilien Vallerand's new wife was there spread quickly and suddenly there were swarms of people passing by the vehicle, both American and Creole, craning their necks to see inside. Even Max had not counted on the amount of attention Lysette's presence would attract.

Lysette stayed away from the windows of the carriage, remaining in the shadows, but still she could hear the excited voices outside, referring to her as *la mariée du diable*

. . . the devil's bride. She looked at Max in amazement. "Why do they call me that?"

"I warned you what to expect," he said. "I'm afraid it doesn't help, *ma petite*, that your hair is such a charming shade of red."

"Why do they take such an interest in me?" she asked in bewilderment. "I have done nothing to anyone!"

"That makes no difference at all," he assured her dryly.

Fortunately the crowd was distracted by the beginning of Governor Claiborne's welcoming speech. Lysette settled back against her carriage seat, enjoying the glimpses of the bustle and motion on the street, wishing she could be outside.

There was a world of alien sights, sounds, and smells just beyond the walls of the carriage: abrasive calls of vendors selling fruit and bread, the barking of dogs, the cries of chanticleer roosters and dunghill fowls. Occasionally she caught a whiff of strong French perfume as fine ladies passed by, and there was a vaguely fishy smell drifting in from the riverfront. Boatmen strolled by uttering ribald curses and language she had never heard before. And as always, whenever Creoles and Americans were in the same vicinity, there were scuffles and arguments, and swift challenges to duel.

Above all the melee Governor Claiborne was striving to be heard. Lysette watched Max's face as he sat opposite her and listened to the speech. Half an hour passed, and the governor was still speaking. "Long-winded politicians," Max muttered, tapping his fingers impatiently.

Lysette's mind wandered as the governor detailed many of Burr's past achievements. Occasionally a phrase or two would interest her, but her attention was easily diverted by the antics of the crowd. "And let us not forget," Claiborne was saying, "the brave young Aaron Burr's actions in the war to secure American independence, single-handedly saving his entire brigade from destruction by the pursuing enemy, exercising the same keen intelligence and fortitude that later characterized his years as the courtroom champion of the common man . . .''

Max snickered. "That's the kindest description of a lawyer I've ever heard."

"It sounds as though Governor Claiborne admires Colonel Burr very much," Lysette said.

"He despises Burr," Max replied, and grinned.

"Then why—"

"Politicians, sweet, often find themselves required to pay homage to their enemies."

"I don't understand—" Lysette said, and stopped as she heard a dull roar that began on the edge of the crowd and grew until it became a great wave of sound. Her eyes widened. "What is it?"

"Burr must have stepped into view," Max said. "Thank God. Claiborne will have to end his speech now." He moved to the door and opened it. "I'm going to stand outside to listen."

"Max, may I—"

"Stay in here."

She folded her arms resentfully and watched him leave the carriage. The tumult outside increased, and she sidled to the window, sticking her head outside regardless of onlookers. There were too many people, carriages and horses—she couldn't see a thing. But she heard a new voice in the distance, a strong and forceful one that cut through the hubbub, greeting the crowd first in French, then Spanish and English. The congregation erupted in hearty applause, shouts, and whistles.

The cheering lasted through the speech's prelude, but gradually Lysette could hear Aaron Burr's voice again.

"There is much I have seen and witnessed on my westward travels," Colonel Burr was saying. "Much of it has pleased me, and much has not. There are riches in this territory . . . riches of goodwill, strength and purpose that would be exploited by those in the nation's councils. There are voices that should be heard, needs that must be addressed . . .''

Lysette strained further out the window, fascinated by that resonant voice. Women scolded their husbands for staring at the flame-haired girl, youths abandoned their quarreling and watched her closely, old women gossiped while old men wished aloud that they were but a decade or two younger.

Standing a few feet away, Max became aware of the growing disturbance, and followed the rapt gazes of those next to him. He sighed ruefully as he saw his wife leaning halfway out of the carriage, craning her neck for a better view of Aaron Burr. Sensing her husband's gaze, Lysette glanced over at him guiltily, and disappeared as quickly as a turtle retreating into its shell.

Smothering a laugh, Max went to the carriage, opened the door and reached inside. "Come here," he said, hooking an arm around her waist and swinging her to the ground. "And don't complain when everyone stares at you."

"Your commerce," Burr continued, "has been crippled by the territory's sudden annexation. And my friends, it will be a long while before the problem is addressed by that United States government I have such intimate knowledge of. You know already that you have been refused American citizenship, and have instead been offered empty promises. They say you are not fit for self-government. *I* say they do not know you!" He was forced to pause as the crowd roared.

"My God," Max said under his breath. "He's treading on the edge of treason. He can't be so foolhardy as to think Jefferson will turn a deaf ear to such statements." He looked down at Lysette, who was wedged against his side and standing on tiptoe.

"I can't see anything," she said. "What does he look like?"

"You'll meet him later," Max promised. "We'll be attending a ball held in his honor next week."

They listened until the crowd showed signs of becoming boisterous and unmanageable. Tempers always ran hot under the Louisiana sun, and inhibitions were weakened from the drinking and feasting that had already begun. Max decided it would be wise to leave early, realizing the sight of Lysette was attracting too much attention. People were staring and pointing openly, eager young men were gathering in groups, and boys were overheard daring each other to run up and touch a lock of her fiery hair.

"It's time to go," Max said curtly, drawing his wife to the carriage. "Or in another few minutes I'll be forced into a score of duels over you." At first he had been amused that his wife seemed to have mesmerized every male between the ages of seven and seventy. But he was surprised to find that a few minutes of it had tested his patience sorely.

Lysette nodded in confusion. "Have I done something wrong?"

Max didn't bother to suppress his scowl. "No. It's nothing." He motioned with a snap of his fingers to the coachman, who hurriedly brought a small stool for Lysette to step up on. She climbed into the carriage, allowing herself one small sigh. Perhaps, she thought, in twenty years or so she would come to understand his quick changes of mood.

Partly for his own reasons, partly as a favor to Claiborne, Max arranged a private meeting with the Spanish minister in New Orleans, the Marquis de Casa Yrujo. Since Aaron Burr's arrival in town yesterday, there had been many comings and goings between the Spanish officials residing in New Orleans. Max hoped he could persuade Yrujo to reveal some pertinent bit of infor-

mation about Burr or Burr's compatriot, General Wilkinson.

Yrujo was an experienced diplomat. His sharp brown
eyes, set deeply in his lean, olive-skinned face, gave nothing away. The relaxed pose of his well-fed body betrayed
no tenseness or uncertainty. Despite the half hour of verbal
fencing that had taken place, Yrujo had not said anything
that exposed Governor Wilkinson as a Spanish agent, nor
revealed what he knew of Burr's treasonous conspiracy.
And there was no doubt in Max's mind that Yrujo knew
a great deal.

"To me it is an interesting puzzle, how Claiborne
managed to enlist your support, Vallerand," Yrujo remarked in a congenial way as the two men talked over
drinks and thin black cigars. The conversation was
coming to a conclusion as both realized that neither
would learn anything from the other. "I have never believed you to be a fool," the Spaniard continued. "Why,
then, do you ally yourself with a man whose control
over the territory is about to be stripped from him? You
have much to lose."

"Stripped away by whom?" Max countered, exhaling
a channel of smoke to the side.

"My question first, *por favor.*"

Max's smile did not reach his eyes. "Claiborne has been
underestimated," he said casually.

Yrujo laughed, openly scoffing at the answer. "You
will have to do better than that, Vallerand! What has he
promised you? I suppose the retention of land grants that
should have been abolished when the Americans took
possession. Or perhaps you are merely hoping to store
up political influence. Do you think it wise to bet that
the Americans will be able to prevent the secession of
Louisiana?"

"My question now," Max said. "You think Claiborne's
control will be stripped away by whom?"

"The answer is obvious," Yrujo said silkily. "Colonel

Burr, of course. That he is hoping for disunion is no secret.''

"Yes. But Burr is doing more than merely *hoping.*" Max watched closely for Yrujo's reaction.

The Spaniard's expression gave nothing away. "That, my friend, is something no one knows for certain. Not even I.''

Max knew that was a lie. If Wilkinson was conspiring with Burr *and* remaining secretly in the Spanish pay, Yrujo had definite knowledge of Burr's intentions.

Leaning forward in his chair, Max renewed the verbal assault. "Recently, Don Carlos, you refused to give Colonel Burr a passport to Mexico. Obviously you had misgivings about allowing him inside Spanish territory. What made you suddenly so suspicious of Burr?''

"I have always exercised caution in my dealings with the man,'' Yrujo said abruptly.

"Not so. You once granted him permission to enter the Floridas.''

The Spanish Minister laughed heartily, but there was little amusement in his eyes. "Your sources, Vallerand, are much better than Claiborne's.''

Silently Max drew again on his cigar, wondering how much Yrujo really knew. Burr and Wilkinson intended to secure the Floridas for themselves, and were undoubtedly trying to keep their true purposes from the Spaniards, who would never voluntarily relinquish the territory. If it were taken from Spain, Yrujo would be held responsible. That prospect had to alarm him.

"Don Carlos,'' Max said quietly, "I hope you won't be deceived by any claims Burr might make that he is trying to serve Spain's interests.''

They exchanged a glance of sharp understanding. "We are perfectly aware,'' Yrujo said after a deliberate pause, "that the only interests the Colonel serves are his own.''

Max decided to take another tack. "Then perhaps you can see your way clear to tell me what you know about the letter of introduction Burr has given to one of the Spanish boundary commissioners here in New Orleans, the Marquis de Casa Calvo.''

"I know nothing about a letter."

"It is suspected that several such letters have been delivered to those who might be sympathetic to Burr's cause." Max studied the tip of his boot as he added, "Including Casa Calvo." Then his golden eyes surveyed the implacable Spaniard once more.

"I am certain I would have heard of it, had Casa Calvo received one. *Lo siento.*"

The finality in Yrujo's voice left no room for deeper prying. Max stubbed out his cigar, annoyed even though he had expected nothing more than what he had gotten. He would dearly love to know what was in that letter, to have some written proof as to Burr's intentions.

Twilight was fast approaching as Max rode home to the Vallerand plantation. He slowed his black stallion from an easy canter to a trot when he saw an enclosed carriage stopped at the side of the road. One of the carriage wheels was broken, and only one horse was harnessed to the vehicle. There was no driver in sight. Stopping by the side of the carriage, Max saw a movement inside. He lightly fingered one of the brace of pistols he always wore when traveling.

"May I be of assistance?" he asked, reining in the stallion as it fidgeted.

A woman's face appeared. She was young and reasonably pretty, and most definitely French, although Max did not recall having met her before. Evidently judging from his appearance that he was a gentleman and not a highwayman, she rested her forearm on the edge of the window and smiled. *"Merci, monsieur* . . . but there is nothing we require. Our coachman will return any moment with help."

"Do not speak to him, Serina," came a voice from

inside the carriage, a strident feminine voice filled with rebuke. "Don't you know who he is?" A second face appeared at the window.

Max stared at the woman with a slight frown, knowing he had met her before but unable to remember her name. She was at least his age, perhaps a little older, her dry white skin stretched over harsh, prominent cheekbones. Her pale green eyes were venomous as they fixed on him, and her lips turned down as if the corners were being tugged by invisible threads.

"Don't you recognize me?" she hissed. "No, I suppose you would not. Vallerands have such short memories."

"Aimée," the younger woman protested softly.

With a shock, Max realized the woman was Aimée Langlois. He had known her when they had both been in their teens. He had even courted her for a time, before he had met Corinne. Back then Aimée had been lovely, although overly prim and prudish. He remembered having teased her, drawing elusive smiles from her, even stealing a kiss or two when her nearsighted aunt had been less than vigilant.

"Mademoiselle Langlois," Max said with unsmiling courtesy, remembering that Irénée had once mentioned that Aimée had remained unmarried. Now, glancing at those pinched-in lips, he knew why. No man would ever have the courage—or the incentive—to kiss her. But what had wrought such a change in her? What had made her so bitter?

Still staring at him coldly, Aimée spoke to the young woman beside her. "This is Maximilien Vallerand, Serina. The man who murdered his wife. You've heard the stories, haven't you?"

Embarrassed, the girl clutched at Aimée's forearm to quiet her.

"He also murdered my cousin five years ago," Aimée

continued. "With no regard for the fact that Arnaud was a mere boy."

"If you will recall, I tried to avoid the duel with Arnaud," Max said stiffly.

Fancying himself a skilled swordsman, Arnaud Langlois had wished to prove himself by besting Max in a duel. He had plagued Max for weeks, trying to provoke him into a challenge, growing increasingly infuriated as Max ignored his efforts. Finally Arnaud had hurled a barrage of insults at him in a public place, giving Max no choice but to challenge the cocky youth. Even after Max had drawn first blood and declared that honor was satisfied, the boy had insisted on fighting to the death.

Remembering the sick feeling of watching the boy's body crumple to the ground, Max stared at Aimée's haughty, hate-filled face. "I am sorry," he said gruffly. "I never wanted to fight him."

"I'm surprised you remember Arnaud. He was just one on a long, long list, wasn't he, Monsieur Vallerand?"

Unable to tolerate any more, Serina broke in. "I apologize for my sister-in-law, monsieur. It has been such an exhausting day, and we—"

"Don't you dare offer excuses for me!" Aimée snapped, and glared back at Max. "Leave us this moment!"

Max would have liked nothing better, but they were alone and unprotected, and no gentleman would leave them in such a situation. "Permit me to wait nearby until your coachman returns," he said. "Night is falling, and it is dangerous to—"

"*You* present the only danger to us," Aimée interrupted. "Therefore, I would appreciate your immediate departure!"

Max gave her a curt nod. "Good evening, ladies," he murmured, and urged the stallion away from the carriage.

Withdrawing to her seat, Aimée glowered while Serina peered out the window at the retreating figure.

"Has he gone?" Aimée finally asked.

"Non. He is waiting farther down the road." Serina glanced at her sister-in-law curiously. "I've never seen you angry before, Aimée. I've never seen you so harsh with anyone."

"That man is a murderer."

"Your brother told me about cousin Arnaud's death, and how Monsieur Vallerand did all he could to prevent it. And as for murdering his wife, nothing has ever been proven, *n'est-ce pas?* There must be another reason why you seem to hate him so."

Suddenly Aimée's eyes glittered with unshed tears. "When I was a girl I foolishly gave him my heart," she admitted. "He gave me reason to believe he cared for me. And then when he met Corinne Quérand, he tossed me aside as if . . . as if I were nothing! How utterly willing he was to be deceived by a vulgarly pretty face and sly smiles!"

"But, Aimée, that is the nature of young men."

Aimée gave her a resentful glance. "Why are you defending him?"

Serina shrugged, looking out the window once more. "He seems to be a gentleman, not the ogre I had envisioned." A half-smile crept over her face. "And I must admit, there is a terribly romantic and mysterious air about him."

"Wait until you have lived here longer," Aimée said grimly. "Anyone will tell you what a cold-blooded monster he is."

Max waited until a carriage arrived to retrieve the two women before he set off down the road. Disturbed by the encounter, he tried to force thoughts of the past from his mind, but they kept returning. He remembered the innocent days of his boyhood, the happiness he had taken for granted, the stern but comforting presence of his father, his reckless adventures with his friends, his careless assurance that he could have any girl he wanted.

Aimée's reticence had been an engrossing challenge,

until he had been introduced to Corinne Quérand—and then he had forsworn interest in all other women. Corinne, with her long-lashed blue eyes, had been mesmerizing. Now he faced those same eyes every time he looked at Justin or Philippe.

It had seemed as if Corinne were two different women. One day she was vivacious, the next alarmingly quiet. She might pout because he did not pay her enough attention, or she might snap at him to stop hovering about her.

Max had naively assumed she would change after their marriage, but her erratic behavior only became worse, and she threw wild tantrums for no reason. However, Corinne's actual hatred of him did not begin until her pregnancy, which for her had been a painful, degrading process. Giving birth to the twins had nearly killed her, and afterwards she had treated her husband with revulsion.

Finally, to try to put their marriage to rights, Max had been reduced to begging her to forgive him for whatever it was he had done. "I'll try to tolerate the sight of you," Corinne had replied contemptuously, "if you'll promise never to touch me again. After the suffering you've caused me, I feel nothing but loathing for you."

After several months went by, he approached her once more, only to have her throw his love back in his face. It was the last time Max ever asked a woman for anything . . . until Lysette.

The thought of Lysette elicited a touch of the old self-contempt. Max despised weakness in himself, and Lysette had definitely become a weakness. She had the same power to hurt him that Corinne had, only this time it was greater. Lysette had broken through the strongest barricades he could build, and now he found himself wanting her with a violence that shook him to his foundations.

As soon as Max reached the house and walked in the front door, Alexandre attempted to corner him. "Max, I have been waiting for your arrival. There is a matter I would like to take up with—"

"It's been a long day," Max said brusquely, shedding his coat.

"Oui, but—"

"We'll talk tomorrow."

"Oui, but . . . I have run into a few unexpected . . . er . . . expenses this month."

"Gambling debts, hmm?" Max strode to the curving staircase while Alex followed at his heels.

"I have left an accounting on your desk."

"Perhaps you could find a less expensive habit to amuse yourself with."

"I could," Alex agree readily. "In the meantime, however, would you . . ."

"I'll take care of it," Max said, continuing up the stairs.

Alex relaxed, a relieved grin spreading across his face. He had expected a blistering lecture, and he was grateful for the reprieve. "Not long ago you would have railed at me for my foolhardiness," he commented.

"I would now, if I thought it would make an impression."

"I rather think that something—or someone—has done much to sweeten your temper, *mon frère!"*

Max did not pause to reply, even when Irénée's voice floated up to his ears. "Is that Max's voice I hear, Alex? Has he had supper? Well, why didn't you ask? Did he *look* hungry?"

Arriving at his bedroom, Max dropped his coat on the bed and sat down with a sigh, wearily contemplating the prospect of taking off his boots. The connecting door, already ajar, was immediately pushed open, and Lysette's head ducked around the corner. Her eyes glowed at the sight of him.

"You have been gone long enough, *mon mari."* Strangely, just the tone of her voice was enough to dispel some of his gloom. She walked to him, intending to give him a welcoming kiss, but he lifted his hands in a gesture for her to stop.

"Petite, wait. I am dusty from the ride back, and I smell of horses besides," he said, his mouth curving in a slow smile. "Let me see what you're wearing."

Lysette turned for his benefit, displaying the ice-blue ball gown with a pretty sweep of her hands, glancing over her shoulder flirtatiously. The gown was partially unfastened in the back, and she could feel the warmth of his gaze as it touched the bared curve of her spine.

"Very nice," he said.

"I am trying to decide what to wear for the ball next week," she informed him. "It will be my first appearance as your wife. Naturally I wish to be presentable."

Max's expression was unreadable, but inwardly he was troubled. Lysette couldn't possibly be prepared for the pointed questions, the razor-sharp curiosity, the small shows of malice she was likely to encounter at the gathering. He was used to it by now, but for someone as sheltered as she had been, the experience would prove distressing.

"You should be warned about what will happen, Lysette," he said quietly. "Yesterday was nothing compared to what the ball will be like. My fall from grace was wellnoted, and memories here are nothing if not long. As you know, some believe you're married to the devil incarnate."

Lysette considered him thoughtfully. Then she came to him, placing her slender hand on the side of his lean face. "But you *are* a devil. I already know that."

Max smiled unwillingly. "Your gown," he murmured, even as he pulled her onto his lap and nuzzled her throat, unable to stop himself.

Lysette twined her arms around his neck and touched her nose to his. "Why were you frowning tonight? Was it your visit with the Spanish minister?"

"In part." Max dipped his head to investigate the shadowy vale between her breasts, his warm breath sending a shiver through her body. "I don't like having so much of my wife exposed to other mens' gazes," he said, his fingertips measuring the amount of skin left uncovered by the deep neckline.

"Oh, but it is a *modest* gown. Other women will be wearing styles far more daring."

"Perhaps, but I'm not married to them," he replied, his hands roaming through the satin folds of the garment.

Lysette chuckled. "Do you think other men will stare?"

"Only vanity, my dear, would produce a question with so obvious an answer." Max grinned as she swatted at his chest. "Yes, dammit, they'll stare." Suddenly his smile vanished, and he was looking at her with apparent seriousness. "And should one pair of eyes stray too long in your direction, I'll wipe the floor with the unfortunate wretch."

"I was not aware you had such a jealous nature," Lysette said, pleased by his possessiveness, her eyes twinkling. Abruptly the world flip-flopped as Max tossed her onto her back.

"Then let me remove all doubt," he said, pulling the hem of her gown up to her waist and climbing further onto the bed, boots and all. He lowered his body over hers, crushing the shimmering material of her skirt between them. Lysette began to giggle at his onslaught of ardor, and struggled playfully as his mouth dragged over her bodice.

"Max . . . my . . . my gown—"

"You have others."

"Yes, but . . ." Lysette stopped and caught her breath as his teeth closed over the satin-covered point of her nipple. Then he kissed her lips again, his tongue slipping into the warm, sweet inlet of her mouth, and all resistance drained out of her limbs. Hands sought the spaces where bare skin could be found . . . lips clung, softness yielded to hardness. Her senses inflamed, Lysette grasped at his hard back, frustrated by the layers of clothing that separated them. "Max . . . I want you."

"You're not ready, my love," he whispered.

"I am . . ." She tried in vain to pull him down to her. Her voice was soft and low, tickling the inside of his ear. "Oh, I am . . ." Raising her fingers to his cheek, she brought her mouth to his.

Max shuddered with desire for the warm, slender body underneath his, and he fumbled with the fastenings of his breeches. Encouraged by his gravelly murmur, Lysette lifted her legs and wrapped them around his waist. And for a long time, there was no sound except the rustling of satin.

Max and Alexandre occupied themselves with drinks in the library while Irénée and Lysette were busy upstairs. "Women," Alex grumbled, "and their everlasting primping."

Max smiled leisurely and lifted a glass of burgundy to his lips. "Why are you so eager to arrive at the ball on time, Alex? I do not believe it is to catch a glimpse of Aaron Burr."

"Little you know," Alexandre replied airily.

"I thought more *recherché* affairs were your preference?"

Alex colored slightly, knowing Max referred to the quadroon balls, lavish gatherings of the town's young bloods and their present or prospective mistresses. Although Alex had not yet found a quadroon girl with whom he cared to make an alliance, he frequented the balls quite often. That was, in fact, what Bernard had chosen to do tonight, something the other members of the family tactfully ignored.

Irénée had been livid when she discovered Bernard would not accompany the family, but she had not been able to vent her feelings with even a single word. Respectable women were compelled to pretend the quadroon balls did not exist. Actually, Bernard's actions were not a great surprise. It was characteristic of him to bow out of something when his absence was sure to be noticed far more than his presence would have been.

Max knew there was another reason Bernard preferred to avoid the company of the family tonight. He was still in a foul temper because of an argument that had taken place only the day before. It had been one of those rare occasions when Bernard had decided to supervise some work on the plantation. Max had returned from business in town to find the entire place in a minor uproar. In his absence, Bernard had ordered the black overseer to be whipped. After being informed of the incident and seeing the marks of twenty lashes on the man's bare back, Max had stormed into the house.

"Damn you," he had raged, grasping Bernard by the front of his shirt, the bloody whip coiled in his hand, "I ought to use this on you!"

Bernard was astonished and defensive. "What the . . . let go of my shirt! What does this have to do with? The overseer? Dammit, Max I had no choice! He disobeyed a direct command. What else was I supposed to—"

"A command to whip one of the slaves for not working hard enough?" Max snarled, letting go of him roughly. "A slave who was sick with fever only last week?"

Bernard looked away uneasily. "Max, I lost my temper. Perhaps I shouldn't have, but it is over now. Let's put the incident behind us, and in the future I'll try not to—"

"*Over now?*" came Lysette's voice from the doorway. She had returned from the overseer's cabin, doing what little she could to assist the doctor while he tended the man's bleeding back. She came into the parlor, eyeing Bernard with disgust and anger. "I wish to heaven it *were* over! But that poor man is suffering and his wife is in hysterics all because you had a fit of *temper*. I can't begin to comprehend—"

"Are you going to allow her to lecture me, Max?" Bernard demanded.

"It's obvious someone needs to!" Lysette retorted. She would have said more, but Max interrupted sternly.

"You've aired your feelings, *petite*. Now I would like to talk to my brother privately."

"But—"

"Lysette," he warned, and waited until she scowled and reluctantly left.

"She obviously doesn't know her place," Bernard muttered. "Now, as I was about to explain, I was only trying to see that the work was being done efficiently. You're always claiming that I don't take on enough responsibility around the plantation, and when I do, you—"

"You'll have no more responsibility," Max said coldly. "Or authority. I'd let the crops rot in the fields before trusting any of the men to your management again."

Thinking back over the scene, Max decided it would be a while before he and Bernard were on comfortable terms. Bernard had been embarrassed and angry at being chastised. If only Bernard had more of Alexandre's softheartedness. Alex would never intentionally harm a living creature. Bernard, on the other hand, seemed to be completely insensitive to others' pain.

Max refilled Alexandre's drink and lounged against the marble mantel, searching for some light topic of conversation. "You realize, Alex, that as an unattached man, you'll be occupied the entire evening with mothers and *tantes* parading their young charges before you. Usually you can't abide such evenings."

"Ah, well," Alex said, "I will bear it for one night."

Max grinned, knowing some maiden had caught his younger brother's roving eye. "Who is she?" he asked.

Alex smiled sheepishly. "Henriette Clement."

"Jacques' youngest sister?" Max inquired with surprise, remembering the last time he had seen the girl outside the milliner's shop with her older brother. "Hmm . . . I suppose you could do worse than a Clement."

"Sang de Dieu, I haven't even *danced* with her yet! Just

because *you've* plunged into marriage doesn't mean the idea holds appeal for *me.*''

Max smiled.''I said nothing about marriage.''

Flustered, Alex cast his mind in search of a reply, and was saved by the sound of the womens' voices. *''Bien,* they're ready now,'' he said hurriedly, setting down his glass.

Following his brother to the entrance hall, Max stopped at the doorway, still holding his drink. At first he did not see Lysette, who was standing beyond Irénée and Noeline, but then the pair moved to the mirror to inspect a coil of Irénée's hair. He stared at his wife, knowing that as long as he lived, he would never forget the sight of her like this.

Lysette smiled, satisfied with the arrested expression on Max's face. Not wishing to be outdone by other women, she had chosen to wear a gold satin gown that outlined her body with exquisite simplicity. Tiny corded-silk shoes peeped out from beneath a hem draped with gold satin. The bodice was cut very low, edged with pearls and white satin insets, while the short sleeves were puffed and slashed with gold and white. Kid gloves covered her past her elbows, leaving her upper arms bare. She and Noeline had artfully braided, twisted, and pinned her hair on top of her head, leaving only a few dangling red curls to trail down her neck and touch her shoulder.

As Max walked to her, Lysette admired the contrast of his ruffled white shirt and cravat against his bronze face. His black coat fit perfectly over his broad shoulders, while his lean hips and thighs were encased in snug white pantaloons. With a touch of jealousy, Lysette realized her husband would certainly attract the notice of other women tonight.

Max's dark head bent, and he kissed the side of her neck. ''You'll have no equal tonight, Madame Vallerand.''

She smiled as he took her wrist and drew her to the

side. "Here," he murmured, taking out a black velvet pouch from his sleeve and handing it to her. "In celebration of our first ball."

"Merci, mon mari." Carefully Lysette pulled out the contents of the pouch, and with wide eyes regarded a bracelet set with a mass of diamonds that seemed too large to be real. She had never been given anything so valuable.

"Does it not please you?" Max asked, frowning at her silence.

"I . . . I . . ." Unconsciously Lysette clutched the bracelet in her fist. "Oh, it is the most beautiful . . . but I could not wear . . . what if I lose it? What if—"

"Then I'll buy you another." Amusement flickered in his eyes, and he pried the piece of jewelry from her fingers, fastening it around her wrist.

"Ah, let me see!" Irénée exclaimed, coming to appraise the bracelet. She turned Lysette's wrist from one side to the other, then beamed at Max. "Quite exquisite, *mon fils.* The stones are of excellent quality."

"I am glad you approve," Max said dryly.

Irénée put her arm around Lysette's shoulders and squeezed. "This is a fine piece with which to begin your collection, *petite.*"

Lysette looked at the diamonds on her wrist with awe. "Is it appropriate to wear with this gown, *belle-mère?*"

"Diamonds," Irénée replied firmly, "are *always* appropriate."

Meeting her husband's smiling eyes, Lysette reached up and wrapped her arms around his neck. "Thank you," she whispered. "You are very good to me, Max." Her soft lips parted as he brushed a kiss over them, and for a moment the pair seemed to forget all else. Finally Alex cleared his throat noisily, alerting them to the fact that it was time to leave.

The ball was being held at Seraphiné, one of the plantations lining the winding river road. Lysette thought the main house was magnificent, with wide galleries and rows of dormer windows built out from the sloping green tile roof. The inside of the house was just as impressive, furnished with venetian chandeliers, richly colored rugs, and massive portraits of prominent Seraphiné ancestors.

Along the sides of the great dance hall ladies fatigued by the dancing rested their feet and the chaperons of eligible Creole girls sat to monitor their charges. Groups of young men positioned themselves nearby, most of them wearing *colchemardes,* small but deadly sword-canes. Hot-tempered youths were wont to quarrel at such affairs, and duels were the natural result of even insignificant disputes.

Alexandre amused Lysette by relating an account of the last ball he attended, at which a duel had exploded in the middle of the room, instead of being conducted outside. Men had chosen sides, benches and chairs had been thrown, women had fainted, and the military guard had been forced to storm inside to quell the riot.

"And what happened to cause the duel?" Lysette asked.

Alexandre grinned. "One of the young men happened to tread on another's toes. It was taken to be a deliberate insult . . . *et ainsi de suite.*"

"Men are dreadful," Lysette said, laughing and placing her hand on her husband's arm. "Why do you not wear a *colchemarde,* Max? Don't you intend to defend your toes if the need arises?"

"No," he replied, his eyes falling to her possessive hand.

"I will defend them for you, then."

There was a ripple of murmurs and speculation as the Vallerands ventured further into the ballroom. Not having expected such immediate attention from the assemblage, Lysette nearly recoiled at the sea of faces turning toward her. Her fingers tightened on Max's arm.

Reminding herself that she had nothing to be afraid

of, she forced a smile to her lips. Suddenly, a pair of intense, jet-black eyes captured hers. Those peculiar eyes belonged to a small, delicate-featured man standing across the room, surrounded by a large entourage. He continued to look at her steadily, causing a light blush to steal over her face.

"It appears," she heard Max's soft drawl, "that you've attracted Colonel Burr's notice."

"*That* is him?" Lysette exclaimed in a whisper. "Aaron Burr? Why, it can't be! I expected . . ."

"What did you expect?" Max asked, now sounding amused.

"Someone taller," she blurted out, and he laughed quietly.

In the distance, Burr murmured something to one of his companions. "And now," Max said under his breath, "he is asking who you are. And if he pays too much attention to you, my love, he's going to have a duel on his hands. Let us hope one of his aides warns him that I'm a much better marksman than Alexander Hamilton."

Lysette blanched, recalling that Colonel Burr had reportedly forced Hamilton, a patriot who had helped write the new Constitution, into a duel which Burr was certain to win. Many had called it cold-blooded murder, for it had been known by all concerned that Burr's duelling skills were far superior to Hamilton's. It was rumored that Burr had shown not one sign of compassion or regret for Hamilton's death.

"Let us have no more talk of duels," she said hastily.

Max began to reply, then was interrupted by the mayor of New Orleans, John Watkins, who suddenly appeared at his elbow. The mayor greeted them effusively and informed them that Colonel Burr desired to meet them.

"We are honored," Max said blandly, and followed the mayor with Lysette on his arm.

Colonel Burr was dressed with the exquisite precision

of a dandy. Lysette liked the fact that although he had lost much of his hair at the front and crown, he did not wear a wig. Max had told her that Burr was at least forty-eight, but the Colonel appeared much younger. His face was deeply tanned, and his smile was quick and self-assured. And those jet-colored eyes were even more remarkable up close, filled with snapping energy and vitality. He smiled at her with the honest appreciation of a man who liked and respected women.

Although a man of Burr's size should have been dwarfed by Max's superior height, the former vice president had a presence and an extravagant charm that held its own. He made a great show of kissing Irénée and Lysette's hand, then looked up at Max.

"Monsieur Vallerand," Burr said. "You must take great pride in being accompanied by such beauty."

"Indeed," Max replied smoothly. "I am well aware of my good fortune."

Burr regarded Lysette with twinkling eyes. "I had heard much of the loveliness and charm of the Creole flowers, but assumed that the tales were exaggerated. I have just discovered that the case was, in fact, understated."

Lysette smiled slightly, unable to help herself. Regardless of his politics, the man was rather charming! "Your facility with words, monsieur, is no less than I had anticipated."

Burr looked at Lysette with warming interest, and Max's nerves bristled. It took considerable effort to maintain his bland expression as he spoke to Burr. "How do you find the climate in New Orleans, Colonel?"

The double-edged question caused Burr to chuckle. "Very pleasant, Monsieur Vallerand. We had quite an agreeable journey down here."

"So I've heard."

"I seem to remember hearing the remark that you own a small shipping business, monsieur. That is rare for a man of your background, isn't it? Don't Creoles as a rule consider anything mercantile to be beneath them?''

"As a rule, yes. But I don't always follow rules.''

"So I've heard,'' Burr said, looking at Max consideringly. "I have been making the acquaintance of many gentlemen in the community, monsieur, most of whom belong to the Mexican Association. May I ask if you happen to subscribe to that organization?''

The Mexican Association was comprised of prominent citizens who desired the liberation of Mexico, and all the attendant trade benefits it would give to the merchants of New Orleans. Anyone who belonged to the group was certain to sympathize with Burr's cause.

"No, I do not,'' Max said politely. "I have found that belonging to organizations of any kind invariably results in . . . unwanted obligations.''

"Interesting,'' Burr commented, his eyes alight with the enjoyment of a challenge. "I hope to talk with you more at a later date.''

"That might be arranged,'' Max replied suavely.

Soon Colonel Burr's attention was claimed by others who wished to be introduced, and Lysette breathed a sigh of relief as Max escorted her away. "I am glad *that* is over,'' she remarked.

"Your impression of him wasn't favorable?''

She wrinkled her nose. "He believes himself to be irresistible to women.''

"Apparently they find him so.'' Max sounded distant, as if his mind were occupied with other matters.

Alexandre interrupted them cheerfully. Having delivered Irénée to her friends who were clustered at the side of the room gossiping, he sidled up to Lysette with a mischievous grin. "My adorable sister-in-law, I humbly request you dance with me. No other woman will do.'' His dark eyes sparkled with enthusiasm and Lysette could not help smiling at him even as she shook her head self-consciously.

"I am not an accomplished dancer, Alexandre. I have not had much experience, and so perhaps you should—"

"I will guide you," he entreated, his tone wheedling. "It is not so difficult, really. My skill will make up for your lack of experience."

Lysette glanced at the mass of couples in the middle of the room, all dancing with a smoothness she knew she was not equal to. People would watch her, and mock her ineptitude. "I cannot—" she started to say, but then Max broke in.

"Why don't you try, *doucette?*"

"I don't think—"

"I'll leave her with you," Max said to Alex. "There are a few gentlemen here I want to speak with briefly." His expression turned ominous. "Do *not* leave Lysette unattended, *comprends?*"

"*Oui, je comprends,*" Alexandre agreed dutifully.

Lysette stared after her husband as he left them.

She turned ruefully to Alex. "It seems I am to dance with you."

Her brother-in-law grinned. "Max can be a trifle overbearing, *non?*"

Lysette made a face. "Perhaps he will soften in his old age."

Alexandre shook his head. "I am afraid he is too much like our father, who became quite insufferable as the years went by." He led her to the edge of the crowd. "Do you see the girl in the green gown? The one with the dark hair."

"No, I do not see—"

"She is tall. There are yellow ribbons in her hair. The blond man dancing with her is her cousin. See her? That is Henriette Clement. I want to pass by her a few times. Make certain you look as if you are enjoying yourself."

Lysette smiled and placed her hand in his. The musicians were playing a slow waltz that easily drew her into

its rhythm. After a faltering beginning, her feet picked up
the sweeping movements, and she found herself actually
enjoying the dance.

"You are more proficient than you led me to believe,"
Alexandre said, guiding her in a perfect circle.

"Has Henriette seen us yet?" Lysette asked.

"Not yet."

"Do you intend to court her, Alexandre?"

"Court her? No, I . . ." Alex looked over her shoulder
and scowled. "She has a fortune *and* a face, a combination that attracts suitors in droves. If I approached her
family with the intention of courting her, I would be called
out by half a dozen jealous swains."

"She seems worth the risk."

"Oh, she is," Alexandre said, and sighed.

Lysette's feet slowed, forcing Alexandre to stop. "Do
you know which of those ladies is her *tante?*" she asked.

"Yes, but—"

"Then go talk to her. If you plead your case well enough
with the *tante,* the battle will be half-won." She gave him
a gentle push. "Go."

"But you are not to be left alone," he said.

"Irénée is right over there, not twenty feet away. I will
go to her. Now, ingratiate yourself with Henriette's chaperon."

Shaking his head, Alexandre left her reluctantly, and
Lysette smiled after him. As she began to move toward
Irénée and her silver-coiffed companions, she was surprised to find her path blocked by a slender youth. The
boy—surely not much older than she—stared at her with
wide, unblinking eyes, and opened and closed his mouth
several times, as if trying to speak. Her forehead gathered
in a frown.

"Oui?" she said with an inquiring glance.

"Madame Vallerand," he said, sounding nervous,
"may I have the honor of this dance?" He introduced
himself hastily, realizing she did not recognize him.

"Théodor Mathurin, madame. W–we met at your wedding."

"Oh, yes." Lysette's frown cleared away. He was one of Max's distant cousins. She smiled and gave him her hand. "Thank you for your kind offer, monsieur, but I find myself quite exhausted."

Mathurin took her gloved hand as if it were a sacred object, reverently touching his lips to the back of it. "Perhaps another time."

"Perhaps."

As she continued to Irénée, Lysette was aware of other hooded stares sent in her direction. One group of young bucks stopped their conversation altogether, watching her every movement. Lysette became absurdly self-conscious, and by the time she reached her destination she felt a blush climbing up her cheeks. Irénée welcomed her warmly.

"Belle-mère," Lysette said, half-amused, half-distressed, "You are enjoying yourself, I hope?"

"Of course I am!" Irénée replied matter-of-factly. "And from all accounts, you are a success, my dear. Why Diron Clement, that sly old gentlemen, was overheard to say you were one of the greatest beauties he has ever seen!"

Lysette laughed self-consciously. "That is a flattering exaggeration, *Belle-mère.* "

"It it not at all an exaggeration!" Irénée nudged a stout, flower-bedecked dowager nearby. "Tell her it is so, Yvonne, tell her!"

Yvonne, an older cousin on Irénée's side of the family, gave Lysette a plump-cheeked smile. "I remember it was the same with your mother when she was a girl. How they all stared when she entered a room!"

"But I am a married woman," Lysette protested. "I do not invite such attention."

"These young blades need no invitation to admire an attractive woman, *ma belle.* How they all envy Maximilien for having chosen you as his bride!"

"I am the fortunate one, madame," Lysette said. "My husband is kind and generous in all ways."

Yvonne regarded her skeptically, then leaned forward to say in a confidential tone, "I'm certain he is, my dear. But mark my words, he will be even *more* generous once you bear him children! It is always so."

Lysette smiled uncomfortably. "I understand, madame."

"As the wife of a Vallerand," Yvonne continued, "you will set the standard for all the young Creole matrons. And we have need of such good examples, with all these brazen American women moving to New Orleans almost daily!" She clucked her tongue, looking displeased. "Shameless creatures—no modesty or delicacy. Why, they think nothing of walking anywhere unescorted, and interrupting their husbands freely! Bah! It is the responsibility of young Creole women to cling fast to the old values. But until you produce children, you will have no authority."

"Yes, that is very true," Irénée said.

Lysette nodded gravely, while inside she wanted to laugh. Being married to Max would not make it easy for her to live the life of a paragon! "I will pray to have them soon, madame."

"*Bien sûr,*" Yvonne replied, satisfied that her admonition had been attended.

They continued to chat until a flutter of perturbation ran through the group of ladies and Lysette half-turned to find the dark figure of her husband beside her. Max greeted Yvonne and his mother quietly, then reached his hand down to Lysette. She took it obediently, and he pulled her up to stand beside him.

"*Pardon* . . . I am stealing my wife for a dance," Max said to Irénée, his fingers closing around Lysette's.

Lysette frowned. "Max, no." She did not want to reveal her lack of grace yet again this evening. Later, she would employ a dancing-master who would help her improve her rudimentary skills, but for now she intended to sit at the side of the room with her mother-in-law.

Max gave me an imperious tug on her hand. "Come, and do not argue with me."

"But your toes . . . I have sworn to protect them. *Non,* I will not dance with you."

"A woman your size could hardly inflict any damage."

"Well, if you are going to be stubborn . . ." Lysette allowed him to lead her away.

"You danced well enough with Alex," Max said, drawing her close and taking her right hand in his.

"You noticed?" she asked, liking the firm, commanding way he held her in his arms.

"I notice everything you do, little one."

Before she could reply, Max whirled her into the dance. Every time one of her steps was too short, or less than certain, he adjusted immediately. His hand was strong on her back, exerting pressure to guide her in the direction he chose. The movement of their bodies was so smooth and light, she felt as if they were flying.

She laughed up at him in surprised pleasure, feeling her skirts sweep around them. "I did not know you could dance so well."

He smiled. "I have many accomplishments you have yet to discover."

"Yes, but . . ." Lysette looked up at him, and the teasing remark she had intended to make vanished from her mind. Hurriedly she lowered her eyes, hoping he had not seen the intense love that had suddenly filled every part of her. Knowing of her feelings might drive him away, or worse, arouse his scorn. There was no way for her to be certain he was ready to accept her love, so she felt she must hold it back until the time was right. But oh, how impossible that was! Don't be impatient, she warned herself.

To her dismay, Lysette felt herself stumble. Max's hand tightened on hers, and he covered her mistake adeptly, taking an extra step to bring them back to the rhythm of the music.

"I am sorry," she murmured, trying to recapture the ease of before. But now her concentration was broken and her thoughts had scattered like fireflies. Once more her steps faltered. Lysette blushed deeply, certain Max would tease her about her clumsiness. "I suppose I am tired, or perhaps it is because people are watching, although I don't know why I—"

"It's all right," Max interrupted, wondering what had caused her disconcertion.

He drew her to the side of the room, and they stopped near tall french doors that opened to the outside gallery. Beyond were long twin borders of flowering shrubs leading to the garden. Young unmarried couples often yearned to sneak out there for stolen kisses, but few found the opportunity. Lysette looked from the dark, star-speckled sky to her husband's enigmatic face, and her heart beat faster.

Circumspectly Max glanced from side to side, then slipped her past the doors in an adept maneuver he had perfected in boyhood. Lysette laughed under her breath as he pulled her through the rustling garden, past tall yew hedges and rosemary-covered walls. All at once she felt wicked and strangely free, and as giddy as if this were a clandestine meeting between secret lovers.

"I am thankful to be a married woman," she said, giggling as Max stopped and swung her around. Throwing her arms around his neck, she clung to him until her feet touched the ground once more. "I believe you would frustrate the most watchful chaperon, Monsieur Vallerand."

He smiled. "Tonight you have no chaperon, madame."

"What if we had met this evening for the very first time, and I . . . what if I were Etienne Sagesse's wife?" The starlight shone on Lysette's face as she looked up at him. The thought of being at another man's side, never knowing Max, was almost frightening. Her whimsical mood changed in a flash, and she held onto him a little tighter. "I could so easily have been his instead of yours. If I hadn't run away, or if Justin and Philippe hadn't found me . . . or if you had decided to give me back to the Sagesses—"

"I would never have given you back." As Lysette stood there in his arms, nestling close against him, Max touched his lips to the top of her head. "And if you had married Sagesse, I would have taken you away from him." Although his voice was soft, ruthlessness was manifest in every syllable. "No matter how I had to do it."

"For revenge?"

"For you."

She was tempted to let the remark pass, but a twinge of stubbornness would not allow it. "No," she said, looking away. "You married me because I had been promised to Sagesse. You wanted reparation for what he did ten years ago. We both know it. There is no need for you to pretend otherwise."

For some reason the statement—which was, after all, the truth—seemed to irritate Max. "I wanted you from the beginning. Even before I knew you were his fiancée."

Lysette sensed his readiness to quarrel, and she sought to soothe him. "Well, we're married now, no matter how it began." She smiled and pulled away, walking by a tiny circular summer house that was nearly engulfed by a mass of climbing roses. The pale pink blossoms were the thornless variety that flowered early in the summer. Max deftly broke off one and handed it to her as they passed by.

Pleased, she lifted it to her nose, enjoying the sweet fragrance.

"I was given a lecture inside by your mother and one of her friends," she remarked, her eyes on the path before them.

"Oh?"

"They said I would stand much higher in your esteem if I gave you children."

"Ah. It's a comforting thing to know I'm understood so well by family and friends." He slid a steely arm around her waist, pulling her back against him. "But as I told you on our wedding night," he murmured against her neck, "don't listen to conventional wisdom."

Lysette frowned anxiously. "Does that mean you . . . wouldn't like it if I . . . if we had . . ."

"If we produced children?" He grinned. "I rather like the idea of having some red-headed Vallerands. With your looks, of course, and my agreeable temperament. But I also like the idea of having you all to myself. It's very easy for you to please me, *ma petite.*"

"Oh, I hope so," she said fervently, the rose dropping from her fingers. She twisted until her arms were wrapped around his lean waist and her hips were pressed against his hard thighs. "I want to make you happy . . . I want . . ."

But his mouth prevented any more words, his kiss lazy, gentle, and devastating. She was left trembling and flushed, and when he began to pull away she clung to him helplessly.

There was a peculiar look on his face, the expression of a man who stood on the edge of a precipice. "Lysette," he said, and there was a distinct unsteadiness in his voice, "after the hell I went through with Corinne, I never intended to marry again. I hadn't the slightest desire to take a wife. And then you—" Max stopped, his mind warning him that he was about to make a terrible mistake. Once, he had sworn on everything he held sacred never to say what he was about to say. He could not, would not, give someone the means to destroy him once more. But his heart pounded violently, seeming to beat a confession up from his chest. "I couldn't help wanting you," he said hoarsely. "I tried not to. God knows I've had my own way too long, and lost too many illusions to be the kind of man you deserve. But I love you."

"Oh, Max," she whispered, her eyes glittering.

He drew her further into the darkness, and his hands searching hungrily over her satin-sheathed form, his head bending over hers as he stole her breath away with deep, smoldering kisses. She fit her body against his, quivering with pleasure as she felt how aroused he was. A protesting moan escaped her as he eased her away from him, withdrawing his hand from her bodice.

"We'll either have to stop now, or see it through," he said huskily, his breath filtering through her hair in strong gusts. "and I'm afraid grass stains don't complement white satin very well."

Lysette slid her hands under his coat and rested them at his waist. "Why don't we go home?"

Max considered the idea for a wistful moment, then shook his head. "And cause a scandal . . ."

She stroked his sides invitingly. "I don't care. Truly, I—"

"No." With a groan, he retrieved her wandering fingers and straightened her gown. "For your sake, we're going to make at least an attempt at respectability."

Her gaze was warm with love and joy as she smiled at him. Taking his arm, she went with him back toward the house where sprightly music and the sound of voices emanated from the open windows.

A shadow disentangled itself from beside the french doors. They stopped on the gallery as Etienne Sagesse stepped forth and spoke. His voice was drawling, his words imprecisely formed, as if he had been drinking. "Well, well," he said, pulling at his disarranged cravat. "Returning from an evening stroll? I trust it was pleasant."

Chapter 11

L ysette searched for Max's hand and felt his fingers close reassuringly over hers.

Etienne's face was stamped with a sneer. "I see you've trained your bride well, Max."

"What do you want?" Max asked curtly.

"Why, to congratulate you. Since I was not invited to the wedding, I haven't had the opportunity before now." His smile was thin and reptilian as he regarded Lysette's flushed face. "Apparently, my dear, you are flourishing under Maximilien's loving attention." He emphasized the last two words precisely. "But, as I recall, so did Corinne . . . for a time."

"If you want another duel," Max said, "you'll have it. Only this time I'll finish it."

"Is that a challenge?"

"No," Lysette gasped, terrified. If another duel took place, there was a chance her husband could be wounded, even killed. She could not bear it. "There is no reason now. Max, *please—*"

"Not a challenge, but a warning," Max said, ignoring Lysette's outburst. His hand tightened to silence her. She flinched at the sudden pain of her fingers being crunched together.

"Do not distress yourself, madame," Etienne said to

Lysette. "I would not dream of disrupting such a cozy marriage. The two of you have much in common. The Vallerand name suits you to perfection, *far* better than mine ever could have." His eyes flickered to Max. "Were it not for me, your wife would still be in Natchez. You owe me, *mon ami*, for having her brought to New Orleans."

Max seemed to consider the remark carefully before replying. "I would like to see all debts between us settled."

For a moment Etienne's face twisted in anger. Lysette held her breath and wondered what had prompted that spasm of emotion.

"Once again you have everything," Etienne said, his speech more slurred than before. "And you wish to be left in peace. But you don't deserve it, not any of it . . . not her. You have never deserved what you had, and once again . . . it will be taken away . . ." He fell silent, leaning back against the wall, watching them through cunning heavy-lidded eyes.

Max moved forward, his hands half-raised.

Lysette held onto his arm. "Don't," she said urgently. "He wants to provoke you. He's drunk. You cannot give credence to anything he says. Please, take me inside."

Etienne was silent, continuing to look at Max.

"Max," she pleaded, "he can do nothing to hurt us."

Max read the concern in her hazel eyes, and his quick-burning rage began to fade. In the past Etienne had presented a threat, but no longer. Lysette was not Corinne, and nothing would take her from him. Forcing himself to relax, he slid his arm around her back. Sagesse stared after them as they went into the ballroom.

Inside they held themselves apart from other people, drawing to a corner and talking quietly. From a distance, some guests commented snidely on a husband paying such marked attention to his wife.

For the moment unconcerned with public opinion, Max bent his head low to hear Lysette's soft voice over the music and the crowd. "Is it possible," she asked, "that even after all these years he feels guilty about the affair with Corinne?"

"I don't know." Max looked grim.

"Perhaps it is different here, but in Natchez a gentleman who drinks to excess is regarded with the utmost scorn and contempt."

"It is no different here."

"It is a scandal for a man of his position to be so intoxicated at a gathering such as this. He seems to want to ruin himself. It is strange . . . just now I actually pitied him."

Max regarded her with a sardonic expression.

"Didn't you?" she asked.

"No."

"I think you did." Gently she tangled her fingers with his. "What did he mean when he said once again you had everything?"

Max shrugged restlessly. "I couldn't say for certain."

"Well, what do you *think?*"

"It reminded me of when we were boys. We used to be friends, good friends, until there was a falling-out."

"Friends?" Lysette said, surprising. "I cannot picture it."

Max grinned ruefully. "Sometimes I can't either. But we were once actually closer to each other than to our own brothers."

"And what caused this falling-out? A girl?"

"No . . ." He took one of the long curls dangling against her shoulder and wound it around his finger, seemingly absorbed in the brilliant red lock. "It was something rather similar to what he said tonight. He believed I had everything, and didn't deserve it." A one-sided smile appeared on his lips. "He was probably right."

"Jealousy, then," Lysette mused, and looked up at him anxiously. "Jealousy is a powerful emotion. And impossible to defend oneself against."

"And what would you know of jealousy?" he asked, the smile deepening in the corner of his mouth.

"A great deal," she said seriously. "Gaspard was always jealous of my father, of his memory. It embittered him. It drove him to hurt all of us, Maman, Jacqueline, and me. The only way Maman could escape from it was to take to her bed as an invalid."

Max let go of her hair and touched her cheek lightly. "And the escape for you was marriage?"

"Oh, no," she whispered. "I married for love, and no other reason."

He smiled. "Somehow I got the impression you were less than willing to marry me."

"I'll remember it the way I want to," she informed him.

His eyes darkened to a smoky shade of topaz, and his thumb strayed along her jaw.

Their reverie was disrupted by the rude clearing of someone's throat. "Er . . . Max," Alexandre said, "Irénée is in a state. She sent me here to tell you to stop fondling Lysette in front of all New Orleans."

The Vallerands left the ball long before it was over. The Creoles, with their love of dancing, would carry on until the early hours of the morning. But Lysette was eager to return home, finding the idea of privacy with her husband much more appealing than staying to be stared at the entire evening. In the carriage Max said little, gazing out the window with a troubled expression.

Lysette questioned Alexandre about his evening, and whether or not he had approached Henriette Clement's aunt.

"Oh, yes," Alex said ruefully. "I hovered around her for at least a quarter-hour, feeling like a complete fool."

"Did you make her like you?"

"That's difficult to tell. The *tante* seems to feel that no innocent young woman would be safe in the company of a Vallerand, not even with ten chaperons present.''

"I can't imagine why," Lysette said, and glanced at Max with a smile. *"Qu'est-ce que c'est?"* she asked softly, while Irénée and Alexandre became involved in a discussion of the Clement family. "Still thinking about Etienne Sagesse?"

Max shook his head, staring at the scenery outside as the carriage sluggishly traveled the muddy road. "I have a feeling something is wrong. I can't explain why. But I'll be glad when we reach home."

Unfortunately Max was proven right. As soon as they entered the house, Noeline greeted them, her usually imperturbable face set with worry. Philippe sat on one of the narrow benches in the entranceway, looking haggard.

"Monsieur, Justin been gone all day," Noeline said tersely. "Ain' come home to eat tonight."

Max turned to Philippe. "Where is he?"

Slowly Philippe stood to face him, his blue eyes bewildered. "I do not know, sir. The pirogue is gone."

"When did you last see him?"

"This morning. Justin was boasting that he sneaked out last night after bedtime. He said he had met some of the crew of a flatboat on Tchoupitoulas Street and planned to go with them tonight. But I didn't believe he would actually do it."

"Oh, my poor Justin!" Irénée cried in distress.

Max cursed with fury, or fear, or perhaps both. Flatboat men were a dangerous crowd for a boy Justin's age to associate with. Bullies and uneducated scoundrels, they lived, ate, and slept on the deck of their boats with no protection against the outdoors. Their idea of entertainment was to swill rye whiskey, brawl, and wallow in unsavory flesh-houses where disease and violence were rampant. When they fought, they bit, kicked, and gouge eyes out, mutilating an opponent without mercy. By now they might have made short work of Justin.

"Which crew?" Max demanded, sounding strangely short of breath. "Which boat?"

Philippe shook his head helplessly.

Max turned to the door, where Alexandre stood with his mouth open. "We have to find him," Max growled.

Alex backed away a step. "Oh, no. I make every effort to steer clear of such fellows. I won't risk my neck merely to rescue your fool of a son, who doesn't want to be found in the first place. Just go to sleep. He'll probably be back by morning."

"Or end up in the river with his throat cut," Max snarled, brushing by his brother and heading outside.

"You won't find him," Alexandre warned.

"Oh, I'm going to find him. And then I'll tear him limb from limb."

Hastily Lysette ran after him. "Max, be careful!" He acknowledged her with a brief gesture of his hand, not bothering to look back. She bit her lip, wanting to call after him again, realizing how terrified he was for his son. Whirling around, she went back to Alexandre, gripping his arm and tugging roughly. "Alexandre, you must go with him! You must help him!"

"I'll be damned if I—"

"He cannot do it alone!"

Irénée took up the fight, helping Lysette to urge Alexandre toward the door. "Yes, you must accompany Max, _mon fils._"

"Maman, I am tired—"

"Think of Justin!" Irénée commanded, pulling at his other arm. "He may be in trouble this very moment. He may be suffering!"

"If there is any justice he is," Alex said through his teeth, shaking off their hands and hurrying after his older brother.

They closed the door immediately, half-afraid he would try to come back in. For several seconds there was silence as they tried to take in what had just happened.

Irénée finally spoke. "Justin," she said, "will no doubt be the death of me." She regarded Philippe sorrowfully. "Why can't he be more like you?"

Suddenly Philippe exploded. "Why does everyone have to ask that? He can't help the way he is, any more than I can help the way I am!" White-faced, he sank back onto the bench. "Everyone is wrong. I am not the good one. He is not the bad one."

Irénée sighed, her face creased with exhaustion. "I am too old and fatigued to discuss this now. Noeline, help me upstairs."

All were silent as the two women left and headed to the curving staircase. Philippe buried his face in his hands, digging his knuckles into his eyes. Filled with sympathy, Lysette sat beside him, thinking to herself how little affection he and Justin had received during their lives. It was Irénée's way to be more scolding than affectionate . . . and then, of course, there was Max, who had long equated love with pain and betrayal. Folding her hands in her lap, she rested quietly, her eyes on Philippe's bowed head.

"Justin is different from me," Philippe finally said in a muffled voice. "Different from all of us. Things are too slow for him—he can't bear to stay in one place too long. He's always wanted to run away. Sometimes I can feel what *he's* feeling . . . it's like being in a cage. I think the world itself is too small for him. He loves father, in his own way, but Justin can't stand to be near anyone who is equally strong-willed."

"Your father does not make unreasonable demands," Lysette said gravely. "Justin must learn to respect his wishes."

Philippe gave a hollow laugh. "Never. Justin will leave first. And they both know it."

Max and Alexandre returned early the next afternoon without Justin. They were both tired, but Max was tense and more agitated than Lysette had ever seen him. His thoughts seemed to race faster than conversation would allow.

"No sign of him," he said hoarsely, downing half a cup of bitter coffee in one swallow. "We found a boatman who claimed to have seen a boy of Justin's description on the waterfront. God knows if he was lying. Justin might have signed on with a crew, but I don't think he would be so—"

"I'm going to bed," Alex mumbled, his face pasty and eyes bloodshot.

Lysette came to stand behind her husband, her hands drifting soothingly over his taut shoulders. "Max, you need rest also."

He motioned Noeline to pour more coffee. "I'm leaving in a few minutes. Bernard will be going with me. I'm going to ask Jacques Clement and one or two others to help look for Justin."

Lysette wished she knew how to comfort him. "I do not think Justin has run away," she said, smoothing his ruffled black hair and sitting beside him. "I think this is another bid for attention. He is staying away deliberately, waiting until he is certain of an uproar before he returns."

Max held the coffee cup in fingers that trembled slightly. "When I get hold of him," he muttered, "he'll have more attention than he ever bargained for."

She took his free hand in both of hers, clasping it tightly. "I know that you're angry with him, my darling, but mostly you're afraid for him. Perhaps you should let Justin know that when you find him."

"And what would that accomplish?"

Lysette ignored the jeering note in his voice. "Justin does not know how you feel about him. You must admit, you're not the most demonstrative of men. Max . . . you and your son must find a way to begin talking to each other."

Max rested his elbows on the table and massaged his

temples. "Justin is to hardheaded to listen to anything I say."

"I believe," she said wryly, "Justin has made the same remark about you on occasion."

Max smiled slightly. "Sometimes I see myself in him," he admitted. "But at his age I was not half so stubborn."

"I'll ask Irénée about that," she said, gently teasing. "I suspect she might not agree."

He brought her hand to his bristled face and pressed his lips against the back of it, closing his eyes. "If I don't find him, Lysette . . ."

"You will," she murmured, hoping desperately that she was right. "You will."

All that day and night the search continued. Max enjoined most of the workers on his own trade vessels to find out what they could. A few boatmen admitted that Justin, or a boy remarkably like him, had been in their company. After a few hours of drinking and gaming, they said, he had left with a waterfront prostitute, and had not been seen again. "How splendid," Bernard had commented upon hearing this bit of information. "Now it seems we must worry about him developing a case of the clap."

"If only that were the worst to fear," Max had rejoined darkly.

After questioning dozens of men and combing through every keelboat, kentucky flat, barge, and raft in sight, the searchers were forced to temporarily disband with the agreement that they would resume the next morning. For two days and nights Max had barely paused to rest his feet, and the strain was telling. Looking very much like the unkempt, unshaven boatmen he had associated with for the past forty-eight hours, he made his way into the house with overcautious movements, blinking hard to say awake.

It was past three in the morning, but Lysette was waiting for him. It tore at her heart to see him so careworn and defeated. She tried to guide him upstairs, but Max refused, afraid that being in a bed would cause him to sleep too soundly. He had time for only a few hours of rest. Together Lysette and Philippe helped him to the parlor and removed his boots. He unfolded his long frame onto a settee, dropped his head in Lysette's lap, and closed his eyes. Philippe left them, anxiously glancing back over his shoulder.

"He just disappeared," Max mumbled, turning his face against the soft line of her thigh, shielding his eyes from the muted lamplight. "No one knows . . ."

Lysette shushed him, stroking his forehead. "Sleep now," she whispered. "You don't have long until morning."

"I keep remembering when he was a baby. Now . . . I can't keep him safe from anything."

"He's a young man," she said, "trying to prove he can take care of himself."

"That's not—"

"Shhh. Just rest. You'll find him tomorrow, *bien-aimé.*"

As Max fell asleep, Lysette watched him for a long time. She shared his concern for Justin and Philippe, and always would. Somehow she had to help bring about changes in the household before the differences between father and son formed a rift too great to bridge.

She dozed lightly, occasionally waking to shift her position and settle more comfortably beside Max. The sky outside changed, darkness lightening into lavender gray. Watching the dawn appear, Lysette rubbed her eyes, careful not to disturb her sleeping husband.

Alertness came in a flash as she heard a scraping sound in the entrance hall. It was the front door opening. Stealthily the intruder crept into the house and paused at the parlor doorway, sensing Lysette's stare.

It was Justin, dirty and disheveled, but looking a good deal better for wear than Max. Silently he looked at Lysette and his father's long, sprawling form on the settee.

Lysette thought of motioning him upstairs and allowing Max to sleep, but Max would want to know about his son's return right away. He would be furious if he did not have the opportunity to confront Justin the moment he entered the house.

"Come in," Lysette said quietly.

At the sound of her voice, Max stirred, and she bent over his dark head. "Wake up," she whispered. "It is over now, *bien-aimé*. He is home."

Blindly Max twisted and sat up, shaking his head to clear away the mist of sleep. "Justin," he said groggily. "Where were you?"

The boy's face was guilty, uncertain, remorseful, but before Max could see any of those emotions, they were quickly concealed. Lysette realized what was coming and nearly groaned aloud as Justin chose to be flippant. "A strange place to sleep," he said casually. "Do you plan to make a habit of it?"

Max's stare was chilling. He fought against the impulse to seize his son and inflict significant damage. *"Where the hell were you?"*

"With friends," Justin said, his expression closed.

"Are you all right?" Lysette asked. "You have not been hurt?"

"Or course I am all right. Why would I not be?"

Lysette winced, knowing that even a touch of humility or repentence on the boy's part would have kept Max from going off the edge.

"The next time you decide to leave," Max said through clenched teeth, "without letting anyone know where you're going or when you plan to return, don't come back."

"I don't have to live under your roof!" Justin exploded. "I don't have to depend on you for anything! You want me to go? Then I'll go, and never look back!" He spun around and darted out the way he had come.

"Justin, no!" Lysette cried, and scrambled up from the

sofa. Max did not move. She stared at him with wide eyes. "You must go after him."

"Let him leave," Max said viciously. "I won't beg him to stay."

Her bewilderment changed to outrage. "Between the two of you I don't know who is more foolishly stubborn!" She turned and hurried after Justin, while Max swore violently.

Lysette winced as her soft-slippered foot encountered a sharp bit of gravel on the front steps. "Ouch!" Painstakingly she hopped to the ground. "Justin, stop this very second! Stop!"

Surprisingly, he did. He stood with his back facing her, his hands clenched at his sides. Lysette hobbled partway along the drive, her face red with frustration. "He has been desperate to find you," she said. "He's had people out looking for you. He hasn't eaten. He hasn't slept, aside from three or four hours on the settee last night."

"If you're trying to make me say I'm sorry, I won't!"

"I am trying to make you understand how worried he has been!"

Justin snorted sardonically.

"You're not fair to him," she said.

"He's not fair to me! He has to have everyone and everything under his control."

Lysette closed her eyes and breathed a prayer for patience. "Justin, please turn around. I cannot talk to your back."

The boy swiveled to face her, his blue eyes radiant with anger.

But Lysette did not retreat. "You don't realize how much he loves you."

"He's not capable of loving anyone," Justin said roughly. "Not even you."

"That's not true."

"And you're a fool for believing in a someone who

murdered—'' He broke off and stared at the ground, his body trembling.

"Do you really believe that?" she demanded, her voice lowering. "Justin, you know your father could never have done something so evil!"

"I *don't* know that." Justin inhaled deeply, his gaze still fixed on the ground. "He could have done it. Anyone is capable of murder. Anyone could be driven to it."

"No, Justin." Cautiously she approached him, noticing the bruises on his bare arms. His hands were scraped and raw. Why was he constantly driven to such violence? "Come inside with me," she said, and with a flash of determination took hold of his wrist.

Justin wrenched his arm away. "He doesn't want me there."

"I suppose that is why he exhausted himself searching for you." She refrained from touching him again. "Justin, did you stay away because you knew it would upset him?"

"No . . . it was . . . I had to get away."

"From your father? From the family?"

"From everything. I can't do what they want. They want me to be a good boy like Philippe, and not ask questions that make them uncomfortable, and not remind them of my mother. Justin's eyes glistened, and he clenched his fists, struggling to master the traitorous tears.

He was a boy, just a boy. Lysette had to repress the urge to put her arms around him and comfort him as she would an unhappy child. "Come with me," she murmured. "Your family has worried enough. And you need to rest." She turned back to the house, holding her breath until she heard his slow footsteps behind her.

Fearing what he might say to Justin before his anger cooled, Max avoided him for the next day and night. Gently Lysette pressed him to have a talk with the boy, and he agreed reluctantly that he would in another day or so, after his meeting with Colonel Burr.

It was nearly midnight when Max welcomed Burr into the library, knowing that Burr was confident of winning yet another wealthy patron to his side. Daniel Clark, a New Orleans merchant with a large fleet of commercial ships and warehouses, had reportedly given Burr at least twenty-five thousand dollars in cash, and several others had matched that sum jointly. Max did not intend to contribute a penny, but he was interested to hear what the ambitious Colonel had to say.

Burr had charmed almost everyone in New Orleans—even the Ursuline nuns. He had been received everywhere with elaborate hospitality. The Catholic authorities and the Mexican Association, which had long agitated for the conquest of Mexico, had granted him their support. It was generally thought that he was planning an attack on the Spaniards, and that he had gained the secret support of Jefferson's government. However, Max had heard enough confidential information from varying sources to know better. Burr was certainly not in league with Jefferson; he was forming a conspiracy for his own gain.

With deliberate bluntness, he asked Burr why he desired this private, highly confidential meeting, when Burr had nearly every man of importance in his pocket. "After all," Max drawled, "one more or less won't make a difference to your plans—whatever they may be."

"You are known to be a man with a most enterprising nature, Monsieur Vallerand. You possess means and intelligence, and you come from an old, renowned family. Frankly, I could not afford to overlook you."

"You neglected to mention my rather blemished reputation," Max said, tigerishly gentle. Obviously Burr had not been informed that he could not stand to be flattered.

Burr shrugged negligently. "All men have their detractors. A few unfounded rumors would never hinder your involvement in my plans."

"Which are?" The two words seemed to charge the air with tension. For a moment there was silence.

"I think," Burr finally said, "you already have an idea about what they may be."

"Not at all," Max lied smoothly.

Refusing a drink, Burr sat in a deep leather chair and pursued a seemingly idle line of conversation. Looking handsome and mysterious, sitting outside the direct pool of light cast by a lamp, he lazily plied Max with questions about New Orleans, his family, his politics.

Max understood Burr's dilemma perfectly. Burr had to risk revealing enough information to gain Max's support, but not give away enough to endanger his plans. The former vice president explained that he intended to use New Orleans as a base from which to conquer Mexico and wrest the Floridas away from the Spanish—if, of course, war happened to break out between the United States and Spain.

After Burr had finished talking, Max smiled with maddening indifference. "And this will be done for whose benefit?"

As Max had expected, Burr refrained from confessing that he planned to be the sole ruler over his new empire. "Let us say," the Colonel dodged, "that the Louisiana Territory will profit."

"I see," Max remarked vaguely.

"And?" Burr prompted. "I can count you among our group, I trust?"

Max let the moment draw out to its fullest before replying. "Unfortunately I find it impossible to pledge support to a cause with such nebulous outlines. Unless you can provide more details . . ."

Burr frowned, surprised at the man's lack of enthusiasm. After the multitude of successes he had enjoyed on his trip westward, the very idea of being refused seemed unlikely to him. "I've provided all the information I can."

Max spread his hands slightly, palms up. "I'm a man with certain responsibilities. And loyalties."

"Loyalties to Claiborne?"

"To what he represents."

"Ahhh . . ." Burr eyed him quizzically, and injected a fine tone of sarcasm into his next statement. "You feel you somehow owe allegiance to a country which has refused to grant your people citizenship."

"Somehow," Max agreed implacably.

"Perhaps you should consider the interests of the territory—and those of your family—more carefully."

"Oh, I have," Max said softly, and the insolence of the statement caused Burr to redden in outrage.

"I can assure you, Monsieur Vallerand, that your loyalties are wrongly directed."

"That may be proven in time. However, for the present I will keep to the course I've already chosen."

Taking Max's refusal as an unpardonable insult, Burr replied with controlled fury. "There will come a day when you will regret aligning yourself with my opponents, Vallerand."

Burr left abruptly, and Max let out a slow sigh, wondering if he had been a fool. It was possible Burr would accomplish all he planned, and New Orleans would someday be part of a new empire separate from the United States. If Max had chosen unwisely, he could lose a large portion of his land, wealth, and property. Burr was known to be a vindictive man.

"He's too confident." Hearing Lysette's voice, Max turned with a questioning look. She stood only a few feet away, wearing a lacy white pelisse that was buttoned from the neck to the floor.

"You listened," he said wryly.

She lifted her nose. "I happened to be walking by. Voices carry very easily from this room, even with the door closed. If you desire privacy, you should try the other parlor."

"I'll remember that," he muttered.

"Monsieur Burr is hardly convincing when he claims to

be acting in the interests of others. He wants power for himself, and the more the better, yes?''

''Yes,'' Max said thoughtfully.

Lysette frowned. ''It is possible that he will succeed? Could he actually create his own empire, and make New Orleans part of it?''

''Perhaps I have underestimated Burr,'' Max admitted. ''I don't think anyone anticipated the public reaction to his journey through the west.'' He laughed shortly. ''He has been greatly encouraged by it. Recently he was heard to say that he expects a king will someday sit on the throne of the United States.''

''A king? Doesn't he believe in democracy, then?''

''No, sweet.''

''Do you, Max?'' she asked, knowing that most Creoles had doubts about the American system of government.

Max grinned and reached for her, swinging her slight body up into his arms. ''Everywhere but at home.''

She persisted in questioning him, even as he carried her upstairs. ''Do you think you'll ever regret not siding with Monsieur Burr?''

''I suppose I might, if he succeeds in taking over Louisiana.''

Lysette wondered why Max didn't seem more concerned. ''If he does, you could stand to lose a great deal, couldn't you?''

''I've made provisions for any circumstance,'' he said, giving her a comforting squeeze. ''Don't forget, the territory's changed hands many times before, and the Vallerands have weathered it quite well. Do you doubt my ability to take care of you?''

''No, of course not.'' Lysette curved her hand around his shoulder, and with her fingertip traced a line from his ear down the side of his neck. ''You didn't sleep well last night,'' she whispered. ''You must be looking forward to bed.''

Max smiled slowly. "There's no question of that, madame."

"You need to rest," Lysette murmured.

He set her by the bed and rubbed his face against the silken fall of her hair, inhaling its sweet fragrance. "What I need is to make love to my wife." His hands locked around the back of her neck, thumbs nudging her jaw upward, and he kissed her. When he lifted his head and dropped his hands, she gave a protesting murmur, craving more of the wine-sweet taste of his mouth.

Clumsily she helped him undress, then began to pull the pelisse over her head, too impatient to attend to the hundreds of silk-covered buttons that fastened it. Max caught the shimmering white fabric at her hips and pushed it back down, whispering they had time, spreading love-words along her neck as his hands went to the top of the pelisse. Each untethered button was celebrated with a kiss, some swift and delicately placed, others slow and lengthy, until the newly-revealed skin of her throat and chest was tinted with a rosy hue.

Max was careful as he pushed her back against the bed and eased her to the mattress. He took his time arranging her hair, pulling it from beneath her shoulders, spreading it in a fiery halo. She watched him through half-closed eyes, catching her breath at the sight of his dark, intent face, tousled black hair, and broad chest. His large hand moved tenderly over her body and the fragile white silk of her pelisse, curving over her hip, rising to her breast.

Gasping, she tried to unfasten the pelisse herself, suddenly desperate to feel him against her naked skin. He brushed her hands aside and kissed her leisurely as he freed the rest of the row of buttons. She responded with a purring sigh low in her throat, relaxing as she felt the welcome tugging and releasing of fabric. Her palms chased over his sinewed back, cherishing the play of hard muscle, the shiver of excitement along his spine and hot mist of sweat on his smooth skin. Then he lifted her arms out of the sleeves, pulling at the folds of silk, extricating her from the garments that had concealed her body from him.

Max was more gentle with her than he had ever been before, even more gentle than the time when he had taken her innocence. He drew his fingertips over her stomach, down to her knees, up the inside of her thighs, while she arched up to him eagerly.

She felt his fingers slide over the entrance to her body and tangle in the downy tuft of cinnamon-red hair. *"Si belle,"* he whispered, caressing until her thighs fell open. "So beautiful . . ." In response to her soft whimper, his fingers slipped inside her wet heat, nudging deep into the velvety passage. His mouth wandered from her shoulder to the crook of her elbow.

Trembling uncontrollably, she rolled to her side, pressing her breasts into his chest, branding him with tender points of fire. She lifted her thigh and draped it over his lean hip, holding him to her in an exquisite trap.

"I love you," Max said raggedly. "Oh, God . . . I didn't know it was possible to love this much."

Lysette buried her mouth in his throat. "Take me now," she whispered. "Now . . ."

Max pushed her onto her back, but instead of settling between her thighs, he bent over her stomach. Lysette flinched in surprise as she felt his tongue dip into her navel. His breath touched the damp hollow before the velvety tip of his tongue intruded once more. She said his name shakily, trying to push his head away from her stomach, but instead he moved lower, seeming not to notice her confusion.

Then his head was between her thighs, and instead of resisting she was passive, shaking, transfixed by the astounding heat of his mouth. Her spine seemed to dissolve. "Stop," she heard herself begin to moan, and her body jolted in an effort to escape the pleasurable agony. But his hands clamped over her hips, keeping her where he wanted her, and he drove her ever faster toward a rising wave of sensation.

It swept over her with devastating force, and she relinquished herself with a broken cry, her fingers clenching in his hair, her heels digging into his naked sides. Wherever she turned he was there, drawing her deeper inside the dark ecstasy. She found herself shattering, falling apart, and she couldn't bring herself to care.

The piercing sweetness began to ebb, and she reached for him with an incoherent cry, frantic not to lose him. She wound her arms tightly around his neck, awareness gradually coming back to her, and she began to cry quietly, spreading kisses over his face and neck. He hushed her with a salt-tinged kiss, his body pressing deeper, penetrating until he could no longer hold back his passion. Feverishly he held onto her, breathing her name with a fierce shudder.

A long time later she was sprawled over his body, while his hands wandered soothingly over her back and buttocks. Spent and satiated, he had not yet found the strength to turn back the covers or reach for the pillows. "Max," she said drowsily.

His answer was a deep murmur in his chest. "Mmmn?"

Her lips found the flat nipple concealed in the covering of heavy fur on his chest, and she kissed its tiny point. "If there is more . . . than what we've just done . . . I don't want to know."

He began to spread long skeins of her hair across his chest and neck. "Why not?"

"Truly, I couldn't bear it."

Murmuring something about her being darling and foolish, Max brought her head to his and kissed her.

It did not seem too much to ask that the family be granted some peace for a while, but apparently that was not possible. The trouble was started unintentionally by Philippe, on his way to a fencing lesson. Justin was supposed to go with him, but as usual, Justin had decided to spend his time with Madeleine Scipion instead. For weeks the girl had displayed interest in not only Justin, but Philippe as well, until the two had tired of arguing over her. Now Justin was the only boy she gave her favors to.

As Philippe dismounted his horse and walked to the establishment of the fencing master Navarre, he was only half-aware of the sound of voices nearby. As usual, his blue eyes were fixed on the ground, his thoughts far removed from the practical day-to-day routine of living. As Justin so often mockingly pointed out, Philippe was a dreamer, not a realist.

Suddenly Philippe was jolted out of his imaginings when a hard shoulder slammed into his, knocking him off-balance. Staggering back a few steps, he looked up in bewilderment. He faced a group of three boys who had just finished their fencing session with Navarre. Excited by their exertions, filled with vigor, they were clearly spoiling for a fight. The bump had been no accident. The leader of the group, Louis Picotte, had clashed with Justin before—it was well-known that they hated each other.

Philippe, however, had no quarrel with anyone, and he preferred to keep it that way. He apologized instantly, something his brother would never have done. *"Pardonnez-moi*—I was not looking."

"It *would* be a Vallerand, of course," Louis sneered. He was a large, husky boy, with the same white-blond hair that characterized the rest of his family. "They think they own every street in town."

Philippe felt his heart sink. "I am late," he muttered, taking a few steps away, but the three blocked his path.

"Your apology wasn't good enough," Louis said, a smirk appearing on his lips.

Philippe raised troubled blue eyes to his. Although not physically weak or of small stature, Philippe was innately gentle and civilized, the kind of young man who Louis instinctively resented. "I'm sorry," he said in a low voice, "for bumping into you. Now let me pass."

For a moment all was quiet. Then Louis' brows gathered together, and he pointed to the ground, smiling thinly. "Get on your knees and say it."

Philippe flushed, wanting to turn and run, knowing that if he did, everyone in New Orleans would know. And then Louis would torment him forever. Looking from one face to another, Philippe saw nothing but hatred, the kind of hatred he and Justin had come to expect after years of being known as the sons of Max Vallerand.

"I won't," he said, staring hard at Louis.

"Then we'll take the matter somewhere private," Louis said, jerking his thumb in the direction of a small lot where hasty duels were sometimes conducted. It was concealed by trees and buildings, and they would not be seen by passers-by. His hand settled on the hilt of the sword at his waist.

Startled, Philippe realized the boy wanted something more than mere fisticuffs. Philippe had resigned himself to being bruised and beaten. After all, Justin had survived it often enough. But swords—it was too dangerous. "No," he said, and nodded in the direction of the fencing master's place. "We'll settle it there. The master often watches such bouts and makes certain no one is—"

"What? Are you afraid?" Louis demanded.

"No, I just-"

"You are. It's what everyone says. You're a coward. If I were you, I wouldn't be so proud of your dirty Vallerand name." Louis spat on the ground. "Your father is a murderer, your brother is a blustering bully . . . and you, a little coward."

Philippe quivered with rage.

"Ah, look at him tremble," Louis jeered. "Look at him—" Suddenly he stopped, wincing as he felt a tiny, sharp blow to the back of his head. He clasped the sore spot and swung around. "What—" Another thud, this time on his chest. Louis stared in disbelief at the sight of Justin, who was lounging behind them and calmly aiming pebbles at him. Justin intently examined a small stone pinched between his thumb and forefinger. "What is it I heard him say, Philippe?"

Philippe gulped with relief and apprehension. "Nothing. Justin, we're late for—"

"I thought I heard him call you a coward." Justin dropped the stone to the ground and selected another from the handful he held. "We know that isn't true. And I also thought I heard him say I was a bully. Well, we *certainly* know that isn't true, don't we?'

"Don't forget," Louis sneered, "I also said your father was a murderer."

Abruptly the handful of pebbles was released to scatter at Louis' feet. Justin smiled vengefully, his blue eyes so dark they were almost black. "Philippe, give me your sword."

"No," Philippe said under his breath, and strode rapidly to his brother. "Justin, not with swords." They understood each other's thoughts clearly. "It should be me," Philippe half-whispered.

"He doesn't want to fight you," Justin said. "He went after you in order to get me."

"Not with swords," Philippe repeated desperately.

Louis called to them tauntingly. "Are you going to let your brother make a coward of you, too, Justin?"

Justin drew in his breath angrily. His eyes met Philippe's, and he vowed, "I'll cut him to pieces before he has time to blink!"

"He's practiced today, and you haven't—"

Louis interrupted them impatiently. "Let's get on with it, Justin."

"Philippe," Justin growled, "give the damn thing to me!"

"Not unless you promise to stop at first blood."

"I can't—"

"Promise!"

They glared at each other, and then Justin nodded.
"Damn you, all right." He reached out his hand. Turning
white, Philippe gave him the sword.

The small group made its way to the lot. By tacit consent, they were furtive and quiet, knowing the duel would
be forbidden if anyone else learned of it. Boys their age
did not usually settle their differences in such a manner—
not for a year or two would it be appropriate. They were
at a dangerous time, just on the verge of adulthood, lacking the maturity to distinguish between games and reality.
Their youthful passions were easily stirred, and they
wanted to test themselves.

Keeping to the rules they had learned at Navarre's,
seconds were appointed. Louis removed his coat slowly,
glancing over his shoulder at the twins. Philippe was
standing with his fists clenched, his tense posture revealing his anxiety. Justin was waiting with unnatural
patience.

Louis almost began to regret challenging the Vallerands. Philippe's gaze had been mild and frightened, but
Justin's devilish blue eyes promised far more to contend
with. Justin's swordsmanship was also quite good, Louis
reflected, almost equal to his own. He had watched Justin
practice at Navarre's, and as the fencing master said, Justin would be superb but for a lack of discipline. Walking
forward until they were separated by only a few feet, Louis
assumed the proper stance.

The group was quiet as they saluted each other and began the match with a click of steel against steel. They tried
a few elementary combinations, each searching out what
he needed to know in order to best his opponent. Double
feint, lunge, parry followed by a quick riposte. Both
moved with fine coordination and equal skill. One of
Louis' companions couldn't help murmuring to the other
that he wished Navarre could see this. It was an effort-
lessly smooth exchange.

Then the contest began in earnest, and the balance tipped. Louis sweated profusely as he fought to keep his concentration. Either Justin was having a freakish spell of good fortune, or he had kept his skill hidden from all of them, even Navarre. His style was wonderfully clean and light, and he was far more agile than anyone could have guessed. In fact, as the match progressed, he seemed to be flippant, as if Louis provided little challenge to him.

Philippe was the only one who was not surprised, but his anxiety did not abate. He alone understood the reckless edge that made his brother so proficient. Justin did not care what happened, and the more time went by, the less anything mattered to him. He was not afraid of pain or solitude, perhaps not even of dying . . . and that frightened Philippe.

Louis jerked back in surprise as he felt the point of Justin's sword touch his shoulder. In disbelief he looked down at the dot of blood on his shirt. Exclamations broke from the boys, and Philippe rushed over to Louis' second.

"Honor is satisfied," Philippe said breathlessly, wiping at the sweat doted on his forehead.

Louis felt sick with humiliation. He saw Justin through a haze of fury, rebelling at the thought that such a minor mistake, one tiny opening of his guard, had led to defeat. His friends would snicker. Even more enraging was Justin's surprising quietness. He would have expected Vallerand to gloat. Instead Justin wore a serious expression as he watched the seconds confer . . . and for some reason, that seemed more contemptuous to Louis than open ridicule.

"It's over," Philippe said, making no effort to suppress the gladness in his voice. He smiled slightly as he saw the relief in Justin's eyes.

"It's *not* over!" Louis snarled, but they paid him no attention.

Justin started toward Philippe, intending to give back

the sword, then stopped as he saw the flash of horror on his brother's face.

"No!" was all Philippe had time to cry before Justin turned swiftly and saw Louis lunging at him.

Startled, Justin felt something pierce his side, looked down and saw the thin blade of steel withdraw. There was a glow of pain. Awkwardly he fell to his knees, staring dumbly at the blossoming stain on his shirt. He pressed his hand to his wet side and collapsed to the ground as his head swam with dizziness. Breathing hard, he caught the scent of his own blood, and he clutched harder at his waist.

"Oh, Justin," Philippe gasped, falling beside him. "Oh, Justin."

Louis was slow to realize what he had done. His friends were staring at him with amazement, and something like disgust. "I didn't mean to . . ." Louis said, and his voice trailed off into ashamed silence. He had done something too dishonorable, too unmanly, for words. Backing away, he turned and fled.

Justin stirred at the sound of Philippe's anxious entreaties, and his dazed blue eyes opened. He turned his face away from the cool grass and looked up at his brother, managing to find his old tone of annoyance. "It's only . . . a scratch."

Philippe gave a choking laugh. "You're *bleeding,* Justin."

"Where is Louis . . . sneaky, goddamned, cowardly bastard, I'll—"

"He's gone," Philippe said, some of his initial fright dissolving. "I think he was as surprised as the rest of us."

Justin struggled clumsily to get up. "Surprised? I'll kill him! I'll—" He broke off and gasped, his side aching. Under his fingers there was a new surge of warm wetness.

"Stop!" Philippe cried, catching him behind the shoulders. "The blood . . . we need a doctor . . . I'll leave you for just a minute and—"

"If you leave me," Justin said with difficulty, "I . . . won't be here when you come back."

"Just-"

"I'm going home, where father will probably finish me off."

"But—"

"Get me home," Justin whispered with an intensity that silenced him.

Philippe tried to staunch the flow of blood with the pressure of his hand, causing a new round of curses from his brother. He did not notice the two other boys standing above them until one of them handed down his wadded-up vest. "Thank you," Philippe said breathlessly, taking the garment and pushing it inside Justin's shirt, over the wound.

"Louis shouldn't have done it," the donator of the vest commented. "I'll never act as his second again."

"There shouldn't have been a duel in the first place!" Philippe said angrily. There was no sound from Justin, who had closed his eyes. His bloody hands were palms-up on the ground.

The boy regarded Justin's long, sprawled-out form admiringly. "He's got courage."

"And the brains of an ox," Philippe muttered.

"He'll win a lot of duels before he's through."

"He'll die before he's twenty," Philippe said under his breath.

Justin's eyes flickered open. They were dark and luminously violet, devoid of their usual snapping energy. Painstakingly he reached up to grasp Philippe's collar, smearing it with blood. "Let's go."

Philippe did not bother to ask how Justin had gotten to town. One of Louis' friends brought Philippe's apple-gray horse, and the three of them pushed and shoved Justin into the saddle. Philippe swung up behind him, checking to make certain Justin was holding the pad over his wound.

"I've got it," Justin said hoarsely, drooping low over the horse's neck. "Go . . . before I fall off."

The ride home was torturous, Philippe suffering every bit as much as Justin. He was terrified that Justin would die.

"Why did you want to fight Louis?" Philippe murmured in bewilderment when they were halfway home. "Do you hate him that much?"

Now that the bleeding had stopped, Justin was feeling more clear-headed. "Little to do with him," he said, his voice weak. "I just wanted to fight. It feels better . . . so much better."

"Better than what?"

"Than not fighting."

"You make no sense. Why does it feel good to hurt another person?"

"When I fight, it's not against a person . . . it's against something else, something . . ."

"Something inside you," Philippe said quietly. It was the essential difference between him and his brother. "Something inside you that wants to destroy yourself," he continued in that same quiet way, "and everyone around you. You won't rest until you've torn the family apart and brought misery to us all."

"No—"

"Until we're all dragged down with you."

"You hate me," Justin said groggily.

"No, I don't hate you. I won't give you the satisfaction of hating you."

Justin knew that Philippe said more to him, but suddenly words became indistinguishable sounds to him, and he felt his eyes begin to roll back in his head. He drifted in and out of a strange dream. They were at the house and hands were reaching up to him, and then he was falling into a deep purple sea, being carried away on the crest of a rising wave. His head ached, his side hurt. He was a little boy again, and his father was holding him. Gently he was lowered to his bed, his head dropping to the pillow, and he rested for what seemed to be hours until he was awakened by a startling sense of aloneness.

"Mon père," he whispered, moving his hand restlessly until it was enfolded in a large, strong one. The vital force of that grasp seemed to bring him back to his senses. He saw his father's tense face, and knew he was angry . . . but at the same time, there was a bewildering tenderness in those golden eyes. His father did not let go of him, not even in the presence of the doctor, and Justin made no move to separate their hands.

Justin writhed in pain as the wound was being cleaned, but he kept silent, sweat dripping off his face. It felt as if a burning poker were twisting in his side. "Aren't you finished yet?" he croaked indignantly when he could stand no more. Maximilien soothed him with a low murmur while the doctor finished. They gave Justin a foul-tasting medicine after he was bandaged, and he insisted on taking the glass in his own hand. His father slid an arm behind his neck and lifted his head up, helping him to drink. Justin found it utterly humiliating.

"I'd rather . . . you shouted and . . . gave me hell," he coughed when the last of the bitter liquid was gone. "Kindness from you is too . . . strange."

"Hell will arrive tomorrow," Max said, rearranging the covers over him. "Right now I'm relieved that you're all right."

"All right?" Justin repeated, making a face.

"It's not a serious wound," Max said, pushing the wet locks of hair off Justin's pale forehead.

"You wouldn't say that . . . if it were yours."

Max smiled. "You'll recover soon enough to hear my opinion of your dueling."

"N–never . . ." Justin yawned widely, the medicine beginning to take effect. His eyes flew open as he felt Max's weight shift. "Are you leaving?"

"No, *mon fils.*"

"Leave if you want," Justin muttered, almost too softly to hear.

"Not yet," came the quiet reply, and the boy relaxed. He reached out for Max's hand once more, and fell asleep holding it.

Chapter 12

❦

"**H**ow is he?" Alexandre asked, starting to pour Max a drink. Max gestured for him to put the bottle down.

"He'll be fine." Max had just come from upstairs, where Justin was sleeping comfortably. Lysette and Noeline were busy helping the distraught Irénée into bed, giving her liberal doses of brandy-laced coffee. "The wound isn't bad, but he is in a state of shock." Max paused and added grimly, "As am I."

"This was a *surprise* to you?" Bernard asked. "I am only surprised it hasn't happened before now."

Alexandre joined in. "Following in his father's footsteps, isn't he?"

Max stared at them both coldly.

"Well, it is true," Bernard said. "Max, you know what the boy is like. You cannot say you weren't expecting this. And you are a fool if you don't expect it again."

A sharp reply was poised on Max's lips, but Lysette's soft voice interrupted him.

"Max," she said, coming into the room and taking his arm, "I do not wish to deprive you of such brotherly compassion and sympathy, but Berté has warmed over some food for our supper. Come, have something to eat."

"I'm not hungry—"

"Just a little something, *bien-aimé,*" she entreated, winsome and coaxing.

With a low grumble, Max turned with her to the doorway. Lysette looked back over her shoulder and gave the brothers a quick, shaming glance before serenely accompanying her husband out of the room. The glare was such a contrast to the sweet expression she had used with Max that Alexandre couldn't help chuckling.

"In her own soft little way," he commented, "she's rather a despot."

"It is not amusing," Bernard said.

"Why not? She is obviously good for Max."

"I wouldn't say so." Bernard took a long drink, staring at the empty doorway. "In fact, I would say she is rather dangerous for him."

"Your reasoning escapes me."

"All the things she is trying to uncover—all the times she has made him face the past, when it is better left alone. Her damned curiosity about Corinne . . . it is all leading to trouble."

Alexandre tilted his head thoughtfully. "You don't like her, do you?"

Bernard's voice was inflectionless. "No, I don't. I don't like the way she stirs up old memories, the effect she has on Max, or on Etienne Sag—" He stopped, but it was too late.

Alex was looking at him with surprise. "Etienne Sagesse? What in the devil's name does he have to do with this?"

"Leave it be," Bernard said sharply.

"God knows she won't have an affair with him, as Corinne did. That can't be what you're worried about."

"I said," Bernard growled, "leave it be."

"It was my fault," Philippe said.

"The hell it was," Justin retorted, and opened his mouth as Lysette lifted the spoon to his lips. She had insisted on feeding him, although Justin could have done it himself. Since Lysette had indulged her invalid mother for so long, it was in her nature to coddle someone who was sick. While Justin had made a half-hearted protest at first, he had quickly become accustomed to it, even snickeringly referring to her as *Maman*.

"Tell me what happened," Max said from the side of the bed, where he sat in a French mahogany chair with a curved back.

As always, Philippe chose his words carefully. "I was having a . . . confrontation with three boys, one of whom wished to provoke me into a duel. I refused, and that was when Justin appeared, and . . ."

"And eagerly picked up the gauntlet," Max said with stinging softness.

Justin's eyes met Lysette's, and he waved away the bowl of soup. "They called him a coward, father," he said without looking at Max.

"And that was reason enough?"

"No, they called me a bully, and you . . ."

"And me what?"

A wave of scarlet crept over Justin's neck and ears. "The same thing," he said, "that you've always been called."

"And what is that?"

"Why ask? You already know!"

"I want to hear you say it."

Justin dragged his hands through his hair several times, looking around the room, as agitated as a caged animal.

"Say it," Max pressed, pinning his son in place with his steady gaze. "For once we're going to face it."

Lysette and Philippe might not have even been in the room. The tension gathered until none of the four of them dared to move or breathe.

"They called you a murderer," Justin half-whispered, and suddenly let out an explosive breath. "It's what they've always said. Everyone. And you find it necessary to ask why I fight? How else am I supposed to . . . I fight for

Philippe and me both! That's the only reason we've survived being your sons. I've never known what it is to have a friend. Neither has Philippe.'' He turned his head to glare at his brother. ''Tell him! In their eyes we're doubly guilty. It isn't as if we're any *common* murderer's sons—we're Vallerands, and that makes them damn eager to spill our blood!''

Max moved to the bed and took Justin gently by the shoulders. ''Listen to me, Justin. I understand everything—''

''No—''

''By God, don't interrupt me! You'll never be able to change what they say. You'll never be able to stop them. The rumors will go on, and you can't crush them, you can't silence them. You can even kill a man, Justin, dozens of them, but the past will not change, and you'll still be my son. Curse that fact if you wish, but you can't change it.''

''What *is* the past?'' Justin demanded, tears suddenly falling down his tanned cheeks. ''What happened? Why can't you say if you did it or not? Why can't you tell me the truth?''

The words hung in the air, while all of them stared at Max.

''There isn't much to tell,'' Max said. ''I married your mother because I loved her. My feelings changed a few years after you were born, when I realized Corinne was having an affair with another man.''

''Who?'' Justin demanded.

''That doesn't matter—''

''Damn you, tell me! Was it Etienne Sagesse?''

Max nodded slowly.

''Why?'' Philippe asked from several feet away. ''Why would she do that?''

''I believe she thought she was in love with him,'' Max said with outward calm. Only Lysette knew of the effort it took for him to speak of the past. ''I was not able to make Corinne happy. That, in part, drove her to someone else.''

"There is no need to make excuses for her," Justin said. "I'm glad she's dead."

"No, Justin. Pity her, but don't hate her."

"Did Etienne Sagesse kill her?" the boy demanded.

"No."

Justin's chin began to tremble. "Then you did?" he asked, his voice cracking.

Max seemed to find it difficult to speak. "No. I found her, already dead."

"Then who . . . ?"

"I don't know."

A mixture of anger and disbelief crossed Justin's face. "But you have to! You *must* know."

"I wish I did," Max said. "I wish I could have found out what happened. And most of all, I wish you had not grown up in the shadow of all this."

Justin closed his eyes and leaned his head back against the pillow. "Can't you tell me any more? Isn't there anyone you suspected? Isn't there anyone who might have wanted her dead?"

"Years ago I talked to Etienne Sagesse, thinking he might be able to reveal something."

"And?"

"He believes I killed Corinne out of jealousy."

"You should have finished him off in that duel," Justin muttered.

"Look at me." Max waited until Justin's eyes opened. "You must choose your fights carefully, my headstrong son. I would rather you be branded a coward than have you jump every time some little bantam throws a challenge at your feet. The more fearsome your reputation, the more others will try to provoke you—and the more you use your sword, the more you'll *have* to. I don't want that for you, or your brother."

"Father?" Justin asked huskily. "How can I be certain you didn't kill her?"

Philippe strode to the bed in fury. "Justin, how can you *ask* that?"

Max did not appear to be angry. "You can choose to believe what I've told you . . . or not to believe it. Either way, my feelings for you will not change. You are both my sons, and I want your safety and happiness above all else."

Justin swallowed hard and lifted himself away from the pillows, leaning toward him. Max put his arms around him carefully, ruffling Justin's hair, murmuring something the others could not quite hear. Lysette noticed Philippe taking a halting step forward, then stopping as he realized the moment belonged to Justin and his father. How unselfish Philippe was, she thought, and reached out to take his hand, her fingers curling around his broad palm. The boy looked down at her, his frown disappearing as they exchanged an understanding smile.

Having accomplished all that he intended in New Orleans, Aaron Burr headed back to St. Louis to plot with General Wilkinson. His journey began overland toward Natchez, on horses furnished by Daniel Clark, the most influential and well-established merchant in the territory. Burr's trip westward had been tremendously successful. By his reckoning, it would not be difficult at all to lead the populace against the Spaniards in order to secure West Florida and Mexico.

Burr was certain he had blinded the Spanish officials, especially Yrujo, as to his true intentions, and had successfully reassured them he had no designs on their lands. In less than a year, Burr reasoned, he would be able to launch an expedition and bring all his ambitions to fruition. And those who had tried to impede his plans—Maximilien Vallerand, for example—would beg to be in his favor.

* * *

The messenger departed from the residence of Don Carlos Martinez de Yrujo early in the morning. As he headed southward out of the city at a circumspect pace, he was forced to rein in his horse suddenly. Two men on horseback, armed with pistols, were blocking his way. Turning pale with fright, the messenger began to splutter in Spanish. Certain they meant to rob him, he protested that he had no money, nothing to offer them. One of them, a darkhaired man with the yellow eyes of a wolf, gestured for him to dismount.

"Give me the letters you're carrying," the dark-haired man said, his Spanish rough but serviceable.

"N–no puedo," the messenger stammered, shaking his head emphatically. "They are private, highly confidential . . . I–I have staked my life on delivering them without—"

"Your life," came the gentle reply, "is precisely what is at stake. Hand over the letters if you wish to preserve it."

Fumbling in the inside of his coat, the messenger withdrew a half-dozen letters, all bearing the official seal used by Yrujo. He wiped his sweating brow with his sleeve as the man leafed through them. One of them seemed to catch the man's interest, and he kept it while handing the others back.

Max looked at Jacques Clement with an ironic halfsmile. "Addressed to Casa Calvo," he said in French. "A Spanish boundary commissioner who has unaccountably lingered in New Orleans."

"Perhaps he likes it here," Clement remarked diffidently.

Max opened the letter, ignoring the faint cry of protest from the messenger. He scanned the contents, his smile fading quickly, then looked at Clement. The golden eyes gleamed with satisfaction. "I love the way the Spanish officials have of wishing a friend a fond farewell, and then—ever so politely—knifing him in the back."

Not understanding their conversation, the messenger watched them anxiously, then dared to interrupt. "Señor, I cannot deliver the letter with a broken seal! What am I to do? What—"

"You're not going to deliver the letter," Max replied, "because I am going to keep it."

A stream of volatile Spanish greeted this statement. It was too fast for Max to follow, but the man's unhappiness was clear.

"He'll probably be imprisoned when they find out," Jacques commented. "They won't excuse him for letting the letter be stolen."

Max tossed a small bag to the messenger, who paused in his barrage long enough to catch it. It landed with a heavy clink in his palm. "That's enough to allow you to disappear. And live in comfort for a long time."

Another mystifyingly fast speech followed. Max glanced questioningly at Jacques. "Are you understanding any of it?"

"Only *esposa* and *hijos.*"

Recognizing the words for *wife* and *children,* Max smiled wryly. "Give him what you have," he told Jacques. "I'll reimburse you later." He tucked the letter in his own coat. *"This* is worth a small fortune."

Max enjoyed Claiborne's astounded expression as he read and reread the letter. "Are the Spaniards aware that we have this?" Claiborne finally asked.

Max shrugged. "It doesn't matter. It won't change their plans."

"This is quite a piece of news," Claiborne said slowly. "Not only do they not trust Burr, they're starting a backlash against him. If this letter is accurate, they'll discredit him completely!" He looked back over the letter. "And the clever bastards are using an American to do it! Have you met Stephen Minor before?''

"Briefly.''

"Did you know before you read the letter that he was in the Spanish pay?''

"No.'' Max smiled casually. "But I can't be expected to keep track of *all* the Americans in the Spanish pay.''

"Insolent Creole,'' Claiborne retorted, nearly beaming at him. "Are you implying that Americans are easily bought?''

"It does rather seem that way, sir.''

Claiborne contained his jubilation and assumed a more statesmanlike expression. "For now all we need do is wait. According to this, Minor will spread rumors throughout the territory that Burr is planning to separate the west from the rest of the nation, unite it with Spanish possessions, and claim it as his own empire. That should set the country ablaze all the way up to the northeast!''

"The rumors should reach St. Louis at the same time Burr does,'' Max agreed.

"I would give a fortune to see General Wilkinson's face. It shouldn't take long for him to disassociate himself from Burr completely.''

Max stood up and extended his hand. "I must be leaving now, sir. If you require me for anything else . . .''

"Yes, yes.'' Claiborne stood up and shook his hand, gripping it more warmly than usual. "Vallerand, you have proved your loyalty this day.''

Max arched a brow. "Was it in question?''

"I did wonder what you may have omitted when you described your meeting with Burr,'' Claiborne admitted. "He is a persuasive man. You might have shared part of his glory by siding with him.''

"I have no desire for glory. Only to keep what is mine,'' Max said seriously. "Good day, your excellency.''

* * *

In an unexpected move, Max appointed Justin in charge
of having the old overseer's house torn down. Lysette was
jubilant at the news, understanding the significance of
Max's decision. The past was losing its terrible hold over
him. He was beginning to discard some of the bitterness
he had nursed for so long. It was a wise choice to allow
Justin to supervise the project. The boy took great pride
in the new responsibility, and it also gave him the opportunity to face his own demons. The twins had also been
victims of the past, and they had been hurt just as much
as Max, perhaps even more.

Philippe, who wanted nothing to do with the project,
applied himself to his studies, perfectly happy in his world
of books. Justin, however, lent his own back to the task,
working alongside a few carefully chosen slaves to pull the
place to the ground. At the end of each day he came home
exhausted and begrimed, but unusually peaceful.

Lysette also had much work to do, but it was of a different sort. It was a challenge to make a place for herself
in the family and community. For one thing, there were
the inevitable points of contention between a daughter and
mother-in-law. Lysette and Irénée disagreed frequently
over the old Creole ways and the changing attitudes of
their small society. Irénée had never been so horrified as
she was the first time Lysette invited some of the young
American matrons of New Orleans to visit the plantation.

"But they are very nice, well-bred women," Lysette
had insisted gently.

"They are *American* women! What will all of my friends
think when they hear of this?"

"Americans are part of New Orleans now, just as much
as Creoles. We attend many of the same gatherings. We
share many of the same concerns."

Irénée stared at her, scandalized. "Next you will be
saying it is acceptable for Creoles and Americans to inter-
marry!"

"Oh, never that," Lysette said dryly.

Irénée's eyes narrowed in suspicion. "Does Maximilien know about this?" she inquired craftily.

Lysette smiled, knowing the older woman was planning to go to Max behind her back. "He approves of it whole-heartedly, Maman."

Irénée sighed in disgust, silently vowing to speak to her son about the matter that very night.

But Max paid little attention to Irénée's complaints, saying he did not see what harm would befall them if Lysette had friendships with a few American women. That was when Irénée began to realize how things had changed. She would no longer be able to influence Max as she once had. He would never take anyone's part against Lysette.

The single-minded interest Max had once shown in his work was now directed toward his wife. Irénée had mixed feelings about that. On one hand, she was happy that Max was finally expressing some of the thoughts and memories he had kept to himself for so long. On the other hand, Irénée could not help resenting the fact that he entrusted these private thoughts only to Lysette. The girl was beginning to know him better than those who had lived with him for years. Lysette seemed to understand him more than his own brothers did . . . or his own mother!

Irénée was also disturbed by the way Max treated Lysette, indulging her every whim, teasing her when he considered her airs too prim or restrained, encouraging her tempers and moments of high dudgeon. It apalled Irénée to see this gentle, soft-mannered girl being turned into a sharp-tongued vixen. Only Max could have taken that sweet-natured creature and done this to her!

Finally Irénée tried to put things aright.

"If Lysette were a child," she said to Max in private, "I would say she was being spoiled. You are encouraging her to think she can have anything she wants."

Max gave her a purely angelic smile, the smile of a man with nothing troubling his conscience. "But she can."

"Lysette is now in the habit of contradicting anyone she

does not agree with. This very morning she was trying to force her opinions on poor Bernard, telling him he should work more and drink less!''

That provoked a laugh from Max. ''In that case I'm afraid she was repeating *my* opinion, Maman. And you know you agree with her. Bernard is becoming a philandering drunkard.''

''That is beside the point! We are discussing Lysette. You are undoing all the good manners her parents instilled in her, unraveling her values, teaching her rudeness and assertiveness. Oh, when I think of the quiet, refined girl who first came to us, and how she has changed—''

''Enough,'' Max said, his amusement vanishing. ''I know your intentions are kind, as always. But Lysette is no more capable of rudeness than you are . . . and as for assertiveness, she has need of more, much more, before I'll be satisfied. You call what her parents taught her good manners? Gaspard taught her to be afraid of men. Her mother taught her that a woman should take refuge in pretend illnesses rather than defend herself against someone else's browbeating. Lysette should be terrified of me, yet somehow she has the instinct not to be. I don't deserve such a gift. God knows I won't be fool enough to throw it away. Lysette has a great deal of inborn courage, and spirit, and I'll be damned if I ask her to pander to the rules of our . . . ,'' he paused and added with a bitter smile, ''quaint little society.''

''Indeed! You forget, Maximilien, that your family and friends are all part of this so-called quaint society!''

''A society that deemed me an outcast ten years ago.''

''You cannot blame—''

''No, I don't blame anyone, not anymore. But I've been exiled for too long, Maman. The shadow I cast falls on everyone I care for, including Lysette. Especially Lysette.''

''This is nonsense!'' Irénée exclaimed. ''Outcast?

Exiled? You know this is not true. You have many friends—''

"Business partners," Max corrected dryly. "Jacques Clement is the only man in New Orleans who calls himself my friend for reasons other than financial profit. You yourself, Maman, have seen the way people cross the street to avoid acknowledging me."

"People still pay calls—"

"To you, Maman . . . not to me."

"You are invited to social gatherings—''

"Yes, by out-of-pocket relatives with an eye on my money, or by those who feel they owe it to the memory of my father. When I attend such gatherings, I'm surrounded by stifled conversations and frozen smiles. You know that if I were anyone but a Vallerand, I would have been forced to leave New Orleans long ago. The gossip lingers like some slow-acting poison. And now . . . now they have my beautiful young wife to stare at in hopes of discovering some sign of abuse. If she appears to be happy, they'll wonder what perverse aspect of her nature allows her to enjoy living with such a cruel, cold-natured husband—''

"Max, be silent! I cannot bear such talk!"

He was quiet for a moment, but Irénée did not recognize in his silence the dread that knifed through his heart whenever he pondered this subject. It was his greatest fear that Lysette might be driven away from him. The hatred and suspicions of others, formerly directed only at him, might be turned against her, his wife. It would be difficult for her to make and keep friends, and there were slights in store for her simply because she was married to him. What if she wasn't strong enough to bear it? What if her love crumbled under the strain and she began to resent him? "In the years to come," he said, "Lysette will need a lion's share of assertiveness. You know what she'll face. She's been too sheltered. It will be difficult for her."

"Max, I think you overestimate the difficulty—''

"If anything, I'm underestimating it. As for the affected manners she was taught by her well-meaning Tante Delphine, I hope she'll rid herself of every last one of them."

Irénée was not paying attention. In a dispute, it was her way never to listen, only to keep repeating her point until the other party agreed out of exhaustion. "You must put a stop to Lysette's unruliness now, or she will soon become unmanageable," she said. "Don't you remember how it was with Corinne?"

Max lost his temper immediately, responding with such a scathing speech that Irénée did not speak to him for days. Eventually, the family learned never to criticize Lysette, unless they wished to face his certain wrath. He did, however, set a few limits unknown to Irénée or anyone else. Max had his own ways of dealing with Lysette when she dared to push him too far.

Utterly frustrated by Max's behavior at one of the Vallerand's Sunday evening *soirées,* Lysette took it upon herself to upbraid him in private. Max had been rude to a guest one of his cousins had brought, a visitor whose political views differed sharply from his own.

Lysette had been mortified by Max's cutting remarks and cold silences toward the man. Max had made the evening uncomfortable for everyone. Usually at soirées there would be music, conversation, and a little dancing, followed by refreshments at eleven o'clock, with the gathering dispersing around midnight. This one ended at ten, before the refreshments were even brought out.

Determined to wring an apology from Max, Lysette approached him in the library, where he had gone with Bernard for a drink. Before she could say a word, Max turned and faced her without surprise. His mouth twisted at the corner. "Have a care," he warned quietly. "I'm in a humorless mood tonight."

"There was no need to be so unpleasant to Monsieur Gregoire just because of one little remark he made about the governor," Lysette said in annoyance. "I've heard you yourself say much worse about Claiborne!"

Bernard looked at them both uncomfortably and set his drink down. "I'm exhausted," he said. "Goodnight."

Neither of them noticed his departure.

Max sipped his drink and crossed his legs comfortably. "When I criticize Claiborne, at least I know what I'm talking about." He shrugged. "Gregoire is an idiot."

"Whether he is or not, the conversation was quite pleasant before you interrupted."

"He had mistaken ideas about Claiborne," Max replied unrepentantly. "It was necessary to correct him."

"Was it necessary to embarrass your mother and all the other ladies present by arguing with him? About a subject as vulgar as politics? I expected your mother to faint!"

"Did you expect me to ignore his digs about my political position?"

"It's not that I'm asking you to be charming, Max. *Civil* would be enough. Whenever we're among others, I'm in constant fear of what to expect from you. You not only insult Creoles, Americans, and Spaniards, you also go out of your way to offend your own relatives!"

"But I offend everyone equally, sweet. That is the democratic way."

"I don't care if you're democratic, I just want you to be nice to people!"

Max's eyes glinted dangerously. He set his drink down, stood, and paced around the library with a measured tread. "This discussion is becoming far too familiar, madame."

"So is the reason for it," Lysette challenged, putting her hands on her hips, finally satisfied that she had provoked him.

Max smiled darkly and closed the library door, so distinctly that it vibrated in the doorjamb. Lysette started in surprise, wondering if he were really angry.

"Max," she said, switching to a placating tone, "will

you at least promise to *try* to be a little more accommodating?''

''You'd like that, wouldn't you?'' He advanced on her slowly, and her eyes widened. ''You'd like everyone to believe you'd managed to tame my abominable temper.''

She shook her head uncertainly. ''No, I merely—''

''You think if I don sheeps' clothing, people might develop some kind of liking for me. I don't want that. I've *never* wanted that.''

''I didn't mean—''

''You think you can reprimand me for my manners, like a mother with her disobedient boy.''

Beginning to feel a twinge of real alarm, Lysette shook her head. What had happened to set his temper off? Quickly she began to calculate how to calm him down. ''Max, it was not anything close to a reprimand. *Mon Dieu,* I am just trying to *help* you.''

''You're trying to change me,'' he growled.

''Change? I would never try to—''

''Into a quiet, domesticated husband who would jump to do your bidding.''

Her mouth sagged open. She did not know whether to laugh or protest her innocence. ''Max, you're not being serious, are you?'' She gasped as he reached out and jerked her hips to his, holding her against the hard bulge of his manhood.

''I'll show you how serious I am.'' He forced her head back with a scorching kiss, increasing the pressure until her mouth opened to admit his searching tongue. His breath rushed against her cheek in a harsh exhalation. He lifted her higher and tighter against his hips, beginning a deep, rhythmic nudging. Caught fast against the warm, thrusting movement, Lysette could not stop a moan from rising in her throat. He smothered the sound and pulled up great handfuls of her skirt, intent on reaching her concealed body.

Lysette was breathing fast when he found the edge of

her pantaloons and slid his hand inside the dainty garment.
"Max," she said weakly, "it isn't that I—"

He interrupted her with another hungering kiss and
pulled her down to the aubusson rug on the floor.

"Here?" she whispered in a daze, her mind registering
confused impressions of the library ceiling, the excitement
in Max's tawny eyes, the startling sound of her pantaloons
ripping.

"Yes, here," came his guttural reply, and he spread her
knees wide as he lowered his body into her feverish, welcoming embrace. "You don't want me to change . . . do
you?"

"No," she cried, quivering as she felt him sliding into
her, gently grinding, filling her with his warmth and hardness.

He braced his feet and pushed deeper, whispering
against her flushed cheek. "Tell me."

"I love you . . . as you are . . . oh, Max . . ."

"No more lectures?"

"No, never . . . please . . . don't stop," she moaned,
suddenly afraid he had decided to torment her.

The faintest of smiles touched his lips. "I won't stop,"
he murmured caressingly, and drove harder, skillfully
drawing her to the brink of excruciating pleasure, letting
her wait for a heart-stopping second, then releasing her in
a flood of rapture. He sealed his mouth over hers, muffling
her helpless cries, riding the urgent movements of her hips
until she relaxed beneath him. The sweet, grasping softness of her body was too much for him, and he reached
his own satisfaction quickly, his final lunges pushing her
a few inches across the carpet.

Languidly she draped her arms over his back and caressed the nape of his neck, while her tongue flirted with
his, inviting more of the love play. Her entire body was
suffused with a tingling glow, as if she had just emerged
from a too-hot bath.

With disconcerting abruptness, Max pressed a short,

husbandly kiss on her forehead and began to rearrange
their clothes.

"Max," she protested, reluctant for the intimacy to end.

He did not reply, only finished buttoning his breeches,
then pulled down her skirt.

"Max, don't you want to—"

"I have work to do," he said, pulling her up from the
floor and brushing another impersonal kiss on her cheek.
Flustered and inexplicably shy, Lysette could not meet his
eyes. "But it is late," she said gruffly. Damn him, he
knew what she wanted!

"I'll be upstairs soon."

She fought against the childish urge to pout. "But
you—"

"Lysette," he said lazily, sliding his fingers under her
chin, "are you going to argue with me?" He forced her
to look up at him.

His expression was stern, but his eyes were filled with
a smoldering light that left her breathless. Lysette felt her
cheeks redden. "No," she heard herself whisper.

"Then go upstairs and wait for me."

She nodded hastily and turned to the door. Before leaving the room, a twinge of pride made her pause and say
with an effort at composure, "I will probably be asleep
when you come to bed."

Max smiled slightly. They both knew full well she would
not be asleep. "All right, *petite.*"

Lysette closed the door behind her and dreamily made
her way to the bedroom, while Max sat down, stretched
his legs out and watched the miniature gilt and marble
vase clock on his desk. He wouldn't go upstairs until he
decided she had waited long enough—provided he could
manage to curb his own impatience to have her again!

Max was a difficult man to live with, but infinitely exciting. There were times when Lysette felt the only safe
place in the world was in his arms. And there were other

times when he would dispel any illusion of safety. During the long, blissful nights they shared, he taught her pleasures she had never dreamed possible. He could be devilishly patient, taking hours to coax her into a state of sensual madness . . . or he could be reckless and wild, setting every nerve on fire and consuming her in the blaze.

Once Lysette would never have believed that one person could have become so necessary to her very existence. She had always enjoyed solitude and privacy, but now the occasional hours she spent alone seemed empty and without meaning. When Max was with her, whether they were talking, arguing, or laughing, she felt a sense of completeness she had never expected to find in marriage. Husbands were supposed to be distant, frequently absent figures, who spent time with their wives only to fulfill certain husbandly duties. But Max kept no mistress, nor was he wont to spend all of his evenings drinking and gambling with the other Creole gentlemen of his acquaintance.

He taught her to dance, stating that he wouldn't tolerate some dancing master's hands on his wife. For hours they waltzed around the empty ballroom, supplying their own music amidst much laughter and argument. Lysette was delighted by her husband's pleasant baritone, and he seemed equally enchanted by her out-of-tune humming.

To distract her from counting every step, Max entertained her with a few of his boyhood reminiscences. During one particularly ribald story, Lysette deliberately stepped on his foot to hush him. Threatening revenge, he caught her around the waist and swung her in the air, causing her to shriek with laughing apologies. Even Irénée had to smile as she came to the doorway and saw how the dance lesson had turned into an undignified romp.

On the occasions when Lysette could free herself from her responsibilities she accompanied Max to the New Orleans waterfront, where the keelboats and barges were so numerous that one could walk a mile across their decks. When one of Max's four ocean trading vessels came into port, laden with European and tropical goods, she accompanied him aboard while the cargo was being inspected and unloaded.

On one occasion Max left Lysette in the care of an officer while he went below with the captain to examine some water-damaged cargo. While she stood at the rail of the deep, high-sided frigate, watching a nearby flatboat unloading the boxes and supplies of a theatrical troupe, many of the crew gathered around her at a respectful distance. Sensing their gazes on her, she turned and started at the sight of the swarthy group. They were a dirty, brawny lot, dressed in strange, loose clothing, their shirts fastened by pegs of wood thrust through the button holes. The tops of their shoes had been cut off, leaving only two or three lace holes.

"Don't be afraid, ma'am," the first officer said. "They just want to look at you."

"Whatever for?"

"Oh, they ain't seen a woman for well nigh a month."

She gave them an uncertain smile, which caused the crew to murmur appreciatively. Gesturing to their feet curiously, she asked in her halting English why their shoes were so odd. Several of them laughed.

"These here is pumps," one of the sailors explained. "When the mate bawls, *all hands reef topsails,* there ain't time fer lace-up shoes."

Intrigued, Lysette asked a few more questions, and then they began to compete for her attention, singing the verses of sea chanteys, showing her a set of brass knuckles, making her laugh by claiming she was a mermaid who had stowed away during their journey.

Coming up from the ship's hold, Max stopped at the sight of his wife smiling at the sailors' antics. A breeze molded the yellow fabric of her gown against the slim shape of her body, while her hair was unbearably bright against the deep blue of the sky. He struggled with a mixture of pride and possessiveness.

"Well, now," said Captain Tierney, stopping by him to admire the picture. "Forgive me, Mr. Vallerand, but I don't envy a man with a wife so comely. If she were mine, I'd keep her locked away out of sight."

"It's a tempting idea," Max said, and laughed. "But I prefer having her with me."

"I can understand that," Tierney said fervently.

When Max discovered Lysette's enjoyment of the theater he began taking her to the St. Pierre, where the prominent members of the community gathered on Tuesdays and Saturdays to enjoy music, drama, and opera. Between acts, people moved around the theater to socialize and gossip.

Gradually it became the habit of many couples to stop by the Vallerands' box and chat idly, for it was noticed that since his marriage, Maximilien had undergone a marked change in character. There was still a certain reserve about him, but his air of cold contempt seemed to have disappeared. His petite wife regarded him with such a complete lack of fear that many people began to reconsider their opinions of him. A man so obviously attached to his wife couldn't be the complete devil they had thought him.

One week an English touring company visited one of the theaters in the uptown section of New Orleans, where many of the Americans were building their shops and residences. Max took Lysette to see the performance, and she was surprised to see a few other Creole couples in attendance. When she remarked on it, Max nodded matter-of-factly.

"Many Creoles—especially the younger ones—are discovering that Americans aren't quite as barbaric as they once thought. And as fast as their population in New Orleans is increasing, Americans will outnumber Creoles in a few years. We won't be able to keep ourselves isolated for long."

"Is that bad?" Lysette asked apprehensively.

"No, of course not. We'll be hardier for it, I think. On the other hand, we'll probably lose many of our traditions . . . and that is regrettable."

Frowning thoughtfully, Lysette turned her attention to the performance, tugging on Max's sleeve when she needed him to translate the more difficult English phrases.

"Maman," Lysette said lightly, laying her hand on Irénée's shoulder as the older woman bent over needlework in the parlor, "I have something to ask you."

"Oui?"

"Would you have any objections if I went through some of the things in the attic?"

Irénée's head remained bent. Her fingers stopped moving. It was clear she was startled. "Why would you desire to do such a thing? If there is something you require, we will buy it."

"No, there is nothing I need." Lysette took her hand off Irénée's shoulder and shrugged. "It's just that . . . Justin mentioned to me that there are some interesting things stored away up there—portraits and clothes, old toys. One of these days, perhaps there will be a need to refurbish the nursery and—"

"Nursery?" Irénée turned sharply and looked at her. "Do you suspect you might be with child, Lysette?"

"No."

"Incomprehensible," Irénée murmured under her breath. At first she had been mildly amused by her son's voracious appetite for his new bride. Now she was beginning to find it vaguely appalling. Noeline smugly attributed it to the voodoo charms she had hidden under Lysette's pillow the first few weeks of the marriage.

Lysette smiled idly. "Now that I've spoken to you about it, I'll just put on an apron and see what I can find up there."

"Wait," Irénée said, and there was an edge in her voice that Lysette had never heard before. "Be truthful with me, child. You are going up there to search through *her* things, are you not?''

Lysette's smile disappeared, and she blushed slightly. "Yes, Maman."

"Pourquoi? What do you hope to find?''

"I don't know," she said truthfully. She was terribly curious about Corinne, and she thought she might understand more about the past if she saw some of the other woman's possessions. Perhaps there might even be some clues that would help explain Corinne's mysterious death. "It will not hurt anyone if I look through a few old trunks and boxes, will it?''

"Does Max know?''

"I'll tell him tonight, when he returns home."

Irénée held back her advice to wait and ask Max first. She hoped Max would be furious when Lysette told him what she had done. Perhaps then he would set the girl back on her heels, and Lysette's untoward curiosity would no longer be given free rein. Max needed to see that he was allowing the girl too much freedom and authority. "Very well," Irénée said evenly. "Whatever you think best. Ask Noeline for the keys to the trunks you wish to open."

Lysette smiled brightly, dropping a kiss on Irénée's head, dislodging the older woman's lace cap.

Irénée sighed and straightened her headdress as she watched the girl fly from the room. "Sweet child," she said reluctantly. "There are simply some things you must learn."

Lysette sneezed repeatedly, waving at a cloud of dust as she struggled with the massive lid of a trunk. She and Justin were in the attic, having cleared a place among boxes and piles of oddities. There was a set of bronze lamps and an old bayonet in the corner. Behind the trunks were a disassembled tester bed, rocking cradle, and wooden tub. As Lysette opened the trunk, its rusted hinges squealed. There was a protesting noise from Justin, who was rattling a key in the lock of another trunk nearby. "*Sang de Dieu,* don't do that again! Worse than fingernails on a slate!"

Lysette smiled. She pulled out a folded quilt, a sumptuous trapunto design of delicate rococo swirls, vines and flowers. Thousands of tiny stitches and much painstaking work had contributed to its exquisite texture. "Is Philippe distressed that you are up here with me?" she asked.

"He said he is glad. Someone needs to protect you if Maman's ghost jumps out of one of these trunks."

Lysette shivered. "Justin, don't!"

He grinned. "Are you scared?"

"I wasn't until now!" She peered at him through the dim attic. Dust motes drifted in and out of the lamp's gentle glow. "Justin, will it upset you if I look through some of these things? If you are—"

"Me? No. I'm as curious as you are. You're hoping to find some clue about who might have killed her, *n'est-ce pas?* You'll do better with my help. I might be able to recognize something you w—"

He stopped speaking as he looked at the quilt she held, his eyes wide. "That's . . . I remember that!"

Lysette looked down at the quilt, her hand smoothing over the intricate swirls. "You do?"

"It was on Maman's bed. There should be a stain on one of the edges. I jumped on her bed once, and made her spill her *café.*" Justin had a far-away look on his face. "She was so angry. I was . . ." He stopped.

"You were afraid of her?" Lysette whispered.

Justin stared at the quilt with dark sapphire eyes. There was no need for him to answer.

"Justin, you do not have to stay up here with me. If it is painful for you—"

"It was strange," he said, "the way it happened. She was there one day, and then the next, she was gone. Completely gone. Father made sure every trace of her was removed from sight."

"What do you remember about her death?" Lysette asked hesitantly. "Did anyone explain it to you?"

Justin laced his fingers together, rested his chin on them, and braced his elbows on his bent knees. *"Grand-mère* did. Then Father was gone for several days. She said he was sick." Justin's mouth twisted. "Sick from drinking, most likely. When I saw him afterwards, he looked to me like the picture of the devil in one of my books—I thought he *was* the devil. I thought he had taken Maman away."

Lysette set the quilt down and bent over the trunk, coming up with an armful of tiny baby clothes and bonnets. "It's not difficult to guess who these belonged to," she said. "Everything is in twos."

Justin reached out and took one of the miniature gowns in his long, calloused fingers. "You can tell them apart. Everything I wore has a rip or a stain. Everything Philippe wore is immaculate."

"I doubt that. Philippe told me once that you are not half as bad and he, not as good as others assume."

Justin ducked his head to hide a slow smile. "He was lying."

Delving deeper into the trunk, Lysette discovered piles of haphazardly folded lace collars, embroidered gloves, delicate painted fans. Corinne, she thought with displeasure, had exquisite taste. Lysette picked up a pair of silk lace gloves and put them down hastily, feeling guilty at sorting through a dead woman's possessions. She also felt a pang of jealousy. All at once seeing these personal belongings made it seem real, that there had been another woman Max had loved enough to marry, enough to pledge his life to. Corinne had known what it was like to share Max's bed, and carry his children. Lysette scowled at the thought.

She heard the rustling and tearing of paper. Sitting up quickly, she bumped her head on the trunk. "Ow! . . ." She clapped her hand over the sore spot, then squinted in the direction of the noise. Justin was unwrapping some

tarnished miniature portraits. "What are those?" she
asked.

"The Quérands, I think. My mother's family." He
handed them to her, and Lysette looked closely at the tiny,
dour faces framed in garnet-encrusted silver. She turned
the objects over, inspecting the spaces between the portraits and the frames, hoping for some hidden note or scrap
of paper. Finding nothing, she looked back at Justin, who
was shaking his head slowly, as if he found her hopeless.

"I suppose you think the name of the murderer is written out for us, and all we have to do is find it."

Lysette glared at him defensively. "Of course I don't
think that!" She peered at the miniatures once more before setting them aside.

As she searched through more trunks, she came across
elaborately beaded and festooned garments, lavish gowns,
dainty undergarments. The clothes were made for a tall,
slender woman. Lysette's sense of being an intruder grew
stronger with each revelation. She found a tiny bronze box
containing two dried cakes of paint, one white, one red.
So Corinne had used paint and rouge, she thought, briefly
cheered by the discovery. Of course, that had been back
in the days when paint was more acceptable.

She frowned as she picked up an ornate comb, decorated with pearls and an egret feather. Caught in the teeth
of the comb were two or three long, dark hairs. Corinne's
hair, she thought, and a cold feeling went down her spine.

"Justin?" she said in a low voice. "Are there any . . .
portraits of your mother up here?" She had to see what
Corinne had looked like. Her curiosity was nearly intolerable.

"I suppose." Justin climbed over an armoire on its side
to a stack of frames covered by a canvas tied with cords.
Pulling out his knife, he cut the cords and tugged at the
dust-laden cloth. Lysette scrambled to her feet, sore from
having been on her knees so long. She made her way to
him and looked over his shoulder at one portrait after an-

other. One was of a very attractive woman—attractive but not astoundingly so.

"Is that her?" Lysette asked hopefully.

"No, it is *Grand-mère*. Can't you see?"

"Oh, yes." In the woman's young, solemn face, there were Irénée's dark eyes. It was a very flattering portrait. Her mouth and nose had been painted to seem more delicate than they actually were. Lysette thought that Irénée was more graceful as an older woman than as a younger one.

"Here is Maman," Justin said, and pulled the portrait aside to show her the next one.

Lysette froze at the sight, unprepared for the overwhelming beauty of the woman. Corinne had been stunning. Her sultry violet-blue eyes—Justin's eyes—were filled with exotic mystery. Sable hair curled around her face and long white throat. Her lips were red, sumptuously curved, drawn with the trace of a delicious pout.

"Did she really look like that?" Lysette asked, and Justin smiled at the plaintive note in her voice. He considered the portrait thoughtfully.

"Sometimes."

Lysette sighed and turned away, walking back to the piled-up trunks and sitting on one. A cloud of dust wafted upwards and swirled around her. She heard Justin snicker.

"What is it?" she asked glumly.

"Your hair is all gray. So is your face."

She glanced at her filthy arms and dress, then at him. Justin's raven hair was covered with gray dust and spider webs, and his face was covered with black streaks. A burst of laughter escaped her. "So is yours."

He grinned crookedly. "I don't think we're going to find anything up here, *Belle-mère*."

"I agree," she said fervently. "*Allons*, Justin. I have seen enough."

She began to climb down from the attic, through a square opening framed with beams, to narrow steps that resembled a ladder. Justin cautioned her to mind her balance. It was a long distance to the cypress floor below. She could be badly hurt if she fell. "Careful," he said, watching her climb down the first few steps. "There used to be a railing, but it was broken."

"Why doesn't someone fix it?"

"Because no one ever comes up here."

Lysette made no reply, concentrating on placing her feet securely. Suddenly the silence was broken by a startling shout.

"What were you doing up there?"

Her entire body jumped at the unexpected noise. Terrified, Lysette felt herself lose her balance and sway backwards. With a sharp cry, she reached out frantically to save herself, her fingers clutching at empty air. Time stopped as she began to fall. Lightning-quick, Justin leaned over the attic opening and grabbed for her, crushing her wrist in a brutal grip. Her feet left the steps and she screamed as she felt herself dangling in mid-air, suspended by Justin's hand wrapped around her arm.

Wildly she looked down and saw a man with dark hair below them. "M–Max!"

But it wasn't Max. It was Bernard, who repeated his furious shout.

Sobbing with fear, Lysette reached for Justin's arm with her free hand. "I have you," the boy said roughly, sweat blotching his dusty face. "You're not going to fall. Can you reach the steps with your feet?"

She strained, but could not touch it. "No, I c–can't—"

"Uncle Bernard . . . damn you," Justin gasped, but a searing pain in his side prevented him from speaking further.

Bernard was strangely slow to move.

Lysette felt the grip around her arm slip a little. "Justin!"

"I'll help," Bernard murmured, approaching the bottom of the ladder.

"Don't bother," Justin snarled, and biting his lip, he used every ounce of his remaining strength to pull Lysette up to the opening of the attic. Her stomach slammed hard against the exposed beam, and she lost her breath. Justin kept on pulling until she was halfway across his lap. She lay without moving while Justin pried her fingers away from his trembling arm and dragged his sleeve across his face. There was an agonizing ache in his side where he had been wounded in the duel. He blinked to clear away the brilliant splotches of color that danced before his eyes.

Bernard appeared at the top of the steps. His face was dark with rage. "You could have waited for me to assist you."

Justin's mouth was dry. He moistened his lips and spoke with an effort. "We didn't have an hour," he sneered.

"And what does *that* mean?"

"Why don't you guess," Justin invited, his voice thick with hostility.

"I demand that you explain what you two were doing up here!"

Ignoring him, Justin bent over Lysette and urged her to sit upright. Dazed, she held her stomach and breathed deeply. "Justin," she said, realizing what he had done. "Are you hurt? Your side—is it bleeding?"

"No, no—" He shook his head impatiently.

Bernard rounded on them both furiously. "You were searching through Corinne's belongings, weren't you? You have no right to do such a thing! I forbid it!"

Justin began to retort hotly, but Lysette silenced him with a touch on his shoulder. She stared at Bernard.

"You forbid?" she repeated. "I was not aware, Bernard, that you were in a position to forbid me anything."

"Or me!" Justin added, unable to keep quiet.

"It's not *decent,*" Bernard said savagely. "Pawing through her possessions just to satisfy your petty jealousies, prying and staring. By God, I hope she curses you from the grave! You have no right!"

His words lashed out through the silence. Lysette was quiet, watching him with luminous hazel eyes. It was uncharacteristic of him, this explosive anger. Until now she hadn't really thought Bernard had a temper. And it had been aroused on behalf of his dead sister-in-law. Something was not right.

She kept her voice very soft. ''Why are you so upset, Bernard?''

''Why—'' He stared at her as if the question were insane. ''I'll inform Max about what you've done as soon as he arrives home. I would not be surprised if he beats you!''

''We'll see,'' Lysette said. ''Now, please leave so Justin and I may descend without further mishap.''

Bernard's face purpled, and he went down the steps immediately. Unfortunately, Justin's temper was still smoldering, and he leaned over the edge of the stairwell to call after Bernard.

''Who appointed you guardian over her belongings, Uncle? She was *my* mother. What was she to you?'' Justin hadn't meant anything in particular by the question, but Bernard swung around as if he had been struck, looking up at Justin with a flash of pure hatred. Uncomprehending, Justin stared at his uncle, his blue eyes as bewildered as those of a child who had been unfairly accused by a respected authority. Bernard turned and left swiftly.

Had Lysette wanted, she could have been the first to rush to Max when he arrived, to tell him her side of the story before Bernard or Irénée spoke to him. She chose not to. Opening the bedchamber door, she discreetly watched Max enter the house. Immediately Bernard and Irénée beseiged him, one appearing angry, the other merely concerned, while Max stared at them both in dumbfounded silence. It was impossible for Lysette to hear what they said, but the tone of their complaints was clear.

Giving a nervous sigh, Lysette closed her door and sat

down to wait at the small satinwood desk by the window. She pulled out a blank piece of parchment and stared at it. Perhaps she should write yet another letter to her mother, or Jacqueline. Max had offered no more objections to her correspondence, and she wrote to them almost weekly. If she persisted, one of them would answer sooner or later. She admitted to herself that she missed her mother, even in spite of Jeanne's illnesses and vacillations. And she missed Jacqueline, and all the advice and gossip her older sister loved to impart. She even missed Tante Delphine, who had been affectionate in her own foolish way.

Depressed and tired, Lysette rested her head in her hands. She did not move until she heard someone come into the room. Glancing over her shoulder, she saw that it was Max.

"Bon soir, mon mari," she greeted him uncertainly, wondering if Irénée and Bernard had succeeded in making a villainess out of her.

Chapter 13

❧❧❧

L ysette stood up quickly, ready to face any inquisition, any display of temper. Max's eyes searched hers, and his stern face softened as he crossed the room to her. Lysette gave a sigh of relief as he gathered her in his arms. The tightness in her chest eased. The familiar scent of him was soothing and pleasant, and the strength of his body elicited a shiver of comfort from the very marrow of her bones.

His lips brushed hers with a velvety kiss, and he sat down in the chair, pulling her onto his lap. "Madame, would you care to tell me what the hell happened today?"

Lysette snuggled against his chest. "I did not expect one little visit to the attic to stir up such trouble."

"You didn't," he said with more than a touch of skepticism.

"You once told me this is just as much my house as it is anyone else's."

"So I did."

"Justin was with me."

"So I heard."

"All we did was open a few boxes and trunks."

"Did you find what you were looking for?"

"I wasn't looking *for* anything. I was just . . . looking."

328

"Ah." His warm hand moved over her back in an idle pattern. "I see the difference."

"And Bernard was so upset, Max." She lifted her head off his shoulder and stared at him earnestly. "It was very surprising. From the way he behaved, one would think . . . one would think Corinne had been *his* wife. He tried to forbid me to go up there again."

Max's face was expressionless, but his voice was gentle. "Is it necessary that you make another excursion to the attic?"

"I don't think so. But all the same—"

"I understand. Bernard can be high-handed at times."

"This was more than high-handed! He—"

"Let me explain my brother. You've always known him to keep his emotions to himself. But occasionally they do surface, and when that happens they do so with an explosion. Today Bernard had a rare burst of temper. Tomorrow he'll be his usual glum self. *C'est ça.* He's always been like that."

"But when he spoke about Corinne—"

"Her death, and the circumstances surrounding it, affected us all. I'm certain Bernard has done his share of wondering what happened to Corinne, and whether he could have done something to prevent it. He may feel a certain measure of guilt. Perhaps that is why he is so protective of her possessions now."

Lysette pondered his explanation. Put in that light, the episode seemed far more reasonable than it had this afternoon. But there was a question in her mind that refused to go away, and she had to ask it, even at the risk of making him angry.

"Max . . . are you certain that Bernard's feelings for Corinne were not something more than brotherly affection?" She rushed on as he gave her a sharp look. "I don't know exactly why I have such a suspicion—it's not something I can easily put into words. But whenever Corinne's name is mentioned, he reacts in such an odd manner. I've heard him say things about her, that she was hypnotic and beautiful . . . And today he accused me of being jealous of her. This afternoon wasn't the first time he and I have exchanged words about her. After I went to the old overseer's cottage—you remember that day?—he told me not to pry into the past anymore, or he would personally put a stop to my meddling.''

Max was still, but she sensed a fine tension in his limbs that had not been there before. "Why didn't you tell me about it before?''

"I didn't know you well enough,'' she said in a subdued tone. "I was afraid of making you angry.'' She peered into his face, trying to read his thoughts. "Are you angry now?''

"I'm looking forward to having a talk with Bernard.''

"You didn't answer my question . . . about his feelings for Corinne.''

"As far as I know, there is only one woman Bernard has ever loved. Ryla Curran, the daughter of an American who settled his family in New Orleans after years of running a flatboat up and down the river. The match was an impossible one . . . she was of a humble Protestant family. But eventually they did have an affair. And she became pregnant with his child.''

Lysette listened carefully, her eyes wide.

"She disappeared,'' Max continued quietly, "without word to friends of family about where she was going. Bernard has searched for years, but he has never been able to find her or the child.''

"When did all of this happen?''

"At the same time Corinne was murdered. No, there was nothing between Bernard and Corinne. He was completely involved with this girl and his unborn child. Losing them affected him deeply—so much so that he's searched for them for years rather than marry anyone else.''

"I didn't know.'' Lysette began to feel ashamed of the suspicions she had had about Bernard. *"Bien-aimé,"* she said tentatively, reaching up to stroke his bristled cheek, "are you unhappy about what I did this afternoon?"

He rubbed his cheek against her soft palm. "Actually I was expecting it, my curious little cat."

"I saw Corinne's portrait," she said soberly. "She was very beautiful."

"Yes." He brushed a wisp of hair off her forehead. "But she didn't have hair the color of sunset." His thumb glided over her lips. "Or a mouth I wanted to kiss every time I saw it . . . or skin as soft as silk." His mouth moved to her ear. "She didn't have a smile that stopped my heart . . . or a way of loving me until we both dissolved in joy."

Lysette's eyes half-closed, and she shifted closer to him, winding her arms around his neck. "I love you," she breathed. But as she moved to kiss him, her wrist bumped against the back of the chair. She winced at the unexpected pain. Max was instantly aware, his amorous mood vanishing.

"What is it?" he demanded.

"Nothing." She groaned inwardly as she realized that the sight of her bruised wrist was going to bring up more questions about today, when she was now perfectly willing to forget the entire matter. Ignoring her protests, Max unwrapped her arms from around his neck, his eyes raking over her slender body. "Max, really—"

"Why did you flinch like that?"

"It's only a little—"

He drew in his breath at the sight of her swollen, discolored wrist. Black fingermarks showed against her pale skin. His mouth hardened, and there was a look in his eyes that made her uneasy. "What happened?"

"Just a little accident. I was coming down from the attic—the steps are so narrow, and there is no railing—and I lost my balance. Justin was quick enough to catch my wrist and pull me back. Now everything is fine. In a day or two my wrist will be perfectly—"

"Did this happen before or after Bernard appeared?" Max was still staring at her wrist.

"Er . . . during, actually. Bernard shouted and startled me, and that was when I fell." Lysette did not tell him how slow his brother had been to offer help. Her perception of things might have been more than a little awry. And Bernard had probably been too stunned to move. Some people were quick to act in such situations, like Justin, while others froze.

"Why didn't Bernard mention it to me?"

She shook her head helplessly. "Max, he was so upset about Corinne's things—"

He lifted her out of his lap and set her on her feet.

"What are you doing?" she asked warily.

"I'm going to get an explanation from him."

"There's no need." She tried in vain to make peace, not wanting to be the cause of trouble between the brothers. "It is all over now, and I—"

"Hush." Gently he took her elbow, holding it in order to inspect her wrist. He uttered a curse that made her ears burn.

"Max," she protested faintly.

"Has Noeline seen this?"

"No."

"She has a salve for bruises."

"Yes. It is terrible. I was there once when she was putting it on Justin. The smell of it made me ill."

"Go to her now. Or I'll see that you do later." He paused meaningfully. "And I assure you, you'd rather do it now."

A few minutes later Lysette sat in the kitchen with Noeline, focusing her attention on the kettles bubbling merrily in the fireplace while the housekeeper attended to her wrist. A housemaid stood at the huge wooden table, cleaning the iron chandelier. Businesslike, Noeline smeared the mustard-green salve on Lysette's arm. The ripe, noxious odor caused Lysette to jerk her head back. "How long must I keep this on?" she asked in disgust.

"Until tomorrow." Noeline smiled a little. "Ah don' think you gonna make babies wid' monsieur tonight, no?"

Lysette raised her eyes heavenward. "I'll be fortunate if he ever comes near me again!"

Noeline's reply was interrupted as Justin appeared at the doorway of the kitchen. Hands in his pockets, he wandered over to them. "What is that odor?" he asked, and clutched his throat, pretending to gag.

Silently Lysette vowed to wash her wrist as soon as she escaped from Noeline.

Justin grinned at her consolingly. "It smells like the devil, *sans doute*. But it does work, *Belle-mère*."

"He know for sure," Noeline said, wrapping a length of cloth around the arm.

"I know what you put in your salve, Noeline," Justin said. He squatted on his haunches and murmured confidentially to Lysette. "Snakes' tongues, bats' blood, toad hairs . . ."

Lysette frowned. "Why don't you go find Philippe? He can help you with some of the Latin lessons you've missed."

Justin made a face. "No need to bring Latin into this. I will leave. But . . ." He glanced at her bandage. He was silent, as if he wanted to say something but was uncertain of the right words. Raking his hand through his black hair until it stood on end, he looked at the floor, the ceiling, and then his gaze met hers.

"What is it?" Lysette murmured, surprised by the shy awareness in his dark blue eyes.

Noeline went to check one of the pots over the fire.

"I didn't mean to hurt you," Justin said gruffly, and gestured to her wrist.

"You helped me, Justin," Lysette said gravely. "I am very grateful for what you did."

Appearing relieved, Justin stood up, dusting his

breeches unnecessarily. "Did you tell Father what happened?"

"About your saving me from falling. Yes, I—"

"No, about Uncle Bernard, and how strange he was this afternoon."

"*Oui.*" Lysette smiled wryly. "Your father seemed to think it was not unusual. He told me your uncle has always been a bit peculiar."

"*Bien sûr,* that's true enough." Justin shrugged. "I'll go now."

Lysette watched him as he left, thinking to herself that the boy had changed somewhat since the duel and his confrontation with Max. He was friendlier, less sullen, as if his dark nature had been tempered by new understanding. Noeline sat down beside her again, shaking her head. "Dat boy was born fo' trouble."

"And what is their complaint?" Bernard asked, looking wounded and upset. "That I did not move quickly enough? I was startled, Max. By the time I recovered my wits Justin had already pulled her back to safety!"

Max's frown did not ease. "Your manner seems to have been rather belligerent. Why is that?"

Bernard hung his head with an ashamed expression. "I didn't intend to lose my temper . . . but all I could think of was how it would upset you, knowing they had been combing through relics of the past. You're my brother, Max. I don't want you to suffer through any more reminders of that horrible time. I tried to tell them that it was better to let things be. I suppose I expressed myself far too strongly."

"Corinne was Justin's mother," Max said. "He has a right to look through her belongings any time he wishes."

"Yes, of course," Bernard replied contritely. "But Lysette—"

"Lysette is my concern. The next time you object to something she does, take the matter up with me. Bear in mind that she is the mistress of this house, and more of a wife to me than Corinne ever was. And one last point—'' Max paused to give his next words emphasis, staring hard at his brother. ''If you ever utter one word to Lysette that she finds even vaguely threatening . . . you'll take up residence somewhere else.''

Bernard's cheeks reddened with suppressed emotion, but he managed to nod silently.

In spite of her prying, Lysette could not find out what had been said in the conversation between Max and Bernard. Ever since then, there had been a distinct tension in the house. Bernard never met Lysette's or Justin's eyes, and they found themselves uncomfortable around him. The episode in the attic had served to engender a special sort of friendship between Lysette and Justin, a sense that they were allies, conspirators—and Bernard seemed to regard them that way.

Lysette came to realize Justin possessed many of Max's qualities, his sharp wit, fierce protectiveness, and deep underlying gentleness. And yet, Justin was young enough to bring out her maternal instincts. She did not understand why he seemed to accept kindness from her when he resented it from others. Max had noticed the boy's unusual docility around her, and made no secret of his approval.

''Justin has known few women like you,'' Max commented one morning as he pulled on his breeches and reached for a clean shirt. ''You may be the first he's ever dared to trust.''

''Do you think he trusts me?'' Lysette asked, pleased at the thought.

''How could he help it?'' Max dropped the shirt and caught her bare heels in his hands, starting to pull her out of bed. ''It's the way you look at someone with those innocent hazel eyes . . .''

''I'm not all that innocent,'' she protested.

''No?'' Inexorably he continued to pull her toward him.

"Not after three months of marriage to you!" She tried to pull down the hem of her gown, which was sliding up to her hips. Her hair trailed along the mattress in a molten river of red. "Max, stop—I do not want to get out of bed yet."

"You told me last evening you would accompany me on an early morning ride." He had recently bought her a small Arabian gelding, a dark chestnut with flashing white stockings. The horse was a more spirited animal than Lysette was accustomed to, and Max was determined to teach her to handle it properly.

"That was before you decided to keep me awake all night." Indignantly she kicked with her imprisoned legs.

Max's eyes gleamed with laughter, and he stopped pulling as her hips reached the edge of the bed. "I didn't plan to."

Lysette looked up at him provocatively. "Then why did you?" She reached out and stroked his chest, her fingers ruffling through the crisp black hair.

He smiled and leaned over her, pressing a light kiss against her lips. "Because you are irresistible. Now get up, or . . ." He stopped speaking, suddenly aware of her soft body underneath his, her legs dangling on either side of his thighs, her breasts warm against his chest. Her gown was twisted around her waist. There was an responsive surge of hunger in his groin. He could not stop his hand from wandering over her silken belly to the fiery thatch of hair that seemed to beckon him.

Lysette's lashes fluttered downward and she made a tiny movement to push him away. His mouth dipped to hers, testing, savoring, reaching deeply. She could not help responding, even though her body was chafed and tender from the long night of lovemaking. He knew how to touch her, knew all the ways to coax and draw forth her desire. As he fondled her gently, she turned her mouth from his with a gasp. "I can't, Max . . . last night was . . . I'm too sore."

His tongue glided wetly over her oversensitive nipple, then down to the undercurve of her breast. She felt a seeping warmth between her thighs as her body readied itself for his possession, and she knew he felt it, too. Lightly his fingers played over her, barely touching the damp, throbbing flesh. "I'll be careful," he said huskily. "You know I will."

Lysette flushed, knowing just how exquisitely careful he could be. "I can't," she said, but he read the indecision in her face. His hands grazed softly over her thighs and knees, back up to her stomach, which quivered tautly at his touch. Involuntarily her naked legs tightened on his hips. He cupped her breasts tenderly and kissed the reddened peaks.

"I'm not hurting you, am I?" he whispered, his warm breath falling against her moist nipples. Her shaking sigh was his only answer. He nuzzled her throat, finding her frantic pulse with the tip of his tongue. "I'll be gentle," he whispered against her breast, and his hand slid once more to the wet tangle of red hair. "Don't you trust me, *doucette?*"

Her eyes darkened at the feel of his long, sensitive fingers, teasing, gently probing. Slowly reason drifted away, and she began to moan, clawing at his sleek back.

With a low murmur, Max groped for the fastenings of his breeches and positioned himself between her thighs. With extreme care he pressed forward, gently courting her swollen flesh until she had engulfed nearly all of him. Drowsy warmth touched his golden eyes as he felt her small hands press against his tense buttocks, urging him deeper. He resisted, not wanting to hurt her. *"C'est bien?"*

"Yes," she whispered, trembling with need of him.

"Lysette . . . I love you . . ." He took a soft bite of her lower lip, and eased fully inside her. "I'll never stop loving you . . . never stop wanting you . . ."

She clung to him with a low cry, burying her face in his neck, overcome with the emotion, and the pleasure.

A little while later, Max strode down the long curved staircase, having been sent out of the bedroom with Lysette's adamant refusal to ride around the plantation with him. After last night's vigorous lovemaking, along with their encounter this morning, she decided she'd find it more than a little uncomfortable to sit on a high-spirited horse for long. He called a cheerful good morning to Noeline, who was passing by with a pile of clean, folded clothes, and the housekeeper smiled. There was no mistaking the tousled condition of his hair, the glow that edged his tanned cheeks, or the relaxed curve of his mouth.

"Missus goin' wid' you dis mawning?" she asked.

Max scowled at her, not wanting to appear overly happy. He had a reputation to maintain. "Have you been asked to take out her riding clothes?"

"*Non, monsieur.*"

"Then obviously she is not accompanying me."

Noeline smiled tranquilly. "*Oui, monsieur.*"

Max winked at her, resumed his scowl, and headed for the front door. The sound of a groan from one of the double parlors caught his attention. Curiously he went to the doorway and saw Alexandre's long body stretched out on the settee, one booted foot braced on the gilded rococo arm, the other resting on the floor. His hair was wild, his face mottled and unshaven, his clothes twisted and wrinkled. There was a sour alcoholic smell in the air, and the pungent sweetness of a whore's perfume.

Noeline must have been the one to pull the drapes closed. Max preferred sunlight in the room. "What a pretty sight," he remarked. "A Vallerand after a night of self-indulgence." He jerked the drapes away from the windows, letting in a flood of brilliant sunshine.

Alex gasped as if he had just been stabbed. "Ohh . . . you evil bastard!"

"Fourth night this week?" Max said casually. "Even for you, this is an excess."

Helplessly Alex tried to burrow into the settee, like a wounded animal seeking refuge. "Go t' hell," he said indistinctly.

"Out of brotherly concern, I feel compelled to find out what is bothering you. At this rate you'll kill yourself by the end of the week."

Alex made a smacking noise, clearing the fuzz from the inside of his mouth, and caught the scent of his own breath. His face crumpled in disgust. He squinted up at Max and raised an unsteady finger to point at him. "You . . ." he said heavily, "tipped your wife this morning, didn' you?"

Max smiled pleasantly.

"I c'n always tell by the disgusting smirk on your face. Tell me . . . married life suit you? Good. One of us ought t' be happy . . . since you ruined it for th' rest of us."

"Oh?"

"Don' look at me with that eyebrow lift . . . ha . . . did you ever think *I* might like t' have a wife . . . woman t' cover whenever *I* felt like it . . . maybe even have chil'ren someday?"

"Why don't you?"

"*Why don' I?*" Alex wobbled to a sitting position, holding his head, groaning. "After you ruined the Valleran' name—you think a decent family would give their daughter to a brother of yours? All fine an' good for you now . . . got Lysette . . . but me . . ."

Alexandre's speech dissolved into incoherency.

"Alex, *tais-toi*," Max said, his amusement replaced by compassion. He sat down in a nearby chair. "Hush." He had never seen his youngest brother so miserable. "I should wait until you're sober before attempting this, but we're going to try talking about it anyway. Agreed?"

"A'right," Alexandre said gamely.

"Now . . . this is about Henriette Clement, isn't it?"

"Yes."

"You're in love with her? You desire permission to court her?"

"Yes."

"But you don't believe her father will give his consent, because he'll assume she could not be content in a marriage with a Vallerand."

"Content? He doesn' think she'll be *safe!* 'Member Corinne?"

"What does that have to do with you?"

"I'm your brother . . . which makes me . . . un . . . . unsuitable . . ."

Max frowned. "You've already asked for his leave to court Henriette, and Clement refused?"

"Yes! Yes!" Alexandre began to nod, and stopped with a wince. "And she loves me . . . I think."

"All right." Leaning forward, Max spoke slowly. "I will take care of it. For your part, I want you to . . . Alexandre, are you listening? Stay here and rest today. And tonight. No more drinking, do you understand?"

"No more," Alex repeated obediently.

"I'm going to tell Noeline to bring you her special remedy."

"Bon Dieu, no."

"You'll do it," Max said evenly, "if you want Henriette. By tomorrow morning I want you looking like a fresh-faced boy."

"I can do it," Alex said after a moment's painful thought.

"Good." Max smiled and stood up. "You should have talked to me about this before, instead of drinking yourself into a stupor."

"I didn' think you could do anything." Alex paused. "Still don' really."

"People can be managed," Max assured him. "If they are approached the right way."

Alex looked up at him quizzically. "Are you going to threat'n a duel?"

"No," Max said with a soft laugh. "I think the Vallerands have had enough of dueling."

"Max . . . if you get Clement to say yes . . . I . . . I'll kiss your feet."

"That won't be necessary," Max said dryly.

Jacques Clement greeted him in the hallway with wry amusement. "I expected you would be here today, Maximilien. Here on your brother's behalf, *oui?* Father will not be surprised to see you. He is having *café* in the breakfast room."

Max leaned his weight against one of the elaborately carved columns framing the wall. He was in no hurry to confront Jacques' father, Diron Clement, who was a venerable, lionesque figure of a man, and in a perpetual bad temper. Descended from the first French settlers in the Louisiana Territory, Creole in every drop of his blood, Diron had no tolerance for those who wished Louisiana to become part of the United States. Or for those who were on friendly terms with the American governor.

The old man was experienced and clever, and had proven himself to be a survivor. Along with Victor Vallerand, Diron had been richly rewarded by the Spaniards for using his influence to soothe the doubt and discontent in the city when they took possession of it from the French forty years before. Now, of course, Diron was wealthy and influential enough so that he never had to do anything he didn't wish.

Victor and Diron had been good friends. Unfortunately, Diron's warm feelings for Victor had not been extended to Max. For one thing, their political beliefs were too sharply opposed. For another, Corinne's death had widened the gulf between them. Diron hated scandals.

Max glanced upstairs. "Jacques," he said speculatively, "has your sister indicated that she feels any sort of affection for Alexandre?"

"Henriette is a little goose," Jacques said. "She always

has been. Tell your brother he could find another girl just like her for far less trouble."

"Does that mean she would not welcome his suit?"

"She fancies herself madly in love with him. And this scenario of star-crossed love—"

"Only makes it worse," Max finished for him. "How does your father regard the matter?"

"He disapproves, of course."

"It would not be a bad match, Jacques."

Jacques shrugged. "My friend, I know what Alexandre is like. You will never make me believe he will stay faithful to Henriette. This so-called love will last a year at most, and then he will take a mistress, and Henriette will be devastated. Better for her to marry without the illusion of love. With a well-arranged match, she will know exactly what to expect."

"On the other hand, perhaps a year of illusion is better than no love at all."

Jacque laughed. "What an American notion. Love before marriage is merely the fashion this year, Max. A temporary one. And I warn you, don't try to convince that crusty old Creole upstairs otherwise, or he'll have your head."

Max saluted him lazily. "My thanks for the warning. I'll go see him now."

"Would you like me to accompany you?"

"I know the way."

The Clement home was designed with simplicity and elegance. The red pine floors were polished to a ruby gleam, the rooms filled with dark oak and fine Persian rugs. As Max walked up the staircase, he ran his fingers lightly over the balustrade, remembering sliding down it when he and Jacques were boys.

Jacques was one of the few Creole sons Max had known since boyhood who had remained a friend. He was constant, dependable, reasonable, neither excessively cynical nor idealistic. Max had long admired him for that.

He stopped in the hallway upstairs, sensing someone's eyes upon him. Looking over his shoulder, he saw that one of the paneled doors was partially ajar. Henriette stared at him through the inch-wide crack, her eyes filled with pleading. She was silent. Max guessed that some watchful aunt was nearby, and Henriette did not dare say a word for fear of detection. He gave her a short, reassuring nod. Throwing aside caution, Henriette opened the door wider, and suddenly there was a burst of chatter from inside the room, a woman's voice, scolding the wayward girl. The door closed immediately.

Max grinned ruefully. He hated the feeling of being the distraught lovers' last hope. He made his way to the breakfast room, hoping to hell he'd know what to say to Clement.

Diron Clement stared at him challengingly the moment he entered the room. A ruff of white hair haloed the top of his head. When he spoke, the edge of a sharp jaw showed through his sagging jowls. Iron-gray eyes bore through Max's, and he gestured to a chair.

"Sit down, boy."

Max had not been called *boy* since his own father had died. He liked the sense of instant familiarity it established. Although Diron had not meant to put him at ease, it had that effect.

"We have not talked for a long time," the old man remarked.

"The wedding, sir," Max reminded him respectfully.

"Non. We exchanged four words at that . . . that tasteless extravagance of a reception. And you stared the entire time at your flamboyant little bride."

Max sternly held back a smile, remembering that most frustrating of evenings. He had not been able to stop staring at Lysette, wanting her as a starving man craves nourishment, but knowing it was too soon to have her. "I regret that, sir," he said politely.

"Do you?" Diron harrumped. "Yes, I suppose you do,

now that you desire my good favor. What about the marriage? Do you entertain regrets about that as well?''

"Not in the least," Max replied without hesitation.

"So you say. And now you've come to plead your brother's case, eh?''

"Actually, my own," Max said. "Since that seems to be your main objection to Alexandre's suit."

"Untrue. Is that what he told you?''

"He has the impression, sir, that were it not for the damage I have wrought on the Vallerand name in the past, his intentions toward your daughter would be welcomed."

"Ah. You are referring to that disgraceful business about your first wife."

Max met his piercing eyes and nodded.

"That was bad," Diron said emphatically. "But my objection to the match has to do with your brother's character, not yours. Foppish, careless boy—he is unsatisfactory in all respects."

"Alexandre is no more foppish or careless than any other young man his age. And he'll be able to provide well for her."

"How is that? I would wager he has run through most of his inheritance by now."

"My father charged me with the responsibility of overseeing the family's finances. Alexandre receives a generous monthly stipend, more than enough to support a family in a suitable manner."

Diron was quiet, glaring at him from beneath massive gray eyebrows.

"Monsieur Clement," Max said slowly, "you know the Vallerands are a family of good blood. I believe your daughter would be content as Alexandre's wife. Discarding all sentimental notions, the pairing is both practical and suitable."

"But we cannot discard these sentimental notions, can we?" the old man shot back. "This entire situation reeks of mawkish sentiment. Is this the foundation for a good marriage? *Non!* These impetuous propositions, these demonstrations and histronics, this gnashing of teeth and beating of breast—this is not love. I distrust all of it.''

All at once Max understood what the old man's objection really was. It would damage Diron's pride, and his reputation for practicality, to allow his daughter to marry for love. It was not the continental way. People would tease and make jest of the old man's decision, and say his iron will was softening. Perhaps they might even dare to say he was influenced by the new American values that were infiltrating the territory. Quite simply, a love-match would embarrass Diron.

''I agree,'' Max said, thinking rapidly. ''That is why I favor the idea of a long courtship—with strict supervision, *naturellement*. We'll allow them enough time to fall out of love.''

''Eh? What?''

''It is only a matter of time, not even a year. You know how fickle the young are.''

Diron frowned. ''Yes, indeed.''

''And then, when all this violent love has faded into indifference, we will marry them to each other. Henriette will probably object to the match by then. It would be a lesson for both of them. Through the years, Alexandre and Henriette will develop the kind of affection for each other that my parents did . . . just as you and your wife did.''

''Hmmm.'' Diron stroked his chin. Max nearly held his breath, waiting for the answer. ''There is something to the idea.''

''It makes sense to me,'' Max said blandly, sensing the old man was secretly relieved to be handed a solution to the dilemma. This way Henriette would have the husband she desired, and Diron's pride would be preserved.

''Hmmm. Yes, that is what we will do.''

''*Bien.*'' Max adopted a matter-of-fact expression. ''Now, about the dowry—''

''We will discuss *that* at a more appropriate time,'' Di-

ron interrupted grumpily. "Dowry . . . how like a Valler-
and.''

"Pretend *not* to love her?" Alex exclaimed. "I do not
understand."

"Trust me," Max said, catching Lysette around the
waist as she passed him. He pulled her onto his lap. "The
sooner you and Henriette convince everyone you are indifferent to each other, the sooner you can marry.''

"Only you could engineer such a convoluted scheme,"
Alex said sourly.

"You want her," Max said flatly. "That is how you can
have her. There is no other way.''

Lysette cuddled against her husband, stroking his hair.
"It was very clever of you, Max.''

"Not at all," he said modestly, enjoying her praise.

Her voice lowered. "I did not realize the extent of your
romantic nature," she said, and he exchanged a slow grin
with her.

Alexandre made a sound of disgust and stood up to
leave. "Max, a romantic nature," he muttered. "I must
be having a nightmare.''

In the weeks to come, Alexandre's romance with Henriette Clement continued on its precarious way. He sat
with her for countless evenings in the parlor, with the entire Clement family in attendance. When he took her on
sedate carriage drives, her mother and aunt accompanied
them. He never dared meet Henriette's eyes in church or
at the balls they both attended. The nearness of Henriette,
and the rigorously imposed distance between them, caused
Alexandre's feelings to ascend to new heights of longing.
It was any young man's idea of a perfect hell, but strangely,
Alexandre was happy.

The tiniest signs from Henriette were significant—the
way her footsteps slowed when she had to leave him, the
flash of her gaze when she allowed herself to look at him.

To his astonishment, he found he had no desire for any other girl. It was with genuine indignation that he reacted to Max's suggestion that he visit some of his former haunts with Bernard.

"Rumors of your new celibate ways are reaching Diron's ears," Max informed him calmly. "He and everyone else knows you're smitten with Henriette. It's time to give the appearance that you are losing interest in her."

"And therefore you wish me to bed down with some . . . some woman of loose morals?"

"You've done it before," Max pointed out.

"Yes, but that was a long time ago. At least two months!"

Max laughed and suggested he find some other way of appearing bored with his pursuit of Henriette. Miserably Alexandre began to ration his visits to the Clement household, making them more and more infrequent, while Henriette strove to appear indifferent to the new flood of rumors.

Lysette pitied the lovelorn pair and told Max as much. "It seems so ridiculous to put them through such trials merely to preserve Monsieur Clement's pride. It makes something very simple into something so complicated."

"It isn't bad for Alexandre to want something he cannot have immediately," Max smiled and leaned down to kiss her. She was sitting at her dressing table, braiding her hair before retiring. "The best things are worth waiting for."

"Such as me?"

"Such as you," he agreed readily.

Lysette frowned in mock reproof, meeting his eyes in the mirror. "As I recall, you did not have to wait long for me at all."

"I waited my entire life for you."

"Hardly! Have you forgotten your first marriage?"

"I've never claimed not to have made mistakes."

"Marrying Corinne Quérand was your worst."

"Yes." He smoothed her brilliant hair and tucked a

glinting tendril behind her ear. "And then for years I
wanted to believe I needed no one. But even at the most
bitter moments, I couldn't stop myself from hoping I would
find someone—" he paused to kiss her temple, "who
would believe in me."

Lysette finished her hair and stood up, her forehead
puckering as she realized how it must have hurt Max to
know that his family—even his own mother—had suspicions that had not faded with time. How could they know
him so little? She had never seen Max treat a woman with
anything but respect. There was not the slightest bit of
cruelty in him.

In spite of his talk about vengeance, Max had not been
able to finish the duel with Etienne Sagesse because he
considered himself to have an unfair advantage. His loyalty to those he loved was unfaltering. He would defend
the members of his family to his last breath. And with
those who were more vulnerable than he . . . how gentle
and caring he was! No, he was not capable of killing a
woman, no matter what the provocation.

"Of course I believe in you," she said, unfurling her
hand along the side of his lean jaw, staring tenderly into
his eyes. She smiled. "I know what kind of man you are."

Suddenly his expression was bleak. "You didn't know
me back then. A hotheaded young fool . . . no one could
be faulted for thinking the worst."

"Maximilien Vallerand," she said, shaking her head.
"You could make a long confession, right here and now,
and I still would not believe you did it."

"I know that." A wry half-smile appeared. He cradled
the back of her head in his hands, tilting her face upward.
"My darling, I appreciate your loyalty. I adore you for it.
But I have great concern over your lack of judgment."

She laughed. "I will not discuss it. Not when there are
better ways to pass the time."

He bent his head, nipping at the corners of her mouth.

"Indeed?" His hand went to the ribbons that fastened her nightrail. "What do you suggest, madame?"

One of the largest balls of the season was being held at the Leseur plantation to honor the betrothal of one of the three Leseur daughters to Paul Patrice, the last unmarried son of a well-to-do New Orleans physician. Usually a doctor's son would not have been considered the most desirable catch for a planter's daughter, but Paul was a handsome lad with exquisite manners and gentlemanly bearing. Only three years older than Justin and Philippe, he was perfectly willing to surrender his bachelorhood in exchange for marriage into a monied family.

"Eighteen years of freedom, and Paul wishes to shackle himself to a wife!" Justin had commented sourly. "Next year, probably a baby . . . *Mon Dieu*, hasn't he thought about what he is doing?"

"He could not do better than Félicie Leseur," Philippe replied, a touch dreamily. "Marriage is not as bad a fate as you seem to think, Justin."

Justin looked at him as if he'd gone mad. Then his mouth curled in a ridiculing sneer. "I suppose *you'll* be married before too long."

"I hope so. I hope I will be able to find the right girl."

"I know what kind of girl you'll choose," Justin continued. "Bookish and sensible, with spectacles pinching the end of her nose. You'll discuss art and music, and all those dreary Greek tragedies, and she'll probably give you half a dozen daughters exactly like her."

Affronted, Philippe closed the Latin book before him. "She will be beautiful," he said with dignity, "and gentle and quiet. And you will be jealous, as you always are when I have something of value."

Justin snorted. "I'm going to sail to the East and have my own harem. Fifty women!"

"Fifty?" Lysette repeated, having just come into the

room. She smiled at Justin. "That will keep you very busy indeed."

He dropped his sneer and gave her an angelic smile. "But if I find anyone like you, *petite Maman,* I'll have only one."

She laughed at his outrageous charm, and her smiling gaze turned to Philippe. "Tonight, *peut-être,* you will catch sight of the girl you dream of. Are you leaving in the carriage with Bernard and Alexandre?" She did not mention Irénée, who was afflicted with a touch of rheumatism and would not attend the ball.

Philippe nodded. "Yes. Father made it clear you and he were going alone in the first carriage."

"Alone?" Justin mused thoughtfully. "Why would Father want to be *alone* in the carriage with you, when he could have Philippe and me there? Well, I suppose he might try to—"

"Justin!" Philippe exploded, mortified at his brother's impudence. He threw a pillow cushion at Justin's head. Justin ducked it with a protest.

Lysette's mouth twitched with amusement. "I will see you at the Leseur plantation," she said gravely, and went back to the entrance hall, where Noeline waited with her bonnet and gloves.

Built facing one of the smaller bayous in the region, the Leseur home was large, simply designed, and stately. One side was bordered by a massive oak that was estimated to be at least three centuries old. Garlands of roses covered the house inside and out. The glitter from intricately prismed chandeliers danced in the most remote corners of the house. Guests filled the outside galleries, while servants moved among them with silver trays of refreshments.

Nearby was the *garconnière,* separately constructed quarters for male guests or family bachelors who required privacy. Several gentlemen accompanied by personal attendants had been in the *garconnière* since early afternoon, drinking, smoking, and discussing the latest events in the city. The ladies had been resting and gossiping inside the house, and now were appearing in the ballroom in their most extravagant gowns. A special orchestra had been summoned from New Orleans to supply the music, and the lively strains of a quadrille filled the air.

"Lysette," Max said as he helped her from the carriage, "A word of warning."

"Yes?" She looked at him with wide, innocent eyes. Too innocent. "What is it, *bien-aimé?*"

"Do not think I haven't been aware that Alexandre has been trying to persuade you to arrange for him to spend a few minutes alone with Henriette tonight."

She appeared to be surprised. "And you think I would help him?"

Max gave her a serious look. "You know it would undo all our careful planning."

"It certainly would," Lysette agreed, arranging the sleeves and folds of her icy pink gown. Molded tightly to her bosom and draped gently over her slim figure, the gown's shimmering paleness contrasted splendidly with her vivid red hair.

"If they manage to give a convincing show of indifference to each other," Max said, "they'll be married in a matter of months. If, however, they are discovered in a clandestine meeting, there is nothing I can do to help them."

"They won't be caught together," Lysette said.

"Alex could lose Henriette over such a trifling thing. You do not understand the extent of Diron's pride."

"I do, I understand perfectly." She tried to move away, but he kept his hands at her waist, staring down at her.

"If I catch you doing something against my expressly stated wishes, my sweet, I promise you will regret it."

She blinked at the quiet threat in his voice. "Max, I have not done anything!"

"Keep it that way," he advised, and let go of her. Lys-

ette left in a mild huff, while Max smiled ruefully after
her, undeceived by her show of wounded innocence. She
was planning something, there was no doubt of it.

Max kept his eye on Alexandre and Lysette both during
the next several hours, but neither of them made a move
to leave the ballroom. He relaxed after a glass or two of
the fine wine being liberally served to all the guests. The
vintage had been made from vineyards on the Leseur plantation.

Max congratulated Leseur, both on the excellent wine
and the match between Félicie and Paul Patrice, and the
two of them engaged in a casual conversation. Soon other
guests came to join them, curious to see for themselves if
the rumors were true, that since his marriage Maximilien
Vallerand had become far less distant and cold.

From a distance, Lysette stood with Alexandre and
watched her husband with a rush of pride. Max was
dressed in stark black and white, a wine glass poised between his long fingers as he conversed with the men around
him. The glow of the chandeliers lent a luminous gleam
to his copper skin and raven hair. His white teeth flashed
in a smile. He looked so virile and handsome that her
heart gave a little skip.

"I've never understood it," Alexandre commented.
"For a man who is universally disliked, Max has always
been beseiged by people trying to gain his attention, ask
for his opinions, solicit his approval. Why is that?"

"He may be disliked," Lysette said, "but he is respected."

"It has not been easy, having him as a brother."

"Why not?" Lysette asked, thinking of all the times
she had seen Max smooth the way for his brothers, doing
what he could to ensure they had whatever they desired,
assuming their debts and responsibilities without one word
of reproach. Alex's statement struck her as being singu-
larly ungrateful. "Max does many things for you, *non?*"

"He does, but . . . for years Bernard and I had to contend with the standards Max set. Everything he did was perfect. And then, for him to fall so utterly in disgrace— it was a disaster for all of us. The Vallerand name was blackened, and the stigma was attached to Bernard and me, as well as Max."

"And you resent him for that?" Lysette asked, her eyes still on Max.

"No, no. I might have, once, but not now. But Bernard . . ." Alexandre stopped, evidently thinking better of what he had been about to say.

"What?" Lysette prompted.

He shook his head. "It's nothing."

"Tell me, Alex, or I will not help you with Henriette."

He scowled. "I was only going to say that Bernard seems to have found it difficult to completely forgive Max. But then, Bernard is the next oldest son. He has always been compared to Max, and found lacking."

"And this is Max's fault?" Lysette asked sharply. Good Lord, what did they want of their older brother?

"I knew you would not understand," Alex said glumly.

Her lips tightened. "You are correct, Alexandre. I certainly do not."

Involved in a leisurely conversation, Max did not notice the exact moment when his wife disappeared. Slowly he became aware of her absence, much as a man awakes from a pleasant midday nap to discover he has slept through the entire afternoon. He politely disentangled himself from the group in the ballroom and wandered past the open doors leading to the outside galleries. There was no sign of a slender figure in pink.

"Dammit, Lysette, what are you doing?" he muttered to himself, immediately drawing the worst conclusion. He headed to the garden at a measured pace, knowing that if Lysette had engineered a meeting between Alexandre and Henriette, it would take place there.

The Leseur garden was large and intricately designed, filled with exotic trees, flowers, and plants from far-off places in Europe and the Orient. Its artificial lagoons were stocked with fish and crossed by charming bridges. An indignant peacock scuttled out of the way as Max strode through the rose-covered arch that marked the entrance to the main path. The way became darker, the lanterns more infrequent, until he reached the corridor of tall yew trees. A fountain of cherubs and spouting fish marked the center of the garden, from which several paths branched off.

Max swore softly. There was no chance of finding his wife, or her fellow companions. The only sensible thing to do was go back to the ball and wait. Just then he caught the sound of footsteps. Quickly he drew into the shadows and remained still, his eyes narrowing on the approaching figure.

It was Diron Clement. Evidently the old man had noticed his daughter's absence. He tromped past Max without seeing him. Max grimaced, taking note of how Diron's head was thrust forward belligerently. There would be hell to pay if he found Henriette with Alexandre. The old man headed to the left, on a path which—if Max's memory served him—led to a tiny pagoda. An unwanted smile pulled at his lips. In his younger days he had made use of the pagoda himself. He still retained a fond memory or two of the place. No, Alexandre would not conduct his tryst there. It was too obvious.

Taking a chance, Max chose the opposite direction, a path which led to a hothouse filled with exotic fruit trees. Keeping to the shadows, he moved stealthily, stopping as he saw the telltale gleam of pink satin. Lysette was standing at the corner of the small structure, fidgeting a little, clearly waiting for someone. An owl hooted in the distance, and she jumped, looking from side to side.

The sight of her there, after she had promised not to take part in any illicit meeting between Alex and Henriette, spurred Max's temper. He decided grimly that this night she would learn she could not tweak his nose and then dance away without fear of retribution.

Lysette sighed, wishing she were back in the ballroom. She wondered nervously if Max had noticed that she was missing. The last thing she wanted to do was cross his wishes, but she had already promised Alex and Henriette that she would do what she could to allow them just five minutes alone. After Max's warning, she had considered reneging on her promise, but that would have been dishonorable. And they were so very much in love. She had tried to imagine what it would be like if she and Max were forbidden to see or talk to each other. The thought was intolerable.

A night owl gave an eery cry. Anxiously Lysette peered into the darkness.

A hard arm snaked around her waist from behind. A large hand covered her mouth as she yelped with fright. She was dragged back against a surface as unyielding as a brick wall. The shock of it paralyzed her. Just as she recovered enough to struggle, prying frantically at the hand over her mouth, she heard a deep, familiar purr in her ear.

"Had I known you desired a tour of the gardens, sweet, I would have offered to accompany you."

Lysette sagged in relief, gasping as the hand was removed from her mouth. "Max . . . oh, Max . . ." Trembling, she turned and wrapped her arms around his neck. "You frightened me!" She dropped her forehead against his chest.

He made no move to comfort her. "I intended to."

Catching her breath, Lysette looked up at him, her arms loosening as she saw his ominous expression.

"Where are they?" he asked.

She bit her lip and looked at the hothouse. The door opened, and Alexandre stuck his head out. His hair was wildly mussed, and his lips were suspiciously moist. "Lysette? I thought I heard—" He froze as he saw Max. They were all silent.

Max was the first to speak. "You have one minute, Alexandre, to say goodbye to Henriette. And make it meaningful. Your separation may be permanent."

Alexandre disappeared inside the building.

Lysette decided to explain as quickly as possible. "Max, I already promised them I would help them, and if you only saw how happy they were when I brought Henriette here you would have understood why I had to—"

"When we get home," he said pleasantly, "I'm going to take you over my knee and ensure that you will not be able to sit down comfortably for a long time."

Lysette blanched. She believed him. Max never made threats he did not carry out. "Max," she said weakly, "I'm not a child to be treated in such a—"

"Obviously," he interrupted with unnerving calm, "you require proof that I meant what I said earlier this evening."

Her arms dropped from around his neck. "I knew you meant it, I did, but . . ." Lysette found she was not above begging. "Max, please, *please,* don't be angry. You must understand—"

"I do understand," he said in that same terribly pleasant way.

"I don't think you do . . ." she began to argue, but suddenly Max was not listening, he was gazing into the distance, his eyes alert. "What is it?" she asked, and began to turn.

In a forceful movement, he yanked her against his body, fitting his mouth over hers. Lysette squeaked in protest at the punishing, painful kiss, and struggled to free herself, but his arms were too tight, and his hot, devouring mouth absorbed all sound. She tried to pull her arms loose, but her elbows were wedged between their bodies.

He angled his head more deeply over hers, his tongue plunging into her mouth. His hand moved down to her bottom, cupping the soft flesh and pulling her high against the swelling, insistent ridge of his manhood. Her vision blurred, and her struggles died away. Convulsively she swallowed, her mouth adjusting to his wet, searing kiss. Sensing her surrender, Max loosened his arms enough to free her hands. She clung to his broad back, writhing closer to his hard masculine body. It was then that he lifted his head, ignoring her soft whimper of desire.

"Ah . . . good evening, Monsieur Clement," he said, sounding completely unaffected by what had just transpired.

Lysette's head snapped around, and she saw Dion Clement's craggy face not five feet away. His subdued glare seemed to bore right through her.

"I was told my daughter Henriette was with you, Madame Vallerand," the old man barked. "Where is she?"

Lysette turned back to Max, looking up at him helplessly.

"I am sorry we are unable to help you, sir," Max said, his thumb brushing lightly over the top of Lysette's spine, "but my wife and I ventured out here in search of privacy."

"Then you have not seen Henriette tonight?"

"I swear upon my honor that I have not."

Unconsciously Lysette curled her fingers into his sinewy midriff. That last part was the truth, she thought. Max had not actually *seen* Henriette. Oh, God, if only Alex and Henriette had the sense to stay inside the hothouse!

Chapter 14

Clement considered them both carefully. Lysette's flustered expression and disheveled gown, Max's unreadable face and obvious state of arousal. They had not been married long, the old man recalled. It was not implausible that the couple had sneaked out to the garden in search of privacy. Giving them a last suspicious stare, he harrumphed and turned his back, walking away to renew the search for his errant daughter.

Lysette looked up at her husband with dazed gratitude. "If you had not been here, he would have found them. Thank you for—"

"Don't thank me." Max let go of her.

Lysette swayed unsteadily, the warmth and excitement he had awakened beginning to fade. She longed to have his arms around her once more. His affection was usually given to her so freely that she couldn't bear to have it withdrawn. She reached out to him tentatively.

"Max—"

He brushed her hands away. "Straighten your gown. You're going to take Henriette back without delay."

Alexandre and Henriette crept out of the hothouse. Lysette glanced at the girl's guilt-stricken face and forced a reassuring smile to her lips. "*Allons*, Henriette—we must go find your *tante*, quickly,"

Timidly the girl drew away from Alexandre and preceded Lysette on the path back to the main house. Alex bit his lip, apparently wanting to call out to her, but not daring to anger his brother further.

Max watched until his wife disappeared from view. Lysette had not looked back once. It was clear he had been cast as the villain of the piece. Thin vales of displeasure carved themselves around his mouth.

Alex gave him a mutinous glare. "Don't you understand anything about love? Don't you know how it feels to want someone until your arms ache to hold her? Are you going to claim that had you been in my place you wouldn't have done the same? Hah! I know how you compromised Lysette in order to force her to marry you. And I feel the—"

Mockingly Max held up his hands in self-defense. "Enough, Alex. I don't give a damn if you see Henriette or not. The choice, and the risk, are yours. But when you enlist the help of my wife, it is my right to interfere."

Alexandre's self-righteous anger vanished. "Of course," he mumbled. "But Lysette wanted to help."

"Of that I have no doubt. She is a softhearted creature, and easily entreated. It presents little difficulty to take advantage of such a gentle nature, *n'est-ce pas?* Don't involve her again, Alex—I won't abide it."

Alexandre nodded, shamed by his brother's words. "Max, I . . . I am sorry. All I have been able to think about is Henriette and—"

"I know," Max interrupted.

"You are angry with Lysette. Please don't blame her. She only did what Henriette and I both begged her to do."

"And what I told her *not* to do."

"You will not punish her, will you?"

Max lifted his brows and smiled derisively. "Why, Alex . . . you seem to believe my wife needs protection from me."

Having returned Henriette safely to her aunt, who had promised she would not confide the events of the evening to Diron, Lysette withdrew to a dark corner of the outside gallery. Sick with dread, she half-hoped Max would not find her, though she knew she would have to face him sooner or later. The crowd of guests inside the house was moving toward the dining room, where midnight supper was being served. The ball had lost its glitter; everything seemed terribly wrong. Frantically Lysette thought of some way to appease Max's temper.

She had crossed him after promising him she would not. That had stung his masculine pride. There was no way she could avoid retribution. Like any other Creole male, Max would not tolerate being openly defied by his own wife. Oh, why had she not considered her actions more carefully? No one, not even she, could blame him for being furious.

She remembered how he had pushed her away after he had kissed her. Max had never rejected her touch before. Folding her arms across her middle, Lysette leaned back against the wall. A hot blush covered her face as she thought of how she had responded to him—and he had only been kissing her in order to mislead Diron Clement! She had never felt so foolish.

She heard footsteps, and saw the shadowy form of a man approaching her. "Max?" The footsteps stopped. Unable to meet his eyes, she stared at the floor. "I—I was wrong," she said humbly. "I wish I could make the choice again. Forgive me. I will not quarrel with whatever punishment you decide." She walked toward him slowly, her voice lowering to a whisper. "But don't be distant, not with me . . . I cannot bear it. Tell me—"

Lysette stopped with a gasp as she came close enough to see his face. It was not Max. It was Etienne Sagesse.

There was a bright, glazed look in his eyes and she could smell the liquor he had been drinking. "Out here all alone?" he said, taking a step forward. "Perhaps you desire someone to relieve your solitude?"

Lysette's heart beat so heavily she could not catch her breath. Her skin crawled as she saw the expression on his fleshy face. He was very, very drunk. She tried to walk around him, but he moved to block her. "Let me pass," she said in a low voice.

"You're hiding from your husband, aren't you?" He advanced another step.

Lysette shrank into the corner. There couldn't be a scene, not involving her and Etienne Sagesse. It would cause a scandal, and another duel. She must get away from him quickly, before Max discovered them.

"He will be here soon," she said.

"You seem to be afraid, m'dear. Of me, or him?"

She did not reply.

Then Sagesse came a step closer. "You have reason to be afraid. You share a bed with a man who killed his wife. How often does he visit you? Every night? If I were in his place, I would use you well."

"He didn't kill her," Lysette said in a shaking voice. "Perhaps *you* did."

Sagesse smiled. "No, it wasn't I. Corinne was no threat to me. And she had given me all I desired—more, actually. Aside from acute boredom, I had no reason to kill her. But Max . . ." His arms stretched out, and he flattened his hands against the wall above her head.

Her chin trembled. "You know what happened to her, don't you?"

"But of course I do," he said truculently, his sour breath wafting against her face.

"Then tell me," she burst out, wondering if he did know something. It was more likely he was toying with her. "Tell me!"

His gaze fell to her breasts, the white gleam of her skin, the red glimmer of a long, coiled lock of hair that fell over her shoulder. "And if I do? What will you offer in return?" he asked, and touched her neck.

Lysette struck him hard enough to turn his face to the

side, then twisted past him. He caught her hair and pulled
her back. She gave a muffled cry of pain. "I'll call for
help—" She dug her nails into his hands, trying to pull
her hair free. "Don't force me to. Max will kill you.
Don't—"

His words struck her cheek in rapid bursts. "If he did
kill me, you know what it would do to him. Your pious
husband—damn his soul—could not tolerate my blood on
his hands. I am too much a part of his past." He wrapped
his burly arms around her struggling form. "For once I'll
know what it is to hold you in my arms. I should have had
you."

"No—"

"You were mine before he ever saw you."

"Stop it!"

"The only one I ever wanted. You should have been
mine."

Lysette cried out as he pulled her hair, and she tried to
claw his face. He shoved a knee between her thighs, and
his hard, bruising hands clutched at her body. His wet
mouth and teeth grazed her cheek. A scream broke from
her lips, and his hand covered her mouth while his other
felt for her breasts. Shuddering in revulsion, she bit his
hand and screamed again.

Suddenly there was a furious shout from behind her,
and Lysette was yanked away with a force that snapped
her head back. She stumbled as she was released, and
steadied herself against a narrow wooden column. Shivering, she watched Justin's slim, dark form step between
her and Sagesse. Some of Etienne's drunken wildness
seemed to fade as he stared at the boy.

Launching himself at Sagesse's bulky form, Justin went
for his throat with a snarl. Sagesse gave him a heavy
swipe across the face. As the pair fought, Lysette flinched
at the sound of each blow. "No, Justin!" Frantically she
looked for help. The guests had noticed the disturbance,
and a crowd, comprised mostly of men, was gathering on

either side of them. Someone pointed to her. She drew as far back into a shadow as possible, pushing back her tumbled hair, pulling up the front of her gown to cover her breasts.

A man darted forward from the crowd, and dragged Justin away from Sagesse. It was Bernard. "Calm down, you fool!" he muttered, struggling to restrain the writhing boy.

"Damn you!" Justin cursed. "Let go! I'll tear him apart!"

Several Sagesse relatives appeared, among them Etienne's brother-in-law, Severin Dubois. They gathered around Etienne, arguing fiercely as they began to drag him away to the *garconnière*. Etienne's behavior had disgraced the entire family. Humiliated, they wanted only to conceal him before more damage to their honor could be done.

Lysette shrank back in embarrassment as she felt a multitude of gazes upon her. She wished she could disappear. Did they think she had brought this on herself? That perhaps she had allowed Etienne to seduce her, as he had seduced Corinne? She started as she heard a voice close by her ear.

"Lysette?" Philippe was beside her, looking down at her with concerned blue eyes. He put an arm around her shoulders, as if he thought she might faint. She leaned against him, taking comfort in his presence. Philippe was so calm and steady . . . so unlike his hotheaded brother, who was still swearing and fighting to be free of Bernard's grasp. Following her gaze, Philippe glanced at his red-faced brother. A faint smile touched his mouth. "He will never forgive Bernard for pulling him off Sagesse," he commented.

"I agree," Lysette said with a shaky laugh.

"Are you all right?"

"Yes, but . . ." She felt a rush of tears come to her eyes. "Where is Max?"

"I think he—" Philippe broke off and looked up as the

chattering crowd fell silent. The congregation parted to make way for Max as he pushed his way through their midst. There was no sound. Even Justin was still, his curses dying.

Max stopped, his gaze darting from Lysette's tear-streaked face to Justin's. Through a scarlet mist he saw Etienne, propped up in the midst of relatives. He experienced an emotion that went far beyond rage. Blood was the only thing that would satisfy him. "By God, I'll kill you," he said in a low, murderous voice that curdled everyone's blood, including Lysette's. Before anyone could move, he had reached Etienne in two strides.

Lysette put her hands over her mouth to suppress a scream as she saw her husband turn into a stranger, attacking Etienne Sagesse in a frenzy. Tearing through the Sagesses, he threw himself on top of the drunken man and smashed Etienne's head against the floor. It took the combined efforts of Bernard, Alexandre, Justin, and Philippe to pull him off.

Severin Dubois stepped forward through the tumult, while Max strained against the arms that held him back. Self-possessed and authoritative, Dubois spoke in a calm voice that reached through Max's blind fury. "There is no excuse for the insult to your wife. Etienne was entirely at fault. On behalf of the Sagesse family, I offer the humblest apologies. All I can do is swear that it will not be allowed to happen again."

"No, it won't," Max sneered. "Because this time I won't make the mistake of letting him live. Get him a sword. I'll finish it now."

"You cannot duel with him," Dubois countered. "He is not in a fit condition. It would be murder."

"Then tomorrow morning."

"It would be murder," Dubois repeated, shaking his head.

Suddenly Etienne's slurred voice interrupted. His relatives had helped him up from the floor. His nose was bleeding, but he made no effort to blot it. "But Max has a taste for murder. And he does it *so* well."

Max stared at the drunken, taunting fool, and nearly trembled in his rage. His arms twitched against his brothers' restraining hands. "Get away from me," he whispered, but Bernard and Alex did not loosen their hold on him.

"Etienne," Dubois said, "be quiet. Do not make any more of a show."

"It is *my* show," Etienne said, and staggered forward, facing Max with a half-grimace that resembled a smile. "And Max's. Why do your women never seem to belong to you, Max? Corinne loathed the very sight of you. And this one . . ." he indicated Lysette with a florid gesture, "you had to steal from me." He looked at Bernard's white face, and then back at Max. A sly expression crept over his face. "For years you've lied to yourself about what happened to Corinne. Why can't you bear the truth? The pieces are all there. And yet you've never put them together. Poor Max . . . you could find the answers under your own roof . . . but *you don't want to.*" He cackled as he saw the bewilderment in Max's eyes. "What a fool you—"

"Etienne, enough!" Dubois snapped, taking hold of Sagesse's collar and dragging him away.

Max stared after them as if in a dream. Abruptly he shook off his brothers' hands, and glanced around wildly for Lysette. She was standing alone near the gallery railing, watching him with wide eyes. The tear tracks had dried on her face, and her long, tangled hair had fallen from its pins to hang past her waist. Casting a grimly threatening glance at the retreating Sagesse, Max went to his wife.

He clasped her narrow shoulders in his hands, while his eyes traveled over every inch of her. She was shaken, but unharmed. The thought that Sagesse had dared to touch her sent a new wave of violence through him.

Lysette could not control her trembling. "He . . . he knows who killed Corinne."

Max curved his arm around her back and pulled her closer. His gaze fell to her downbent head. "Did he hurt you?" he murmured, smoothing her hair gently.

"N–no." She felt his lips touch the top of her head. Closing her eyes, she clutched her arms around his waist. His warm hand kneaded her tense shoulders and rigid spine until she relaxed against him with a gasp of relief. He held her until the trembling stopped, and then kissed her temple with a comforting murmur.

Lysette protested as she felt his arms fall away from her nestling form. "Take her home." She heard the soft growl of his voice over her head, and she looked up in surprise as he urged her to Alexandre. Max's face was unreadable, but there was something in his eyes that frightened her.

"What are you going to do?" she asked.

Max bent his head and kissed her tear-salted cheek. "I'll be home soon."

"Come with me now," she begged.

But Max paid no attention to her plea, only exchanged a glance with Alex and left.

"Max!" she cried, both angry and fearful, taking a step after him.

Alexandre took her arm. "He'll be all right, Lysette. He is only going to talk with Severin and one or two of the Sagesses. I am certain Jacques Clement will be there to help mediate." His attention turned to Bernard, who was standing nearby. "Are you going with him?"

Bernard shook his head. "I'd be of little use," he said, and added venomously, "Especially since I wish we had let Max kill the insolent bastard."

Justin's low voice cut through the silence. "If father doesn't, I will."

They glanced at the boy, who had been forgotten in the disruption. Alex frowned, while Bernard laughed scornfully. "Little braggart," Bernard said.

Lysette went to the boy immediately, taking his hand and pressing it between her own. "Justin, don't say such things."

"I watched Sagesse all evening," he said roughly. "While he was watching you. When you disappeared, he went to look for you. That was when I followed him, and—"

"Thank you," she interrupted with a wan smile. "Thank you for rescuing me. Now it is all over, and we can—"

"I saw him go out to the gallery," Justin continued, his voice quieting to a half-whisper. He turned until his back was to the others. His intense stare did not waver from her face. "By the time I reached one of the doors, he had taken hold of you. I ran forward, and brushed past someone who was standing on the side of the gallery. Standing and watching the two of you. It was Uncle Bernard. He wasn't going to lift a finger to help you."

She shook her head, not understanding what he thought was significant. "Justin, not now—"

"Don't you understand? Something is wrong, wrong, when a man won't defend a member of his family, no matter what the feelings are between them. It was not only an offense against you, but against father, and me, and—"

"I am tired," she said, unwilling to hear more. Tempers were too high, and the boy was clearly incensed. All of this could be sorted out later.

Lysette huddled in bed alone, her teeth chattering. Her gaze moved restlessly over the dimly lit room. The events of the night kept churning through her mind, and she could not rid herself of the feeling that something terrible had been set in motion, something neither she nor Max could change.

She had never seen Max completely out of control, as he had been tonight. For a moment she had thought he would kill Sagesse right before her eyes. *Bonté Divine,* what am I thinking? She pressed her hands to the side of her head to drive away the dark images. But they persisted mercilessly, as did the echo of Etienne Sagesse's voice.

You have reason to be afraid. You share a bed with a man who killed his wife . . .

Max has a taste for murder . . .

And Max's deadly-quiet vow—*By God, I'll kill you.*

Lysette groaned and turned over, burying her face in the pillow. The house was silent. Alex and everyone else had retired, while Bernard had chosen to spend the night somewhere else. They had all agreed not to mention anything about the evening to Irénée.

It seemed that hours dragged by before Lysette heard the sounds of someone's arrival. She bolted up to a sitting position, then jumped out of bed, hunting for a pelisse to cover her gown. Just as she reached the bedroom door, Max stepped inside. He did not appear surprised to find her awake.

"I am so glad you are home," she said, going to him immediately, slipping her arms around his waist. But her relief diminished quickly. She sensed the unfamiliar tension in his body, a simmering violence that would not long be contained. His hand swept down her back, and he hugged her briefly before holding her away in order to look at her.

"Ça va?" he asked quietly.

"Oh, yes, I am fine. Now that you are here." A perplexed furrow gathered between her brows as she tried to read his mood. "Is there going to be a duel tomorrow?"

"No," he said, his mouth straightening into a harsh line.

"Well . . . I am certain we will have no more trouble from Etienne Sagesse, now that his family is—"

Max laid a finger over her lips, silencing her. "Go to sleep."

"But you—"

"I'm going to have a drink downstairs."

"I will join you."

"Not tonight."

"But I wish to—" she tried to argue. He turned her in the direction of the bed and gave her a gentle push. Fuming, she flopped down on the mattress in a gesture of childish pique.

The clock struck two, and still Max had not come to bed. Twice Lysette crept downstairs and saw his shadow as he paced back and forth across the library floor. What was making him so overwrought? What was he contemplating. She stood in the hall, wondering if she should go to him when she heard him striding out of the library.

Instinctively she fled for cover, darting into one of the double parlors. Max came into view. His cravat was missing, and his clothes were uncharacteristically disheveled. Lysette frowned as she saw him go to the front door. Was he leaving? She could not let him go anywhere tonight, not in this dangerous mood . . . not when such dreadful suspicions were plaguing her.

"Max?" she said, emerging from the parlour. "Wait . . ."

He stopped with his hand on the doorknob, a scowl on his face.

Lysette gathered up her courage and tried to appear casual. "Where could you be going at this time of night?" she asked.

He stared at her stonily. "Go to bed, Lysette."

"Come with me."

He turned with a curse and opened the door.

"Max, wait!"

The note of desperation in her voice stopped him. Eyes narrowing, he looked at her once more with a scrutiny that stripped away all pretense. Lysette felt a trembling in her knees, and she damned herself silently. "Why are you leaving?" she asked, short of breath.

"I won't be long."

"You . . . y-you can't go."

His gaze fell to her fidgeting hands. Lysette stilled them immediately, but it was too late. He had read all the signs of her fear. "You've never looked at me like this before," he said slowly. He closed the door, an odd, chilling light in his eyes. "Tell me what thoughts are running through your mind, my sweet."

"I–I . . ." She swallowed and tried to steady herself. "I want you to come to bed with me."

"Your uppermost thought," he prompted, with gentle, malicious insistence. "Tell me why you're so anxious to keep me here."

She shook her head helplessly.

"You're afraid of what I'll do, aren't you?"

"No," she protested, her voice catching in the middle of her throat. "No, it's not that."

He seemed calm and controlled, but she sensed his growing ferocity. "Then go upstairs and get into bed."

Only a fool would have disobeyed him. Lysette stood resolutely still, although part of her longed to flee upstairs. He had never been this way with her before, and it made her uneasy. "Max, don't," she said in a small voice.

His expression turned ugly, as if her timid manner had enraged him. "Don't what?"

"I can't talk to you when you—"

"You're frightened of me, aren't you?" He came closer, and it took all her nerve to keep from moving. "Just what do you think I'm capable of?"

"Frightened?" she repeated. "No." Saying it out loud gave her strength. "No, of course not." And then she realized it was true.

Max didn't understand how much she trusted him. And he was trying to leave the house at a time when he belonged with her. She intended to remedy the situation immediately. "Is it so unreasonable for a wife to ask where her husband is going in the middle of the night?"

"Most women would have the sense to assume their husbands are seeing a mistress."

Sharp words rose to her lips, but Lysette bit her tongue to hold them in. She had learned from past experience that Max could not argue with her when she didn't snap back at him. "But you don't have a mistress," she said, and reached out to brush the backs of her knuckles against his taut midriff. He flinched as if he had been touched by a live coal. *"Bien-aimé,* can't your plans for tonight wait until morning?"

Max looked at her derisively. "No."

"Then . . . I will not try to stand in your way." Looking dejected and lonely, Lysette raised vulnerable hazel eyes to his. "But . . . would you hold me for one minute before you go? I keep remembering what happened tonight, and I . . ." She bit her lower lip. "Just for a minute?"

Max hesitated. "I can't. You don't understand. I—"

"Half a minute." She blinked as if to fight back tears. "You're going to refuse me when I need you?"

"Dammit, I . . ." He scowled and did not move as she stepped closer and draped herself against his chest. Gingerly his arms slid around her back. His foul temper did not prevent him from noticing the sweet scent of her hair, the warmth of her body beneath the thin cambric gown and robe, or the feel of her breath as she pressed her face into his shirt.

"It always feels so safe in your arms," she whispered. Her hands crept up his back, and she felt his heart beat faster under her cheek. "Are you still going to beat me for what I did tonight? For helping Alexandre and Henriette?"

The hostile edge to his voice was gone as he replied. "I never said one word about beating you."

"You said you were going to take me over your knee and—"

He interrupted her with an exasperated sigh. "Do you actually think I would raise a hand to you?"

"You sounded very sincere," she said dubiously. He

responded with a string of soft curses that caused her face to turn red. Abashed, she turned her cheek to his shoulder. "I am sorry for what I did. You wouldn't listen when I tried to tell you before."

Max was nearly overcome with the urge to cuddle her close, cover her with kisses and endearments, tell her that she could do whatever the hell she wished as long as it pleased her. Gritting his teeth, he began to ease her away from his chest. She snuggled tighter against him.

"Kiss me before you go," she begged. "Just once."

"Lysette, you're trying to—"

"Half a kiss?"

Relenting with a scowl, he gave her a quick peck on the lips and let go of her. Lysette concealed her triumph, knowing now that nothing was going to keep him from her bed tonight.

"That wasn't a kiss at all," she said, giving herself the license to pout.

"It was exactly half. Now let go of my neck."

She refused to move. "I never thought you would be so stingy."

He glared at her. "Here," he said distinctly, "is your goddamn kiss. And then I am leaving. *Comprends?*"

Lysette nodded, closing her eyes and turning her face upward.

He took her head in his hands and touched his lips to hers. Voluptuously the tip of his tongue edged the inside of her mouth. He exerted pressure to widen the tender opening of her lips, and his tongue roamed skillfully inside her mouth.

Lysette pressed her breasts against him to relieve the sweet ache in her chest. Her hands slid to the back of his neck, and her fingers curled over the edge of his collar, digging into his thick black hair. With one hand Max tilted her head back, while his other palm settled at the base of her spine and pulled her belly flat against his. She responded languidly, her senses sliding into a warm pool of awareness.

When he released her, she gasped for air, falling back a step. He followed her movement, catching her hips in his hands, towering over her small, bare-footed figure. "Max," she whispered, sensing that his restless energy was turning to her. "Listen to m—"

He seized her mouth again, too hungry to stop himself. A tremor raced through him as he molded her body against his. Growling softly, he pulled down the top of Lysette's robe, baring her white shoulders. His self-restraint unraveled until his only thought was that he had to be inside her, hearing her sweet murmurs in his ear, feeling the nerveless quivering of her body as he thrust within her.

"I love you," she moaned, tilting her head back as his avid mouth wandered down her throat. Gently his teeth sank into her skin, and she arched against him, her heart stopping in pleasure. Her shaking hand moved over his abdomen until she reached the hot, burgeoning ridge straining against his breeches. Greedily she caressed him, her breath quickening in anticipation, and he covered her hand with his.

"Little witch," he said thickly, his mouth roving over her shoulder. "You knew one kiss would lead to this."

"So did you," she whispered.

His aroused body sent a demanding message to his brain, and suddenly he could not bring himself to care if the entire world went to hell. He snatched her up in his arms and strode to the stairs. Resting her head in the crook of his shoulder and neck, Lysette nuzzled past the top of his shirt. He smelled earthy and male and exciting. She strung kisses along the side of his neck, while her fingers plucked at the buttons of his shirt.

Reaching the bedchamber, Max carried her inside and paused long enough for her to close the door. As soon as the task was accomplished, he lifted her higher and covered her mouth with his, licking her love-bruised lips. Her head was spinning, and she could hardly stand as he lowered her feet to the floor. Unsteadily she made her way to the bed, fumbling with her robe and gown. The folds of cambric fell to the floor, and she stepped out of the circle of cloth, her body feeling deliciously unburdened. She pushed back the rumpled sheets on the bed, then sat on the edge of the mattress to watch Max, who was stripping off the last of his clothes.

Feeling her gaze on him, he looked up, catching his breath at the sight of her slender limbs, partially concealed by her long red tresses. Eagerly she reached out as he came to the bed, her small hands settling on his lean flanks. Whispering her love to him, she buried her face against the thin line of hair on his flat stomach. An absorbed look stole over his features, and he slid his fingers into her hair, his thumbs caressing her temples.

She took the heavy length of his manhood in her hands, her fingers tightening and loosening in the rhythm he had once taught her. Intent and aroused, Lysette bent her head, reveling in her sensual power over him. Her lips opened to slide over his silky-taut flesh, and her tongue flickered along the pulsing vein on the underside of the tumescent shaft. Closing his eyes, Max endured the torture for as long as he could, until he groaned and eased her away, his nerves close to exploding.

Wrapping his arms around her, he dragged her to the center of the bed with him. She shivered at the feel of his hard, naked body against hers, his seeking mouth on her breasts, his hands moving expertly over her tender flesh. His shaft pressed against the inside of her thigh, and she writhed in anticipation. "Take me now," she whispered, her open hands trembling against his back. "Now . . . Max, please . . ."

Rolling her onto her back, he spread her thighs and braced his elbows on either side of her head. There would be no games tonight. He wanted her too much. Lysette looked up into his golden eyes and whimpered his name. Her hands reached over her head and clasped his, their fingers lacing together. He penetrated her with a flex of his hips, working surely into the soft depths of her body. She tensed, gripping his hands until her fingers turned white.

"Lysette," he whispered, afraid he had hurt her. She appeared not to hear him. He began to withdraw, but her hips undulated, luring him to press inside once more. He sank deeper, kissed her trembling eyelids, her parted lips, the tiny crests of her nipples. Back and forth he moved, stoking the fire within her, taking fierce satisfaction in her purring sighs.

Slowly he rotated his hips, and she shuddered, her eyes flying open in astonishment. He repeated the movement, circling once, twice, and smothered her scream with his lips as she was overcome with ecstasy.

Lysette blinked several times as she drifted back to awareness, filled with lassitude. It took all of her strength to drape her arms around Max's body. Wearily she kissed his neck. Her contentment was curtailed abruptly as his body shifted, and she realized he was still hard and full within her. She shook her head with a protesting moan. "Not again . . . I can't . . ."

He continued to move, keeping her helplessly impaled on the swollen length of his manhood. Against her will, her body tightened, the tension beginning anew. She dug her fingers into his hard, broad back. The sensations ripened, more acute than before, until the madness swept them both, and they strove together until all feeling shattered into rapture.

"It seems like a dream now," Lysette said, the sheet falling to her hips as she rolled onto her stomach. Max lounged beside her, propped up on one elbow. They had been talking for some time. Max had wanted to know the details of her encounter with Etienne Sagesse, and she had reluctantly told him everything. His temper had eased somewhat, and although he was still wrathful over the incident, Lysette did not fear he would fly into another rage.

"Etienne was so intoxicated that it was impossible to make sense of what he was saying," she mused. "But he seemed to believe that he knew exactly who killed Corinne."

Max retreated into a frowning silence, absently stroking the silky line of down on her back.

She peered at him quizzically. "Max, how is it that he is certain of what happened to her, and you aren't?"

He sent her a sardonic look. "Etienne was her lover. Lovers are privileged to information that husbands are not. Obviously Corinne confided something in Etienne that he assumes I also know." He sighed moodily. "All I'm certain of is that I didn't kill her."

Lysette chewed her lip thoughtfully. "Etienne has ruined himself. No one will be able to meet his eyes without feeling scorn or pity. No family will want him to wed one of their daughters. No one will invite him anywhere. What do you think his family will do with him?"

"I have several suggestions to offer," he said darkly.

"I think I know why Etienne drinks so much."

"He's an undisciplined swine."

"No, because of this . . . this pained affection he bears for you."

"Pained affection?" He looked at her as if questioning her intelligence. "I would like to know where *that* notion came from, madame."

"Well, you said you were as close as brothers at one time. And there was a falling-out because Etienne was jealous of everything you did and had. It is possible to love and hate someone at the same time, *n'est-ce pas?* That was how he felt about you. How he *still* feels. He seduced your first wife because he wanted to hurt you. He insulted me because he knew it would make you angry. Somewhere inside he carries a burden of guilt for this, yes? That is why he drinks.''

"I don't give a damn why he drinks. But if he comes near you again, I'll—"

"No, no, no . . . don't say it!" She decided to divert him. "Er . . . you will tell Irénée today about what happened, *d'accord?*"

He shook his head. "There is no reason for her to be told."

"Yes, there is! Her friends will tell her if we do not, and she will be angry with us all."

Max scowled. "I don't have time to recount the story thrice over, sit with her while she had a *coup d'apoplexie*, and then reassure her for an hour until she calms down. You tell her."

"She is *your* mother."

"I'll have Alexandre tell her."

"Irénée will not believe him when he says everything is all right. Or me, for that matter. You are the only one who can reassure her."

"She'll believe you. She adores you." Max grinned and pulled her underneath him. "Say you'll tell her." He turned his head to the side as she hit him with a pillow. "Say you will."

"Never!"

"You will," he said, and caught her wrists in his hands, pinning them on either side of her head. Lysette stared up at him challengingly.

"It is *your* place to deal with Irénée, not mine."

"That, my sweet, is a matter of opinion. And when our opinions differ, you will defer to me."

"Ogre," she muttered. "You cannot force me to do anything."

"I'll have your promise before the night is through," he said, inwardly enjoying her defiance.

"How? You've already said you won't beat me."

He smiled slightly. "There are other forms of coercion, *enfant.*"

She stared up at him curiously, pondering his meaning, until she read the intent in his gaze. Her eyes rounded, and she made a sudden, sincere effort to escape. "No—"

No other word left her lips, as his mouth stifled her every sound. Expertly he seduced and took possession of her writhing body, and rewarded her helpless submission with infinite pleasure.

New Orleans was ablaze with gossip about the controversy. The rivalry between Etienne Sagesse and Maximilien Vallerand was well-known, but the events at the Leseur ball were outrageous. The scandalous story of Sagesse's drunken advances on Vallerand's lovely red-haired wife was recounted until the wildest rumors scattered from one household to the next.

It was said that the young Madame Vallerand had been half-naked out on the gallery. One witness was certain he had heard Vallerand swear to take revenge on every member of the Sagesse family, no matter how distantly related. Someone else claimed that Vallerand had threatened to strangle his second wife as he had the first, if she was ever caught even looking at another man.

As he went to his small shipping office in town, Max was well aware of the increased attention he received. It had taken little to reestablish all the old mistrust and suspicion. Wherever he went, there was scurrying excitement in his wake. Not since before his marriage had women given him those glances of fearful attraction, as if he were some dangerous animal to be desired and yet avoided. Men regarded him with measuring, subtly challenging gazes, like small boys facing the schoolyard bully. Filled with disgust, Max concluded his business as quickly as possible. Obviously, it was his lot in life to be hounded by scandal whether he deserved it or not.

When he returned to the plantation, he saw several carriages stopped on the long drive in front of the main house. It was not Irénée's usual at-home day. Frowning, he walked in and removed his gloves and hat. There was a steady hum of voices coming from the parlor.

Before he went to investigate, Lysette appeared. "Irénée's friends," she whispered, taking his arm. "Don't show yourself. We don't want anyone to faint." She led him hastily to the library. Max allowed her to tug him forward, while he filled his eyes with the sight of her. She was dressed in a vivid blue day gown trimmed with frothy white lace.

"Your mother has had a wonderful morning," she informed him, closing the library door. "Everyone from far and near has visited to hear her version of last night. It matters not in the least that she wasn't even there!"

Max laughed and bent to kiss her. "She can't embellish it any more than others have."

"How is our reputation?" she asked against his lips.

He smiled, suddenly feeling better. "Ruined."

"Hmm. No worse than the first month we were married." She sighed. "For a while I was certain we were improving."

"We were. Given enough time, we will again. The scandal could fade in as little as ten, twelve years."

Lysette smiled impishly and pulled his head down again. "So be it. We'll just have to keep to ourselves until then."

His lips skimmed softly over hers. "Madame Vallerand," he breathed, "you could make hell itself seem appealing."

She nestled against him with a contented sigh. "Wherever you go, *bien-aimé*, I'll be certain to follow."

Late that night Lysette was awakened as Max lifted his arm from around her waist and got out of bed. She mumbled in protest, missing the warm weight of his body next to hers. "Wh–what are you doing?"

"I must leave for a little while."

"Leave?" Confused, she shook her head and rubbed her eyes, struggling to a sitting position. *"Leave?"* she repeated groggily. "Why?"

"I have some business to take care of."

"Oh, Max . . ." Sleepy and irritated, she pushed her hair out of her face. "Didn't we discuss this *last* night?"

"We did." He pulled on his breeches and hunted for his discarded shirt. "And I should have taken care of it then," he added sardonically, "but I was distracted."

"Can't this business be seen to in the daylight?"

"I'm afraid not."

"What are you going to do?" she demanded. "Something dangerous?"

"No."

"Something underhand? Illegal?"

"Not entirely."

"Max!"

"I will return in two hours or so."

"I do not approve," she muttered. "I am certain this has nothing to do with Etienne Sagesse. I know it could not possibly be another woman. But I have a bad feeling, and you should heed a woman's instinct when—"

"Go to sleep," he whispered, pushing her back down, kissing her forehead. He tucked the covers around her. "When you wake, I'll be here beside you and everything will be all right."

She couldn't help pleading with him. "I trust you, I do, but—"

"Shhh." A feather-light kiss brushed her lips.

Lysette closed her eyes tightly, folding her arms across her chest. "Then go," she said in annoyance. "I don't care at all what you do."

"Lysette, there is one thing I should tell you."

"What is it?"

"If you try to follow me, I'll find out quickly. And I would have no compunction about tying you to the bed to keep you here."

Lysette felt herself turn crimson. "I wouldn't try to follow you, I wouldn't."

He laughed softly. "Good. Because tying you to the bed might lead to more . . . distraction."

"Please go," she said through her teeth, and turned on her stomach, covering her head with a pillow. He smiled and bestowed a light pat on her buttock.

A light, drizzling rain greeted Lysette in the morning, and she dressed more warmly than was usually required for a September day. Her simple velvet dress was made of a dull, rust-colored red that brought out the ruby glow of her hair. She parted her hair in the middle and gathered it loosely at the back of her head.

A faint groan of awakening came from the bed, and she looked over her shoulder at the mass of tangled sheets and long hair-dusted limbs. As he had promised, Max had returned during the night. Refusing to give any explanation of where he had been, he shed his clothes, smothered her questions by making love to her, and promptly went to sleep. Lysette was irritated by his evasiveness, but she was also relieved to have him back.

Standing up from her dressing table, she walked over to the bed, her hands resting on her hips. "So, you're awake," she said pertly.

Max made a sound that was neither confirmation nor denial.

"Bien," she continued, "because I did not intend to let you sleep a moment longer."

One golden eye squinted open.

"I want you to be tired today," she said. "I hope you're *exhausted,* my sneaking, close-mouthed husband, who cannot resist skulking away in the middle of the night for some clandestine activity you cannot even—''

''No, no, don't say clandestine,'' he mumbled. ''That word is not appropriate.''

''Then tell me what you did, so I may choose a more appropriate word.''

''No.'' He yawned hugely, rolling on his side away from her. ''Ring for breakfast, wife.'' He was startled out of his wits by her sudden cry of horror.

''Max!'' Her eyes widened and her hands flew to her mouth.

He twisted and shot up, the sheet falling below his waist, his black hair flying as he looked from right to left. ''What? *Qu'est-ce que c'est?''* His eyes met hers. She was staring at him utterly appalled, her face pallid. ''Lysette—''

''Turn around,'' she said anxiously.

Frowning quizzically, he complied. Lysette reached out to him, timidly touching one of several long, red scratches on his back. It looked as though he had been attacked by some fanged creature. ''What happened to your back?'' she demanded.

Baffled, Max shook his head, and then he realized what she was referring to. He relaxed with a rueful grin. ''Don't you remember?'' He reached around and dragged her across his lap. Bending his head, he touched the tip of his nose to hers, looking straight into her eyes. Mesmerized, Lysette felt as if she were drowning in the depths of gold. ''Don't you remember, *petite?''* he repeated huskily.

Her nostrils flared as she drew in a breath of surprise and consternation. ''I–I . . . you . . . you're not *possibly* implying that I . . . that *I* did that!''

He smiled lazily. ''I assure you, no one else was in a position to do so.''

''I *can't* have.'' she said weakly. Although, upon re-

flection she did recall a moment last night when her hands
had been on his back, and he had been . . .

Suddenly she went scarlet.

Max grinned. "I see you do remember."

Lysette was overcome with agonizing remorse. "Does
it hurt?" she asked in a small voice.

"No, no," he soothed. A devilish glint appeared in his
eyes. "Although I can't say I relish the prospect of soap
and hot water this morning."

She moaned, covering her face with her hands.

Realizing how distressed she was, Max abandoned his
teasing, trying to pry her hands away. *"Doucette,* listen
to me," he entreated, scattering kisses over her cheeks,
pulling her head to his chest and smiling against her hair.
"It doesn't hurt. I swear it." He murmured against her
crimson ear. "Last night you were so beautiful . . . so
passionate . . . I love the moments when you forget yourself, when you're wild in my arms . . ."

He tried to kiss her, but she was too upset, and he
finally released her with a laugh. "You may as well
reconcile yourself to the fact that it won't be the last
time."

Lysette wriggled off the bed. "Yes, it will," she cried,
and ran to the door while he grinned after her.

As the door swung open, she stopped abruptly, watching in amazement as Philippe raced up the stairs in apparent panic. "Where is Justin?" he cried as soon as he
saw her. "Is he home?"

"I do not know," she said, stepping into the hallway
and partially closing the door while Max pulled on a robe.
"Why? What is the matter?"

Philippe fought to catch his breath. "I was in town for
a lesson," he gasped. "I h–heard . . . *Bon Dieu,* I heard
that Etienne Sagesse . . ."

Lysette stared at him in bewilderment, gripped by an
ominous chill. Philippe was quaking visibly. She felt Max's
presence behind her, and she leaned back against him,

thinking feverishly that whatever had happened, she would not doubt him. "Go on," Max said, opening the door wider. "What about Sagesse, Philippe?"

The boy cringed. "I heard that he was found last night in the Vieux Carré, near Rampart Street . . . Etienne Sagesse has been murdered."

Chapter 15

The full weight of the suspicions against Max were revealed by the visit of Jean-Claude Gervais, the captain of the *gens d'armes*. Gervais, the highest-ranking police official in New Orleans, would not have come himself unless the situation was extremely grave. Captain Gervais fervently wished himself to be in anyone's shoes other than his own. He had not forgotten the favor Maximilien Vallerand had done him not long ago, putting a few words in the right ears to ensure the *gens d'armes* were provided with new arms and equipment. And now he was repaying the man by intruding on his privacy, and questioning him in regard to murder. Gervais suppressed his discomfort and assumed an impassive expression as he was welcomed into the Vallerand home.

"Monsieur Vallerand," he began, standing ramrod-straight as Max closed the library door to afford them privacy. "The reason I am here—"

"I believe I know why you're here, captain," Max said dryly. He walked to a set of crystal decanters and held one up with an inquiring glance.

"Non, merci," Gervais said, although he sorely desired a drink.

Max shrugged and poured himself a brandy. "Sit down, if you wish. I have a feeling this might take a while."

"Monsieur Vallerand," Gervais said, lowering his bulky frame into a deep leather chair, "I must begin by saying this is not an official—"

"I know you have many questions, captain. In order to save time, let us both be as brief and direct as possible." Max smiled slightly. "We'll save small talk for a more pleasant occasion, *oui?*"

Gervais nodded, and took a deep breath before beginning. "Is it true, monsieur, that you threatened Etienne Sagesse's life the night before last, on the premises of the Leseur plantation?"

Max nodded. "Sagesse had just made insulting advances to my wife. Naturally I desired a duel with him. But I was persuaded not to pursue the matter because of his condition."

"Yes. I have been told he drank." Only a Creole would understand the delicate significance Gervais placed on the last two words. The phrase was an indictment of his masculinity, honor, and character. It was unpardonable for a Creole not to have control over his appetite for liquor.

Gervais clasped his hands together loosely, resting them on his plump thigh. "Monsieur, your present wife and Monsieur Sagesse were at one time betrothed, were they not?"

Max's eyes narrowed. "They were."

"The Sagesse family claims that you stole her from Etienne. How exactly was that accomplished?"

Max was about to reply when there came a gentle knock, and the door was pushed open. Lysette peered in at the two of them.

"Oui?" Max said abruptly.

"I would like to listen, if it would not displease you. I promise not to interfere. Not in any way."

Max considered her request briefly, then glanced at the other man. "If the captain has no objections. Captain Gervais, my wife, Lysette Vallerand."

Gervais did not reply. He was staring in a stupefied

manner at the woman before him. She was like some exotic flower, a bright and lush flower that could survive only in sultry climes. Her slender, voluptuous figure was clad in a velvet gown of a hue that emphasized her lustrous ruby-red hair. Her soft red lips brought thoughts to mind better left undisclosed.

She was the stuff of fantasy, an erotic vision a man would conjure during lonely contemplation in a solitary cell, or on board a China-bound ship with no hope of feminine companionship. And yet, in the midst of all that sensuous allure, her eyes were unspeakably innocent, and her voice, childishly sweet. The contrast was too delightfully stimulating. Even with her imposing husband in the room, Gervais could not squelch the heat that had begun in his loins the moment he saw her. Now he understood the furor that seemed to erupt whenever this woman's name was mentioned. He felt his face begin to glow, and he stirred discreetly in the leather chair.

Max gave the silent man a glance of understanding . . . perhaps even sympathy. "Captain?" he prompted.

Gervais started. "Oh, yes . . . no, I am afraid . . . that is . . . it is possible that the questions I must ask may be distressing to Madame Vallerand."

"We may be frank in front of my wife," Max said, and motioned for Lysette to join them. She closed the door and perched on a small chair nearby. *"Maintenant,* Captain Gervais . . . where were we?"

"Ah, yes. The, ah, theft of Etienne Sagesse's betrothed."

"Theft?" Lysette repeated, unable to help herself. "Of *me?"* Max took a sip of his drink to cover a wry smile, reflecting that not even a minute had passed before she'd broken her promise not to interfere. "Oh, I must explain," Lysette continued. "I left the Sagesse home of my own accord—because of Monsieur Sagesse's improper and ungentlemanly behavior toward me. At the invitation of Maximilien's mother, Irénée, I came to stay here—she was

an acquaintance of my mother's, you see—and then I took
ill. And, during my extended visit and convalescence, I
fell in love with Maximilien and accepted his offer of marriage. I was not stolen from anyone. It is very simple,
voyez-vous?''

"Indeed," Gervais muttered. She smiled at him, and
he forced himself to look at Max, his eyes feeling sun-
dazzled. "Monsieur Vallerand, you dueled with Monsieur
Sagesse over this . . . ah, matter . . . did you not?"

"Yes."

"Would you say it deepened the enmity that already
existed between you?"

"No. In fact, I ended the duel prematurely."

"Why?"

"I was aware of a feeling of . . . pity for him. Any man
who was there will concur that I could have easily killed
him on the spot, in legitimate defense of my honor. But I
have finally reached the age, captain, when a man desires
a measure of peace and tranquility."

Gervais nodded, although he did not fully believe the
latter claim. A man did not marry a woman such as *that*
if one desired tranquility!

"I even dared to hope," Max continued, "that the open
feuding between the Sagesses and Vallerands might come
to an end." His brows quirked as he saw that even Lysette
was looking at him skeptically. "It's true," he said mildly.

"Even with the certain knowledge of his relationship
with your first wife?" the captain asked.

"Hatred is a draining emotion," Max replied. "It leaves
room for little else." He glanced at Lysette. "I finally
began to relinquish it when I realized how much richer
life could be without it." His attention moved back to the
captain. "Not that I forgave Sagesse, you understand. His
betrayal struck deep, and I have as much pride as any
man. But I became tired of nursing the old bitterness, and
I wished to put the past behind me, where it belonged."

"But Sagesse made that impossible?"

"I wouldn't say that. There was virtually no communication between us after the duel."

Captain Gervais asked several more questions about the affair between Corinne and Etienne, and then he changed tacks. "Monsieur Vallerand, you were seen by two witnesses in the Vieux Carré last night. Your purpose there?"

Lysette did not move or speak, but her pulse began to beat heavily until she could feel it thrumming in every vein of her body.

"I was visiting a quadroon woman."

Both Lysette and Captain Gervais flushed. Mariame? Lysette thought wildly. What had he been doing with Mariame? Why had it been necessary for him to visit her? She blinked as she realized Captain Gervais was speaking to her. "Madame Vallerand, if you wish to leave the room—"

"I do not wish to," she said distantly.

Dismayed, Gervais resumed the questioning. "Your mistress?" he asked Max, whose reply was shamelessly matter-of-fact.

"Yes, for several years."

Lysette did not hear the rest of the interview. Her mind buzzed with distasteful possibilities. Either Max had lied to her and was still keeping Mariame as a mistress or he was lying to Captain Gervais in order to cover up the true reason he had been in the Vieux Carré.

Finally Captain Gervais stood up to indicate the questioning was over. "Monsieur Vallerand," he said solemnly, "I feel obligated to bring certain facts to your attention—unofficially, of course."

Max inclined his head, his eyes alert on the captain's face.

"It is important for the people of New Orleans to feel the law is being executed as competently as before the American possession," Gervais said. "You, monsieur, with your influence, are more aware than most of the disorder that exists everywhere. The populace has little faith in any of the institutions of government—including, I am sorry to say, my own police force. Etienne Sagesse was of an old and recognized family, and his death is considered a great loss. People demand quick retribution for such a crime. Moreover, a fair trial cannot be guaranteed to anyone. The court system is in turmoil. One would be a fool to hang his life on the hopes of absolute fairness and justice.''

Max nodded slowly.

''Especially,'' Gervais added, ''when several prominent men in the community have come forth to denounce you. One of these men is the judge of the County Court. They are calling for your arrest. And it is more than simple sword-rattling, monsieur.''

''Do any of these men, by chance, belong to the Mexican Association?'' Max asked.

''Many of them, I believe,'' Gervais hesitated. ''Perhaps all.''

Burr's friends. Max smiled cynically. The associates of Aaron Burr were calling for his arrest, most likely having promised Burr they would do what they could to take his revenge on Max for his disdain of their cause. There could be no better opportunity than this.

''I am giving you time to make plans, monsieur.'' Gervais looked at him squarely. The warning was unorthodox, but he had not forgotten his debt to Vallerand. ''Because I shall be forced to arrest you soon.'' He paused. ''Incidentally, have you been made aware of how Monsieur Sagesse was murdered?''

Max shook his head.

''He was strangled,'' Gervais said. ''It takes great strength, monsieur, to kill a man of Sagesse's size in such a manner.'' He looked pointedly at Max's heavily-muscled chest and shoulders. ''Not many men could have accomplished that.''

Lysette could not make a sound as Max guided the captain to the front door. She pressed her fists against her abdomen. "It isn't happening," she whispered. "It isn't real." It was a dream, a horrible dream, and she was going to wake up soon.

A minute that seemed like a year went by, and then she was aware of Max's return. He dropped to one knee beside the chair, taking both her cold fists in his big, warm hand. "Sweet," he murmured. "Look at me."

She gave him a fixed, frantic stare.

"I did see Mariame last night," Max said. "I had to make arrangements for her son—by another man—to flee the territory. He's an octaroon. Last week he was discovered having an affair with a white woman. His life is in jeopardy. You may have heard what they do to . . . well, we won't go into that. A few days ago Mariame sent me a message asking for help. Knowing what the boy means to her, I could not refuse."

Lysette had barely listened to the explanation. "What Captain Gervais said about giving us time to make plans . . . he has given us time to get away. He meant escape, didn't he?"

"Yes." Max sighed. "That is what he meant."

"We have only a day—perhaps less—we must be gone by tonight! It will not take long to pack, we don't need much at all. Mexico? No, France. we'll go to France, and—"

"We're not going anywhere," he said gently.

Lysette gripped his coat lapels. "Yes, we are! I don't care where we live, as long as I can be with you, and if you stay, they'll—" Her voice cracked. "I believe what Captain Gervais said. I believe him, and you must as well!"

"I did not kill Etienne Sagesse."

"I know that, I do. But we will never be able to prove it, and if we could, no one would listen. The American authorities won't want to listen. They want to show their power over the Creoles, and to take down a man of your position would make them feel as if they were finally in control of the city. They will convict you, take you away from me. We have to go. Don't you understand? If anything happens to you, I won't want to live! I *won't* live!'' Lysette burst into tears as she saw the refusal in his eyes.

''They won't convict me,'' he said, his face understanding but firm. ''And we're not going to run anywhere. We're going to stay here and face what comes.''

''No!'' she said, jerking away as he tried to comfort her. ''No, don't say anything else!'' Rapidly she gained control of herself. ''I am going upstairs to pack for both of us. Tell Noeline to have the trunks brought out. No, no, I will tell her.'' She jumped back as he reached out for her. ''Don't touch me!'' She steadied her quivering chin and took a hiccuping breath. ''I am leaving for France tonight, and you can either stay and be hanged with your principles, or go with me and be happy. It shouldn't take you long to choose!''

Lysette stormed out of the room, and then, lightning-swift, reappeared at the doorway. ''And while you are considering your options,'' she hissed, ''you might think about the fact that by now you have probably ensured that I am pregnant. Our child will need a father! And if *that* doesn't perturb you . . .'' Her eyes slitted. ''Then I swear by all the saints that if you stay here to be hanged, I'll *still* go to France, and find someone else to marry! Think on *that!*'' Whirling around, she went upstairs, while Max stared after her dumbfounded.

The house was still as a tomb, except for the sounds of Lysette's hasty packing. Heavily veiled and grief-stricken, Irénée had taken Noeline with her to the cathedral, where she spent several hours taking counsel from an old, familiar priest, and praying brokenly for forgiveness for her son. She had not been able to speak to Max, or even look at him, as she left the plantation.

Of course, Max reflected, it had not crossed Irénée's mind that he might *not* have been Sagesse's murderer. For years she had lived with the belief that he had ended Corinne's life. He wondered bleakly how Irénée could still love a son she thought to be a cold-blooded killer.

Prowling in and around the house until early evening, Max pondered the idea of escape and rejected it. Long ago he had acquired holdings in Europe, in case his property in Louisiana was ever jeopardized. If forced to flee, he had the means to keep himself and Lysette in comfortable style for the rest of their lives. But the years of exile, being haunted by his reputation, always looking over his shoulder in fear of retribution from the Sagesses or their kin . . . no, he and Lysette would never be happy. And the kind of vendetta the Sagesses would declare would be extended to his children. His sons' lives would be in danger, until someone paid for the crime Max was accused of. He had to stay here and fight to prove his innocence.

He stopped at the foot of the double staircase and glanced up at the second floor. Bewildered and afraid, Philippe had closeted himself in his room. Justin, as usual, was nowhere to be found. A maid scurried by Max and went up the stairs carrying a bulky leather valise, while Lysette's high-pitched voice urged her to hurry. Max shook his head slowly. No one could fault the woman he had wed for lack of spirit. He set his foot on the first step, intending to go up and put a stop to the useless packing.

Max stopped at the explosive sound behind him, as Justin threw open the front door and burst into the house like a madman. "Father!" Justin shouted. "Fath—" The boy skidded to a halt in front of Max, all tense, trembling energy. The drizzling mist from outside had soaked into his clothes and hair, and he stood there heedlessly dripping on the rug.

Automatically Max reached out to steady him. "Justin, where have you—"

"F–following," Justin stammered, clutching at Max's arms, "following U–uncle Bernard." He tugged impatiently. "He is in town, drinking and gaming at *La Sir-ène.*"

Max was hardly surprised. "He has his own ways of dealing with family misfortune, *mon fils.* God knows he's had to suffer through enough of it. Let him be. Now—"

"No, *no!*" Justin pulled at him tenaciously. "You have to talk to him."

"Why?"

"There are some things you must ask Bernard." Justin's stabbing blue eyes met his father's.

"Such as?"

"Ask him why he resents Lysette so much. And why he let her fall from the attic. Ask him why he stood on the gallery, watching her with Sagesse, and didn't try to help her! Ask him where *he* was last night!"

"Justin," Max said impatiently, "it is obvious that, for whatever reason, you and Bernard have quarreled. But right now there are more important—"

"No, nothing is this important!" Justin clung to him obstinately. "Ask him" he insisted, "how he felt about my mother! And then ask what Etienne knew that made him so dangerous to Bernard!"

Max shook the boy roughly, startling him into silence. "No. *Stop it!*"

Justin closed his mouth.

"I understand that you want to help." Max's hands bit into the boy's wiry arms. "You don't want me to be blamed for the murder. But that gives you no license to cast groundless accusations at others, especially members of your own family. You may not be fond of Bernard, but—"

"Come with me," Justin begged. "Talk to Bernard. If you do, you'll see what I'm trying to tell you. It is the only thing I will ever ask of you." Justin abandoned his humble pleading and let his temper flare. "Damn you, don't try to claim you haven't the time! What else were you planning to do tonight? Waiting to be arrested?"

Max studied him, his face implacable, while Justin held his breath. Then Max nodded slightly. "All right."

Justin threw his arms around his father and buried his head against his chest, then jumped away abruptly. "There is little time. We shouldn't use the main road—"

"We'll have to," Max said. "By now the other routes have turned to mud." He strode to the door, while Justin scampered after him.

Renée Sagesse Dubois sat alone in the parlor with the sealed letter in her lap, staring at it with red-rimmed eyes. It was addressed to Maximilien Vallerand. She remembered watching Etienne write it just before the duel. Etienne had sealed it himself, adamantly refusing to tell her the contents. He had told her to give the letter to Maximilien, if Vallerand proved the victor.

Numbly Renée wondered why Vallerand had spared Etienne's life then, why he had ended the duel without real bloodshed. Etienne had mentioned it more than once in the months afterward, seeming to have even greater contempt for Maximilien.

Since the duel, Renée had tried to give the letter back to Etienne. He insisted each time that it remain in her possession, with the same instructions. Upon his death, he wanted her to place the letter in Maximilien's hands.

But she could not. In spite of the promise she had made, Renée could not face the man who had killed her brother. "I am sorry, Etienne," she whispered. "I cannot do it." Beginning to cry, she knocked the letter to the floor, and hunched over in grief.

After a long spasm of sobbing, Renée regained her composure. Her eyes were drawn again to the letter. What could Etienne have written? What were his true feelings for the man who had been his friend, enemy, and ultimately his murderer? Leaning over, Renée snatched the letter up and broke the scarlet wax seal.

She began to read, using her fingers to wipe the stream

of tears from her cheeks. The first page was too cryptic to
understand. Frowning, she turned to the second. "Oh,
no," she murmured, the letter trembling in her hand.
"Etienne . . . how can this be?"

The light was beginning to fade as Justin and Max rode
along the cool, mist-shrouded road. They had not exchanged a word since leaving the plantation. Max wondered what madness had possessed him to head to town
with Justin. If, by some miracle, they reached their destination without Max being arrested, then what? He would
gain nothing by talking to Bernard, who was probably too
deep in his cups by now to form a complete sentence.

What did Justin think he would read in Bernard's re-
plies? Why was Justin so determined to involve Bernard
in this sorry tangle? Max had to grit his teeth to keep from
telling his son that he was going to turn back. But as Justin
had pointed out, the boy had never asked for anything
from him.

Justin increased their pace until the horses' hooves were
slogging a desperate canter through the mud. They came
to a curve and slowed, seeing four riders a short distance
ahead. The riders fanned out instantly, forming a half-
circle as they approached the pair. Max recognized Severin Dubois, Etienne's two brothers, and a Sagesse cousin.
It wasn't difficult to figure out their purpose—they had
formed a lynching party to avenge the death of one of their
own. Max's hand flew instinctively to his side. He swore
under his breath, realizing that in his haste to leave the
house, he had forgotten his brace of pistols.

Justin cut his horse sharply to the right, preparing to
flee.

"No, Justin," Max said hoarsely. The riders were too
close; it was useless to run. Either not hearing him or
ignoring the command, the boy continued on his reckless
path. One of the Sagesses held his rifle by the barrel and
used the heavy maplewood stock as a club. Suddenly Jus-

tin felt a brilliant burst of pain at the back of his head, and everything went gray. Dazed he tried to clear away the mist before his eyes. Darkness wrapped itself around him, and he succumbed helplessly.

Max jumped from his horse and caught Justin's limp form as it slid from the saddle.

The horses stamped and shuffled. Severin Dubois watched calmly as Max lowered his son to the ground. "Justice is uncertain these days," Dubois remarked. "We felt it best to take matters into our own hands."

Max breathed a sigh of relief as he turned Justin's head and saw that the injury didn't appear to be serious. He stripped off his cloak to cover the boy. "I'm sorry," he whispered to his unconscious son, smoothing the lank black hair, pressing a kiss on Justin's pale forehead.

"He won't be harmed any further," Severin said. "We'll leave him here. Unless, of course, you try to make things difficult."

Max stared at Dubois with cold hatred, not resisting as one of the Sagesses began to bind his wrists.

Etienne Sagesse's sister was the last person Lysette had expected to call that evening. Still, she welcomed her with irreproachable politeness. She was sorry for Renée's loss, even though she had no liking for the woman.

Etienne's sister had been nothing but unfriendly during the time Lysette had been forced to stay in the Sagesse home. Renée had gone out of her way to make it clear that Lysette was far from her choice as a sister-in-law.

Lysette now found it ironic that for the first time the two of them had something in common. Renée had just lost a brother, and Lysette was on the verge of losing a husband.

"Where is Monsieur Vallerand?" Renée demanded without preamble. Lysette could not help staring in amazement. From what she remembered during her brief stay with the Sagesses so many months ago, Etienne's sister had possessed an icy composure that had been unshakable. At the moment she seemed to be an entirely different woman. "I must speak to your husband," Renée said rapidly, refusing to go into the parlor. *"Immédiatement."*

"I am afraid he is not here," Lysette said.

"Where is he? When will he return?"

Lysette gave the older woman an assessing glance, wondering what her game was. Had the Sagesses sent her to work some bit of mischief? "I do not know," she said truthfully.

"I have something for him. Something from my brother."

"Oh? What is it?"

"A letter. Etienne wished it to be given to Monsieur Vallerand when he died."

Lysette nodded coolly. No doubt the letter was some last bit of insulting nonsense. Only Etienne would find a way to taunt Max from the grave. "If you wish to leave it with me, I will see that my husband receives it."

"You do not understand. It tells everything, all about the past . . . the affair . . . *everything.*"

Lysette's eyes darkened. "Please, let me see it. Please." Hastily she reached for the letter, taking it out of the other woman's hands before it was offered. Bending her head over it, Lysette turned partially away, a swath of hair falling forward to hide her face. Certain phrases leapt out at her, and unconsciously she read them aloud, her eyes skimming over the scrawling lines.

> *"What a blind fool love makes of you, Max. Perhaps I should have let you keep your illusions . . .*
>
> *. . . I understand you well enough to be certain you would rather shoulder the blame for a crime you did not commit than believe your own brother was capable of such betrayal . . .*
>
> *. . . I gave you what you wished . . . I watched you wallow in self-delusion, while I—"*

Lysette broke off and looked at Renée. "Bernard?" she said wildly.

Renée regarded her with reluctant pity. "So the letter claims. After Corinne's affair with Etienne ended, she began a liaison with Bernard. She admitted as much to Etienne, and also told him of her plans to expose her affair with Bernard, if Bernard did not agree to run away with her."

Lysette rifled through the letter frantically.

> . . . *there is no doubt Bernard found the idea of doing away with her much more appealing than enduring her companionship in a lifetime of exile. Given the same choice, I might have strangled the bitch myself. But making it appear as though the unfortunate, cuckolded husband had done the deed . . . that was a master touch, worthy only of a Vallerand.*

"Etienne writes that your husband was a fool for not considering the possibility of an affair between Corinne and Bernard," Renée said. "Etienne scorned Maximilien for ignoring what he could have seen if he'd only cared to look."

"But . . . Max believed that Bernard was very much in love with someone else."

"Yes, an American girl."

"Bernard made her pregnant, and she ran away—oh, what was her name—"

"Ryla Curran," Renée interrupted. "In the letter Etienne makes a different claim. Bernard was interested in the girl, but *never* had an affair with her."

"How did Etienne know this?"

"Because it was Etienne, not Bernard, who seduced her." Renée smiled bitterly. "Unfortunately she wasn't the first young girl Etienne ruined—or the last."

Lysette went cold, wondering what it would do to Max

to discover what Bernard had done. Her mind reeled. "Bernard killed Etienne," she said.

"I believe so. Of course, there is no proof, only—"

"He did!" Lysette insisted. "Bernard must have been convinced the night of the Leseur ball that Etienne would not keep his silence much longer, not with his drinking, and . . . yes, Bernard must have killed him! Only for this second murder, Max will pay in full measure. Oh, I must do something, show this to someone—"

"Do not panic," Renée said. "There is time. All that is necessary is to show the letter to the authorities when they come for your husband." Her lips thinned. "Unless Maximilien has already fled the territory. Has he?"

Lysette responded with a scathing glance.

Renée began to ask something else when they were distracted by a sudden intrusion.

"Max?" Lysette asked, whirling around. "Where—" The words died away on her lips.

Justin was leaning against the doorframe, gasping and panting, having run for miles without stopping to reach home. His face was bluish-white under its tan. Every inch of him was soaked and spattered with mud. "Lysette, I . . . need help . . . where is Alexandre?"

"He is with Henriette and the Clements," she answered automatically. "Justin, what—"

The boy interrupted her with a hoarse call toward the stairs. "Philippe! Philippe, damn you, come here!"

Philippe appeared at the top of the stairs, took one look at his brother, and began to hurry down. Justin glanced beyond Lysette to Renée Dubois. The sight of the visitor seemed to sharpen his wits. "How neighborly of you," he said, staring at Renée. A spasm of hatred crossed his face. "Keeping my . . . stepmother company while your husband and your brothers butcher my . . ." Dizziness overtook him, and he crumpled against the doorway, holding his head. "My father," he finished with a gasp, and reached out to Lysette as she drew closer. He held onto her, oblivious to the mud on his clothes and hands. "They took him," he gasped softly, afraid he was going to faint. ". . . I don't know where. They'll kill him . . . Oh, God, they might have already."

The small group led Max's horses off the main road and through mud-bogged side avenues. The Sagesses were grimly determined to punish the man they were certain had murdered Etienne. In this territory, where power seemed to change hands almost monthly, the definitions of right and wrong were variable. The only certain means a man had of extracting justice was to rely on his own family.

Hands bound behind him, Max waited tensely while they took his horse's reins and rode to the remotest edge of the Sagesse plantation, out among fields left to lie fallow for a season. When they stopped near a grove of trees and began to dismount, Max took action, kicking his horse into a sudden leap sideways, hoping the reins might be yanked out of Severin Dubois' grasp.

Dubois took the end of the rope binding Max's wrists and pulled, toppling him to the ground. Max landed on his side with a grunt of pain. There was no laughter or jeering at his ignominious descent. This was a serious business, and they were acting not out of petty vengeance, but moral obligation.

Although he knew it was hopeless, Max struggled as he was lifted to his feet. The first blow came with blinding force, whipping his head back and sending a stab of pain through his skull. Before he could draw breath, there was a torrent of relentless blows that increased until his ribs cracked under the strain. Again his head was snapped to the side, and he felt his body begin to sag. Dark and light hovered around him, and all sound dissolved into a jumbled roar. His energies were no longer directed toward resistance, but endurance. Although some distant part of

him knew what was happening, consciousness began to
drift in and out of his reach in elusive waves.

Renée looked blank with surprise. "You say my husband has taken him?" she asked. "Severin and—"

"Yes!" Justin snarled. "Your entire accursed family!"

"How long ago?"

"I don't know. I . . . half an hour, perhaps."

Renée came forward, lightly touching Lysette's shoulder. "I did not know about this. They must have decided
on this very quickly."

"Like hell you didn't know," Justin muttered.

Renée's cool eyes flickered to his angry blue ones.
"Your insolence won't help anyone, little man." She returned her gaze to Lysette. "I might know where they
have taken him, but I am not certain. My carriage is just
outside."

"Why would you want to help me find him?" Lysette
asked woodenly, barely taking notice of Philippe as he
joined them.

"It was wrong of Etienne to keep silent for years when
he knew that Maximilien was innocent. It was not your
husband's fault that he was the object of Etienne's irra-
tional jealousy. No one can make reparation for what
Etienne has done, and no one—"

"Perhaps," Justin interrupted icily, "we could make
speeches later, and try to find my father before your family
stretches his neck several inches." Grunting with pain, he
pushed open the front door and gestured mockingly to the
carriage.

Quickly Philippe escorted Lysette outside, and Justin
took Renée's elbow in a hard grasp. She glared up at him.
Although she was a tall woman, he possessed almost every
inch of his father's height. "You are ruining my gown with
your dirty hand, boy!"

Justin did not let go of her, using her to maintain his
precarious balance. "Tell me where we're going and why

you think he's there," he said as they went down the front steps. "And why I should not believe you're leading us on a merry chase to keep us from finding him." It did not bother Justin that he was addressing a well-respected society matron several years his senior, in such a rude manner.

"I have already explained why I wish to help," Renée said haughtily. "And we are going to a field on the northwest corner of my plantation, a private and secluded place." A trace of malice entered her voice. "With trees aplenty for hanging. Severin had a man severely beaten there once before. I know, because I followed him."

"And the man's offense?"

They stopped at the door of the carriage. Renée shoved his hand away from her elbow. They faced each other, and she decided to shock the arrogant boy into silence. "Severin suspected him of being my lover," she said. Pleased with her own boldness, she waited for a youthful blush that never came.

"Was he?" Justin's dark eyes were far too adult for a boy his age.

To her annoyance, Renée was the one that blushed as she climbed hastily into the carriage.

The Sagesses had gathered underneath an ancient oak tree and wrapped a rope around the thickest limb.

"We'll wait until he comes to," Severin Dubois said, and the men grunted as they lifted Max's heavy, slumping body onto the saddle of the fidgeting black stallion. Sensitive and fiery-natured, the horse could not tolerate the nearness of anyone other than his master. Max was the only one who could ride him.

Tomas Sagesse, Etienne's youngest brother, slipped the noose around the unconscious man's neck, tightened it, and gingerly took hold of the stallion's reins. "I will not be able to stay him for long," he said.

"You must. I want Maximilien to be awake," Severin replied. "I want him to know."

When the horse was allowed to walk away, Max's body would slowly come to dangle in mid-air. His neck would not be broken. He would hang there with his windpipe closed off, choking and strangling. Justice, as far as Severin Dubois was concerned. He wandered closer to the agitated horse, and stared closely at Maximilien's bloodied face. "Open your eyes, Vallerand. Let's have done with this!"

At the sound of the unfamiliar voice, the horse side-stepped, and the noose tightened. Max's long black lashes stirred, his eyes half-opening. His head lifted from the stallion's withers, easing the constricting pressure of the rope. Severin had expected to see anger, resentment, pleading in his face, but the golden eyes were emotionless.

Painstakingly Max parted his swollen, bruised lips. His voice was a mere scratch of sound. "Lysette . . ."

Severin frowned. "I shouldn't worry about your wife, Vallerand. I suspect she'll rejoice at being rid of such a cold-blooded bastard as you."

Max was possessed with agonizing worry, wishing what Severin had said were true, for he did not want Lysette to grieve, and he knew it was inevitable.

"Do it now," Severin said, motioning for Tomas to release the horse's reins. "Now, while he's still awake."

All of a sudden, they heard a woman's desperate cry. *"Nooo!"*

From a distance they saw one of the Sagesse carriages, its wheels mired in mud, and a woman stumbling across the field toward them. Tomas raised his hand to slap the horse's hindquarters, but Severin stopped him with a curt command. He had just seen Renée emerge from the carriage. Stormy anger appeared on his face as he watched his wife and Vallerand's two sons follow.

Lysette fell and picked herself up quickly, hurrying across the soft, sinking earth. She quaked with fear as she saw that no one was holding the reins of the horse. There was a noose around Max's neck, and the rope was secured to the tree limb above him. He was badly beaten, and his eyes were closed. She spoke in a low, shaking voice, terrified of startling the horse. "You've made a mistake," she said, going to Severin with outstretched hands, holding out the half-crumpled letter. "Look at this—please—don't do anything until you look at this letter."

Tentatively Tomas reached for the reins of the horse, but the stallion flinched, wall-eyed, his huge body tensed and ready to explode with movement. Lysette thrust the letter at Severin and stared at the horse, mesmerized, realizing exactly how delicate the thread between life and death was. A thousand prayers flashed through her mind. The paper rustled as Severin turned a page, and the stallion tossed his head impatiently.

Slowly Lysette began to walk toward the trembling stallion, step by hesitant step. "Don't be afraid," she whispered. "Stand still for a moment longer, just a moment—"

The horse went rigid, and Lysette stopped, while her heart took a sickening plunge. "No," she said softly. "Just a little more time . . . Oh please, I can't lose you, Max . . ." One step, then another, and she was forced to stop again as the animal snorted and stamped. Tears streamed down her face as she looked at the taut rope. Max might fall at any moment.

Suddenly she was aware of Justin's quiet voice behind her. "I'll cut the rope. Don't move."

The boy's thin, dark form moved behind the horse to the oak tree. There was a knife in his hand. As lithely as a cat, he began to climb.

"Stop, boy," Severin Dubois said, pulling a flintlock pistol from his breeches. Justin continued shimmying up the tree trunk as if he hadn't heard. "Boy—" Dubois said again, and Lysette interrupted quietly.

"Put away the pistol, Monsieur Dubois. You know my husband is not guilty."

"This letter proves nothing," he replied.

"You must believe it," she said, her unblinking gaze on the scene before her. "It is written in your own brother's hand." She had never thought she would feel such agony in her life. Everything she held dear, her only chance at happiness, was poised precariously before her. It could all be snatched away in one cruel second.

"A hand that was none too steady, by the look of it," came Severin's reply. "Etienne often tried to pass off entertaining nonsense as the truth. Why should this be different?"

Renée confronted him, clear, cold, and sensible. "Stop tormenting the child, Severin. For once be man enough to admit you have been mistaken."

A breeze caught the folds of Lysette's skirt and caused it to flap. At the movement of the red flag of velvet, the stallion jerked and twisted, breaking free at last. With a silent scream, Lysette saw her husband's body fall through the air with nightmarish slowness.

But the rope was no longer tethered. Justin had sawed through it.

Max's body hit the soft earth and was still. A chilling breeze ruffled his black hair.

Chapter 16

Severin glanced at the prone form on the ground, and turned back to Renée and the letter. "And if this letter is true Renée?" he asked with a sneer. "If Bernard was indeed the one who killed Corinne? That has no relevance at all to this matter. Maximilien murdered your brother because Etienne could not leave his pretty little wife alone."

"Why would Maximilien have resorted to murder if he desired Etienne's death?" Renée demanded. "Etienne gave him every opportunity to do it honorably! Maximilien could have killed him at the duel—but he did not. He could have demanded satisfaction at the Leseur ball, and ended it with a sword right then, and no one would have thought the worse of him. But he did not. Oh, Severin, you know the truth of what I am saying!"

After pulling the noose away from his neck, Lysette pillowed Max's head and shoulders in her lap. His shirt was in tatters, his clothes wet and muddy. If only she had a cloak, something to protect him from the rain. She curved herself over and around him, her tears falling freely as she saw how they had beat him. "My darling . . ." Her fluttering hand searched for his heartbeat, and she panicked until she felt a pulse on the side of his neck. "You're safe now," she crooned, stroking his hair, wiping

407

the blood from his face. He groaned faintly, and she reassured him with a murmur. "I am here, *bien-aimé.*"

His shaking fingers clenched in her velvet skirt. He had been plummeting through cold, empty darkness, and suddenly he was caught in gentle arms. Pain gnawed at him with sharp teeth, and instinctively he strove to bury himself deeper in the sweet, soothing warmth so close by. A woman's voice fell tenderly on his ears. His mind struggled with questions, and he tried to roll to his side, only to be stabbed by icy-hot knives. He recoiled in shock and pain.

"No, be still, darling," Lysette whispered, pressing him back. "Everything is all right." She looked up at Justin, who was standing just a few feet away, seeming dazed. Her expression hardened with determination. "Justin, tell Monsieur Dubois we are taking your father home."

Justin nodded shortly and went to Dubois, who was still quarreling with his wife.

"What purpose have you for defending him?" Dubois demanded, his face reddening.

Renée discarded her aggressive posture, knowing now that she had hit her mark, it was time to allow him to appear the victor. "I am not defending him," she said, her voice noticeably softer. "It is just that I desire the *real* murderer of my brother to be punished. Won't you to try to find Bernard? *There* is your justice, if you are able to pry the truth out of him."

"Perhaps we will," Severin said harshly, and raised his voice for all to hear. "Where *is* Bernard?"

No one answered. Lysette thought quickly, wondering what was best for Max's sake. If there were only herself to think of, she would invite them, *encourage* them, to find Bernard and do what they pleased with him, as long as she never had to see his loathsome face again. But Bernard was Max's brother, and it was Max's right to decide how to handle him.

"Bernard is at home," Lysette spoke out. "He accompanied his mother to church today. He usually resides in our *garconnière.*"

Justin and Philippe glanced at her discreetly, knowing she was lying. "She is right," Justin said. "You'd better go now, if you hope to find him. I would not be surprised if he leaves soon, and chooses to stay the night in town." There was no mistaking the vicious sincerity of his tone as he added, "How I hope he receives his comeuppance!"

"Monsieur Dubois," Lysette said, and Severin met her gaze evenly, showing no trace of regret for what he had done to her husband. "I would like to retain possession of the letter. It is the only evidence I have that might prevent Captain Gervais from arresting Maximilien."

"First I must know," Severin replied, "how forthcoming you and your family intend to be with the authorities regarding your husband's condition."

In other words, she could have the letter if she gave her word she would not tell Gervais or his lieutenants how the Sagesses had brutally beaten her husband. Lysette swallowed back her impotent fury, thinking that the authorities would do nothing in any case. But her hatred of Dubois and the Sagesses would last the rest of her life, and she promised herself that eventually they would be paid in full for their actions. She did not have to look at Justin to know he was thinking the same. "In exchange for the letter, we will keep our silence," she vowed. "Please help the coachman pull the carriage out of the mud before you go. I must take my husband home quickly, or you may yet have succeeded in killing him."

"Of course," Severin said, his brusqueness concealing his discomfort. He was not a soft-hearted man, nor was he capable of real contrition. But something about the way Vallerand's young wife stared at him elicited an unwanted feeling of shame. She was no bigger than a child, yet she sat with her arms around her husband as if protecting him from all the evils of the world.

"They are a strange pair," Dubois muttered to Renée

sotto voce, turning away and gesturing the Sagesse brothers to the mired carriage. "She could not possibly understand what he is, or she would not defend him so."

"Perhaps she is the only one who understands what he is," Renée said pensively. She glanced back with sudden melancholy. "I wish she had been Etienne's. She might have been able to change him."

Max moved sluggishly from the depths of oblivion into painful awareness. His eyes opened, and he found himself in a cocoon of velvet softness. Carefully he pondered this strange situation, and step by step recalled what had happened. He decided he had not died. He was in too much pain to have died. Searching tentatively with his hand, he found wet ground, a clump or two of straggly grass, the muddied hem of Lysette's skirt. Her gentle fingers were in his hair, stroking and smoothing.

"It won't be long now," she said, bending over him. "We'll be home soon, Max."

Max heard the distant sound of voices. He needed to see what was happening, to regain some of his control. "Help me up," he said through a rush of shivering.

"Max, no—"

"Help me," he rasped.

Slowly Lysette eased him into a half-sitting position, supporting his body with hers, biting her lip at the sound of his low groan. If only she could take his pain into herself. She would rather bear it than have him suffer one moment more.

"Lysette," he said, "why . . ."

"Not now," she interrupted, gentle but unyielding. "I will explain everything soon. Rest for now."

The Sagesses and their brother-in-law rode away toward the road leading to the Vallerand plantation. Renée's carriage moved along the side of the field and came to a stop nearby, and she opened the doors herself, giving rapid orders to the coachman.

Philippe came to crouch by Lysette. "I do not understand," he said. "Bernard is at *La Sirène*. Why did you tell them he was at home?"

"To allow us time," she said, aware that her husband was listening intently.

"Time for what?" Philippe asked.

"To warn Bernard before they find him," she replied.

"No," Philippe said in outrage. "Why should Bernard be warned? Why shouldn't we allow the Sagesses to have him?"

Lysette was about to answer when Justin appeared. Ruefully he rubbed the back of his head and managed a grin as he met Max's eyes. "Hello, father."

"Bernard—" Max said with an effort, and Lysette interrupted quickly.

"We're going to move you into the carriage now, *bien-aimé.*"

After binding his ribs, they half-dragged, half-carried Max to the vehicle and lifted him inside. In the midst of the process, Max lost consciousness once more, making Lysette wonder with growing dread how badly he was hurt, and if their well-intentioned clumsiness had just worsened his injuries.

While Renee and Philippe settled inside the carriage, Justin took Lysette's arm and drew her a short distance away. His face was lined with exhaustion, but his expression was one of grim determination. "I'll go to Bernard," he said quietly. "What should I say to him?"

"Tell him . . ." she paused. "Tell him that the Sagesses are looking for him. For tonight at least, I believe he can safely hide in the new warehouse Max built on the riverfront." She frowned. "How are you going to reach town?"

Justin nodded back in the direction of the black stallion, which had bolted only a short distance away and was grazing warily underneath a tree. "I'll take father's horse."

"You can't," Lysette protested, knowing how volatile the stallion was.

"I can," Justin said flatly.

Lysette knew that he would not make the claim unless he was certain. She would not give her consent, however, until one point was made. "I am placing my trust in you," she said. "That you will do as you say, and not allow your own temper to best you. Give the message to Bernard and leave. No accusations, no arguments. I am trusting you not to lift your hand against him, Justin. Will that be too difficult for you?"

His blue eyes did not move from hers. "No." He took her small hand, lifted it to his lips, and pressed the back of it against his cheek. "Take care of him," he said huskily, and walked her back to the carriage.

La Sirène was filled with all the noise, music, and good-natured brawling of any slightly disreputable drinking establishment on the waterfront. On any other occasion, Justin would have relished the opportunity to visit the place. It was the kind of place he liked, making no pretense at sophistication, yet discriminating enough that the vulgar, blustering Kaintocks from up the river were not welcome.

As soon as he entered the place, he was accosted by a gaudily-dressed whore. "I've seen you before," she purred, winding her perfumed arms around his neck. Her accent was purely American. "No one else has those blue eyes. I'll make you real glad you came here tonight, honey."

"Not now," he said in terse English, unwrapping her arms and setting her aside. "I haven't the time. Excuse me."

"You're a little gentleman, ain't you? With all that dirt and those clothes, I thought you was a river boy." She rubbed her heavy breast against his arm. "Let's have a drink, m'lord."

Ignoring her, Justin pushed through the crowd to the gaming-rooms in the back. He located his uncle with little effort. Bernard was sitting at a table with a small group of his cronies, idly rearranging a hand of cards.

"Bernard," Justin interrupted, "I have a message for you."

Bernard looked up in surprise. "Justin?" His dark eyes snapped with dislike. "Get out of my sight. And don't bother me here again."

"The message is from Lysette." Justin smiled coolly as he saw that the other gentlemen at the table were beginning to lend their attention to the exchange. "Would you like to hear it in private, or should I say it in front of everyone? Lysette said to tell you—"

"Insolent whelp!" Bernard threw his cards down on the table and stood up, yanking Justin to the corner. "Now tell me, and then begone with you!"

Justin shook off his hand, and stared at his uncle with hot blue eyes. "It would have been three murders," he murmured. "Because of you they nearly killed father this evening."

"What nonsense is this?"

"Lysette's message," Justin said, "is that the Sagesses know you were the one who killed Etienne—and they are looking for you. If you value your life, you'd better find a way to disappear. Quickly. Lysette suggests you spend the night at the new warehouse on the *quai.*"

Bernard did not react at all, except for a violent twitch at the corner of his mouth. Then he looked away, and when he returned his gaze to Justin's face, the naked truth was there to see. "It's a lie," he said, looking ill. "It's a bluff of yours, to make me admit to something I—"

"Perhaps it is," Justin replied. "Why don't you stay and find out? I think you should." He smiled thinly. "Really."

Bernard stared at the boy in incredulous fury. A score of emotions crossed his haggard face, and he lifted his hands as if he would throttle Justin.

Justin did not move. "Don't try it," he said softly. "I'm

neither a drunkard nor a helpless woman—not your favored sort of victim at all.''

"I regret nothing," Bernard said hoarsely. "The world is better for being rid of Sagesse . . . and your whore of a mother."

Justin flinched. Silently he watched as his uncle staggered from the room.

After Max had been attended to by the doctor, Noeline satisfied herself by adding yet more bandages and salves of her own, and then hanging an array of charms over the doorway. Lysette did not dare remove them, having been assured by Noeline that they were very powerful. "I suppose they can't hurt," Lysette reflected ruefully.

Max slept for three or four hours, and then awakened with startling abruptness. "What happened?" he demanded, cursing in pain as he sat up, putting a hand to his battered ribs.

Lysette hurried to the bedside with a glass of water. While he drank thirstily, she picked up the thin sheaf of paper on the bedtable. "Max . . . Etienne Sagesse's sister brought this earlier today. He told her it was to be given to you upon his death."

He looked at her face, detecting the strange mixture of concern and dread in her eyes. "Read it to me," he said, setting down the glass.

She read the letter without inflection, trying to keep her voice steady. When she finished the first page and came to the first mention of Bernard, she did not look at Max's face, but sensed the torrent of outrage, fear, and fury that swept over him.

"No," he said softly.

She continued to read, the letter trembling in her hand. Before she reached the end, Max had snatched the leaves of paper and crushed them, his face white under its tan.

"Sagesse was a lying drunkard," he muttered viciously.

"Max, I . . . I know you don't want to believe it, but—"

"But you do," he sneered. "It makes things much easier, doesn't it? Pin the blame on Bernard—someone you have no great liking for in the first place—and then the mystery of what happened ten years ago is over. Never mind that Sagesse had no more honor than a gutter rat. It's obvious you're perfectly satisfied with a drunken bastard's explanation of it all. But it didn't happen that way, damn you!"

"And why are you so certain of that?" Lysette retorted, forgetting her concern and pity, smarting under the sting of his words. "Because Bernard is your brother?"

"Damn you," Max repeated harshly. "Where the hell is he now?"

She replied irately. "It's possible Bernard is hiding in the new warehouse on the waterfront. He knows the Sagesses are looking for him. But he might already be on his way out of the territory."

Max pushed back the light sheet that covered him and moved his legs over the edge of the mattress.

Lysette watched him with surprise and dismay. "Max, what are you doing? No, you're not well enough to go anywhere, least of all to confront—*Nom de Dieu*, you were beaten within an inch of your life today. You can't—"

"Help me get dressed."

"Absolutely not!" With horror she looked at his battered and bruised body as he stood up and made his way to the bulky armoire. He began to search for his breeches, cursing profusely. "Max, stop it," she cried. "You'll do terrible harm to yourself!"

"Get my clothes," he said through gritted teeth, "or I'll call for Zac to help."

"We'll send someone to tell Bernard whatever you wish—Philippe or Justin—I'll even go. But you can't—"

"I have to see him."

"Why? You know he'll deny everything!"

"I'll know when I see him if it's true or not."

Realizing that arguing would do no good, she fought the urge to cry. "Max, please," she whispered. "Today . . . for a few moments when I thought you might die—"

He turned and gave her a look that seemed to scorch her soul. "No," he said huskily. "Not now. We'll talk later." He could not deal with a show of emotion from her now. He would need all his strength to face Bernard. "Get my clothes, *doucette.*"

Struggling with her feelings, she bit her lip and went to the armoire, yanking out a shirt.

The outline of boxes, furniture, and bales of cotton was briefly illuminated by moonlight as one of the warehouse doors swung open. A tall, slightly stooped form filled the doorway, then stepped inside. All was dark again. There was no sound or movement until a quiet voice cut through the stifling air.

"I'm here, Bernard. Alone."

The silence lasted a few more seconds, and then there was a shuffling and scraping in the corner. "Max?" A match was struck.

Max watched as his brother lit an oil lamp. "Be careful with that," he said tersely. "After what I've been through today, I'm in no mood to deal with a warehouse fire."

"After what *you've* been through," Bernard said, sounding shaken. "My God, I've been hiding here for hours, actually in fear for my life. Justin told me . . ." His voice died away, and he gave a shocked gasp as he saw his brother. The oil lamp wobbled in his grip, and he sat it on a nearby crate. "Max . . . oh, God . . . what happened?"

The soft yellow light played over Max's swollen face, purple with bruises, marked with blood-crusted scrapes. His golden eyes seemed to gleam with a demonic light. "That is what I came here to ask you. What happened to Etienne Sagesse, Bernard? What happened to Corinne?"

Bernard backed away, looking afraid. "Max, don't listen to what others say. You have to help me."

"I want the truth," came the chillingly soft reply. "Enough to let you buy your life with it. But if you lie to me, Bernard . . ."

"What are you saying?" Bernard demanded, his voice bewildered. "I'm your brother! Are you threatening me? You couldn't hurt me, Max, you—"

"Believe me, you don't know what I could do," Max said in a raw whisper.

Evidently Bernard believed him. "What do you want me to say?" he asked, quivering.

"Tell me about the woman and bastard child you've been looking for all these years."

Bernard spread his hands wide. "I . . . don't know what you—"

Max interrupted with a snarl as sharp as the crack of a whip. "You had no affair with Ryla Curran, did you?"

"No," Bernard said, his dark gaze falling to the ground.

"Etienne was the one who seduced her." At his brother's nod, Max continued slowly. "But you did have an affair, Bernard. With my wife."

There was no answer.

Without thinking Max pulled out a dueling pistol and leveled it at the center of his brother's chest. There was no unsteadiness in his hand. "You had an affair with Corinne," he said. "Why?"

Mesmerized, Bernard stared, not at the pistol but at Max's face. "Y–you know what kind of woman she was, Max. I . . . it just happened . . . I had no control over it, or her . . . there was no harm, she had already cuckolded you with Etienne. And then I started to believe she was half-insane. She wanted me to run away with her, leave everything . . . I told her I couldn't do that to you, but she persisted. And one day I had one of my rages. She drove me to it. You know how it is when I . . . before I knew it, my hands were around her neck. I knew you

would be better off without her—you can't deny that
you were. She made your life hell, everyone knew that
she—"

"No more," Max whispered. There was no need to ask
about Sagesse—now all the answers were obvious. The
urge to kill was throbbing in his veins. Beads of sweat
trickled down his face. The walls of the warehouse seemed
to be squeezing closer. Suddenly he felt trapped in the
airless building, caged in with a stranger who was his
brother . . . a stranger who had *never* been his brother.

"Max, you must help me," Bernard said, sensing the
moment of anguished vulnerability. "I have no money.
The Sagesses will kill me if I don't get away. And if they
don't find me, the authorities will. Help me. In spite of
what I've done, I'm still your brother—"

Max interrupted with a harsh, grating laugh. "There's
a ship to Liverpool . . ." He paused to take a breath,
feeling as if his lungs could not take in enough air. "A
ship leaving at dawn. Captain Tierney will allow you
aboard, no questions asked. I don't care where you go.
Just don't come back. If I ever see you again . . ." He
paused. "God help me, I will kill you."

"Max—" There was a note of pleading in Bernard's
voice.

"Don't. Don't ask for anything else," Max warned.
Inch by inch he forced himself to lower the pistol, but the
wild intensity still burned in his eyes. Concentrating
fiercely, he walked away, conscious of nothing but the soft
light and silence behind him. The moment he reached the
warehouse door, the lamp was extinguished.

In spite of the clamoring of Aaron Burr's associates,
Max was not arrested. Etienne's letter, combined with a
discreet nudging from Governor Claiborne and a most unexpected silence from the editor of the *Orleans Gazette*,
convinced the Municipal Council and the *gens d'armes* to

satisfy themselves that the absent Bernard Vallerand had indeed been guilty of the crime.

Perhaps those influential men in conspiracy with Aaron Burr could have pressed the issue further, but they were occupied with more demanding matters. By that summer of 1806, Burr had gathered men and supplies at a small island on the Ohio River in preparation for his conquest of Mexico and the West. However, the rumors that had dogged Burr ever since his trip to New Orleans proved his undoing.

Abandoning what he saw as a sinking ship, General Wilkinson changed sides and added his warnings to those President Jefferson had already received. The president eventually issued a proclamation calling for Burr's arrest, at the same time that one of Burr's coded letters to Wilkinson was published in a prominent newspaper.

Lysette talked with Max in private about Bernard, but he never revealed what had been said in the warehouse. She questioned, hinted, provoked, but he remained stubbornly silent. Finally she had to accept that in this matter he preferred to deal with his feelings in his own time and way.

When Irénée was told about what Bernard had done, she was as grief-stricken as if he had died. It was difficult for a mother to accept that her child could be capable of such evil, and the shock of the news seemed to age her immeasurably. However, she possessed a core of inner strength that sustained her, and she informed the household with dignity that Bernard's name was never to be mentioned in her presence again.

It was not long before Lysette discovered she was with child. The news could not have come at a better time. There was little room for bitter reflection on the past when they were possessed with such joy. Lysette was amused by Max's attitude that she had accomplished something quite remarkable. *"Vraiment,* it is not all that unexpected," she teased him. "As your mother says, the only remarkable thing is that it took this long!"

"If you give me a daughter," he had told her, enfolding her in his warm embrace, "I'll lay the world at your feet."

"I might decide to give you a son," she said. "Wouldn't you like another son?"

He shook his head with a grin. "No, *petite*, we need more women in the family."

Max had been excluded from Corinne's pregnancy, as was the usual way, and in truth, none of it had been significant to him until the twins had been born. With Lysette, however, he took an indelicate interest.

If there had been a question in anyone's mind about whether or not Maximilien doted on his wife, it was forever banished. Each time Lysette experienced a twinge of discomfort or a trace of nausea, the family physician was summoned, and soundly berated if he did not arrive immediately. Irénée told one of her friends in strictest confidence that despite the doctor's protests, Maximilien insisted on staying in the room while Lysette was being examined. It was indecent, horrifying! The elderly ladies exclaimed over it with horrified delight during an entire Thursday afternoon.

In the spring Alexandre married Henriette Clement, and the wedding proved to be an occasion of great happiness for all concerned. For a while it had seemed that the scandal of Etienne Sagesse's suspicious death would prevent Diron Clement from allowing his daughter to marry a Vallerand. But the old man was persuaded to see the rightness of the match, and he gave his consent with a show of calculating authority, terrified that someone might see the soft-hearted motives beneath all his scheming.

Lysette was thrilled when she received a letter from her sister Jacqueline, a kind of gentle-spirited latter asking for her forgiveness for the long silence between them. It led Lysette to hope that Jeanne and Gaspard would relent soon and recognize her marriage to Max. At Lysette's insistence, Jacqueline and her elderly husband came to stay at the plantation for nearly a month. Although Max disliked the intrusion on his privacy, he endured the visit because it brought Lysette such happiness.

Shortly after Alexandre's wedding, Philippe left for France to continue his studies, and visit all the places he had read and dreamed of for so long. Although the family begged and prodded Justin to go as well, the boy chose to stay behind, declaring he had no interest in moldy museums and ancient ruins. With his brother gone, Justin prowled around New Orleans alone, sometimes standing at the riverfront for hours and eyeing every departing ship as though it had been his only chance of escape.

Lately Justin was quiet and withdrawn, his boyishness and sense of mischief slipping away day by day. The events of the past fall, the injustice that had been done to his father, the cruelty of the Sagesses and his own uncle, seemed to confirm some terrible inward suspicion he had carried with him all his life. It seemed as if his worst fears about human nature, including his own, had been proven accurate.

With his family Justin was loving but guarded; with all others he was remote. Girls were attracted by his sullen handsomeness, but they were not spared from his stinging cruelty. Older women occasionally succeeded in luring him to their beds—Renée Dubois among them—but his liaisons were purely physical, and any mention of love ended the affair immediately.

Lysette was at a loss to know what ailed Justin, but Max seemed to understand. "He'll change in time," he told her. "Someday Justin will come to realize that all these formidable defenses he's building aren't necessary."

"How can you be certain?"

One of his brows arched expressively. "Didn't *I* change after I met you?"

Lysette gave him a perturbed frown. "Yes, but you were thirty-five years old!"

Max laughed softly. "It might take Justin that long, *ma petite*. The Vallerands are slow to change their ways."

"What a comfort you are," she said darkly, and then gave a gasp of laughter as he swept her up in his arms. "Be careful," she said, one of her hands coming to rest protectively on the firm swell of her stomach. "Or must I remind you of my delicate condition, monsieur?"

"I'm always careful with you," he said, his golden eyes smiling down at her.

"You are handling me as if I were a sack of potatoes." She looked at her ungainly form and added ruefully, "But I suppose I cannot fault you, as that is what I resemble."

Max kissed her forehead. "You're the most beautiful woman I've ever known." His nose brushed against hers as he moved his attention to her curving lips. "And the most distracting, in every way." He smiled and whispered against her cheek, "And your condition makes you even more exciting than you were before."

Lysette pulled her head back. "Don't tease, Max."

His lips wandered to her soft, tempting throat. "I see I'll have to prove it to you."

She giggled and kicked her slippers off, and the shoes thumped down the stairs as he carried her up to their bedroom.

Much later they lay together in the tumbled bed, feeling as if they were the only two people in the world. Lysette drifted her palm over his chest, while her head nestled against his shoulder. Her happiness was almost too great to bear. No matter how much time went by, she could never take this for granted, having him, being his. "Sometimes it frightens me," she whispered, "thinking about how I nearly lost you. I still remember how it felt, and I—"

He touched his fingers to her mouth to silence her, and his thumb smoothed over the soft curve of her lower lip. "That is all behind us, my love. We're going to share a long, long life together."

"I hope so."

"We will," he replied, and leaned over her with an arrogant smile, pressing her back againt the pillows. "Do you doubt my word?"

"Oh, no." Lysette smiled against his lips, her fears melting before the steady warmth of his love. She slid her arms around him as he moved over her. "No, *bien-aimé*, I wouldn't dare."

Now that you've enjoyed
Lisa Kleypas'
ONLY IN YOUR ARMS,
sample another of Avon Books'
Romantic Treasures—
LADY LEGEND
by Deborah Camp

Copper-Headed-Woman is a legend among Indians and whites alike for her healing arts, but to Tucker Jones, a wounded soldier whom she nurses back to life, she is a woman . . . a woman he intends to make his . . .

She looked up from her work, and sent him another one of those heart-soaring smiles. God, she's a beauty! he thought. His groin tingled, tightened. He wanted to please her, to earn her respect again after losing it yesterday.

"I think a man should learn to take care of himself *and* his family. Work should be shared and not labled as 'his' and 'hers.' "

"I believe you're trying to turn my head, Tucker Jones."

"Maybe, and soften your heart toward me a little. I do mean what I say, Copper. I'd like to learn how to survive in this country. It would please me no end to know as much as you about providing for yourself. You were tossed into this vast country and lived in a cave. You did for yourself without proper clothing or weapons." He shook his head in amazement. "You're the stuff of legends."

She made a scoffing sound. "You could survive if you had to, Tucker. The spirit gets strength from hardship."

"Is that an old Indian saying?"

She nodded. "And true." Copper knitted her brow. Her breasts moved freely beneath her bodice, winning Tucker's avid interest.

"I dreamed of you last night." His admission prompted the response he'd wanted. She stopped working and fixed her wide, earthy eyes on him. Her lips parted, but she didn't say anything. For once, he'd rendered her speechless.

"In fact," he continued, "I dream of you most every night." He let a grin crawl slowly across his face as lucious bits of his nightly vision harkened back to him.

"What kind of dreams?" she asked, although she told herself this was most probably a trick. Men were known to say just about anything to get a woman's interest.

"You really want to know?" he teased.

Copper swallowed hard and nodded. Tan his hide! He knew she wanted to know how she figured into his dreams. Tucker crossed his arms and ankles and angled his gaze upward in contemplation. Copper tried to appear only mildly curious. She sensed, however, that he could hear her pounding heart.

"We were in a glade where the shadows were damply cool. You were wearing some slip of a thing . . . yellow as sunshine, and your hair was loose and free."

"What were you wearing?" she interrupted.

He shrugged. "Damned if I know. I was too busy looking at you to bother with me." His gaze flickered over her. "I could have been as naked as a new chick. All I know for sure is that you're an eyeful, Copper."

She ducked her head and busied herself over the hide again, scraping with a new intensity. She recalled what he looked like naked and found herself wishing she could see him again that way. His body fascinated her with all its swirling, sable hair and ropy muscles. She'd seen more muscular bodies, but she liked his because it was sturdy and still graceful. When his leg was healed, she knew that his would be a light-footed, fluid gate.

"In the dream you looked at me with encouragement and tenderness," he said, his voice a little foggy, as if he were speaking to himself. "Your eyes told me that I could touch you and love you, so I took you in my arms and we kissed. Kiss." He frowned. "Such a small, trifling word for what we did. The earth trembled beneath us and the sky whirled like a kaleidoscope above us. You melted into me and I was lost in you. It was the most . . . what I mean to say is that it was . . ." Words failed him and he grappled for just one that would describe the maelstrom. "Rapture." He felt utterly foolish the moment he released the fanciful word, but the appreciation in her expression redeemed him. For once, he thought, he'd said the right thing to her.

"All that from one kiss?" she asked, so softly he had to strain to hear. All sound seemed to have diminished. She heard no birdsongs, no shuffling of hooves, no whisper of wind. All she heard was her pulse booming in her ears, responding to his tender words. She wanted to believe that a kiss could move the earth and lower the heavens so that mortals could reach up and touch them. More importantly, she wanted him to make her believe such things were possible.

"It was some kiss, Copper." He picked at the leather nap covering his thigh. "The kind that can bring a man to his knees."

FREE BOOK OFFER!

Avon Books has an outstanding offer for every reader of our Romantic Treasures.
Buy three different Avon Romantic Treasures and get your choice of an Avon romance
favorite—absolutely free.

Fill in your name, address and zip code below, and send it, along with the proof-of-
purchase pages from two other Avon Romantic Treasures to:

AVON ROMANTIC TREASURES
Free Book Offer
P.O. Box 767, Dresden, TN 38255.

Allow 4-6 weeks for delivery.

- -

(Please fill out completely)
AVON ROMANTIC TREASURE FREE BOOK OFFER!

Name_____

Address _____

City_____ State_____ Zip_____

Please send me the following FREE novel:

_____ 76214-5 SPELLBOUND   _____ 75673-0 DEVIL'S DECEPTION

_____ 75921-7 DREAMSPINNER   _____ 75742-7 BLACK-EYED SUSAN

_____ 75778-8 CAUGHT IN THE ACT   _____ 76020-7 MOONLIGHT AND
                                                  MAGIC

I have enclosed three completed proof-of-purchase pages.

Offer good while supplies last. Avon Books reserves the right to make substitutions. Limit
one offer per address.

Offer available in U.S. and Canada only.
Void where prohibited by law.   Offer expires September 30, 1992.

```
76150
0 71001 00450 2
ISBN 0-380-76150-5
```

Proof
-of-
Purchase